SPIRITWALK

SPIRITWALK

Charles de Lint

A TOM DOHERTY ASSOCIATES BOOK
NEW YORK

Portions of this work—"Ascian in Rose," "Westlin Wind," and "Ghostwood"—
were previously published in limited editions by Axolotl Press/Pulphouse Publishing,
in 1986, 1989, and 1990 respectively. "Merlin Dreams in the Mondream Wood" first
appeared in issue #7, 1990, of *Pulphouse, the Hardback Magazine.*

Grateful acknowledgments are made to:

Susan Musgrave for the use of a quote from her novel *The Charcoal Burners,* McClel-
land and Stewart, 1980.

Ingrid Karklins for the use of a quote from the liner notes of her cassette, *Kas Dimd;*
copyright © 1989 by Ingrid Karklins. For information about Karklins's music, write:
Willow Music, 500 Terrace Drive, Austin, TX 78704.

Ron Nance for the use of a quote from "Jackalope Blues," which first appeared in
The Magazine of Speculative Poetry #2; copyright © 1985 by Ron Nance.

SPIRITWALK

This book has been printed on acid-free paper.

A Tor Book
Published by Tom Doherty Associates, Inc.
175 Fifth Avenue
New York, N.Y. 10010

Tor® is a registered trademark of Tom Doherty Associates, Inc.

Library of Congress Cataloging-in-Publication Data

De Lint, Charles
    Spiritwalk / Charles de Lint.
        p.   cm.
    ISBN 0-312-85204-5
    I. Title.
PR9199.3.D357S66   1992
813'.54—dc20   92-823
                                                                      CIP

First Edition: May 1992

Printed in the United States of America

0 9 8 7 6 5 4 3 2 1

In prior appearances, some of this material bore dedications that I'd like to repeat here. *Spiritwalk* is for:

MaryAnn Harris
Claire Hamill
Alan Stivell
Robin Williamson
Midori Snyder
Kristine Kathryn Rusch
Dean Wesley Smith

To which I'd like to add, at this time:

Terri Windling
Ron Nance
Charles R. Saunders

My thanks to them all for inspiration and support.

There are graves in the forest:
in its moss,
the bones of memories.

    —Wendelessen;
     from "Names"

AUTHOR'S NOTE

Spiritwalk is related to another book of mine, *Moonheart*. A familiarity with the events in that previous novel is recommended, though not, I hope, altogether necessary.

CONTENTS

SPIRITWALK

TAMSON HOUSE, OTTAWA, ONTARIO

Extract from "Chapter Three: Mystical Buildings and Other Structures," first published in *Mysterious North America* by Christy Riddell (East Street Press, 1989)

ON SEPTEMBER 23, 1906, one of Canada's most notorious lumber barons went for an afternoon ride in the Gatineau Mountains and never came back. He left behind a flourishing lumber business and an extensive trail of theories, rumors and conjectures. He also left behind the architectural oddity known as Tamson House.

To this day, the mysterious whereabouts of Anthony Tamson is no more certain than it was on the day of his disappearance. Adding to the mystery surrounding one of the major figures of the turn-of-the-century Canadian business world were the subsequent disappearances of both his son Nathan in 1954 and his reclusive grandson James in 1982.

There was a funeral for James—known in literary circles as "Jamie Tams"—but it was a closed-coffin affair and rumors persist that there was, in fact, no body interred. The current owner, Sara

Kendell, James Tamson's niece, is proving to be as much of a recluse as were her forebears and is rarely seen in public.

Tamson House is situated in the heart of a residential district known as the Glebe. The house takes up an entire city block east of Bank Street, is fronted on three sides by residential streets, and on the fourth by Central Park. The general appearance from any view is that of a long block of old-fashioned town houses set kitty-corner to each other. There are three towers, one each in three of the structure's corners; an impressive observatory, oddly unaffected by light pollution from the city, occupies the fourth.

Inside, there is a labyrinth of corridors and rooms, an impressive library and a garden surrounded on all four sides by the house, the actual acreage of which is subject to question as evidently no two measurements have come out equal.

Beyond the odd disappearances and reclusive nature of most of its owners, not to mention its existence as an architectural curiosity, Tamson House is listed in this volume for two further reasons.

The first is that while much of Ottawa's downtown core is built upon a limestone headland, the area surrounding Tamson House was originally fenland, reclaimed by those who settled the area. Before the arrival of European explorers and settlers, however, the native peoples of the area spoke of a sacred island in the fens, the location of which, legend has it, is where Tamson House now stands.

The island was considered a gateway to the spiritworld, the place from where the manitou came to visit the world of men. Until the coming of the Europeans, the island was a regular site for the *jessakan,* or conjuring lodges, of shaman from local tribes as well as those from tribes that lived as far as a thousand miles away. Curiously, there was never any protest made when first Philemon Wright and then Braddish Billings brought settlers into the area in the early 1800s, subsequently cutting off shamanistic access to the island.

A more current reason for Tamson House's inclusion in this volume is that over the years—particularly from the time that James Tamson took ownership, late in 1954—the house has proved to be a haven for certain individuals who might be considered "outsiders" to normal society. It has been home not only to an impressive array of poets, artists, musicians, scholars and writers, but also to those not traditionally considered to be involved in the arts, but who still communicate in terms not readily accepted as the norm.

So circus performers have lived there, side by side with those involved in occult studies; it has been home to strippers and Bible students, martial arts *sensei* and chefs, gardeners and hedgerow philosophers; it has been a waystop for travelers from many lands as well as backpackers and hikers from closer to home.

What draws them to Tamson House is a sense of community, the opportunity to collect their strengths in a safe haven before they must go out once more to face the world that lies beyond the house's walls. Most remain for no more than a few weeks or months, a year at the most, although there do appear to be a few permanent residents.

There is no hidden sign or handshake required to gain admittance, no secret societal obligation involved for those who find welcome in Tamson House. The harmony that lies behind its walls appears to have an indefinable source, but it has such potency that, according to some previous residents, those who might bring discord with them feel so uncomfortable once they've stepped through one of the house's many doors that they don't remain long enough to cause any harm.

Regardless of its history, visitors to Tamson House will certainly be struck by the "feel" of the building—a sensation akin to that found in certain other places that we remember forever, our subconscious memory stirring in recognition of some hidden facet of mystery that stands revealed, if only for a moment.

MERLIN DREAMS IN THE MONDREAM WOOD

MONDREAM—an Anglo-Saxon word which means the
dream of life among men

> *I am Merlin*
> *Who follow the Gleam*
> *—Tennyson*
> *from ''Merlin and the*
> *Gleam''*
> *(''gleam'' =*
> *inspiration/muse)*

IN THE HEART of the house lay a garden.

In the heart of the garden stood a tree.

In the heart of the tree lived an old man who wore the shape of a red-haired boy with crackernut eyes that seemed as bright as salmon tails glinting up the water.

His was a riddling wisdom, older by far than the ancient oak that housed his body. The green sap was his blood and leaves grew in his hair. In the winter, he slept. In the spring, the moon harped a windsong against his antler tines as the oak's boughs stretched its green buds awake. In the summer, the air was thick with the droning of bees and the scent of the wildflowers that grew in stormy profusion where the fat brown bole became root.

And in the autumn, when the tree loosed its bounty to the ground below, there were hazelnuts lying in among the acorns.

The secrets of a Green Man.

"When I was a kid, I thought it was a forest," Sara said.

She was sitting on the end of her bed, looking out the window over the garden, her guitar on her lap, the quilt bunched up under her knees. Up by the headboard, Julie Simms leaned forward from its carved wood to look over Sara's shoulder at what could be seen of the garden from their vantage point.

"It sure looks big enough," she said.

Sara nodded. Her eyes had taken on a dreamy look.

In was 1969 and they had decided to form a folk band—Sara on guitar, Julie playing recorder, both of them singing. They wanted to change the world with music because that was what was happening. In San Francisco. In London. In Vancouver. So why not in Ottawa?

With their faded bell-bottom jeans and tie-dyed shirts, they looked just like any of the other seventeen-year-olds who hung around the War Memorial downtown, or could be found crowded into coffeehouses like Le Hibou and Le Monde on the weekends. Their hair was long—Sara's a cascade of brown ringlets, Julie's a waterfall spill the color of a raven's wing; they wore beads and feather earrings and both eschewed makeup.

"I used to think it spoke to me," Sara said.

"What? The garden?"

"Um-hmm."

"What did it say?"

The dreaminess in Sara's eyes became wistful and she gave Julie a rueful smile.

"I can't remember," she said.

It was three years after her parents had died—when she was nine years old—that Sara Kendell came to live with her Uncle Jamie in his strange rambling house. To an adult perspective, Tamson House was huge: an enormous, sprawling affair of corridors and rooms and towers that took up the whole of a city block; to a child of nine, it simply went on forever.

She could wander down corridor after corridor, poking about in the clutter of rooms that lay spread like a maze from the northwest tower near Bank Street—where her bedroom was located—all the way over to her uncle's study overlooking O'Connor Street on the far side of the house, but mostly she spent her time in the Library and in the garden. She liked the Library because it was like a museum. There were walls of books, rising two floors high up to a domed ceiling, but there were also dozens of glass display cases scattered about the main floor area, each of which held any number of fascinating objects.

There were insects pinned to velvet and stone artifacts; animal skulls and clay flutes in the shapes of birds; old manuscripts and hand-drawn maps, the parchment yellowing, the ink a faded sepia; Kabuki masks and a miniature Shinto shrine made of ivory and ebony; corn-husk dolls, Japanese *netsuke* and porcelain miniatures; antique jewelry and African beadwork; Kachina dolls and a brass fiddle, half the size of a normal instrument. . . .

The cases were so cluttered with interesting things that she could spend a whole day just going through one case and still have something to look at when she went back to it the next day. What interested her most, however, was that her uncle had a story to go with each and every item in the cases. No matter what she brought up to his study—a tiny ivory *netsuke* carved in the shape of a badger crawling out of a teapot, a flat stone with curious scratches on it that looked like Ogham script—he could spin out a tale of its origin that might take them right through the afternoon to suppertime.

That he dreamed up half the stories only made it more entertaining, for then she could try to trip him up in his rambling explanations, or even just try to top his tall tales.

But if she was intellectually precocious, emotionally she still carried scars from her parents' death and the time she'd spent living with her other uncle—her father's brother. For three years Sara had been left in the care of a nanny during the day—amusing herself while the woman smoked cigarettes and watched the soaps—while at night she was put to bed promptly after dinner. It wasn't a normal family life; she could only find that vicariously, in the books she devoured with a voracious appetite.

Coming to live with her Uncle Jamie, then, was like constantly being on holiday. He doted on her, and on those few occasions when he *was* too busy, she could always find one of the many houseguests to spend some time with her.

All that marred her new life in Tamson House was her night fears.

She wasn't frightened of the House itself. Nor of bogies or monsters living in her closet. She knew that shadows were shadows, creaks and groans were only the House settling when the temperature changed. What haunted her nights was waking up from a deep sleep, shuddering uncontrollably, her pajamas stuck to her like a second skin, her heartbeat thundering at twice its normal tempo.

There was no logical explanation for the terror that gripped her—once, sometimes twice a week. It just came, an awful, indescribable panic that left her shivering and unable to sleep for the rest of the night.

It was on the days following such nights that she went into the garden. The greenery and flowerbeds and statuary all combined to soothe her. Invariably, she found herself in the very center of the garden, where an ancient oak tree stood on a knoll and overhung a fountain. Lying on the grass sheltered by its boughs, with the soft lullaby of the fountain's water murmuring close at hand, she would find what the night fears had stolen from her the night before.

She would sleep.

And she would dream the most curious dreams.

"The garden has a name, too," she told her uncle when she came in from sleeping under the oak one day.

The House was so big that many of the rooms had been given names just so that they could all be kept straight in their minds.

"It's called the Mondream Wood," she told him.

She took his look of surprise to mean that he didn't know or understand the word.

"It means that the trees in it dream that they're people," she explained.

Her uncle nodded. " 'The dream of life among men.' It's a good name. Did you think it up yourself?"

"No. Merlin told me."

"*The* Merlin?" her uncle asked with a smile.

Now it was her turn to look surprised.

"What do you mean *the* Merlin?" she asked.

Her uncle started to explain, astonished that in all her reading she hadn't come across a reference to Britain's most famous wizard, but then just gave her a copy of Malory's *Le Morte d' Arthur* and, after a moment's consideration, T. H. White's *The Sword in the Stone* as well.

"Did you ever have an imaginary friend when you were a kid?" Sara asked as she finally turned away from the window.

Julie shrugged. "My mom says I did, but I can't remember. Apparently he was a hedgehog the size of a toddler named Whatzit."

"I never did. But I can remember that for a long time I used to wake up in the middle of the night just terrified and then I wouldn't be able to sleep again for the rest of the night. I used to go into the middle of the garden the next day and sleep under that big oak that grows by the fountain."

"How pastoral," Julie said.

Sara grinned. "But the thing is, I used to dream that there was a boy living in that tree and his name was Merlin."

"Go on," Julie scoffed.

"No, really. I mean, I really had these dreams. The boy would just step out of the tree and we'd sit there and talk away the afternoon."

"What did you talk about?"

"I don't remember," Sara said. "Not the details—just the feeling. It was all very magical and . . . healing, I suppose. Jamie said that my having those night fears was just my unconscious mind's way of dealing with the trauma of losing my parents and then having to live with my dad's brother who only wanted my inheritance, not me. I was too young then to know anything about that kind of thing; all I knew was that when I talked to Merlin, I felt better. The night fears started coming less and less often and then finally they went away altogether.

"I think Merlin took them away for me."

"What happened to him?"

"Who?"

"The boy in the tree," Julie said. "Your Merlin. When did you stop dreaming about him?"

"I don't really know. I guess when I stopped waking up terrified, I just stopped sleeping under the tree so I didn't see him anymore. And then I just forgot that he'd ever been there. . . ."

Julie shook her head. "You know, you can be a bit of a flake sometimes."

"Thanks a lot. At least I didn't hang around with a giant hedgehog named Whatzit when I was a kid."

"No. You hung out with tree-boy."

Julie started to giggle and then they both broke up. It was a few moments before either of them could catch their breath.

"So what made you think of your tree-boy?" Julie asked.

Another giggle welled up in Julie's throat, but Sara's gaze had drifted back out the window and become all dreamy again.

"I don't know," she said. "I was just looking out at the garden and I suddenly found myself remembering. I wonder what ever happened to him . . . ?"

"Jamie gave me some books about a man with the same name as you," she told the red-haired boy the next time she saw him. "And after I read them, I went into the Library and found some more. He was quite famous, you know."

"So I'm told," the boy said with a smile.

"But it's all so confusing," Sara went on. "There's all these different stories, supposedly about the same man. . . . How are you supposed to know which of them is true?"

"That's what happens when legend and myth meet," the boy said. "Everything gets tangled."

"Was there even a *real* Merlin, do you think? I mean, besides you."

"A great magician who was eventually trapped in a tree?"

Sara nodded.

"I don't think so," the boy said.

"Oh."

Sara didn't even try to hide her disappointment.

"But that's not to say there was never a man named Merlin," the boy added. "He might have been a bard, or a follower of old wisdoms. His enchantments might have been more subtle than the great acts of wizardry ascribed to him in the stories."

"And did he end up in a tree?" Sara asked eagerly. "That would make him like you. I've also read that he got trapped in a cave, but I think a tree's much more interesting, don't you?"

Because her Merlin lived in a tree.

"Perhaps it was in the idea of a tree," the boy said.

Sara blinked in confusion. "What do you mean?"

"The stories seem to be saying that one shouldn't teach, or else the student becomes too knowledgeable and then turns on the teacher. I don't believe that. It's not the passing on of knowledge that would root someone like Merlin."

"Well, then what would?"

"Getting too tangled up in his own quest for understanding. Delving so deeply into the calendaring trees that he lost track of where he left his body until one day he looked around to find that he'd become what he was studying."

"I don't understand."

The red-haired boy smiled. "I know. But I can't speak any more clearly."

"Why not?" Sara asked, her mind still bubbling with the tales of quests and wizards and knights that she'd been reading. *"Were* you enchanted? *Are* you trapped in that oak tree?"

She was full of curiosity and determined to find out all she could, but in that practiced way that the boy had, he artfully turned the conversation onto a different track and she never did get an answer to her questions.

It rained that night, but the next night the skies were clear. The moon hung above the Mondream Wood like a fat ball of golden honey; the stars were so bright and close Sara felt she could just reach up and pluck one as though it were an apple, hanging in a tree. She had crept from her bedroom in the northwest tower and gone out into the garden, stepping secretly as a thought through the long darkened corridors of the House until she was finally outside.

She was looking for magic.

Dreams were one thing. She knew the difference between what you found in a dream and when you were awake; between a fey red-haired boy who lived in a tree and real boys; between the dreamlike enchantments of the books she'd been reading— enchantments that lay thick as acorns under an oak tree—and the real world where magic was a card trick, or a stage magician pulling a rabbit out of a hat on "The Ed Sullivan Show."

But the books also said that magic came awake in the night. It crept from its secret hidden places—called out by starlight and the moon—and lived until the dawn pinked the eastern skies. She always dreamed of the red-haired boy when she slept under his oak in the middle of the garden. But what if he was more than a dream? What if at night he stepped out of his tree—really and truly, flesh and blood and bone real?

There was only one way to find out.

Sara felt restless after Julie went home. She put away her guitar and then distractedly set about straightening up her room. But for every minute she spent on the task, she spent three just looking out the window at the garden.

I never dream, she thought.

Which couldn't be true. Everything she'd read about sleep research and dreaming said that she had to dream. People just needed to. Dreams were supposed to be the way your subconscious cleared up the day's clutter. So, ipso facto, everybody dreamed. She just didn't remember hers.

But I did when I was a kid, she thought. Why did I stop? How could I have forgotten the red-haired boy in the tree?

Merlin.

Dusk fell outside her window to find her sitting on the floor, arms folded on the windowsill, chin resting on her arms as she looked out over the garden. As the twilight deepened, she finally stirred. She gave up the pretense of cleaning up her room. Putting on a jacket, she went downstairs and out into the garden.

Into the Mondream Wood.

Eschewing the paths that patterned the garden, she walked across the dew-wet grass, fingering the damp leaves of the bushes and the low-hanging branches of the trees. The dew made her remember Gregor Penev—an old Bulgarian artist who'd been staying in the House when she was a lot younger. He'd been full of odd little stories and explanations for natural occurrences—much like Jamie was, which was probably why Gregor and her uncle had gotten along so well.

"Zaplakala e gorata," he'd replied when she'd asked him where dew came from and what it was for. "The forest is crying. It remembers the old heroes who lived under its branches—the heroes and the magicians, all lost and gone now. Robin Hood. Indje Voivode. Myrddin."

Myrddin. That was another name for Merlin. She remembered reading somewhere that Robin Hood was actually a Christianized Merlin, the Anglo version of his name being a variant of his Saxon name of Rof Breocht Woden—the Bright Strength of Wodan. But if you went back far enough, all the names and stories got tangled up in one story. The tales of the historical Robin Hood, like those of the historical Merlin of the Borders, had acquired older mythic elements common to the world as a whole by the time they were written down. The story that their legends were really telling was that of the seasonal hero-king, the May Bride's consort, who with his cloak of leaves and his horns, and all his varying forms, was the secret truth that lay in the heart of every forest.

"But those are European heroes," she remembered telling Gregor. "Why would the trees in our forest be crying for them?"

"All forests are one," Gregor had told her, his features serious for a change. "They are all echoes of the first forest that gave birth to Mystery when the world began."

She hadn't really understood him then, but she was starting to understand him now as she made her way to the fountain at the center of the garden, where the old oak tree stood guarding its secrets in the heart of the Mondream Wood. There were two forests for every one you entered. There was the one you walked in, the physical echo, and then there was the one that was connected to all the other forests, with no consideration of distance, or time.

The forest primeval, remembered through the collective memory of every tree in the same way that people remembered myth— through the collective subconscious that Jung mapped, the shared mythic resonance that lay buried in every human mind. Legend and myth, all tangled in an alphabet of trees, remembered, not always with understanding, but with wonder. With awe.

Which was why the druids' Ogham was also a calendar of trees.

Why Merlin was often considered to be a druid.

Why Robin was the name taken by the leaders of witch covens.

Why the Green Man had antlers—because a stag's tines are like the branches of a tree.

Why so many of the early avatars were hung from a tree. Osiris. Balder. Dionysus. Christ.

Sara stood in the heart of the Mondream Wood and looked up at the old oak tree. The moon lay behind its branches, mysteriously close. The air was filled with an electric charge, as though a storm were approaching, but there wasn't a cloud in the sky.

"Now I remember what happened that night," Sara said softly.

Sara grew to be a small woman, but at nine years old she was just a tiny waif—no bigger than a minute, as Jamie liked to say. With her diminutive size she could slip soundlessly through thickets that would allow no easy egress for an adult. And that was how she went.

She was a curly-haired gamine, ghosting through the hawthorn hedge that bordered the main path. Whispering across the small glade guarded by the statue of a little horned man that Jamie said was Favonius, but she privately thought of as Peter Pan, though he bore no resemblance to the pictures in her Barrie book. Tiptoeing through the wildflower garden, a regular gallimaufry of flowering plants, both common and exotic. And then she was near the fountain. She could see Merlin's oak, looming up above the rest of the garden like the lordly tree it was.

And she could hear voices.

She crept nearer, a small shadow hidden in deeper patches cast by the fat yellow moon.

"—never a matter of choice," a man's voice was saying. "The lines of our lives are laid out straight as a dodman's leys, from event to event. You chose your road."

She couldn't see the speaker, but the timbre of his voice was deep and resonating, like a deep bell. She couldn't recognize it, but she did recognize Merlin's when he replied to the stranger.

"When I chose my road, there was no road. There was only the trackless wood; the hills, lying crest to crest like low-backed waves; the glens where the harps were first imagined and later strung. *Ca'canny,* she told me when I came into the Wood. I thought go gentle meant go easy, not go fey; that the oak guarded the Borders, marked its boundaries. I never guessed it was a door."

"All knowledge is a door," the stranger replied. "You knew that."

"In theory," Merlin replied.

"You meddled."

"I was born to meddle. That was the part I had to play."

"But when your part was done," the stranger said, "you continued to meddle."

"It's in my nature, Father. Why else was I chosen?"

There was a long silence then. Sara had an itch on her nose but she didn't dare move a hand to scratch it. She mulled over what she'd overheard, trying to understand.

It was all so confusing. From what they were saying it seemed that her Merlin *was* the Merlin in the stories. But if that was true, then why did he look like a boy her own age? How could he even still be alive? Living in a tree in Jamie's garden and talking to his father . . .

"I'm tired," Merlin said. "And this is an old argument, Father. The winters are too short. I barely step into a dream and then it's spring again. I need a longer rest. I've earned a longer rest. The Summer Stars call to me."

"Love bound you," the stranger said.

"An oak bound me. I never knew she was a tree."

"You knew. But you preferred to ignore what you knew because you had to riddle it all. The salmon wisdom of the hazel wasn't enough. You had to partake of the fruit of every tree."

"I've learned from my error," Merlin said. "Now set me free, Father."

"I can't. Only love can unbind you."

"I can't be found, I can't be seen," Merlin said. "What they remember of me is so tangled up in Romance, that no one can find the man behind the tales. Who is there to love me?"

Sara pushed her way out of the thicket where she'd been hiding and stepped into the moonlight.

"There's me," she began, but then her voice died in her throat.

There was no red-haired boy standing by the tree. Instead, she found an old man with the red-haired boy's eyes. And a stag. The stag turned its antlered head toward her and regarded her with a gaze that sent shivers scurrying up and down her spine. For a long moment its gaze held hers; then it turned, its flank flashing red in the moonlight, and the darkness swallowed it.

Sara shivered. She wrapped her arms around herself, but she couldn't escape the chill.

The stag . . .

That was impossible. The garden had always been strange, seeming so much larger than its acreage would allow, but there couldn't possibly be a deer living in it without her having seen it before. Except . . . What about a boy becoming an old man overnight? A boy who really and truly did live in a tree?

"Sara," the old man said.

It was Merlin's voice. Merlin's eyes. Her Merlin grown into an old man.

"You . . . you're old," she said.

"Older than you could imagine."

"But—"

"I came to you as you'd be most likely to welcome me."

"Oh."

"Did you mean what you said?" he asked.

Memories flooded Sara. She remembered a hundred afternoons of warm companionship. All those hours of quiet conversation and games. The peace that came from her night fears. If she said yes, then he'd go away. She'd lose her friend. And the night fears . . .

Who'd be there to make the terrors go away? Only he had been able to help her. Not Jamie nor anyone else who lived in the House, though they'd all tried.

"You'll go away . . . won't you?" she said.

He nodded. An old man's nod. But the eyes were still young. Young and old, wise and silly, all at the same time. Her red-haired boy's eyes.

"I'll go away," he replied. "And you won't remember me."

"I won't forget," Sara said. "I would never forget."

"You won't have a choice," Merlin said. "Your memories of me would come with me when I go."

"They'd be . . . gone forever . . . ?"

That was worse than losing a friend. That was like the friend never having been there in the first place.

"Forever," Merlin said. "Unless . . ."

His voice trailed off, his gaze turned inward.

"Unless what?" Sara asked finally.

"I could try to send them back to you when I reach the other side of the river."

Sara blinked with confusion. "What do you mean? The other side of what river?"

"The Region of the Summer Stars lies across the water that marks the boundary between what is and what has been. It's a long journey to that place. Sometimes it takes many lifetimes."

They were both quiet then. Sara studied the man that her friend had become. The gaze he returned her was mild. There were no demands in it. There was only regret. The sorrow of parting. A fondness that asked for nothing in return.

Sara stepped closer to him, hesitated a moment longer, then hugged him.

"I do love you, Merlin," she said. "I can't say I don't when I do."

She felt his arms around her, the dry touch of his lips on her brow.

"Go gentle," he said. "But beware the calendaring of the trees."

And then he was gone.

One moment they were embracing and the next her arms only held air. She let them fall limply to her sides. The weight of an awful sorrow bowed her head. Her throat grew thick, her chest tight. She swayed where she stood, tears streaming from her eyes.

The pain felt like it would never go away.

But the next thing she knew she was waking in her bed in the northwest tower and it was the following morning. She woke from a dreamless sleep, clear-eyed and smiling. She didn't know it, but her memories of Merlin were gone.

But so were her night fears.

The older Sara, still not a woman, but old enough to understand more of the story now, fingered a damp leaf and looked up into the spreading canopy of the oak above her.

Could any of that really have happened? she wondered.

The electric charge she'd felt in the air when she'd approached the old oak was gone. That pregnant sense of something about to happen had faded. She was left with the moon, hanging lower now, the stars still bright, the garden quiet. It was all magical, to be sure, but natural magic—not supernatural.

She sighed and kicked at the autumn debris that lay thick about the base of the old tree. Browned leaves, broad and brittle. And acorns. Hundreds of acorns. Fred the gardener would be collecting them soon for his compost—at least those that the black squirrels didn't hoard away against the winter. She went down on one knee and picked up a handful of them, letting them spill out of her hand.

Something different about one of them caught her eye as it fell, and she plucked it up from the ground. It was a small brown ovoid shape, an incongruity in the crowded midst of all the capped acorns. She held it up to her eye. Even in the moonlight she could see what it was.

A hazelnut.

Salmon wisdom locked in a seed.

Had she regained memories, memories returned to her now from a place where the Summer Stars always shone, or had she just had a dream in the Mondream Wood where as a child she'd thought that the trees dreamed they were people?

Smiling, she pocketed the nut, then slowly made her way back into the House.

ASCIAN IN ROSE

ascian—one who casts no shadow

> *I saw old Autumn in the*
> *misty morn*
> *Stand shadowless like silence,*
> *listening*
> *To silence.*
> *—Thomas Hood,*
> *from "Autumn"*

ONE

1

She was running along a downhill stretch of the Gatineau Parkway, an asphalt ribbon that cut through the wooded Gatineau Hills. The grass on the verge swallowed the sound of her footsteps, but not the ragged rasp of her breathing. Panic shrieked through every nerve end. The moon was fat and swollen above her, but she cast no shadow.

Her mind was empty, except for her fear. She couldn't remember her name. She didn't know where she was. She didn't know who was chasing her. All she knew was that they were closing in.

Terror drummed in her chest—a monster that consumed her with a will of its own. It wailed through her nervous system, a banshee howl that gained intensity with every pace that closed the gap between herself and what she fled.

And then she stumbled.

She fell with bruising force against the ground. Flailing her arms, she landed in a sprawl. One hand clawed at the grass, trying to stop the force of her momentum. The other was closed in a fist so tight that her knuckles were white. Sobbing for breath, she began to haul herself to her feet, but then they were there, a circle of them standing all around her.

Not one of them appeared out of breath.

They were squat ugly creatures, body hair covering their lower torso and legs like wiry trousers, their upper bodies hairless and pale. Wide noses split their flat faces. The heads were triangular, reptilian almost. Thick dirty-white hair like a Rastaman's dreadlocks hung to their broad shoulders. Their eyes were a deep green and, in the moonlight, gleamed like the reflective retinas of a cat.

She turned slowly, panting for air, taking in their watching stance, the grins that split thick lips, the utter silence with which they encircled her. They cast shadows, thick and crouching on the grass. Something in their eyes, in the alien set of their features, told her that the chase, by and of itself, held a certain pleasure for them.

"P-please . . ." she tried, but knew before she spoke that whatever she said would mean nothing to them. "I don't . . . I never . . . don't . . ."

Had they been willing to listen, she wouldn't have known what to say. Her mind was empty, filled only with emotion. Fear. Raw, paralyzing fear.

The circle opened then and another of the creatures walked slowly toward her. There were bones woven into his hair—small bones like those of a bird, or a rodent, or a man's fingers. His phallus stood erect between his legs, its tip shiny. The lust in his eyes was not a carnal lust for her body, but a lust for the hunt. She was the game, those eyes told her, and she had quit the chase too soon.

"Run!" he told her, the word issuing like a grunt.

"P-please . . ." she tried again.

He carried a short staff, bedecked with bones and shells and feathers tied to it by leather thongs. He raised it and she cringed, waiting for the blow, but then there was a new sound in the night. A distant throbbing like thunder. He hesitated, staff still lifted. His nostrils flared as he turned his head toward the source of the sound.

Light blossomed at the top of the hill, the thunder resolving into the roar of an engine. When the machine topped the rise, it appeared to be bathed in a halo of light. The leader of the creatures grunted—they were words, but they were unintelligible to her. Like ghosts, for all their bulk, the creatures melted into the night.

The leader was last to go. He touched her knee with the tip of his staff and pain fired there, lancing up her thigh. Then he, too, was gone.

She collapsed forward, crouching on her hands and knees in the damp grass, rough sobs heaving up her throat. That was the position in which the headbeam of the chopped-down 1958 Harley-Davidson caught her. The big motor whined down as its rider brought the machine to a halt. He shut off the engine, but the headbeam stayed on, as he had it wired to the bike's accessory terminal. With just a six-volt battery powering it, he had about fifteen minutes of light. Kicking out the stand, he rested the Harley's weight on it.

"Hey."

The voice was gentle, but she didn't look up. The rider took off his black helmet and laid it on the seat of the Harley, then stepped cautiously toward her, approaching her as though she were a wild animal that would flee at the slightest provocation. His gaze darted left and right, looking for whatever had left her in this condition, but the night was quiet. The only sound was the creak of his boots as he knelt down by her, close, but not close enough to frighten her.

"Hey," he said again. "How bad are you hurting?"

This time she looked up. She saw a broad-shouldered man, the eagle of a Harley T-shirt stretched tight against a weight lifter's build. His jeans were greasy, his boots black. His face was roughly sculptured, as though an artist had roughed it out in clay but never gone back to finish it. Long black hair was drawn back in a ponytail. He cast a shadow that stretched out long in front of him, almost touching her.

"P-please . . ." she mumbled as though it were the only word she knew. Where was her name? Where was her past? She knew enough to know that she should have one, but while she could remember a thousand details about the world, anything personal was simply a blank.

"Nobody's going to hurt you anymore," the man said.

He reached a hand out to her and she cringed back. The tightly closed fist opened convulsively and a small round white disc fell on the grass between them. Moving slowly, he picked it up and held it up to the light thrown by the Harley's headbeam.

"Shit," he said, looking at that bone disc. His gaze returned to her. "Where did you get this?"

Fear filled her eyes. "I . . . I don't know."

"That's okay. Nobody's going to hurt you. What's your name?"

Tears brimmed. "I don't know."

He studied her for a long moment. She was pretty in a way he couldn't define—not any one thing on its own, but everything together. There was a tanned glow to her skin. Her hair was a chestnut red and tied back in a French braid. She wore jeans and a white blouse with a frill around the neckline. Adidas on her feet. No purse. The big green-gray eyes, wet with tears, regarded him, still afraid.

"I know I don't look like much," he said, "but I hope you'll believe me when I tell you that I won't hurt you. Tell me where you want to go and I'll take you there, okay?"

"I don't . . . I don't have anyplace. . . ." The words were barely a whisper.

"You're scared, right?"

Numbly, she nodded.

"Do you want to try to trust me?"

A weak shrug.

"You can't stay here on your own."

"But I . . . I . . ."

This time he moved forward, and as the flood of tears broke, he held her against his shoulder. At first she went stiff and pushed weakly at him, but he was too strong. Then she went limp in his arms.

"Everything's going to work out," he said. "It usually does—though it doesn't seem like it at the time." He spoke soothingly, as though to a wounded animal. "My name's Blue—funny name for a guy, right? But you should hear what my old lady saddled me with. . . ."

2

In the bedroom of her small chalet in Old Chelsea, Emma Fenn woke suddenly to lie staring up at the pooling shadows of her bedroom ceiling. The three-room building creaked to itself. Outside, choruses of crickets and frogs vied with each other. In the combination living room/kitchen, the metal hands of the old mantel clock above the fireplace were edging toward midnight.

Emma had owned the chalet for a short enough time to still wake each morning with a warm sense of ownership. She had a mortgage, true enough, but the building and its acre and a half of land were still hers. The sense of proprietorship made up for the half-hour drive to and from the city where she worked five days a week.

But it was almost midnight now, not morning, and what filled her as she lay staring up at her ceiling was only an emptiness and nothing more. She sat up, tugging a pillow up behind her. Half-asleep, she became more and more awake as she explored her feelings—or rather her lack of them.

While she never considered herself emotionally unstable, she was still aware of her easy susceptibility to sudden mood swings. She was either bubbling with happiness, or vivid with anger, or mind-numbingly bored, or hopelessly sad—but never this. Never just . . . empty. It wasn't the bleakness of a depression, either. There was simply nothing there.

Why am I doing this to myself? she wondered. Of course I've still got feelings. It's not like someone came along while I was sleeping and just stole them all away. . . .

Some vague memory stirred at that ridiculous thought. She had the oddest feeling that something strange *had* happened to her this evening, but she couldn't pinpoint it for the life of her. Getting up from the bed, she padded barefoot out through the living room to the bathroom. There she flicked on the light and blinked at its glare. Once her eyes had adjusted to it, she leaned forward to look at herself in the mirror.

Her familiar features leaned toward her in the mirror. Nothing different there.

She sat down on the toilet, jumping with a start when something touched her bare calves. It was only her cat, Beng. Lean and black, Beng was a gangly eight-month-old stray that had appeared one morning on her doorstep not long after she moved in, and never left. According to a book she was reading at the time, "Beng" was a Romany word for the devil, and since the cat looked as though he had more than a bit of the devil in him, she decided that the name fit him to a T.

"Do you think it's time for breakfast?" she asked as she hoisted him onto her lap.

Beng purred noisily, pushing his head against her arm while kneading her lap. Emma got no pleasure from the cat's familiar ministrations. After a few moments, she put him down on the floor again and drifted into the living room. Past twelve. She opened her front door and stared through the screen at the night.

What's wrong with me? she thought. Why do I feel as though someone's snuck in and stole away a part of me?

She called up some memories. Office politics—Gina playing her against their supervisor—but while she could perceive that it wasn't a very nice thing to do, she couldn't muster any anger at Gina tonight. All right. Jimmy dropping her for that anorexic model bimbo of his. That hurt was only three weeks old. But while she could remember the pain of the moment, and her subsequent anger, right now she didn't feel anything.

This was starting to get scary, she thought, except those emotions, too, were more something she realized she *should* be feeling than what she actually *was*.

Beng wrapped himself around her legs until she bent down and cradled him in her arms. Closing the door, she retraced her way to the bathroom, shut off the light, and went back to bed. She lay there in the dark, sensing the house around her, the night beyond its walls, Beng curled up and purring on her stomach, but still couldn't call up one genuine feeling that wasn't a secondhand memory.

The cat, had he been able to speak, might have mentioned one more oddity to her. When she was in the bathroom with the light on, she had cast no shadow. But whatever languages Beng knew, there weren't any that he shared with his mistress.

3

Blue held her until the flood of tears subsided into sniffles. The headbeam on his Harley had gotten a little dimmer. To save his battery, he left her for a moment to shut it off, then came back and sat near her, keeping his distance now so that she wouldn't feel threatened.

"The way I see it," he said, "is we've got two choices. Either we camp out here for the night, or I take you somewhere."

The moonlight was bright enough for him to see her stiffen, even if he couldn't make out her features.

"I . . . I told you . . ." she began haltingly.

"Okay," he said quickly. "No problem—or at least nothing we can't handle. I know a place in town where you can stay long as you want. Are you game?"

She nodded slowly.

"We're going to have to find a name for you. I can't just go around calling you 'hey you.' "

"I'd like one like yours—a color."

"Sure. Black and Blue—wouldn't we make a pair?"

"But I can't think of a name. I . . ."

"Don't force it," Blue said. He looked down at the button-sized bone disc in his hand. "Maybe I'll just call you Button." His smile was lost in the dark.

"B-button?"

She was like a mouse, Blue thought, all trembling and scared and lost in the middle of a field. "Sure," he said. "Why not? We can think up a better one later. But first we'll find ourselves a more comfortable place to hang out in—what do you say?"

"Okay."

"So let's go."

He fitted her with his spare helmet, then pushed his own down over his thick hair. Warning her to hang on, he kicked the bike into life and headed down the parkway, the big engine throbbing under them.

She held on, leaning close against him. He could feel her breasts through the thin material of his T-shirt, her arms tight around his waist. Her closeness woke memories he didn't want to deal with, but he couldn't help realizing how much he'd missed having someone to care about. Someone to cruise with and hang around with in the House. Someone who could maybe care for him. . . .

Pushing those feelings away, he concentrated on the bike, on the wind in his face and the asphalt unrolling underneath him, but it was hard to ignore her, hanging on to him as if he was her anchor in a world gone strange. No name. No identity. He could see how that'd screw you up. But sometimes, he thought, it could be a blessing. It all depended on what you'd been. Who you'd hurt, and how bad. And maybe how bad you were hurting yourself.

They crossed a bridge in Hull, over the Ottawa River into downtown Ottawa. The hour was late and there was little traffic, so he just took Bank Street all the way down to the Glebe. At Patterson Avenue, he turned left, gunning the bike up the quiet street to O'Connor. There was a control button for a garage door on O'Connor, mounted on the Harley's handlebars. Blue thumbed it as he turned onto O'Connor, and the door slid open. A moment later he was parking the bike alongside four others and killing the engine. The door closed automatically behind them, rolling smoothly on its rollers.

"Well, here we are, Button," Blue said. "End of the line."

His passenger got off and stood uncertainly beside the Harley. Blue removed his helmet, then helped Button with hers. In the light of the garage they got their first good look at each other. Button spotted the small gold earrings in each of Blue's ears. She seemed less nervous now. Their gazes met and Blue saw that something in his eyes seemed to satisfy her that she was in safe hands.

"I don't know about calling you Button," he said as he looked at her. "It's not that you aren't cute as a . . ." And then he noticed something else—she wasn't casting a shadow. He kept the shock from his face as she spoke.

"I like the name," she told him. She swayed slightly and put a hand to the seat of the Harley to keep her balance.

He couldn't stop staring at the floor where his own shadow lay across the cement where hers should have been. Keep it cool, he told himself. But this was some weird shit.

"Tired?" he asked, keeping his voice level.

She nodded. "What is this place?"

"Just the garage where I keep my bikes and tools. The place belongs to friends of mine and I'm just sort of looking after it. . . ." The strangeness of finding her, of the bone disc and her lack of a shadow, dissolved under a flood of memory. He couldn't stop the look of pain that crossed his features. "On a permanent basis, looks like. Come on. I'll show you where you can crash."

He led her out of the garage into a long hallway that just seemed to go on forever.

"It's huge," Button said.

Blue nodded. "Takes up a whole block. It's called Tamson House after . . . after the guy that owned it. But he's been—"

Button stumbled and Blue put an arm around her to help keep her on her feet. He was just as happy not going into why things were the way they were. He glanced back at his lone shadow following them up the hall, half surprised that there was any substance to her at all. He thought of the late-night movies he loved. Vampires didn't cast a shadow—not in the old Hammer flicks anyway—but he told himself to can that shit. Besides, it was reflections in a mirror, not shadows. And you didn't find vampires flaked out on the side of the Gatineau Parkway. You didn't find vampires, period, except when he thought of some of the weird shit he *had* seen go down. . . .

With Button leaning heavily against him, he took her upstairs to one of the bedrooms and tucked her in, dressed as she was. All he took off were her running shoes. She was asleep before he drew the comforter up to her chin.

Blue sighed as he looked down at her. He put his hand in his pocket and withdrew the small bone disc she'd been clutching when he'd found her. No shadow. No memories. Something was brewing, no doubt about that. He wondered if bringing her here had been such a good idea. He couldn't have just left her there, but after what happened the last time he saw one of these little bone discs . . .

He sighed again. There was going to be shit to pay, no doubt about it. Trouble was, he didn't know if he was up to it—not on his own.

"But what've you got to lose this time?" he asked softly. The room swallowed the words and Button stirred in her sleep. What with one thing and another, he'd pretty well lost it all before.

Shoving the disc back into his jeans, he left the room, closing the door softly behind him. A few doors down the hall, he turned in to what had been Jamie's study—the room they'd called the Post-man's Room after the mailman who'd hung out there all through one long mail strike. Jamie's computer sat on the desk, the green screen glowing like a cyclops's eye in the dark room. A small green cursor pulsed in one corner. Jamie had called the computer Memoria, but Blue had another name for it.

There were no messages on the screen as Blue sat down in front of it.

4

Button slept deeply, nesting in the flannel sheet and comforter like a cat. All around her, the vast building that was Tamson House stirred and creaked. At another time, the curious building, the strange bed, the unfamiliar noises might have kept her awake. But tonight they lulled her sleeping mind, allowing a crack in the wall that hid her memories from her to open ever so slightly.

She remembered herself as a teenager and a meeting she had one day with another girl the same age as she was—sixteen going on forty. They bumped into each other as she was coming out of the Classics Bookshop in the National Arts Centre building and the other girl was coming in. Mumbled "excuse me's" died in their throats as something sparked between their gazes.

Button was an outgoing personality, but it was all surface. She hung around with the other kids at school, doing her best to fit in, though all the while a different set of values from dates and proms and boyfriends filled her head. She read Yeats and Dylan Thomas and K. M. Briggs, paying only lip service to whatever bands were currently popular with her peers. She read the classics and kept a journal instead of a diary. She drew whenever she could—fine-line pen-and-inks, sketches, watercolors, all in the Romantic tradition of Burne-Jones and William Morris. She held animistic beliefs and was positive that everything from the moon and seasons and winds to the trees and mountains and lakes had its own individual personality.

Though she could never explain how she knew it at the time, in that chance encounter, in that other girl's eyes, she saw a kindred soul looking back into her own gaze, *knowing* just as she *knew*. In that moment a curious relationship was born between the two.

The other girl's name was Esmeralda Foylan. Her father was Cornish, her mother Spanish, so her name reflected a touch of either culture. They exchanged addresses and phone numbers, but when Button went to call Esmeralda that night, she found herself setting pen to paper instead. She drew an ink sketch of two tousle-haired waifs on an autumn cliff, the wind blowing their tattered clothes tight against their thin bodies. Under it she wrote, "Autumn meets the West Wind on a distant shore," and mailed that instead of phoning.

Esmeralda didn't phone either. She wrote poetry and stories, it turned out, and she sent back a letter addressed to "My Lady of Autumn" and went on to tell a story relating to the drawing Button had sent her. She signed it "a Westlin Wind."

In the years that followed they corresponded regularly—even though they lived in the same city. Button went on to become a commercial artist, while Esmeralda took to university life and lost herself in her studies. They saw each other only two or three times in all those years, and although they got along splendidly, each knew some irretrievably precious thing would be lost if they allowed their relationship to go too far beyond the exchanging of letters.

What they had was a truly Romantic love, unsullied by physical concerns. Neither had leanings toward a lover of the same sex, but what they had went beyond a platonic relationship. It was something only two women could share, though it had deeper levels than a simple friendship. They were two souls united by some curious bond. To see each other, to do things together, would only bring the relationship down to a mundane level that would steal its magic.

For magic was what it was.

In time they drifted apart, the letters becoming more sporadic, finally one or the other not replying until neither had heard from the other in years. But the magic never died. That spark that flew between them at that first chance meeting lived on, long after the letters stopped. Then one day Button received a card in the mail. The outside was a reproduction of a Rackham print from his illustrations for *Rip Van Winkle*. It showed a raggedy girl, holding a cat, while behind her another figure climbed the boughs of a dead tree that were hung with red blossoms. It reminded Button of the first drawing she'd sent, all those years ago. Inside the card it said:

My dear Autumn friend,

I heard a whisper on a sister Wind. She said the waves have carried a blade of Winter across the seas and its point is aimed for your heart. Oh, beware, dearheart, beware. The knives of Winter are ever cruel. I fear they will cut you deep.

your Westlin Wind

Button stirred restlessly as she slept, remembering, but then her dreams changed from memories to those dreams we all have, dreams that shift and flow like chameleons and have only as much meaning as we wish to put to them. When she woke in the morning, all she retained of them was one word. A name. Esmeralda.

5

Blue's fingers danced on the keyboard and the words HELLO, JAMIE appeared in green letters on the screen. There was a moment's pause, as the cursor moved to the next line. Blue rested his chin on his hands and watched the screen as a reply appeared under his greeting.

HELLO, BLUE. BROUGHT HOME A GUEST, DID YOU?

"You ever miss anything?" Blue asked.

NOT WHEN IT HAPPENS IN THE HOUSE, the computer replied.

There was more to Tamson House than its vast size—secrets an outsider could never guess. Otherworlds bordered the world in which it was originally built by Jamie Tams's grandfather. Tamson House straddled more than one of them. The spirits of Jamie's father and grandfather were a part of its essence. When Jamie died—at the end of that war between the druid Thomas Hengwr and his darker half—his spirit had joined those of his forefathers to become a part of the House with them, living in its foundations and walls, seeing through its windows.

Since their return from the Otherworld that last time, Jamie's spirit had been dominant. It was Blue who discovered that his friend could still speak to him through the computer that sat in the Postman's Room. That computer was never turned off now.

"There's something strange about her," Blue said. "She doesn't have a shadow."

The cursor pulsed for a long moment, as though in thought. Then the word ASCIAN appeared on the screen.

Blue typed in ??.

COMES FROM THE LATIN, Jamie replied. TWICE A YEAR IN THE TORRID ZONES, THE SUN IS AT ITS ZENITH AND THE PEOPLE LIVING THERE DON'T CAST A MERIDIAN SHADOW.

"We're not living in a torrid zone."

THEN PERHAPS SHE'S A CHANGELING. SOME FA-ERIE DON'T CAST SHADOWS EITHER.

"And maybe I'm the bogyman," Blue said. "Come on, Jamie."

YOU'RE TALKING TO A DEAD MAN, AREN'T YOU?

Blue stared at the screen. There was that. He sighed. Taking out the bone disc that Button had been carrying, he set it on the desk beside the keyboard.

"She was carrying one of those bones," he said. "Like Hengwr's Weirdin."

!?

"Yeah. That's what I thought, too. This one's not like the one

Sara found. It's got what looks like a mask on one side and a stick or staff on the other."

The computer hummed to itself for a moment; then a block of information appeared all at once on the screen.

SECONDARY: FIRST RANK

21. A) THE MASK—PROTECTION, CONCEALMENT, TRANSFORMATION, NONBEING
    B) THE WAND—POWER

Blue read the information through, shaking his head. All he knew about the Weirdin was the little he'd heard from Jamie back when Thomas Hengwr was still alive. It was some kind of an oracular device, like the Tarot or the *I Ching,* only it had a druidic origin. It was composed of sixty-one two-sided flat round discs, made of bone, with an image carved on either side. Each image meant something, but knowing how to put it all together was a subtle study that Blue had never had enough interest in to work on.

"What's all that supposed to mean?" he asked finally.

AT FACE VALUE? Jamie replied.

"Sure."

IF THE BONE RELATES TO YOUR GUEST, IT MEANS SHE'S EITHER UNDER SOME ENCHANTMENT, OR SHE DOESN'T EXIST BUT WE'RE SUPPOSED TO THINK THAT SHE DOES, OR SHE HAS SOME MEASURE OF POWER. PERHAPS IT ALL RELATES TO HER; PERHAPS NONE OF IT DOES. WHERE DID SHE GET IT?

"She doesn't know. She doesn't know who she is, or where she's from." In a few brief sentences, Blue described his encounter with Button and what little he knew of her to date.

SHE HAS NO PAST—NO IDENTITY? Jamie asked. KNOWLEDGE OF THE WORLD, BUT NO KNOWLEDGE OF WHERE SHE FITS IN?

"That's about it," Blue replied. "So what does it mean, Jamie?"

TROUBLE.

"Yeah. I kind of figured that. But what can we do?"

There was a long pause. The computer made a humming sound

that seemed to resonate throughout the House. Finally a response appeared on the screen.

WAIT UNTIL SHE WAKES UP?

Blue leaned back in his chair and rubbed the back of his neck. He hated waiting for anything, but he didn't suppose he had much choice. He couldn't just go roust her after putting her to bed an hour or so ago. Who the hell knew what she'd been through before he found her? He remembered the feel of her against him, the guileless look in her eyes. . . .

"Shit," he muttered. Leaning forward again, he signed off. GOOD NIGHT, JAMIE.

Directly under that, the cursor flitted across the screen, leaving behind the words, GOOD NIGHT, BLUE.

Sighing, Blue got up and went to bed. He had the feeling that tomorrow was going to be a long day.

6

The night was almost gone when two men walked down into Central Park from where they'd parked their car on Bank Street. They settled on a bench that gave them a long view of the south side of Tamson House. One of them took out a pack of Export A and shook a cigarette free.

"What do you think, Joey?" Chance asked as he lit up. "Is that some place or what?"

He tossed the match onto the pathway in front of the bench and leaned back, smoke drifting from his nostrils. His hair was long and slicked back from a high forehead, his eyes a pale blue and close-set. He wore jeans, a tan cotton shirt open at the neck and a summer-weight sports jacket.

"It's something all right," Joey replied.

At six-foot-four and two hundred and sixty pounds, Joey Martin topped his partner by four inches and outweighed him by eighty pounds. He was dressed similarly, though on him the clothes were more serviceable than stylish. His hair was cropped short in a military style.

"Got to be two hundred rooms," Chance said, shifting his

weight so that he was leaning forward now. "I mean just *look* at the place."

"When're we gonna start breaking heads?" Joey wanted to know.

"Be cool, Joey. This is just a recon, nothing more. I just wanted to check the place out. We got a job to do and that comes first. Fact that Farley's the local watchdog is just icing on the cake—now you remember that."

"Yeah, but he owes you."

"Course he owes me," Chance said. "Everybody owes me something. I just choose my own time to collect it, that's all. So don't push me, Joey. I don't like being pushed."

Chance turned to face the bigger man. For all his size, Joey looked quickly away, hunching his neck into his shoulders.

"I didn't mean nothing," he mumbled.

Chance punched him lightly on a meaty shoulder. "I know that, Joey. You just get excited." He took a final drag on his cigarette and flicked it out onto the grass. "But you have to learn how to be patient. See, we're businessmen now. We're wearing our colors in here now"—he tapped his chest—"where only we can see them. We don't just go wading into places and break heads anymore. We think things through. We're looking for the profit, now. The percentages, Joey."

"I don't know about that kind of shit," Joey said. "All I know's breaking heads and partying, Chance. That's all I know."

"And that's why you've got me," Chance said.

Joey nodded happily. "So when're we breaking some heads?"

Chance sighed. He let his gaze follow the length of Tamson House. "Soon enough," he said. "But not right now." He stood up and shook loose another cigarette. "Right now it's time to see if this gizmo that Our Lady of the Night gave us can do its job."

He took a small oval stone from his pocket and pointed it at the House, panning slowly along its length. When it was pointing near the O'Connor Street end, the stone began to glow softly. Chance looked down at the pale golden glimmer and smiled as he put it away.

"Bingo," he said. "She's there."

"I don't like working for these fags," Joey said.

"They're not fags, they're Faerie," Chance told him.

"Same difference—they're all queer, right, Chance? I'd like to break their heads."

You're like a big dumb dog, Chance thought, looking at his partner. You don't understand shit, all right, but I wouldn't swap you for the world.

"Come on, Joey," he said. "Let me buy you a doughnut."

"A chocolate doughnut?"

Chance lit his cigarette, then led the way out of the park to where their car was parked on Bank Street. "Sure," he said. "Any flavor you want, Joey."

He looked back at the block-long structure that was Tamson House one more time before getting into the Mustang. That's one fucking monster of a place, he thought. You could hide an army in there. It might be smart if he renegotiated their fee—upped it to where they could hire some more muscle without it having to come out of what they were already getting.

"Who do you know that's looking for some work?" he asked Joey as he slid into the passenger's seat.

TWO

1

"Esmeralda," Button said as she came into the kitchen.

Blue turned from the stove where he was frying up chopped vegetables for an omelet. The kitchen had a name, like most of the rooms in Tamson House. It was called the Silkwater Kitchen, but Blue never could remember why. It was a bright sunny room, with an old Coca-Cola clock over the door and a cassette player up on top of one of the cupboards. An Ian Tamblyn song was currently spilling from the pair of Braun speakers on either side of the tape machine.

"Esmeralda?" Blue asked. "What's that—your name?"

Button shook her head. "I just woke up with it in my head. It's someone I know . . . I think."

"Does she live in town?"

"I seem to remember letters. . . ."

Blue sighed and turned to give the vegetables another stir. If it was a friend who lived in town, a first name wasn't much to go on. And if it was a correspondent . . . well, the world was a big place.

"Don't be mad," Button said softly from the table in the nook. She was sitting with her feet up on a chair, hugging her knees.

"Mad?" Blue took the frying pan off the burner and came to sit with her at the table. "I'm not mad, Button. What makes you say that?"

She gave a little shrug. "I don't know. You just seem mad."

"Frustrated, yeah—but *for* you, not at you. I just want to figure out a way to find out who you are."

"Me, too."

Before he realized what he was doing, Blue covered one of her hands with his own. "I know, Button," he said.

She clutched his hand tightly, a desperate look in her eyes. The intimacy of the moment stirred Blue's own needs again. He wanted to fold her into his arms, but instead he gently disengaged their hands and stood up to return to the stove.

"So—are you hungry?" he asked in a voice that was a little too bright.

He scraped the vegetables into a bowl. Pouring a stirred egg, herbs and milk mixture into the frying pan, he waited until it was half-cooked, dumped the vegetables on top of it, then folded the omelet over. By the time he had their breakfast on the table, a steaming cup of coffee beside each plate, he had his own feelings under better control. When he looked at Button, something deep and warm lay waiting in her gaze for him, but she seemed to know enough to talk of other things.

"Do you live here all alone?" she asked. "Sort of like a caretaker?"

Blue shook his head. "I guess you could call me a caretaker, but I don't live here alone. There's just no one around this weekend. See, Tamson House is a strange sort of a place. It draws people to it—but only the right kind of people. They're the kind of people who are a little different. They don't always fit the norm, at least not in the outside world, and that can get a little hairy. Everybody needs a bit of a quiet space once in a while, a place they can just be themselves, and like Jamie always says, 'This is a place where difference is the norm,' so nobody has to try and fit in here because everything fits in."

"Jamie's the man who owns the House?"

"No, he's . . ." Ever since he'd discovered that Jamie's spirit was a part of the House still, that they could talk to each other through the computer, Blue couldn't say the simple words "he's dead." He didn't know what it was that Jamie was, but it wasn't dead no matter what anybody—Jamie included—had to say about it.

"The House belongs to Sara Kendell," Blue said finally. "She's Jamie's niece, see? Anyway, since she's off traveling right now, I'm sort of looking after the place for her." Off traveling. Right. Which was a very simple way of saying that she was in one of the Otherworlds with the Welsh bard Taliesin at the moment, undertaking her own bardic studies.

"What do you do when you're not here?" Button asked around a mouthful of omelet. "I mean, what kind of a job do you have?"

"This is like a full-time job," Blue said with a smile. "Or did you forget the size of this place?"

Button smiled back. "That's right. I felt like I should have a map just to get down here for breakfast."

"I'll give you a tour later."

"Great."

They ate in silence then, until both their plates were clean. Button blotted up the last of her egg with a piece of toast, then leaned back in her chair.

"So do you have a, you know, a girlfriend or anything?" she asked offhandedly.

The question hit Blue with a flood of memories. For a moment he was back there at the end of that war between the druid Hengwr and his monstrous evil half. He could remember. . . . They were in the House, fighting off the enemy's creatures, their own allies almost as strange. Norindian elves. The little manitou Pukwudji. A pair of wolves. Not to mention Tucker from the RCMP. Oh, they'd had it all—shaman magic and bardic magic and just plain guns and duking-it-out fisticuffs—but none of it had been enough. It had still taken Jamie's life to end it.

Only Jamie wasn't dead, Blue never stopped trying to tell himself. Not like dead was supposed to be. But things just weren't the same anymore anyway. How could they be? Everything had changed. They'd been like a family, only after the casualties there wasn't much of a family left. Fred had died. And Sam. And Jamie.

And when it was all over, Sara didn't stay much in the House, so she left it to Blue to look after. And things didn't work so well between him and Sally. . . .

"It didn't work out the way it was supposed to," Blue said softly.

"I didn't mean—" Button began.

"That's okay," Blue said. "I want to tell you. The last woman I was close to—her name was Sally. Sally Timmons. We went through some bad shit that wasn't her fault or mine—we just got caught up in what was like a war. I used to ride with the Devil's Dragon and I wasn't much of a human being. Man, I had the colors and the bike and the Dragon was everything. But the Dragon turned on me and I was on a downward slide until I ran into Jamie.

"He pulled me up and brought me here and then he and Sara sort of showed me what it was like to be a real person—not just some animal cruising with a machine between his legs, see? Now, I'm not cutting down my bikes, Button—they're like a lifeline for me, out there on the road. Sometimes they're all that keeps me sane. But you can have the chopped-down Harley and not be an animal, you know?

"So I was doing good, here in the House, learning things about myself, learning about how the world works and how I could fit into it—like sliding through it, not smashing my way through. By the time I met Sally I was doing pretty good. But then this trouble came up and I . . . Christ, Button, I scared the shit out of myself.

"Now I know it was a time for that kind of thing—we had to fight or die, it was as simple as that—but by the time it was all over I just couldn't handle the way I'd gone back so quickly to what I'd been. It was like the violence was always there inside me, just aching to get out. It's like it's always going to be sitting there inside me.

"When that war was over and we got ourselves back home, I had a lot of trouble handling that. I hid it pretty good from most people—Christ, there weren't many left to hide it from except for Sara and she was caught up with her new beau—but I couldn't hide it from Sally. You can't hide that kind of thing from someone when you're living with them.

"Sally tried helping me, but I just couldn't take her concern. Things got real bad between us and she just had to split. . . ."

Blue had been staring at the table while he talked, the words spilling out of him in an undammed flood. Suddenly he looked up, straight into Button's gaze. What am I doing? he thought. What am I laying all this shit on her for?

"Look," he said. "I guess you got a little more than you were asking for with that one simple question. I'm sorry. I don't usually run on at the mouth like this."

"That's all right."

She sat there, looking at him with those guileless green-gray eyes until Blue stood up suddenly from the table.

"I've got to check a few things on my bike," he said. "The carb's acting up and . . ." His voice trailed off. All he wanted was to get away. Motormouth here needs the time to clear his head, he felt like he should tell her, but all he added was, "I won't be that long."

"I'll do the dishes," Button told him.

"Great. Okay." He turned abruptly and left the kitchen.

Button stood there for a long moment, then set about washing up. When she was done, she wandered aimlessly down one of the long hallways. A doorbell rang just as she reached the rooms fronting O'Connor Street. She called for Blue, but when there was no answer, she stepped up to the door and opened it herself.

2

Chance and Joey parked the Mustang on O'Connor Street, near the corner of Clemow. They left it with its nose pointed north for a quick getaway. Construction on the Central Park bridge blocked the street going south.

"Now be cool," Chance told his partner as they approached the nearest door of Tamson House. A few discreet questions in the right places had told him what he wanted to know. The girl was what they were after and there was only Farley living here at the moment. In other words, nothing was going to come up that he and Joey couldn't handle by themselves. "If Farley or anybody else answers, I want them out of the way, fast. If it's the girl, we snatch her and run. Got it?"

"Yeah, but Farley—"

"We're not getting squat for Farley," Chance said. "If he's there, great, we got ourselves a bonus. If he's not, we play it like I laid it out. *Got* it?"

"Sure, Chance," Joey said, plainly unhappy, but unwilling to push the point.

Chance took the seeking stone out of his pocket and pointed it toward the House as they approached. It glimmered eerily in his hand, brightening as they neared the second doorway north of Clemow. The House loomed above them, three stories high here and continuing down the block in a facade that made it look like a row of houses tucked snugly one against the other, although it was in fact all one structure.

"We're getting lucky," Chance said.

He hit the bell, then tapped his foot impatiently as they waited for someone to come. Joey took up a position on the other side of the door, a tire iron held down beside his leg where it couldn't be seen by anyone happening to look at them from across the street.

"Okay," Chance murmured. "This is it."

The door opened and he had one quick look at their quarry. She stood framed in the doorway, chestnut hair tied back in a messy French braid that looked like it had been slept on and wearing blue jeans and a dusty rose sweatshirt. The stone flared in his hand.

"Grab her!" he cried.

Shoving the stone in his pocket, he snatched the tire iron from Joey's hand and ran for the car. By the time he had it pulled up to the curb in front of the doorway, Joey was half-carrying the girl under one arm to join him. She struggled in Joey's grip, but she might as well have fought a gorilla for all the good it was doing her. He had a big meaty hand clamped across her mouth to stop her from screaming.

Joey tossed her into the back of the Mustang. He slapped his seat back into place and got in as the car was already starting to roll. Chance grinned as he booted the gas. The Mustang burned rubber as it tore north on O'Connor and took a quick right at Patterson.

"Piece of fucking cake!" he cried as the car squealed around the corner.

Behind him, the girl lunged toward the front seat. Joey gave her a shove that sent her floundering back.

"Try that again and he'll break your face," Chance told her. He shook a cigarette free from its pack and stuck it in the corner of his mouth, eyeing her in the rearview mirror all the while. Beside him, Joey leaned over his own seat, watching her as well.

Button cowered under Joey's baleful eye. "P-please," she said. "What are you—what do you want with me?"

"We don't want nothing, sweetheart," Chance said. "But we got somebody who's paying us a pretty penny to deliver you to her tonight. Let me give you a hint—she's got skin so white you'd think she was dead, and hair so black it's got to be dyed. Ring any bells?"

Button stared at his eyes in the rearview mirror, her mind flooding with an image of the hunters that had tracked her down last night before Blue had come to rescue her. She hadn't mentioned them to Blue because, no matter what she didn't know about herself, she knew enough to know that things like that didn't exist in the real world. She had to have imagined them. But looking into Chance's eyes, hearing something that was almost a whisper of awe in his voice, she knew that those creatures had been real. And whatever had sent them after her had sent these men as well.

"Please," she tried again, but Chance only laughed.

"There's nothing like hearing a woman beg, right, Joey?"

Joey nodded slowly, his gaze never leaving their captive. " 'Cept maybe breaking her head," he said.

Button pressed herself into the corner of the backseat on the driver's side of the car, trying to get as far as she could from him.

"I don't know about you," Chance said to his partner. "You never like to just fuck a broad like an ordinary guy?"

Joey frowned. "Sure," he said. "I just like to break 'em open when I'm finished, that's all."

"You don't get asked back to a lot of parties with an attitude like that," Chance told him. He slicked back his hair with a free hand and laughed again.

3

Blue entered the garage and flicked on the lights. Standing in the doorway, he looked at his bikes. The two vintage Harleys stood side by side. A third was in pieces on the far side of his workbench, cannibalized for parts. A rebuilt Norton, a BMW and a scooter he'd been fixing up for Sara were on their stands near the Harleys, while two trail bikes and a Yamaha he was working on for the guy who'd tracked down the third Harley for him stood in a line along the back wall.

Sighing, Blue closed the door behind him, then slumped in the car seat that was bolted to the floor across from his workbench. It had come out of the last car he'd owned—a '67 Chevy that he'd sold for parts, minus the seat. There was a can of Budweiser on the floor by his boots. When he picked it up, it sloshed. Half-full. Leaning back, he downed the flat beer, then crushed the can, tossing the empty into the metal garbage barrel beside his workbench.

Nice going, he told himself. There he'd been, supposedly helping Button except instead of pumping her for information—like what the hell she was doing out on the parkway last night, and where she'd got the Weirdin bone, and how come she didn't have a fucking shadow—instead of doing something to help her, he'd just dumped all his problems on her. Way to go, man.

It had to be her eyes. Every time he looked in them, he just got lost. He wanted to help her, but he saw something in those eyes that could help him and like some kid getting laid for the first time, he'd just shot his load, never stopping to think about her.

He wondered what the hell she'd thought of it all. She had to think he wasn't playing with a full deck. She'd be having second thoughts about hanging in here where he could maybe help her—and he wanted to help her. But he wanted her, too, and that was the trouble, wasn't it?

He leaned forward and stared at the concrete floor between his boots. Needed a cleaning. Just like his head. It wasn't like him to dump his problems on somebody else, but maybe that was the other problem. The one thing he'd learned from Jamie and Sara was that you couldn't go through life on your own. Give and take. And it had to balance out. It was just as important to take as to give. Sally had told him as much, just before she split.

Should have listened, man, he told himself. But he never seemed to learn. There were a lot of should-haves in his life.

Well, right now he had to try and dope out Button's problem. He'd lived with his own for so long, a little longer sure wasn't going to change anything. As he stood up from the car seat, a doorbell rang. Besides ringing by the door that they were set into, all the bells were wired to ring in certain parts of the House. The Postman's Room. Sara's Tower. The garage. . . . They were all tuned different, so he could tell that this was from one of the doors on O'Connor—the second-closest to Clemow.

He started for the door that led into the House proper, but before he could reach it, the lights in the garage began to flicker rhythmically. That was Jamie's way of calling him.

Trouble.

Pushing through the door, he ran down the hall and spotted the open door right off, but by the time he reached it, all he could hear was the sound of squealing tires. There was nothing in sight. He ran back toward the Silkwater Kitchen, calling Button's name. Something knotted in his stomach when he got no response. Wasting no more time, he headed for the Postman's Room, taking the stairs two at a time. There was a message pulsing on the screen when he got there.

TWO MEN TOOK YOUR BUTTON RIGHT OFF OUR DOORSTEP, it said. Following that was a brief description of the men and their car, followed by a license-plate number. As Blue started for the door, the computer beeped loudly. Blue turned back to look at the screen. IT'S TOO LATE TO CHASE THEM, Jamie said. YOU'VE GOT TO TRACK DOWN THE CAR AND HOPE IT WASN'T STOLEN. The plate number was repeated under that, the green letters and numbers pulsing.

"You got any bright ideas as to how we're going to do that?" Blue asked.

Jamie gave one name in reply. TUCKER.

Blue nodded. Right. The intrepid Horseman. "Have we got his number?" he asked.

When the digits flashed on the screen, Blue grabbed the phone from the desk beside the computer and dialed the number. He didn't want to be doing this. He wanted to be out there, hunting down the suckers that'd snatched Button.

"Inspector Tucker," a familiar voice said as the connection was made.

"Hey, John," Blue said. "I need some help."

"Glen Farley," Tucker replied. He used Blue's real name just to raz him. "How's the bike biz?"

"I don't have time for farting around," Blue said. "I need a favor—fast."

"Have you got trouble?" Tucker asked immediately.

Blue could tell by the tone of the inspector's voice that he was remembering the same things that Button's arrival had woken in Blue. Unspoken was "more of that weird shit."

"Nothing like before," Blue said. At least he hoped to Christ it wasn't. "I've got a license number and I need a name to go with it—can you do it?"

"What's it for, Blue?"

"Just something personal—guy ripped something off from my workshop and I want it back."

"You start breaking heads, Blue, and I can't help you."

"It's nothing like that, John."

There was a moment's silence. Come on, Blue thought. We owe each other, man. Finally Tucker sighed on the other end of the line.

"Shoot," he said.

Blue read off the number.

"If it gets back to me that you fucked somebody over," Tucker said, "I'll come looking for you, Blue."

"Yeah, I know. Wearing a nice red jacket and one of those funny flat hats. Is this going to take long?"

"Give me half an hour," Tucker replied and hung up.

Blue cradled the receiver and rubbed his knuckles in his eyes.

YOU DID WHAT YOU COULD. Jamie's words dropped from the cursor as it crossed the screen.

"If I'd done what I should've done in the first place," Blue replied, "she never would've been snatched, period." He paused, staring at the screen. No, he thought. He'd had to worry about his own problems instead. "Christ, Jamie," he said. "What's going on?"

Before Jamie could reply, another doorbell rang—one of the ones on Patterson Avenue.

YOU'D BETTER GET GOING, Jamie said.

"What do you see?" Blue asked.

YOUR BUTTON IS BACK.

Blue took off for the far side of the House as the doorbell rang again. By the time he reached the appropriate door and flung it open, a familiar figure was just turning away.

"Jesus!" Blue cried. "What happened to you, Button?"

The face that turned back to look at him was familiar, too, but at the same time it was a stranger's face. Button, but not Button. It was in the eyes again, Blue realized. These were flat, almost expressionless.

"What . . . what did you call me?" the woman said.

As she took a half step back, Blue noted that she didn't cast a shadow.

"Button . . .?" he said, no longer so sure. What the *hell* was going on here?

"You can't . . . *how* can you know . . .?" She shook her head slowly. "Only my dad ever called me . . ." She took another step away from him. "You couldn't. . . ." She clutched a cloth purse to her chest, confusion plain in her features, but her eyes still registered flat.

Blue stepped out onto the stoop. "Listen," he began. "I don't know what—"

"This is a mistake," the woman said. "I should never have come here. I . . . I . . ." She turned and bolted.

For one long moment Blue watched her go; then he took off after her. Catching her was no problem. He didn't like forcing her, didn't like grabbing her shoulders, using enough force to keep her from slipping free, but he wasn't going to let her go.

"We've got to talk," he said as gently as he could.

He looked into those green-gray eyes, still flat, still expressionless, and a shiver went through him. They had to be twins. He held her for a long moment before the fight went out of her. He let her go then, ready to grab her if she bolted again, but not wanting to scare her.

"You . . . you know me, don't you?" she said. Her voice, too, was flat. Button's voice, but without her intonations, the way her words rose and fell.

"If I don't know you, I know your twin," Blue said.

"I don't have any siblings."

"We've really got to talk," Blue told her. "Do you want to come inside?"

She nodded slowly and let him lead her inside.

THREE

1

There was a Faerie holt at the northeast end of Gatineau Park's Lac la Pêche, a small wood sacred to the native manitou that immigrating Faerie had named Rathbabh and taken for their own. It lay in the Borderlands between the Seelie Courts of Kinrowan and Dunlogan, what Faerie called Ottawa, and that part of the Gatineau Mountains still held by Dunlogan's Laird.

Once a sainly place, blessed by the presence of the Good Folk who shaped their spells deasil rather than widdershins, it had been abandoned when Kinrowan and Dunlogan fell on hard times and drew their borders in closer to their Lairds' keeps. Bogans and other unsainly creatures haunted it in the years that followed until the recent arrival of a new Mistress of the Night to the continent that Faerie named Loimauch Og, the West Fields of the Young. Her name was Glamorgana and she took that holt for her own.

She sat now in the dun under Rathbabh's central mound with her bard at her side and impatience in her heart. Faerie lights glimmered near the ceiling, glinting on mica embedded in the dirt walls. Furs lined the floor. Glamorgana sat on a fox's pelt, fingering a spellbag of badger fur. Her bard sat on the hide of a spotted doe, a small wire-strung harp in his hands. He played an idle tune, a half-smile on his lips.

"I can't 'bide waiting," his mistress muttered, not for the first time that day.

"Your trouble," her bard told her, "is that you count time by men's reckoning."

Glamorgana glared at him. "Take care, Taran," she said. "With Durkan beyond my reach, I might well spill your guts in his place."

The bard shrugged. "Durkan told you no lies," he replied mildly. "Kinrowan *was* ready for the taking. It wasn't his fault or mine that the sea led us astray."

Their voyage across the Atlantic had taken twice the time it should have. When they arrived, expecting to find Kinrowan an easy replacement for the lands they had lost at home, they found instead a rallying Laird and a Court under the protection of a giant-killing Jack—no match for a woodwife accompanied only by her bard and a small pack of unsainly gnashers. Kinrowan's strength was such now that they dared not even cross her borders, having to send human agents in their place.

"No," Glamorgana agreed. "It wasn't his fault—but I'd have his heart all the same, if he were here, and I might still have yours for speaking up for him."

Taran hid a sigh. It was because of that sort of deed that they'd had to flee in the first place—and far this time. Not just from one county to another, across a loch or on the far side of a moor. No. This time their flight took them into exile straight across the sea to Loimauch Og.

The bard was not happy here. The secret resonances of which only a bard could be aware were too unfamiliar in these hills. He had no peers. No one to exchange news or tunes with. No one except for Glamorgana and her gnashers.

He gave the gnashers a glance. The creatures lay sleeping in various heaps along the far wall of the dun, all except for one.

Smoor was the chief gnasher and he sat upright, fingering the ornaments on his staff and returning the bard's glance with a glare. Oh, this was fine company for a bard, was it not? A curse on his mother and father for never blessing him, with water or with fire, so that the only folk to take him in were unsainly ones such as these.

"Be content," he said then, as much to his mistress as to himself.

"Content?" Glamorgana demanded. "With this?" She waved a hand around the poorly furnished dun. "I've known corpses to have better lodgings."

"Then allow me to offer a word of advice," Taran said. "When you have her tonight, play no more games. Cut her open on a gray stone and read what you seek in the spill of her red blood."

Glamorgana's teeth flashed white as she smiled. "Bloodthirsty words for a bard."

"Bards weary as well," he replied.

Glamorgana reached into her spellbag and drew forth a handful of Weirdin bones. She let them fall back into the bag, one by one. She'd stolen them from a druid, long ago, and they had served her well across the years. But they could tell no futures now. They could point no paths. Not since the fetch had stolen one in its escape. But they'd have it back tonight. The missing bone, the fetch and, in the end, the hidden talisman, too. She didn't need the bones to tell her that.

Her teeth gleamed in another smile. "Wearying, are you?" she asked her bard.

Taran met her gaze, wary now, knowing he might have spoken too freely. Whatever else she was, Glamorgana was still his mistress. "Time lies heavy in this land," he said.

Glamorgana's smile widened. "Your trouble," she told him, "is that you count time by men's reckoning."

Taran lowered his head, accepting the rebuke. By the back wall, the chief gnasher snorted with laughter until Glamorgana turned to look at him.

"Be not so quick to laugh," she said in a soft deadly voice. "It wasn't a bard that lost her on the open green last night."

Smoor stared down at his feet.

Are we not a happy clan? Taran thought, schooling his face to reveal nothing of what he felt inside. We bow and scrape before her as though she were the Queen of Faerie she thinks herself to be, rather than the woodwife she is. But she had magics—more than either he or the gnashers did—so they did her bidding. And how will it be when Glamorgana gains her talisman? he wondered. He was surprised to find himself hoping that the girl would win free so that such a day might never come.

<h1 style="text-align:center">2</h1>

Chance found his Faerie Queen on the night of a full moon in late spring. He was cruising Eardley Road, up by Lac la Pêche, burning off the previous night's partying. He'd slept all day, waking up around six to a house full of crashed-out bikers and their women. He had a foul taste in his mouth that the first cigarette of the day just made worse. Grabbing a couple of beers, he went out to sit on the front porch of the farmhouse and stare at the bikes cluttering its lawn.

The farm was a part of the holdings of the Devil's Dragon—a getaway place where they could party it up without bringing down any heat. It lay outside of Saint-François-de-Masham, and the closest neighbor was a few miles to the east. North, west and south were the Gatineau Mountains. Finishing his beers and a third smoke, he got up suddenly, straddled his bike, and just went cruising. By the time he pulled in by Meech Lake, his head was clear. Taking out a crumpled Export A pack, he dug a joint out from between the cigarettes and stuck it in his mouth. It was while he was getting his lighter that she came out of the woods and approached him.

All Chance could do was stare. She was tall and built like a dream, skin creamy white, hair black as wet tar, with big dark eyes that just seemed to swallow him up. All she had on was some kind of filmy nightgown that left nothing about her body to his imagination. Chance took the joint from between his lips and blinked hard. She was still there when he opened his eyes. He put his bike on its kickstand and tried to still the thunder of his heart. All he wanted to do was jump her, right then and there.

Play it cool, he told himself. Slicking back his hair, he collected himself and lounged on his bike.

"Nice evening for a walk," he said.

The woman gave him a smile that woke a throb in his crotch. She didn't say a word.

"You're new around here, aren't you?" Chance tried again.

The woman closed the distance between them until she was trailing her fingers along the chrome of his bike's extended forks. "New come to this place, yes," she said, "but older and far stranger than you could ever imagine."

There was a foreign quality to her voice—an accent that Chance couldn't quite place. But he grinned at the challenge in her words.

"Oh, I got a pretty good imagination, babe," he said.

"Do you now?" she replied.

Chance didn't get a chance for a comeback. The woman opened her mouth and then to his horror, a snake emerged from between her lips. Not some little noodle, but a fucking huge snake, as big around as her mouth was wide. It came straight out, unblinking gaze fixed on his face, then slid up along her nose, wrapping back into her hair to rise above the top of her head. There it studied him again, forked tongue flicking as the remainder of its length emerged from her mouth to wrap around her shoulders, the tip of its tail resting in the hollow of her throat. It had to be three feet long.

"What do you know of Faerie?" she asked him.

"I . . . uh . . ."

Chance was stunned. His joint fell from limp fingers. He had a vague feeling that he should be disgusted at that thing coming out of her—a snake the color of a corpse's skin—but instead he had a hard-on so big that it hurt as it strained against the crotch of his jeans.

"Let me teach you," the woman said.

She took him by the hand and led him into the woods by the lake. He followed in a daze. The snake slithered from her shoulders to his, crossing by the bridge their arms made between their bodies. He was hers, long before she stripped him, laid him down on the hard ground and mounted him, the snake entwining between their bodies. By the time he came inside her, he knew he'd do anything for her.

"I need a human like you," she told him as he lay there spent, the spill of her black hair tenting over him. She continued to straddle him, playing with the hair on his chest. "A dark rider—a dragon. Will you be my agent in the lands of men?"

"You . . . you got it, babe," Chance muttered, his voice hoarse.

He met her gnashers later, squat ugly creatures that didn't look anything like the fairies in the Disney movies his old lady used to take him to when he was a kid, but by then it didn't matter. He was hers, body and soul.

3

Her name was Emma Fenn.

Blue took her up to the Postman's Room and wouldn't let her talk until he'd served them both up a steaming mug of tea. That was one of Jamie and Sara's things—always going for the tea when things needed talking over. She sipped the hot liquid, gaze roaming the room, from the crammed bookshelves to the single unblinking eye of the computer's screen set into the old rolltop desk where Blue was sitting.

"You feeling a bit better?" he asked.

Her gaze left the screen to settle on his face. A cassette was playing at low volume in a small tape machine in the corner of the room—a recent Claire Hamill album that was an a cappella interpretation of the seasons. Everything, percussion and all, was done only with voices. Blue always thought better with music playing. Right now he figured he needed about thirty albums' worth.

"What I feel is stupid," Emma said. She set her tea mug down on the side table by her chair. "I don't really know why I'm here."

"There had to be some reason you were ringing our bell."

"Yes, well . . ." She pulled her purse up from the floor by her feet and sat with it on her lap, playing nervously with its button fasteners. "I had a friend who lived here for a while and she . . . well . . ." She looked everywhere but at Blue. "You're going to think I'm crazy."

"Try me anyway."

She took a deep breath, let it out slowly. "Okay. That's why I came so I might as well just . . . I had a dream a couple of nights ago—a funny kind of a dream. There were these . . . creatures. They grabbed me, right out of my house, and took me . . . I don't know. Out into the bush somewhere, to where this couple was waiting for us in a glade—a guy playing a harp and a woman . . . honest to God, she looked like she'd stepped right out of one of those old Hammer flicks."

"Love 'em," Blue said.

A vague smile touched her lips. "Well, I guess you know what I mean. Dracula's daughter or something. Black hair, white, white skin, slinky black dress, red-lined cape. . . ." She gave him an apologetic look.

"That's okay—you're doing fine."

"They wanted this talisman they thought I had. I knew I didn't have whatever it was, but it seemed familiar at the same time—you know how things make sense in a dream, but don't later?"

"Yeah. What kind of a talisman was it?"

"Well, they never described it, if that's what you mean. She called it the Autumnheart—like it was all one word—sometimes, but then later she called it Summer's End. It was weird. That guy was sitting there playing this little harp. Those . . . creatures were sitting around in a circle, just watching. And she had me pressed up against this stone outcrop, laughing at me, telling me she knew what I was up to.

"When I tried to tell her I didn't know *what* she was going on about, she made me reach into this bag and pick out a little bone button that had some symbols on it. The bag was full of them. When I opened my hand to show her the one I'd picked, she got all excited and said to the guy, 'I told you she knows!'

" 'Wait a minute,' I told her. But before I could do anything she was grabbing at me and her hand . . . her hand . . . it went right inside me. It was like she was pulling me out of me." Perspiration beaded Emma's brow as she spoke, her gaze going off into some far distance now. "I hit her—just shoved her as hard as I could away from me—and took off. There was this weird wailing sound then, and suddenly I was running, through the woods, and those creatures of hers were after me and . . . and . . ."

"And what?" Blue asked as her voice trailed off.

"I woke up." She gave him a lopsided smile. "I woke up and I was safe in my bed, except I still felt like I was being chased—somewhere else. Like the dream was going on, only I wasn't part of it anymore. You see what I mean? Just talking about this makes *me* think I sound crazy. But I've had the dream again—two nights running now and I feel . . . God, this sounds stupid . . . I really feel like there's something missing in me. It's like I can't feel things anymore. I can't laugh or get mad or . . . Is this making any sense?"

"It gets worse," Blue said.

"What do you mean?"

"You checked out your shadow lately?"

"My . . .?" Emma lifted a hand up against the light coming through the window and her face went pale at the lack of a shadow. Her gaze, when it lifted to meet Blue's, wasn't so expressionless anymore. Behind its flatness was a raw streak of fear.

"This friend of yours," Blue said. "The one that lived here. What was her name?"

"Esmeralda," Emma said. "Esmeralda Foylan."

"Oh, Christ," Blue said. He rubbed his face with his hands.

"You know her!" Emma cried. "And that's how you know what my dad used to call me. I must have told Esmeralda once and she . . . she . . ." Her voice trailed off again as Blue shook his head.

"I want you to meet somebody," Blue said. "This is going to seem weird, but he can help you, so hang in there."

"What . . . what do you mean?"

Blue pointed to the computer screen. "Emma, I'd like you to meet Jamie."

The cursor darted across the screen, leaving the words HELLO, EMMA—PLEASED TO MEET YOU behind them.

Emma just stared at the screen, her mouth shaping a soundless "O."

4

Chance never had any doubts about the existence of Faerie—not after that bit with the snake. Glamorgana showed him her gnashers later—"Usually you can only see Faerie when they wish to be seen," she told him, which was just as well as far as Chance was concerned. Christ, they were ugly. He met her bard, too. Taran, like the Lady herself, could have passed for normal if he'd just put on some real clothes. Instead the bard went for soft leather trousers with something that looked like a minidress on top. And a cloak. He liked this green cape thing and wore it all the time like he thought he was some kind of superhero.

Chance didn't much care for the bard. He figured there wasn't anything between the bard and the Lady, but he still saw Taran as a competitor for her affections.

He did his first job for her a week or so after they met.

"I want you to fetch me a hob," she told him.

"A what?"

"Do they teach you nothing in your schools?"

Chance shrugged and lit up a smoke. "They teach all kinds of crap, but who listens?"

"I see," Glamorgana said, hiding her irritation. "Well, a hob, my dragon, is a small Seelie Faerie—a little wizened man the size of a child. The one I want is named Rutherglen Cam."

"Seelie?" Chance asked. "Like with flippers?"

Glamorgana sighed. "There are two Courts of Faerie," she explained. "The Seelie and the Unseelie. Seelie means sainly—blessed."

"Right," Chance said doubtfully. "You want me to get you a hob. No problem. Where do I find him?"

She gave him a seeking stone and explained how its glowing would guide him; then she gave him a thin white rope made of a material Chance didn't recognize. "Faerie living so long in the cities of men can't be bound with either cold iron or the holy word anymore," she told him. "But this will do—witches' rope." Chance took it gingerly. The last thing she did was rub an ointment into his eyes so that he could see into Faerie. Chance didn't find that it made any difference until Joey was driving him into Ottawa, and then . . . oh, Christ, then.

They seemed to be all over the place. Weird little wizened beings—those were the hobs, he guessed—and others. Black dogs that only he could see. Men and women riding little ponies. Things that looked like they had scales instead of skin. All this, side by side with the everyday reality of cars and buses, skanky secretaries in tight skirts and CFMPs and bozos in their three-pieces.

"You see that horse there?" he asked Joey once.

They were stopped at a red light, waiting for it to change. Joey looked all around. "What horse?" he asked.

Chance watched the tall black horse cross the intersection and trot off up the Sparks Street Mall. "Nothing," he said, rubbing at his eye. "I was just pulling your leg." Joey gave him an odd look, but then the light changed. "Take a right here," Chance said as they came up to Laurier.

They found the hob in a back alley off Laurier—the seeking stone glimmering brightly in Chance's hand as he pointed it at what appeared to be a rubbie sleeping off a drunk in a mess of newspaper and trash.

"That's him," Chance said. "Get him, Joey."

"But, Chance—"

"Just get him!"

The rubbie woke at the sound of their voices, but before he could flee, Joey had him in a headlock and was dragging him back to the car. Chance quickly bound their captive with the rope Glamorgana had given him. Joey looked into the backseat where they threw him and saw a frightened old wino, but the Lady's ointment let Chance see the little hob for what he was. The little man acted like the ropes were burning him where they touched his skin.

"What are we doing with this guy?" Joey asked.

"He's a Faerie," Chance told him. "We're snatching him for Our Lady of the Night." Chance wasn't stupid—he hadn't told any of the other Dragons about what he'd found out in the woods near Lac la Pêche—but Joey was different and Chance had told him the whole score. The secret was safe with the big galoot. Joey'd been his partner since day one, and besides, the poor guy was too stupid to really understand anyway.

"What does she want with a fag?" Joey asked.

Chance shrugged. "Guess we're going to find out. Let's go, Joey."

Glamorgana paid them well—in both gold and, at least for Chance, her favors. It was a good gig. An easy one. And that night they got to sit in as Glamorgana cut the little hob to pieces. Tough little bugger, Chance thought, watching the proceedings with interest. All he had to do was talk, but the little man wouldn't give up squat. Still, in the end Glamorgana found what she wanted. She was looking for a power—something she could turn on Kinrowan's Laird and the giant-killing Jack so that she could have the place for her own. It took time—Chance and Joey brought in two more Kinrowan Faerie before the Lady's gnashers got a chance sniff of what she was looking for in a snug little house in Old Chelsea.

Because the house was in the Borderlands between Kinrowan and Dunlogan, the gnashers had done the Lady's work for her that time. But it took Joey and me to clean things up, Chance thought with satisfaction as he checked their captive in the rearview mirror. Nice little piece of ass, this one. Maybe the Lady'd give her to Joey if there was anything left of her after tonight.

They pulled into the Dragon's farm outside of Saint-François-de-Masham, having the place to themselves for a change.

"It's a little stopover," Chance explained to Button as they dragged her out of the car. "But don't worry—things're going to pick up real soon."

Button shivered at the grin that appeared on Joey's lips.

5

Emma exchanged her armchair for a straightback, which she brought over to the desk. Leaning closer to the computer, she asked Blue, "How did you get it to do that?"

"I don't do anything," Blue said. "Jamie's got his own mind."

"You mean like . . . Artificial Intelligence?"

"You could call it that, I guess."

Emma looked at the computer. "But that's just an old IBM model—I mean, it's so small."

"It's connected to something a whole lot bigger," Blue said. Yeah. Like would you believe the whole frigging house?

Emma shook her head. "I've read about stuff like this—you know, like in that William Gibson novel—but this . . ."

"This is for real," Blue said.

AS ARE YOUR DREAMS, Jamie added.

Emma numbly stared at the screen.

"What're you talking about, Jamie?" Blue asked.

THERE'S NO OTHER EXPLANATION. WHAT EMMA THINKS TO BE A DREAM HAS TO BE REAL. SOME CREATURE OF FAERIE HAS MANAGED TO SPLIT THE TWO HEMISPHERES OF HER MIND. BUTTON HAS THE RIGHT HEMISPHERE—THE SIDE THAT'S RESPONSIBLE FOR VISIO-SPATIAL ABILITIES, THE EMOTIONAL OR ARTISTIC SIDE OF THE BRAIN. EMMA HAS THE LOGICAL HEMISPHERE. EACH OF THEM HAS SUBSTANCE, HENCE THEIR LACK OF SHADOW. THERE WAS ONLY SO MUCH MATERIAL TO WORK WITH.

"That . . . that's impossible," Emma said in a small voice. She looked to Blue for confirmation, but he was shaking his head.

"We've . . . ah . . . seen this kind of thing before," he said, remembering how the druid Thomas Hengwr had become two separate entities.

"But it's not so cut-and-dried," Emma said. "You can't get by on just one side of your brain—can you?"

I USED THAT DESCRIPTION MERELY TO SIMPLIFY THE EXPLANATION, Jamie replied, BUT THE THEORY DOES FIT YOUR PRESENT DIFFICULTIES.

Emma looked away. "Oh, Jesus," she mumbled.

"Look," Blue said. "We're going to help you."

"Help me? I have to be insane to be listening to this."

Blue nodded. "So where's your shadow?"

"I . . . it . . ."

"Right. And just who the hell was your twin that got snatched out of here just before you arrived?"

"I . . ."

"She woke up this morning with the name Esmeralda in her head," Blue said. "I guess that's just a coincidence, too?"

The computer beeped loudly and the words LIGHTEN UP appeared on the screen.

Blue glared at the screen for a moment; then he nodded. "I'm sorry," he said to Emma. "I . . ." He didn't know how to explain what he felt about Button. Christ, he'd only just met her. But what she had was something that called out to him—something Button's twin sitting here beside him didn't have. Right side, left side. Who cared about brains. It was something in Button's heart that touched him.

I REMEMBER ESMERALDA FOYLAN. Jamie's words slipped across the screen. SHE STAYED HERE A LONG TIME AGO—THAT WAS BEFORE YOUR TIME, BLUE. I REMEMBER SHE LEFT US SOMETHING. . . . The computer made a soft humming noise, occasionally broken by a sound that was almost like an old man's cough, as it searched its memory files. YES, I THOUGHT IT HAD BEEN ENTERED. SHE LEFT US A BOOK ENTITLED *THE TALE OF THE SEASONS,* A COLLECTION OF ANIMISTIC VERSE—QUITE GOOD, TOO.

"We used to write to each other," Emma explained. "And we took on other personalities in our letters." She fetched her purse and pulled out a sheaf of letters, poems and drawings. "I was Autumn and she was a Westlin Wind."

I SENSED THAT IN YOU, Jamie said. AND IN BUTTON, TOO. AND OF COURSE ESMERALDA—SHE *WAS* LIKE A WIND. NOT FLIGHTY SO MUCH AS . . . EVERYWHERE AT ONCE.

Emma looked surprised. "What?"

THE SPIRITS THAT MAKE UP THE WORLD SOMETIMES CHOOSE HUMAN HOSTS, Jamie explained.

Emma looked to Blue for help, but he just reached for the clutter on her lap. "Can I see these?" he asked.

"The top one came in the mail just a week or so ago," Emma said as she passed them over. "I hadn't heard from her in, oh, a long long time."

Blue read the card that Button had dreamed of, then held it up to the window. "Can you see this, Jamie?" he asked.

Emma gave him a strange look, but then Jamie's words began to cross the screen again: IT SEEMS TO BE A WARNING. SHE KNEW THAT DANGER WAS APPROACHING YOU, EMMA, AND TRIED TO WARN YOU.

Emma looked at the card again. "I remember feeling weird

when I first read it, but we—well, I just took it as a sort of poetic way of saying, why don't we get in touch."

NO, Jamie replied. FROM THIS IT WOULD SEEM THAT YOUR ENEMY—THE WOMAN IN YOUR DREAM, I SUPPOSE—HAS ONLY RECENTLY ARRIVED ON OUR SHORES. FROM YOUR DREAM IT'S OBVIOUS THAT YOU HAVE SOMETHING SHE WANTS. I WONDER WHAT THIS TALISMAN IS.

"Let's get Button back first," Blue said. Emma started at the name and Blue gave her an apologetic glance. "I guess it sounds strange to you, but that's just what I called her. We've got to call her something, right?"

Emma nodded slowly. Then she pulled a sheaf of paper from the pile in Blue's hand. "Look at this one," she said. "The last stanza. I've read these all through again since that dream and this one seems to . . . I don't know . . . talk about some kind of power. Maybe I'm just making something out of nothing, but . . ."

Blue wasn't much for poetry, but he dutifully gave it a look, holding it up to the window so that Jamie could read it, too.

> That gift was yours, my heart
> to call to sleep the trees
> and dream their dreams
> the berry red and the laden bough
>   their poetry, your poetry
>   their music, your music
>   their strengths, your strength
> through Winter's long
> and bitter night
> oh, guard that gift, my heart
> and guard it well

THAT'S IT, Jamie said.

"What is?" Blue asked.

THE TALISMAN—IT'S A PART OF HER. IT IS HER— OR AT LEAST THE HER SHE WAS. WHO KNOWS WHICH ONE OF THEM HAS IT NOW.

The phone rang suddenly, making both Blue and Emma start.

"Got a pen and paper?" Tucker asked without any preliminaries when Blue answered.

"Yeah. Shoot."

"Okay. I doubt the car's stolen. It's a '78 Mustang registered to an Edward Chance."

Blue hesitated in his writing, then added the address that Tucker gave him under the name. "Eddie Chance?" he asked. "You're sure?"

"I thought you'd recognize the name," Tucker said. "One of your old pals from your biking days. Well, he's still riding with the Dragon, at least he is according to a source I've got with the Ottawa cops. I had him run Chance's name through Ceepik. No outstanding warrants but he's got a record as long as his arm, Blue. He's one of the new biker breed, now. You know—sports jackets and suits, pushing dope and women, running scams. Nice guy."

"This is one I owe you," Blue said.

"I see in his file where you've had a run-in with him before, haven't you? Put him in the hospital just before you dropped your colors?"

"Yeah, we've had our differences."

"The guy's scum," Tucker said, "but I meant what I said before. You fuck him over and I'll have to come for you."

"It's not that kind of problem," Blue said.

"I'm offering to help, Blue."

"And I appreciate it. But it's just something I've got to handle myself. Thanks, John."

There was a moment's pause and Blue knew that he wasn't kidding the inspector. The only reason Blue didn't want Tucker's help was because he didn't want his hands tied by legalities, and they both knew it. But they did owe each other. Blue just hoped Tucker would remember that.

"Okay," Tucker said finally. "Just remember—don't get caught. I don't want to hear about it after."

The line went dead before Blue could add anything. Cradling the phone, he looked at Emma. "Well, now we know who snatched Button. His name's Chance. He's a biker that rides with the Dragon and if he's involved, then his partner Joey Martin is, too. Maybe the whole local chapter."

"Bikers?" Emma said. "What would they want with me?"

THEY MUST BE WORKING FOR THE WOMAN IN YOUR DREAM, Jamie said. IF SHE IS FAERIE, SHE'LL NEED HUMAN AGENTS.

"And what better than the Dragon?" Blue said. He handed Emma back her package of letters. "I've got to go check this out."

"I'm com—"

Blue cut her off. "Trust me in this. You don't want to get involved in what's going down. The best thing you can do right now is wait here for me. Nothing—and I mean *nothing's* going to hurt you while you stay inside the House. It's got ways of keeping undesirables out." And keeping other folk in, he added to himself. He hoped Jamie knew enough to keep Emma here until he got back because he didn't want to have to go out tracking down Emma just when he got back with Button.

"But . . ."

"Will you just do this one thing for me—trust us that far? You can talk to Jamie or explore all you want, just stay inside the House."

"All right."

"Thanks. Believe me, soon as something comes up where you can help, I'll be the first to ask you to step in, but with what's going down right now, I'll be able to do a better job by myself where I don't have to worry about anyone else."

The words BE CAREFUL appeared on Jamie's screen.

"Count on it," Blue said. "You just take care of things here, Jamie." As he got up to go, Emma caught his arm.

"If . . . if something happens to . . . Button," she said, "what'll it do to me?"

Blue glanced at Jamie's screen, but the message BE CAREFUL hadn't changed. "Let's hope to Christ we never find out," he said.

Then he stepped out of the room and was gone.

6

The address that Tucker gave Blue was in Mechanicsville. Been a long time, Chance, Blue thought as he pulled his bike up in front of the house. He left his helmet hanging by its strap from the Harley's handlebars. The Mustang wasn't in sight, but that didn't necessarily mean anything. He meant to go in hard and fast— Chance would just have to take the hand he'd dealt himself and that'd be all she wrote.

When he reached the front door, he kicked the heel of a boot against the paneling by the lock. The door sprang open with a crack like a gunshot and then Blue was inside, roaming through the house. Come on, he thought. Be here, for Christ's sake. But the house was empty, upstairs and down, with no clue that Button had ever been brought here.

Outside again, Blue looked up and down the street, but no one paid him any attention. Chance's neighbors had probably seen the Dragon's bikes pull up too often to get involved with any weird shit going down here.

Okay, he thought, putting his helmet on again. Where now?

He kicked the Harley into life and headed downtown to make the rounds of the bars and bike shops. He didn't get lucky until late in the afternoon when he got to Judy Kitt's place in Sandy Hill. It was a biker's garage, run out of the garage in back of her house. Judy looked up from the old Norton she was working on at the sound of his motor.

"Hey, Blue," she said, wiping her hands on her greasy jeans. "How's it hanging?"

She was a skinny little thing with a frizz of blond hair held back with a hairband. Blue liked the way she handled herself. Even the biggest badasses backed down when she got on their case.

"I'm doing okay," he said. "Nice bike—yours?"

"Nah. I'm fixing it up for Hacker. I like the way these English bikes ride, but I hate the way you have to baby them." She checked out his Harley with an experienced eye. "Don't tell me you're bringing that in to me."

Blue laughed. "No. I'm trying to run down a guy—name of Chance. Runs with the Dragon."

Judy nodded. "Yeah. I've seen him around. Slick-looking guy. He's always got that big ape with him."

"Joey."

"Gives me the creeps, that guy."

"Know where I can find them?"

Judy gave him a hard look. "Thought you were finished messing around with the Dragon, Blue."

"Who's says I'm messing around? I just want to find a guy."

"Sure. But your eyes say it's ass–kicking time when you do."

"So what's it to you?"

Judy held up her hands between them. "Hey, back down, big boy. This is me. Judy. Your friend, remember?"

"They snatched a girl—right in front of the House, Judy. I've got to get her back. I've been running around the better part of the afternoon trying to get a line on him and come up with zip-all."

"You tried the Dragons themselves?"

Blue shook his head. "I'm not exactly on their list of favorite people."

Judy started to walk back into her garage. Opening a small icebox, she tossed Blue a beer, then took one out herself. Popping the can open, she took a long swig.

"I needed that," she said. She closed her toolbox and sat down on its lid. "Let me think a minute."

She closed her eyes and leaned back against the wall. Blue sat down on an upended crate across from her and worked on his own beer while he waited. After a few minutes Judy sat up again. Her gaze settled on him.

"They've got a place in Quebec," she said finally. "Up around Saint-François-de-Masham. Be a good place to take someone you'd snatched."

Saint-François-de-Masham, Blue thought. Up on Highway 366. To reach it, you had to go up old Highway 105 past Old Chelsea. That had to be the place.

"Could you tell me how to get out to the farm?" he asked. "I've heard of the place, now that you've mentioned it, but I've never been out there."

"I'll draw you a map," Judy said. She took the stub of a pencil out of her back pocket and, ripping the label off an oil container, started to draw on the back of it.

"Judy," Blue said when she was done. "You're a dream." He folded the map and put it in his pocket, then gave her a quick kiss on the forehead, before he went for his bike.

"Hey!" Judy cried. When Blue turned, she was rubbing her forehead with a greasy hand. "Watch that smooching stuff, buster."

Blue grinned as he got back on the Harley. "Put it on my tab," he called back.

"You don't have a tab," Judy told him, but he'd already kicked his bike into life so he couldn't hear her. "Don't let the bastards catch you on their home turf," she added as he drove away. She watched him go down the street with a frown. Then, sighing, she finished her beer and went back to work on the Norton.

7

Emma couldn't stay in the Postman's Room with the computer. The way it talked like a real person just gave her the creeps. She wandered down the long halls of Tamson House, feeling like she'd gotten lost in a fun house. The halls and rooms just went on and on, as if there were no end to them. Finally she couldn't take it anymore. Making her way downstairs, she ran to the first door she saw. She tried to fling it open, but it wouldn't budge. Fiddling with the lock didn't help either.

Trapped.

The weight of the House around her, the sheer strangeness of it all made her panic—but it was a strange sort of a panic. Her head was filled with a welter of confusion, but at the same time a part of her mind had her logically walking down the hall, trying door after door. By the tenth one, she looked around for something to throw through a window. A large vase was close at hand. She picked it up, approached the casement with the vase upraised, and then things just got weirder.

The air moved around her, swirling like a wind, pushing her back from the window. She tried to throw the vase as she was forced back, but the thrust of the air pushed it aside with a strong gust. It shattered on the floor of the hallway, shards spraying around her. She flung up her hands to protect herself, then stopped when she held them up against the light. She turned to look behind her. No shadow.

"Oh, Jesus. . . ."

The lights in the hallway began to flicker and she heard a distant beeping sound. Backing away from the mess she'd made, she returned slowly to the Postman's Room, following the computer's high-pitched signal. When she reached the room, she stayed by the door, staring at the machine.

"Please," she said. "Just let me go."

Words appeared on the screen. She was determined not to go closer to read them, but after long moments she knew she might as well. She sure wasn't going anywhere. Crossing the room, she sat down by the keyboard. WE ONLY WANT TO HELP YOU, the message said.

"I don't want any part of this," she told it.

THIS IS NOT SOMETHING WE BEGAN, Jamie replied.

She picked up the sheaf of Esmeralda's letters and flipped through them. "I've got to be crazy," she said. She looked at the screen, the way she would have looked at another person if there'd been one in the room. "How can something I dreamed be real?"

FAERIE HAVE GLAMOURS TO CLOUD PEOPLE'S MINDS, Jamie told her. I BELIEVE THAT WHAT YOU THINK WAS A DREAM ACTUALLY HAPPENED. IT'S ONLY BY THE MACHINATIONS OF YOUR FOE THAT YOU REMEMBER IT AS A DREAM.

"Right," Emma said. "If I can talk to some Wizard of Oz sentient computer, dreams might as well be real, too." She looked around the room. "Come on. Own up. There's someone running that computer, but I just can't see you—right?"

YOU ARE PARTIALLY CORRECT, Jamie replied. I'M NOT PART OF THE COMPUTER. I MERELY USE IT TO COMMUNICATE.

"So where are you hiding?"

There was a long pause; then finally the words I'M NOT HID-ING—I AM THE HOUSE ITSELF appeared on the screen.

Emma stared numbly at them. "I had to ask," she muttered.

I HAVEN'T SEEN ESMERALDA IN A VERY LONG TIME, Jamie went on, obviously intent on taking their communication along a new slant. SHE LIVED HERE FOR ONLY A YEAR OR SO, BUT WE GREW VERY CLOSE IN THAT

TIME. I'VE OFTEN THOUGHT OF HER, HOPING SHE
WOULD COME BACK ONE DAY. . . .

Jesus, Emma thought, rubbing her face. This was all she needed:
a nostalgic computer.

HOW IS SHE?

"We haven't really kept in touch," Emma said. "That card was
the first I'd heard from her in ages."

WAS THERE AN ADDRESS ON THE CARD OR ITS
ENVELOPE?

Emma nodded her head, then remembered what it was she was
talking to. "Just a Post Office box number," she said aloud.

TOO BAD. IF WE COULD CONTACT HER . . . The
cursor paused for a moment, before continuing on across the
screen. IT'S POSSIBLE THAT SHE KNOWS MORE THAT
COULD HELP US, BUT SENDING A LETTER WOULD
TAKE TOO LONG.

"The box is in London, anyway," Emma said.

ONTARIO?

"No. England. It's not much help, I guess."

The screen stayed blank for a long time then and Emma began
to be afraid that whatever it was that was communicating to her
had gone away. The computer gave her the creeps, but even it was
better company than being all alone in this place.

"So," she said. "How'd you . . . ah . . . end up being a house?"

What an insane question. But it was an insane situation.

THAT'S A LONG AND NOT ALTOGETHER PLEASANT
STORY, Jamie replied after a moment or so.

"We've got lots of time. At least, it doesn't look like I'm going
anywhere."

"Think again."

Emma jumped at the sound of the voice, turning in her chair as
though she'd been shot.

"Jesus!" she cried when she saw Blue in the doorway. "You
scared me half to death."

She'd never even heard him come in. He stood there with a
black leather jacket on over his T-shirt. There was a set of binoculars around his neck and he held a shotgun in one hand.

"I know where they've got her."

"You do? Where?"

"Up around where you live. The Dragon's got a farm up in the Gatineaus. It's the only place they could've taken her."

"Are you going there now?"

Blue nodded.

"Are you taking me?"

"Are you game?" he asked. "I've got the feeling you should be there. I mean, if you and Button are two halves of the same person . . ."

He frowned and Emma was pleased to see that the whole concept bothered him as well. Then she wondered just what had gone on between her other half and him.

"Well, it just makes sense for you to come," Blue added. "But if you don't feel you can handle it . . ."

Emma stood up quickly. "Let's go before you change your mind," she said. "I'm going batty in here."

The computer beeped loudly before they could leave the room. Blue crossed over to read the message on its screen. WHY ARE YOU TAKING THAT SHOTGUN?

"Come on, Jamie. You think they're just going to hand her over if I ask them nicely?"

THE LAST TIME—

Blue cut the words off before they could flow across the screen. "I know what happened the last time." In the Otherworld. When he'd gone berserk fighting those creatures. He still couldn't handle the way the violence had come back to him so easily. Like it'd never gone away. "Maybe this is just what I am, Jamie," he said after a moment. "Maybe what I know best is violence and the shit that goes with it."

YOU USED TO WORK ON GENTLER ARTS. YOU AND SARA. YOU TAUGHT HER AS MUCH AS SHE TAUGHT YOU.

Blue could almost hear Jamie's voice as the words touched the screen. It would be gently reprimanding.

"I'm not giving up one for the other," Blue said softly. "And Sara's not here anymore." Was that another of his problems? he wondered as the words left his mouth. Did he feel that he'd been deserted—first by Jamie, then by Sara and Sally? Or did he feel he'd driven them away?

DO WHAT YOU HAVE TO, Jamie replied.

Blue nodded, hearing the regret that would have been there if Jamie could speak. He turned slowly away. "Come on," he said to Emma. "How did you get here?" he added as he led the way to the garage.

"I drove."

"You're parked on Patterson?"

She nodded.

"Okay. We'll get my bike and I'll drop you off at your car. Then you can follow me out. Can you take this with you in the car?" He handed her the shotgun. "I won't get ten blocks with it on the bike—cops'll stop me, sure as shit."

She took it gingerly.

"This could get rough," he warned her.

She swallowed thickly. "I guess . . . I guess that's just sinking in." The weapon was heavy in her hand. "What are you planning to do?"

"Did you ever hear the legend of St. George?" Blue asked her. Emma nodded.

"Well, that's you and me, Emma. We're going up against a Dragon—just like he did."

8

Judy took the Norton out for a spin when she was finished working on it. When she got back, she readjusted the carburetor until it was finally running as smoothly as she wanted it to. Shutting off the engine, she went to get herself a beer. As she was popping the tab, she thought about Blue's visit.

The Dragon. Snatched some girl. And wouldn't you know that Blue'd have to go out like some knight in greasy armor to get her back.

"Aw shit, Blue," she muttered.

Putting down the beer, she went over to the wall and picked up the phone.

FOUR

1

The room they put Button in was on the second floor of the farmhouse. It had a bed with crumpled dirty sheets and an old blanket, and a window that was painted shut, overlooking the backyard. Past the yard were fields with the Gatineau Mountains rising up green behind them. The floor was a litter of cigarette butts, beer cans and other trash.

Joey shoved her into the room, then slammed and locked the door. Button staggered, arms pinwheeling for balance. When she came up against a wall, she leaned against it for a long moment and caught her breath. She took in her surroundings distastefully, then made for the window. Clearing a space on the floor in front of it, she knelt down and stared out at the freedom of the fields and mountains that couldn't be hers. She leaned her arms on the windowsill, her head on her arms, and the afternoon passed.

What made the waiting hardest was not knowing what her captors meant to do with her. At least they weren't last night's creatures, she thought. No. They were bikers. Maybe that was worse. She was still flushed from the remarks of the men downstairs who had greeted her arrival with whoops and catcalls; the sleazy women, with their cold appraising eyes.

But thinking of bikers brought Blue to mind. With no past to retreat to, she went over and over her memories of the little time she'd spent with him in that big strange house he was looking after. Sometimes she half-expected to hear him come roaring up to the farmhouse on his bike to rescue her—just like he had last night— but then she'd realize that he didn't even know where she'd been taken. He might even think that she'd just taken off.

She wondered if she'd ever known anybody like him before. God, it was hard to have nothing to connect her to the rest of the world. The world was there inside her—knowledge of everything from current events and history to how to make her way around Ottawa. But it was impersonal. Like something she'd read about, not places she'd actually been. She could call the city up, street by street, but not where she fit into it.

Maybe she was married and had kids, though that didn't feel right. Even having a boyfriend didn't feel right. So did she just live on her own? What did she do for a living? And what in God's name did these men want with her?

She twisted the bottom of her sweatshirt in her hands, then looked down at it. Even it wasn't hers. She hadn't wanted to put on her dirty blouse this morning, so she'd poked about in the closet of the room Blue had left her in until she'd found something she liked. It was comfortable. She probably liked casual clothes. She—

"Oh, Blue," she said softly. "I wish you'd come get me."

She put her head back down on her arms and stared listlessly out the window. The afternoon passed, time dragging like a cloud's slow movement on a windless day. But then she heard footsteps on the stairs, her door being unlocked, and everything started to move in a confusing blur again.

"Okay, babe," Chance said from the doorway. Joey loomed up behind him, a feral glitter in his eyes that gave his dull features a frightening cast. "Time to get this show on the road."

2

Blue and Emma stopped in at her place so that she could change into clothing more suitable for the bush, then headed off to the Dragons' farmhouse, Blue leading the way, Emma following in her car. At the turnoff to the farmhouse, Blue kept right on going. He didn't stop until they were well beyond the buildings. Pulling his bike off the road, he indicated to Emma that she should just park by the side. When she joined him, she was carrying the shotgun.

The spot Blue had chosen had a good vantage point from which they could overlook the farm. He gave the place a slow once-over with the binoculars, marking the various cars and bikes parked on the lawn and by the barn. There were some rusted hulks off to one side of the barn, but the Mustang was there, right in front of the house, along with a pickup truck and a beat-up Trans Am. He counted nine bikes. Four or five Dragons were lounging on the farmhouse's porch. There'd be more inside, he knew.

"The car's there," he said, turning back to Emma.

"What are we going to do?"

Blue rubbed his face. "Play it by ear, I guess. There's too many of them for me to take them head-on—best to wait until it gets dark, anyway. I'll go down then, see if I can sneak her out, or maybe get the drop on them."

"What about me?"

"I want you to keep watch. If things get hairy, I need you to get out of here and go for help. I've got a friend you can contact." He pulled a scrap of paper out of his pocket. On the back of it, he wrote in Tucker's home and business phone numbers. "But I'm hoping we can pull this off without any fireworks."

"God, I'm scared," Emma said. She held up her hand. "Look at me shake."

Blue nodded. "I know the feeling."

Somehow, knowing that he was nervous, too, just made Emma feel worse. Blue studied the farm again through the binoculars.

"I've been wondering," he said as he turned back to her.

"About what?"

"Well, why they were chasing just Button and not you, too."

Emma didn't have an answer for that. Shrugging, Blue turned his attention back to the farm. It was past six by the time they got into place. As the hands of Emma's wristwatch slowly reached seven, Blue stiffened suddenly.

"What's happening?"

"I see her," Blue said, his voice grim.

Through the binoculars, he could see Button being led out between Chance and Joey. When Chance got on his bike, Joey shoved Button toward it. She got on the back with a jerky motion. Scared. Once she was in place, Joey got onto a three-wheeler with a car engine behind the seat. Blue held his gaze on the scene as the two bikes started up, waiting until he was sure the two men were leaving on their own. He nodded to himself as the bikes turned in their direction.

"Somebody's smiling on us," he said. Dropping the binoculars so that they bounced against his chest, he turned to Emma. "Let's go."

"Will you tell me what's happening?"

"Chance and his buddy are taking her away on their bikes and you and me, Emma, are going after them."

He ran down toward his own machine, letting Emma follow at her own pace, still carrying the shotgun. When they reached the trees where Blue had hidden his Harley, he waited for her to catch up.

"Once they go by," he said, "get ready to move out fast."

"Shouldn't we just stop them on the road?" Emma asked. She held up the shotgun.

"Wouldn't I love to," Blue said, but he shook his head. "Trouble is, at the speed they'll be going, there's too much chance that Button'll get hurt. We've got to follow and look for a spot to take them out."

Just then the bikes roared by—Chance with Button on the back in the lead, Joey's three-wheeler right behind. As Blue had expected, neither man paid any attention to Emma's car parked on the side of the road. He knew what they were thinking—who was going to mess with the Dragon?

"Let's go!" he cried.

He started up his Harley and headed for the road, dirt spitting behind its rear wheel as it sought traction in the rough sod. By the time he was on the road, Emma had just gotten into her car. Putting the shotgun on the floor by the passenger's seat, she started it up and sped off after Blue's already diminishing figure.

3

It was Chance who spotted them first. Checking his rearview to look at Joey, he saw the bike and car coming up behind them. He flashed on the car—the way it'd been parked alongside the road. Just waiting for them to go by. He didn't know who was driving it, but the biker had to be Blue. He wasn't sure how Blue'd tracked them down, but it couldn't be anyone else.

Just like the last time, he thought. You, me and a girl, Blue. But I got a hole card like you won't believe. He grinned, thinking of what the Lady's gnashers would do to Blue; then he realized that she wouldn't be too happy with him bringing shit down on her home turf.

He lifted his hand to get Joey's attention. Nice thing about a three-wheeler. It was hard to unbalance. Not like a Harley. He pointed behind them, nodding to himself when he was sure that Joey had seen their pursuit and would take care of them. The three-wheeler fell away as Joey slowed down, then went into a skidding 180. Joey aimed his machine right at the oncoming bike and car, front end lifting from the ground as he cranked up the gas.

Chance fed more gas into his own bike with a hard twist of his wrist and he shot ahead, leaving them all behind.

4

Weasel laid his head back against the steps of the farmhouse, grinning as he watched Shotgun and Ruthie getting ready to go at it. He looked like his namesake, lean and dangerous, with a knife-hilt protruding above the top of either boot, thin brown hair and a long scar that ran down the side of his left cheek.

Man, those girls were like a pair of cats, he thought. Always at each other's throats. Shotgun was a big blonde, jeans fitting like a second skin, her large breasts jostling in a torn T-shirt that was a couple of sizes too big. Ruthie was small and dark-haired, built almost like a boy, but who cared, the way she'd go down on a guy—any guy, so long as he had the Dragon colors on the back of his vest.

"Two-to-one Shotgun gets creamed," Beard said from behind him. He was like a Tennessee mountain man, a wild thatch of dirty blond hair sprouting everywhere. Even his arms and shoulders were covered with a pelt of hairy growth.

"Come on," Weasel said. "All she's got to do is smother Ruthie with her tits."

"You been counting how much brew Shotgun's been putting back today?"

Before Weasel could respond, they all heard the roar of engines coming up the road. The two women looked away from each other.

"Guess the boys are . . ." Beard's voice trailed off as a string of motorcycles turned into the yard. Not one of the riders was wearing colors.

Weasel stared, jaw hanging slack. He lost count of how many bikes there were after the first fifteen or so. There had to be twice that number. And then three pickup trucks pulled up in the rear.

"What the fuck?" he muttered, standing up.

Shotgun and Ruthie drifted toward the porch, their fight forgotten. Beard stood up and was joined by the rest of the Dragons inside the farmhouse.

We are in deep shit, Weasel thought as he did a quick calculation as to how many bodies they could field against this invasion. The roar of bikes was like thunder in the farmyard. Then, one by one, the riders shut their machines down. In the forefront, a woman in black leather revealed a frizz of blond hair as she took off her helmet. With the helmet off, Weasel had no trouble recognizing her.

"You tired of living, Judy?" he asked.

Recovering from his surprise, he swaggered over to where she straddled her bike. She gave him a cold stare back, then jerked a thumb over her shoulder.

"It took me an hour to get this crew together," she said. "Give me a little more time and I can put together three times this many."

"You got some kind of a problem?" Weasel asked.

Beard was standing beside him now, the other Dragons spreading out across the yard, but Christ, there were only twelve of them here, including the women. Course they had the guns, if some of these dumbfucks were smart enough to bring 'em out. He shot a quick glance to either side and was happy to see that at least Danny and Stern had used their heads. Danny was carrying a repeat shotgun, Stern a hunting rifle. He could see that Judy hadn't missed the weapons either.

"Let's keep this real simple," she said. "Eddie Chance and Joey Martin snatched Blue's girl. We want her back."

Weasel started to laugh, but she cut him off.

"Think about it, asshole," she said. "You want the city closed off to you?"

"Somebody been feeding you happy pills?" Weasel asked. "Fer-crissakes, you'd think —"

"No garage or shop'll deal with you. No bar'll serve you. Every time you set up a deal, the man'll be breathing up your ass. Are you starting to get the picture?"

"Listen, bitch. You try to pull any of that shit and you're dead meat."

Judy put her bike up on its kickstand, and got off. Tossing her helmet onto the ground, she walked right up to Weasel.

"Come on," she said, a feral look in her eyes. "Let's you and me get it on, Weasel."

She stood in front of him, relaxed, ready. Her face told him she didn't give a shit. He thought about the things he'd heard about her and hesitated. Even if something got started, there were still too many of them for the Dragons to come out ahead.

"You and me, Weasel. Let's go."

"Just what the fuck do you want?"

"The girl."

"She's not here. Chance just took off with her."

"Then how's about this," Judy said. "You stay out of it and we stay out of it. We leave it between Chance and Blue. Whatever happens, happens, and we all go on the way we were going—business as usual."

Weasel glanced at Beard and the big man shrugged. "Chance's pretty full of himself," Beard said. "Always saying he can handle anything."

Weasel nodded. They'd come up here to party, not to get fucked over like this. And seeing how Chance wouldn't even share that little piece of ass he'd snatched—well, fuck him.

"You've got a deal," Beard told Judy.

"You come after any one of us and that deal's off," she said.

"I'm saying you got a deal," Beard said, his voice lowering. "Don't push your luck."

Judy nodded. "Okay." Whatever else Beard was, he was a man who kept his word. "You seen Blue around?" she tried.

"What do you think?"

"Right." Judy went back to her bike. Picking up her helmet, she took the machine off its kickstand. The large man who sat on the Norton beside her leaned close.

"What now?" Hacker asked softly.

"Well, we didn't see them coming in, so I guess we'll just see where the road takes us going the other way."

"Can we trust them?"

Judy looked at Beard. "I think so." Kicking her bike into life, she gave the Dragons a wave, then led the way out of the farmyard.

"Are we letting them get away with this?" Weasel asked Beard.

The big man looked at him. "Chance that big a friend of yours?" he asked.

"He rides with us."

Beard nodded. "Yeah. He wears his colors a lot—under that sports jacket he's got on half the time. Besides, I gave them my word."

"Turk isn't going to like this. Chance's been bringing in a lot of bread."

Turk was the president of the Ottawa chapter of the Dragon.

"It's the bread Turk likes, not so much Chance," Beard said. "Chance did his bit to set things up, but now that the business end of things is running smoothly, well, the guy's too fucking ambitious—you know? We only got room for one main man, Weasel.

What goes down today, it could solve a lot of future problems." He laughed at Weasel's frown. "Come on, man. Lighten the fuck up, would you?"

Weasel nodded.

"Who's for more brew?" Beard called to the other Dragons.

One by one they made their way back to the farmhouse.

5

Blue didn't have time to think. By the time he realized that Joey was turning, the big man was already roaring down the road toward them. Blue hit the brakes, swerving into the ditch as Joey came at him. The Harley skidded in the dirt. Before the bike could trap him under it, Blue jumped free. Bushes broke his fall, but he still hit hard.

Farther down the road, Joey played chicken with Emma's car, running her into the ditch as well. The car came to a dead stop. Emma slumped in the seat and the car stalled. Oh, Christ, Blue thought. If she's hurt . . . He started for the car at a run, pain lancing in his side. Might've cracked a rib.

By the time he reached Emma's car, Joey had turned around and was coming back. Blue reached in across Emma's limp form and came up with the shotgun. As Joey came up broadside, Blue turned and fired, aiming low. The blast caught out the front wheel and the bike spun out of control, skidding sideways down the road until it spilled over in the ditch. Joey went flying.

Blue ran up to where Joey lay and thrust the barrels of the shotgun into his face. "Where's he taking her?" he demanded.

"Fuck—fuck you."

Joey was in bad shape. One leg was twisted under him, broken for sure. Some ribs were probably broken, too.

"You can still come out of this alive," Blue told him.

Pure hate blazed in Joey's eyes. "We . . . we got magic on our side," he said. "The fags'll make me better."

Blue didn't know what he was talking about. He sat back on his heels, laying the shotgun across his knees. He didn't think he could use it on Joey, but Jesus, he *had* to get after Chance.

"Guess I'll just sit here and watch you die," he said, making out like he thought Joey's wounds were worse than they were. "Anybody comes along to help you, and I'll blow a hole in them."

"Chance . . . Chance'll get 'em to fix me up. He'll . . ."

His words trailed off as he looked past Blue's shoulder. Blue turned fast, bringing up the shotgun, then saw it was only Emma.

"You," Joey said. "You're . . ." His face clouded with confusion as he looked at her. "You're supposed to be at the lake with . . . with Chance."

Blue grinned. "Thanks, Joey," he said as he stood up. He took Emma by the arm. "Let's go—we're losing time."

"What . . .?"

"Are you all right?"

"Shook up, but—what happened?"

Blue got her into the passenger's side of the car and took the wheel himself. The ditch wasn't deep and he didn't think he'd have a problem just backing the car out. "Joey thought you were Button and it screwed him up. Good thing, too. He might be stupid, but he's stubborn as hell. He'd never have told us anything."

"I didn't hear him tell you anything."

"He said Chance was taking her to the lake—closest one to here is La Pêche. That's got to be it. Come *on,*" he added to the car when it wouldn't start.

"Are we just going to leave him . . . lying there?" Emma asked.

The engine finally turned over, coughed and started. "What do you think?" Blue asked. It took some rocking back and forth before he could back the car out. "You want to bring him along?"

"Well, no. But—"

"Hang on," Blue said. He booted the gas, power-shifting until they were barreling along the road in fourth gear.

6

Judy brought the long cavalcade to a halt when they reached the wrecked bikes. She shut off her engine and the others followed suit. In the ensuing quiet, she walked over to where Joey lay, blinking up at her like a hurt animal.

"Blue's bike's over here," Hacker called.

Judy bent over Joey. "What happened?" she asked, but the big man wouldn't answer.

"He's in bad shape," Hacker said as he joined her.

Judy nodded. "Let's clean up after Blue and call it a day," she said. "We'll load the bikes in a couple of the pickups and drop Joey here off with the Dragons."

"What about Blue?" one of the other riders asked.

"I think this evens the odds," Judy replied. She turned to them all. "Hey, thanks for backing me up."

They hauled the bikes onto the beds of the pickups. Joey protested, but they put him in the back of the third truck.

"You coming?" Hacker asked.

Judy was looking on down the road. "This goes on to Lac la Pêche, doesn't it?" she said.

Hacker nodded.

"I think maybe I'll check out how things end."

"You want some company?"

Judy smiled. "Not a crowd—but you'd be welcome."

They waited until the rest of the group was ready to go. When the long line of bikes took off, followed by the three pickups, they stayed behind, watching them go.

"You think Blue's okay?" Hacker asked.

Judy nodded. "I just figure he might be wanting a ride home."

Starting up their own machines, they headed off down the road.

FIVE

1

Twilight was thickening in Rathbabh when Glamorgana's gnashers bound Button to a squat granite outcrop. Smoor stood nearby, staff in hand, glaring at Chance, who was watching the proceedings with a smirk. Soft music came from Taran's harp where he sat in the deepening shadow of an old maple tree. The bard's eyes were expressionless as he watched Glamorgana approach. The woodwife carried a naked knife in one hand. Its blade was long and finely honed, with two blood grooves running close to its false edge.

The gnashers stepped away from the stone at an abrupt motion of Smoor's staff. Using the edge of the knife, Glamorgana cut open Button's sweatshirt, baring her upper torso.

"Is the metal so cold?" the woodwife asked pleasantly at Button's shiver.

Taran withdrew his hands from the strings of his harp and a deep quiet settled over the glade.

"I've had time to worry at this riddle of the hidden talisman," Glamorgana continued, "but it took my bard's words to give me the answer. Spill her red blood on a gray stone, he told me, and then I knew. The talisman is your heart, sweet thing." Cutting through Button's bra, Glamorgana laid her hand on Button's bared breast. "That pulsing organ that beats so wildly under my hand."

Taran frowned and laid aside his harp, remembering the words spoken that couldn't be recalled. He'd spoken rashly, letting his bardic spirit unravel the riddle through him, but he wasn't pleased. He had no stomach for more blood-spilling. Not like Glamorgana's human agent. He watched under hooded eyes as Chance took a few steps closer to the stone. The biker slicked back his hair with a quick motion of his hand, a look of anticipation on his face.

"And it needed to be your heart, sweet thing," Glamorgana said. "The wild heart—the heart that knows no logic, only emotion. I think I knew it all along, or why let your other half go?"

She played the tip of the knife across Button's belly as she spoke, smiling as the stomach muscles contracted at the contact.

"I can feel the moment growing," Glamorgana said. "The time is ripe to free the talisman from its pretty sheath." She bent over, her face close to Button's. "Surely you feel it too?"

Button's eyes were huge with raw panic. She strained against her bonds, the ropes burning at her wrists and ankles. Glamorgana kissed her lightly on the brow, then straightened, the blade held ready in her hand. Then the gnashers raised nostrils to the air.

"Don't even try it," a voice said, dark with anger.

Glamorgana turned slowly from the stone to see Blue standing at the edge of the trees, the shotgun in his hands, bore trained on her. Behind him was a twin to the woman her gnashers had bound to the rock—the wild heart's logical half.

"What's this?" Glamorgana said lightly. "A rescue?" But she laid the knife down on the stone beside Button.

Taran stood up under the maple. Glamorgana mocked the man in his grease-stained jeans and leather jacket, but the bard in Taran saw beyond the man's simple anger and plain garb. This was a hero, stepped straight from the old tales. An old heart beat in that young breast.

"Take care," he said, so softly that the words carried no farther than his own ears. And he didn't know if he spoke to the man or to his mistress.

2

They had spotted Chance's bike as soon as they pulled in by Lac la Pêche. Blue parked the car beside it and killed the engine. Stepping out of the car, he looked all around them for some clue as to where the biker had taken Button.

"Listen," Emma said.

That was when Blue heard the harping that led them to the glade where Button was bound to an old gray stone. The music made Blue think of Taliesin, and for one moment he thought he saw Sara's bard standing there under the maple, the small harp at his feet. But then he aimed the shotgun at the woman with the knife, a raw red fire burning up through his nerves. He almost pulled the trigger when the woman mocked him.

"Step away," he said, making a small motion with his weapon.

But the tall woodwife merely regarded him, one hand straying to a bag at her side. "So forceful," she said. "And he sees into Faerie, too. Can he see my gnashers as well?"

She made a small motion with her hand, but Blue had been ready for it. He'd spied the gnashers straight off. As they moved forward at her signal, he turned slightly, fired at them, then pumped a new shell into the breech. The bore swung back to cover Glamorgana, Chance and the bard before they had a chance to make a play.

But Blue wasn't prepared for the effect of his shot on the gnashers. He'd just wanted to scare them off. They were standing far enough back so that they'd get stung by the little steel pellets, but not badly. Instead, they were howling as if he'd shot them from close up. It was the iron in the steel pellets. And Faerie can't abide iron—not Faerie such as these, unused to the haunts of men.

A humorless smile tugged at Blue's lips as he saw the woman's dismay. He turned slightly toward the gnashers, saw them thrashing about, clawing at where the pellets had struck them, but still approaching him. He fired a second time, smoothly pumping up a new shell again. This time they backed away.

"I'll only ask you one more time," he said. "Step away from the stone."

"Oh, I think not," Glamorgana said.

Her hand lifted from her spellbag, cold witchfire flickering in her closed fist. But before she could throw it, before Blue could shoot, Taran sprang forward. One hand tore the spellbag from her shoulder so that it fell to the ground, the other closed about the fist that wielded the witchfire.

"You fool!" Glamorgana cried.

She spun out of his grip, but the witchfire ran down her arm. The flames charred Taran's hand, but only the smallest spark had touched him. Glamorgana screamed, the witchfire enveloping her in a sheet of white flame. She stumbled against Chance and the two staggered in a macabre dance that lasted only moments before the witchfire consumed them. The flare of their dying blinded every one of them watching. When they could see again, it was to see a cloud of ash settling where they'd stood.

"Jesus Christ," Blue said softly.

The gnashers howled. When Blue turned to them, shotgun raised, Smoor tossed down his staff and the creatures fled.

Emma clutched Blue's arm. "Blue . . .?"

He looked at her, seeing his own shock mirrored in her face; then he shook his head slowly. "Button," he said softly.

He went to the stone and cut her free, enfolding her in his arms.

"I prayed you'd come," she mumbled into his shoulder. "I didn't believe you would, but God I prayed."

Blue took off his jacket and wrapped it around her. "You think I'd let them just take you?" he asked. Button didn't answer. She just hugged him tighter. "It's going to be okay now," he told her. "Can you hang in for a moment? I want to see to the guy that saved our asses."

When she nodded, he left her leaning against the stone, his jacket wrapped tight around her, and moved to where the bard knelt, clutching his burnt hand. Laying down the shotgun, Blue went down on one knee so that their faces were level.

A twisted smile touched Taran's lips. "I'll be . . . I'll be playing no songs of this night's work," he said.

"We owe you a big one, man," Blue told him. "Let me see that hand."

Taran held out the hand. It was shriveled and black—a bird's talon now, not a human hand. It wouldn't be fingering a harp's strings anymore.

"Witchfire burns . . . clean," the bard said. "But painful."

"Jesus."

While Blue talked to the bard, Emma slowly approached the stone. She stared at her twin's face. As Button's gaze met her own, something fired between them. Gingerly, Emma reached out to touch her twin. Like a movement in a mirror, Button lifted her own arms. When their hands met, they each felt their gazes spin. A rushing sound filled Emma's ears. Vertigo overcame her so that she fell to her knees, eyes shut fast. When she opened them again, Button was gone and she was clutching a dusty rose sweatshirt and a leather jacket.

"What the hell . . .?" she heard Blue say.

She turned to him, tears in her eyes. She could feel again, though it wasn't quite the same as before. There was a sense of sharing present inside her now. The memories she had for the past two days were doubled, strangely imposed on each other. She looked at Blue and saw him through Button's eyes. Her eyes. Their eyes.

"She . . . she's not gone, Blue," she said softly. "But it's not just Button anymore."

She hugged the jacket and sweatshirt against her chest. She wanted him to say everything was okay again, but she wasn't sure that it was. Button wanted him, but she didn't even know him.

"I guess it's got to be like . . . starting over again," he said finally.

She nodded, not trusting herself to speak. She looked up at the darkening sky through the boughs of the holt's trees and felt something else stir inside her as well. The wild heart. That power that Glamorgana had sought, that could never have been hers. A wind touched her cheek, blowing in from the west.

Be strong, my heart, she thought she heard it say in a voice low and husky, as she remembered Esmeralda's to be. *Guard that gift and use it well.*

Use it? she thought. She could feel the stir of tree roots underfoot, could almost understand the words spoken above her, leaf to leaf. They told her what to do. She rose from where she knelt and went to the bard. When she touched his hand, that Autumn Gift drew the pain away. She couldn't heal, but she could ease. Taran looked up, his eyes shining as his bardic nature recognized what moved through her. Then she turned to Blue.

Holding the jacket and sweatshirt close in the crook of one hand, she lifted a hand to touch his cheek and could feel the tension ease in him as well.

He closed his fingers around hers and squeezed them lightly before letting her hand go. "Look," he said.

The moon had risen, casting its light into the glade. Emma looked at where he pointed, then shook her head.

"What is it?" she asked.

"You've got your shadow back."

SIX

"IS THIS a private party, or can anyone join in?"

Blue looked over to Emma's car as they came out of the woods and saw Judy sitting on the hood. Hacker leaned up against a headlight, one heel hooked onto the bumper. Their bikes stood beside Chance's.

"What the hell are you doing here, Judy?" Blue asked.

Judy slid down from the hood. "Cleaning up your messes," she replied. "We took your bike into town and dropped Joey off with the Dragons."

"Thanks."

"I see you found her." Judy was plainly curious about both Emma and Taran.

"Yeah. We got lucky," Blue replied. Found her and lost her again, all in a few minutes. Real lucky. Got himself a one-handed bard, too, and a woodwife's spellbag, complete with a set of Weirdin. That'd please Jamie, anyway.

"Anybody need a ride?"

Blue shook his head. "I'll take Chance's bike into town. Taran here needs a place to stay and I think the House is just what he's looking for. But I wouldn't mind the company."

"You got it," Judy said. "Ah, about Chance. You didn't . . .?"

"I never touched him."

"It's just that we heard gunshots. . . ."

"I was just scaring off some wildlife. But Chance is gone and I don't think he'll be back."

He gave Judy Taran's harp to strap onto the back of her bike and put Glamorgana's spellbag in his own saddlebag. Then he turned to look at Emma.

"Are you going to be okay?" he asked.

She nodded.

"Well . . . see you around then."

He started to get on his bike, when she called his name. He turned slowly.

"Come see me tomorrow?" she asked. "For dinner?"

"You sure?"

"I'm sure." She touched his jacket, which she was wearing now. "You can pick this up then."

Blue smiled. "You got a date."

"And Blue?" She handed him the cut-up sweatshirt. "Thanks for being there."

Blue held the sweatshirt in his hand and watched her walk to her car.

"Do I hear those heartstrings soaring?" Judy asked Hacker in a stage whisper.

Blue turned to her but he didn't have the energy to summon up the growl she deserved. "Let's ride," he said.

He got onto his bike, Taran perching uncomfortably behind him, and they followed Emma's car out from the lake and down the road.

WESTLIN WIND

> O wild West Wind, thou
> art of Autumn's being,
> Thou, from whose unseen
> presence the leaves dead
> Are driven, like ghosts from
> an enchanter fleeing. . . .
> —Percy Bysshe Shelley,
> from "Ode to the West
> Wind"
>
> O Western wind, when wilt
> thou blow?
> —Anonymous,
> from "O West Wind,"
> c.1530
>
> And when you come,
> will you remember me?
> —Christy Riddle,
> from "The Old Friends that
> Autumn Sends"

ONE

1

She'd forgotten just how big the House was.

It stretched the length of the long block in a facade of old-fashioned town houses that were set kitty-corner to each other, expertly disguising the unalterable fact that it was one enormous building. The illusion was completed by each facade having its own stonework stoop and working front door. She let her gaze drift over the steep gables running from cornice to ridge, the well-worn eaves overhung with vines, the odd dormer window thrusting out from the top floor. Towers rose from three of its corners, but she could only see two from where she stood on Patterson Avenue.

She'd forgotten its size, but not its comfort. Nor its mystery.

In dreams she had come back to walk the long halls and rooms, sometimes empty, sometimes filled with people of every shape and creative persuasion, drawn to the House as once she had been, for the refuge it offered from the less forgiving confines of the world outside. No matter how far she traveled—in distance, or in time—she could never forget any of it. Not the secret park inside with its disconcerting tendency to appear so much larger than it was. Not the Postman's Room and the long talks with Jamie over tea. Not the Library, where she'd spent longer hours still, reading and writing.

She chose a door at random, her leather-soled shoes clicking softly on the stonework stoop. The scent of lilacs drifted toward her from the clump of blossomed trees two entrances down. Laying the palm of her hand against the door, she felt the swirl of the wood grain press against her skin. Her reflection looked smokily back at her from leaded windows set in the polished wood.

"Hello, Jamie," she said softly. "Do you remember me?"

For she was no longer the young girl who'd once found refuge in Tamson House. The image the windows cast back was of a tall woman, gold and brown hair falling to the small of her back, gray eyes serious in a fine-boned face. Her faded blue raincoat looked washed-out in the reflection. The leather carpetbag at her feet was no more than a smudge of shadow. She had changed in so many ways. In others, she hadn't changed at all.

When she took her palm away from the wood, the door swung silently open. A small wind rose up at her feet, tossing her hair. Not until it gusted away did she step inside.

It was very much like walking into the reflection. The sense of smokiness was deeper here. The building's age lay warm and thick in the air. It smelled as comfortable as the scent of a favorite old shirt, brought out of a drawer scented with a potpourri gathered and dried in the deeps of autumn. The wallpaper was a fading Morris design. The carpet was worn, but still plush underfoot. A hallway stretched for as far as she could see in either direction.

Cocking her head, she appeared to listen to some unseen speaker. She touched a hand to the pocket of her raincoat. A rustle of paper answered her touch; then she turned to her left and began to walk down the long hallway.

2

The elders of the Djibwe taught that there were three parts to a man: *wiyo,* the corporeal body; *udjitchog,* the soul, which is the seat of the will and allows him to perceive things, to reason about them, and to remember them; and *udjibbom,* the shadow, which is the eye of the soul, awakening it to perception and knowledge. When a man travels, his soul ranges before or behind him, but his shadow walks with him.

As Migizi of the Black Duck totem set about constructing his *jessakan,* his conjuring lodge, his soul rested by a stand of honeysuckle nearby, looking to the west. The sweet smell of the honeysuckle reached Migizi where he worked, but stronger was the scent of sweetgrass and dirt underfoot. He thrust four birch poles into the soft ground, one for each of the cardinal points. These he connected with shorter lengths of cedar, fastening them to the poles with leather thongs. Four connecting one pole to another, then four and four and four again. Sixteen in all.

On one pole, that which faced Nanibush, the ruler of the west, he fastened a small pine bough. Between the north and east poles, he strung a strand of braided leather festooned with *migis* shells, the small bones of birds, and wooden beads that rattled against each other whenever the wind moved them. Over the east and south poles, he hung a number of deerskins, stitched together and so perfectly cured that they were as supple as cloth. Inside the lodge, he placed his *buankik,* his water drum—a hollowed cedar log covered with deerhide and partially filled with water.

His shadow was the first to become aware of the new presence approaching his *jessakan,* warning him with a twitch that started at the nape of his neck, then traveled up, behind his eyes. His soul turned to look down from under the honeysuckles. The shells, bones and beads of the conjuring lodge rattled in a stronger gust of wind; the deerskins flapped. Migizi himself could feel not a breath of that wind, though he stood no more than two feet from the eastern pole.

"Nanabozho," he murmured.

But he knew it wasn't the great uncle manitou playing a trick on him. Migizi was familiar with the manitou, enough to recognize and put a name to all the mysteries, great and small. Some came— wind shadows, small thunders—for the smoke of the tobacco Migizi offered from his spirit pipe: they told him secrets in return. Others came only to watch, though they, too, would accept his tobacco.

This manitou took no tobacco, and told no secrets. It came only to watch, drawn to Migizi's side whether he conducted a cere- mony or not. Like the other manitou, it brought only its shadow into his company. Unlike the others, it brushed up against his leathery brown skin and touched his moose-hide shirt and leggings with airy fingers. It traced the beadwork designs of the bandolier that held his sacred tobacco pouch and spirit pipe. It fingered his long graying braids. It whispered in his ear, but the words it spoke were of a language that no Djibwe knew.

It had no name. None that Migizi knew. None, he was sure, that it even knew itself.

It was because of this manitou that Migizi had constructed his conjuring lodge today. He meant to ask Nanibush if this manitou was an errant soul, lost from Epanggishimuk, the spirit land in the west where Nanibush ruled and the spirits traveled after death. For sometimes, because of its strangeness, that was what Migizi per- ceived it to be. A lost soul of a dead manitou. Not the shadow of a living one. He meant to ask Nanibush to guide it home so that it might be born again, the line of its clan unbroken.

For manitou, like men, had a *madjimadzuin*—a moving line, an earthly Milky Way connecting those who had gone before with those who followed. The Milky Way stars that rode the skies at night were part of an enormous bucket-handle that held the earth in place. If ever it broke, the world would come to an end. So it was with the chain of *madjimadzuin*. When it broke, a clan ended.

His conjuring lodge shook again, shells and bones and beads rattling, deerskins slapping against the poles. Taking out his spirit pipe, he filled its soapstone bowl with a pinch of tobacco, which he lit from the coal that he carried in a small clay jar for that purpose.

"Be patient," Migizi said, not unkindly, to the strange manitou. "I mean to help you."

He left the smoke as an offering for it, then settled himself on the ground inside the *jessakan,* legs crossed, eyes closed, his shadow settling like a cloak upon his shoulders. He drew the deerskins down until he was enclosed in a warm, dark cocoon. Now the smell of sweetgrass and freshly turned earth was very strong.

"Me-we-yan, ha, ha, ha," he sang softly. I go into the conjuring lodge to see the medicine.

Filling his spirit pipe again, he set it on the ground in front of him. He let a stillness fall over him, a quiet that had its source in his *skibdagan,* the medicine bag that hung from his belt where the dream objects of his totem lay hidden from prying eyes. Untying the bag, he set it down by his knee and fingered the *wadjigan* inside, one by one.

A carved stone. Black duck feathers gathered together with a twist of leather. The polished shell of a baby turtle. Bone beads. The claw of a lynx. A small piece of wood, rubbed smooth by the stones of a river. Clamshell charms, filled with herbs and salves, kept sealed with pine-tree resin.

Tapping the water drum with his other hand, he sang again.

"Ka-ka-mi-ni-ni-ta." We spirits are talking together.

He lit the spirit pipe and the conjuring lodge filled with its smoke. He alternated then, between the pipe and the drum, the dream objects of his *skibdagan* and the chant.

The *wadjigan* spoke to his totem, Nenshib, the Black Duck. The drum talked to the *animiki,* the thunders, and asked for their aid in speeding his message to where the sun, moon and stars set. The smoke called to Nanibush, the grandson of Grandmother Toad and ruler of the west.

His shadow lay across his shoulders, listening. Outside, the unusual manitou circled his *jessakan,* making its deerskins flap. By the honeysuckles, his soul looked westward once more.

3

The Postman's Room was on the second floor, in the part of the House that faced O'Connor Street. Laying her carpetbag on the floor against the wall in the hallway outside, she stood in the doorway and looked in. The rush of memories that stirred in her now was the strongest she'd felt since she'd entered Tamson House.

The room hadn't changed at all.

The old rolltop desk that housed Jamie's computer, Memoria, shared the west wall with a hearth and mantel, and a sideboard laden with knickknacks and curios. A window overlooking O'Connor Street was set in the middle of the east wall. The remaining wall space was taken up with bookshelves, stuffed to overflowing with fat volumes and slim folios. In front of the desk was an old-fashioned wooden secretarial chair with a swivel seat, faded green cushions and wooden arms. The other furnishings consisted of a pair of overstuffed club chairs near the window, each of which had a small fat ottoman before it, the low table between the chairs, and the double floor lamp behind them, its brass base and stand gleaming in the light that came through the window.

Her memories were so strong she could almost see Jamie sitting there in one of the club chairs, looking up at her appearance in the doorway, smiling a welcome as though she'd never left. As though he were still alive.

She'd never realized just how much she'd missed him.

By the window, a set of small silver chimes tinkled, though the window was closed. Her hand returned to the pocket of her raincoat to touch the letter there.

But then he wasn't really dead, was he? At least not in the common sense of the word. Because he was still here, in the House. A part of its walls and foundations. Sensing, hearing, smelling, tasting through its wood and stone. Seeing through its windows. And here, in the Postman's Room, his presence was stronger than ever. As though this was the heart of the House. And that was how it should be. Jamie always had been its heart.

The computer made a beeping sound to get her attention. When she looked at it, the cursor moved across the screen, leaving behind it a short trail of words. She started to step into the room when a voice stopped her.

"I wouldn't go in there."

A wind rose up at her feet, rustling the cloth of her skirt and raincoat, flicking the ends of her hair against the small of her back.

She turned quickly to find a young man in the hall beside her who took a fast step back at her sudden movement.

His hair was short and dyed an extreme blond, with a quarter-inch of black roots showing. Dark eyes watched her carefully. He had a slender frame and wore jeans and a Billy Bragg T-shirt with the arms torn off. The T-shirt had a logo that read "Talking with the Taxman About Poetry." He appeared to be in his late teens.

He stopped moving when she faced him, but looked ready to bolt. She found a smile.

"I'm sorry," she said. "You startled me." Her voice had the faint cadence of a British accent. "What did you say?"

Her smile and the soft tone of her voice calmed him.

"It's just—you shouldn't go in there. Blue doesn't like it and it makes the House act weird."

"Act weird?" she asked. "What do you mean?"

He shrugged. "Lights start flickering and sometimes it can feel like there's an earthquake or something, shaking things up down in the cellar. You're new here, right?"

She shook her head. "I used to live here—a long time ago. This room and I are old friends."

"Well, it's your funeral. I just thought I'd tell you. And Blue's not going to like your poking around in there."

"Who is this Blue?"

"I guess it was a real long time ago that you lived here—everybody tells me that he's been here forever. He kind of runs the place, though the House itself has got a way of letting you know where you can go and what you can do. It's like there's all these people staying here and nobody messes things up."

She nodded. "I remember that." Some things never changed. "Are there many guests staying here just now?"

"There's a few full-timers—like me and Blue and this weird one-handed guy who spends most of his time in the garden. Right now I guess there's maybe, I don't know, twenty people?"

"And is this Blue around?"

"No. He's at the hospital. His girlfriend came down with something weird a couple of weeks ago and he's been sitting with her, so he hasn't been around much lately."

"I see." She pushed a loose strand of hair away from her shoulder so that it fell down her back once more.

"This is going to sound weird," he said, "but when you first turned around there was this wind . . .?"

She gave him a blank look, then remembered. "It must have been a draft," she said with a smile. "Old houses like this get them, you know. What's your name?"

"Tim Gavin. I'm writing a play. A musical. It's about what happens to kids when their parents split up. I know that sounds depressing, and I'm keeping it serious, but it's not going to be all downbeat. I'm going to lighten it up some."

His eyes took on a real glow as he described the project.

"It sounds like it could be a winner," she said.

"Well, maybe. Nobody's much interested in it—I've got no credibility, you know, 'cause this is just my first one. That's why I'm staying here. If I had to pay rent somewhere, I'd be too busy working some dead-end job to do any writing."

"I know exactly what you mean."

"Do you write, too?"

"Sometimes. Mostly just the kinds of things that have a very limited audience of one: me." She smiled. "My name's Esmeralda Foylan."

"Are you here to do some writing, too?"

Esmeralda shook her head. "I'm here to see some old friends—and perhaps make some new ones."

She offered him her hand. Giving her a quick grin, Tim stepped forward and shook.

"Do you want to come have some coffee or tea?" he asked. "Most people are using the Lobo Kitchen on the north side of the building, but I keep my stuff with Blue's in the Silkwater Kitchen—that's the one that overlooks the garden."

"I remember it," Esmeralda said. She smiled, hearing the old familiar room names of the House dropping so casually from Tim's lips. "After the long drive from the airport, some tea would be lovely. But first I have to talk to someone."

Tim followed her gaze as it went into the Postman's Room. "There's a phone in the kitchen," he said.

"The person I want to talk to is in here," she said.

"But there's no one in—"

"You go ahead and put the water on—I shouldn't be long."

Tim gave her an uncomfortable look. He hesitated in the hall-way, flinching slightly as she entered the study. When nothing happened, he moved to the doorway and looked in.

Esmeralda didn't look up as she sat down in front of the computer. "I won't be long," she repeated.

"Okay," Tim said. "I can take a hint. But Blue's—"

"Just going to have to live with it," she said.

She waited until she sensed him walking down the hallway before turning her attention to the words that were still on the screen.

THANK YOU FOR COMING, they said.

"Not even a hello, Jamie?" she asked.

The chimes by the window tinkled again, and then a new series of words spilled out from behind the cursor as it dropped two lines and sped across the screen.

4

Smoor had changed in the months since his mistress had been slain. Unlike his brothers, who had fled into the hills the night of her death, fled not to return, he had crept back into the glade once the humans were gone. He took up the ashes of his mistress and her human puppet in his hands and spat on them, then smeared some of the mixture on his face and torso. More of it he had swallowed, and then the convulsions dropped him to the ground, pain like a fire inside, burning behind his eyes, shrieking as it swept like lava through his nervous system. He wept and tore at the grass, howling and gnashing his teeth, until finally, with the dawn, the pain left him.

And he was changed.

No longer the simple squat gnasher, with a face like a toad's and a mind so simple it could only follow, never lead. Like a phoenix, knowledge had risen up from the ashes of the dead to wing into his mind. The woodwife knowledge of his slain mistress. The human knowledge of her pet.

Autumn sped by and the long months of winter. By the time spring touched the Gatineau Hills, he was ready to leave the solitary holt where he'd hidden away for half a year. In that time he had assimilated what the ashes had given to him.

And he was changed.

He could bide the touch of iron now and understood the ways of men—that a gift from his mistress's human puppet. From the ashes of his mistress herself, he had acquired a woodwife's Faerie lore. He could farsee. He could change his shape to walk among men or Faerie as one of their own. His own strengths were undiminished.

There was only one price set by the shades of his mistress and her puppet: in payment for what they had given him, the Autumn Heart and her friends must die. It was an easy debt for him to discharge for he had his own score to settle with them.

So now he walked in human form down a corridor of Ottawa's General Hospital. He paused at the doorway of a private room and looked inside. The woman on the bed lay very still, an IV tube in one pale arm, the lights of monitoring units blinking behind her. The man sitting by the bed looked up, eyes bloodshot and haunted.

What the man saw was an orderly in hospital greens, pausing at the door. What Smoor saw were two victims, one already half-dead. He gave the man a solemn nod, then moved on down the hall, a thin smile touching his lips once he was out of sight.

Soon, he thought. Within hours, the Autumn Heart would belong to him.

5

It was a bizarre tale that Jamie related, the words appearing on his screen almost faster than Esmeralda could read them. Some of it she had known already. She had been there at the beginning—three thousand miles away, but aware enough to send her warning across the Atlantic. And she had been there at the end. Briefly. Like a murmur of wind, fanning the spark of Emma's Autumn Gift into a glow. But she hadn't known the details that fell between her warning and the tale's resolution. She hadn't watched the glowing ember subsequently fade, the spark die, the darkness return.

The first she knew that all was not as it should be came to her in a waking dream that showed Emma's familiar face, the features now pale and drawn, the promise of the gift that lay within no longer hidden, but fled. Then the letter arrived at her Chelsea flat, a letter from a dead man, and she knew that it was too late for warnings and that words could not be enough.

And so she had come. Returned to the city of her youth. To the strange rambling house that now served as the body of one of her dearest friends.

She read the last of what was on the screen, then leaned back in the chair, absorbing what she'd been told. Her gaze strayed, not quite focused, until it fell upon a small leather bag that lay on the desk's blotter. Here were the Weirdin that Blue had brought back from the glade.

Blue, she thought. Who was this man? Jamie's friend, Emma's lover. She felt as though she should know him, but knew they'd never met. Not on this turn of the world's wheel.

The bone discs clicked against each other with a muffled sound when she picked up the bag. She'd found references to them in druidic texts, studied the meanings of the symbols inscribed on either side, understanding them with a familiarity that had long since ceased to surprise her. It was often that way for her with old things—ancient languages, the placement of stone circles, the bardic calendars of the trees, oracular devices. She'd always had an instinctive grasp of their meanings, their relationships with the past, and with the world as it was now and might come to be.

The bones were worn and smooth to the touch. She could feel the ridges of their inscriptions, smoothed as well. By time. And much use. Their age tingled against her fingers, the years rising up from them through the pores of her skin to spark and flicker in her mind.

A quick glimpse, she thought. Not a full reading, just a glimpse into where we are. Where we're going.

She drew three of the bones out of the bag and laid them out in a row on the blotter.

Secondary, First Rank: The Acorn, or Hazelnut. For hidden wisdom and friendship.

That was Emma. Or herself. Perhaps both.

Secondary, Second Rank: The Forest. A place of testing and unknown peril.

The peril was Emma's . . . unless . . . It depended on who was being tested, she realized.

Tertiary, Mobile: The Eagle. Release from bondage.

Who was imprisoned? Emma in her coma? Or were the bones riddling deeper than that? Release could mean many things. A release from a way of life. Release from life itself.

The computer beeped and she looked at the screen. It went blank for a moment; then Jamie's words appeared.

THE TROUBLE WITH ORACULAR DEVICES IS THAT WITHOUT A CLEAR QUESTION THEY TEND TO MUDDY THE ISSUE.

Esmeralda nodded. "And sometimes the best thinking is done when you're not thinking at all."

EXACTLY.

"What do you think this means?" she asked, pointing to the bones.

THAT THEY ARE TELLING US SOMETHING VERY PRECISE WHICH WE AREN'T CLEARHEADED ENOUGH, OR WISE ENOUGH, TO UNDERSTAND AT THE PRESENT.

"In other words, 'What was the question?' "

WHEN YOU DON'T DO A FULL READING, IT HELPS TO BE VERY SPECIFIC.

Esmeralda looked at the bones for long moments, clearing her head of all thoughts to let an intuitive leap come if it would, but she had too many questions tangled up inside her to be able to attain the required inner quiet. Sighing, she replaced the bones in their bag.

"I need to think," she said, "without thinking. A cup of tea with a playwright sounds about right at the moment."

YOUR OLD ROOM'S WAITING FOR YOU.

She smiled. "The Blue Dancer's Room," she said softly. "High in the southwest tower. I used to dream about princes in there,

Jamie, and they all looked like you. Did you know I had a crush on you? I think half the women staying here at the time did."

UM . . .

"An embarrassed computer. A blushing house." Her smile widened as she rose from the chair. "I'll talk to you later, Jamie."

Her good humor lasted all the way down to the Silkwater Kitchen and through her visit with Tim, but when she finally took her carpetbag up to her old room in the southwest tower, not even the room's familiarity could stop its fading. Instead, it added to her growing sense of disquiet.

The Blue Dancer's Room, like the rest of what she'd seen of the House so far, hadn't changed at all. By now she shouldn't have been surprised, but the room was almost too familiar. The books she'd left behind when she went away were still on the bookshelf. One of Emma's watercolors hung above the mantel. Below it was a clay South American whistle in the shape of a bird that she'd borrowed from Jamie one night before she left. The patchwork quilt that her grandmother had given her was still on the bed. The room was neat, and dust-free. And it looked as though she'd just left it this morning. As though all the intervening years were just a dream. Pages in someone else's journal that she'd read instead of lived.

She felt dislocated from herself. Talking to Jamie had woken old feelings that she'd thought she'd forgotten. And the House, this room . . . She had traveled three thousand miles to help a friend. Now she felt as though she'd traveled through time as well. Into the past.

She stayed long enough to put away the contents of her carpetbag, then went back downstairs, troubled by more than what had initially brought her here.

6

A deep quiet lay inside Migizi. He dreamed awake, his gaze traveling far beyond the confines of his conjuring lodge. He tapped his water drum and chanted. He spoke to his totem through the fingering of the dream objects of his *skibdagan*. West his gaze ranged, and farther west, beyond the sight of his soul. He lit the spirit pipe again, but Nanibush remained hidden, refusing the invitation of smoke that Migizi offered.

The deerskins of his lodge finally shook in response to his seeking, but it wasn't the ruler of the west approaching. He heard a puckish laughter. His eyes flickered open in time to see the head and upper torso of a small, thin, brown figure poke into the lodge. Its wizened face, bewhiskered like a cat's, flashed a grin in his direction as it drew the sacred smoke into its lungs; then the little being was gone, and the deerskins lay still.

Memegwesi, Migizi thought. The sound of their laughter diminished as the little band of mischievous manitou left the area of his *jessakan.* He lifted a deerskin flap in time to see the last of them slip away into the woods.

"Choose another old man to play your tricks on!" he called after them. "This one has serious business to conduct."

There was no response, but he hadn't expected any. He retied his medicine bag to the beaded belt at his waist and replaced his pipe and tobacco pouch in his bandolier. As he left the lodge and stood erect, muscles still supple despite his sixty-three winters, he caught another glimpse of motion from the corner of his eye.

Like the *memegwesi,* the strange manitou was leaving as well.

"I will try again," Migizi told it. By the honeysuckles, his soul stirred and drifted down toward the lodge. "Dreams walk quicker by moonlight, following Nokomis's light west. I will ask her to bear our message to her grandson."

The strange manitou paused as though listening to him, then faded in among the trees and was gone. But it would be back. Whether he spoke to the west or not, it would return. Troubled and alone. The discord within it setting up an echoing disturbance that distressed the balance of bird and animal, plant and stone, in ever-widening ripples.

It was the manitou's presence that kept him from reaching Nanibush, Migizi realized. He would need a stronger medicine to overcome its influence—a medicine he didn't have, unless the moon's light would add enough strength to his call. *Wabigwanigizis* would be her aspect tonight—a moon of blossoms. Not the strongest moon, but strong enough if she would help.

He walked up the slope to the hilltop and sat down cross-legged, his shadow resting beside him, his soul ranging in the shadows of the woods at his back. Birch and pine, maple and cedar. Their sap could already hear the call of Nokomis's light, edging the eastern horizon, waiting for old man Mishomis to set in the west.

Migizi touched his medicine pouch and closed his eyes. He would try again.

7

Esmeralda waited for Blue in the garage where he kept his motorcycles. She sat on the '67 Chevy car seat that was bolted to the floor across from his workbench and looked around at the organized mess of tools and machines. She found it odd that Emma would have ended up with a biker, though he had to be more than that if he was also a trusted friend of Jamie's.

She tried to imagine what he'd look like, talk like, who he was. She pictured the kids in their leathers in London's East End, then the stereotypical bikers from B-movies, and finally gave up trying. Closing her eyes, she leaned her head back against the car seat and looked for the silences hidden within. Not to dream. Just to be quiet.

She was so successful that when the garage door suddenly opened, she started upright, disoriented. A gust of wind fluttered some litter at her feet, then rose to wind her hair about her neck and face. The roar of the big Harley-Davidson as it entered only served to confuse her more. It was followed by a second machine.

Esmeralda pulled the hair from her face and forced herself to sit quietly. When the two machines were turned off and the garage door had rumbled shut again, she let out a sigh of relief for the blessed silence that followed. She watched the riders as they removed their helmets.

The man had to be Blue. He was big, broad shoulders bulging tightly in a black T-shirt, long black hair pulled back in a ponytail. His features were roughly chiseled. Gold earrings glinted in each earlobe. The woman looked tiny compared to him. She was all in black leather with a cloud of frizzy blond hair and delicate birdlike features. She was the first to notice Esmeralda sitting there watching them.

She touched her companion's arm. "Blue?"

He turned to look, a frown creasing his face when he saw Esmeralda. "Who the hell are you?" he demanded.

"I could be a friend."

He balanced his helmet on the seat of his Harley and shook his head. "Friends are people you know. And they don't show up in your space, hanging around like they owned the place."

This was Emma's lover?

"I'm a friend of Jamie's," she said. "An old friend."

Some of the suspicion left his face. "Well why didn't you say so in the first place?"

"You never really gave her any time," his companion told him.

"Sweetness and light here is Judy," Blue said, motioning to the blond woman with a thumb. "But she's right. I've never had a whole lot of patience and I'm wired a little tight these days, but that's no excuse. It's just that people don't usually come in here. The House knows it's my . . ." His voice trailed off. "I guess you haven't been around for a while, right? It's just that Jamie—"

"I know what's happened to him. He told me."

"He . . .?"

"He's the one that said I should wait for you here."

From the way Tim had acted earlier that day, Esmeralda had already gathered that not too many people were aware of Jamie's continuing presence in Tamson House. Blue's confusion now confirmed that.

"I'm here about Emma," she added. "My name's Esmeralda."

"Esmeralda? You're the one with the poems who sent Emma that warning?"

She nodded.

He looked at her with an expression that she couldn't read. "Let's go grab a beer," he said, "and I'll fill you in."

After picking up a six-pack of Millers from the fridge in the Silkwater Kitchen, they went up to the Postman's Room to talk. Esmeralda and Judy sat in the club chairs, while Blue pulled the swivel chair away from the desk, positioning it so that he could comfortably talk to them and look at Jamie's screen at the same time.

"After it all went down last year," he said, "Emma and I ended up together. It wasn't the quickest romance on record, and not the smoothest at the start, but I've screwed up enough relationships in my time. This time I was going to stick it out—it was that important to me, you know?

"Anyway, things were going good, except for one thing—Jamie filled you in on what happened with Glamorgana and everything, right?"

Esmeralda nodded.

"Well, what happened was, Emma acted like it never went down. Not any of it. She just couldn't remember anything about splitting into two different people, about Glamorgana—none of it. It's like it went right out of her mind. What she remembered was getting messed up by some bikers and me and Judy and Hacker just happened to show up to pull her out. I mean, she sees Taran here around the House—Glamorgana's bard, right?—and she honestly believes that the first time she met him was here."

"That kind of thing happens," Esmeralda said. "It's a defense mechanism of the mind. When events are too disturbing, or they simply don't fit into one's worldview, the mind convinces itself that they never happened."

Blue nodded. "Yeah, Jamie said something like that. It's just weird. Because I remember. Taran's living proof that it went down. . . ."

"What about you, Judy?" Esmeralda asked.

Judy shrugged. "I wasn't there—not for the weird stuff."

"So what do you make of it?"

"I keep an open mind."

"It happened," Blue said flatly.

"I believe you," Esmeralda said. "In a way, I was there myself." Judy's eyebrows lifted questioningly, but Esmeralda simply went on. "What happened after that?"

"Well, I stopped going on about it to her," Blue said. "I figured, what's the point? What difference does it make? But then she started getting more withdrawn over the winter. Moody, first. I thought maybe it was cabin fever—Ottawa winters can do that to a person."

"I remember."

"But it didn't go away when the weather warmed up. Got worse, in fact. So then a couple of weeks ago I was supposed to meet her to go to an opening at a gallery—"

Esmeralda didn't blink at that, but she revised her opinion of him again. There was definitely more to him than the face he presented to most of the world.

"—only she never showed. I tried calling her. No answer. Finally I drove up to her place and found her lying in her bed like she was dead. I didn't know what to think. I thought maybe she'd OD'd on something, so I brought her into town. I didn't want to take her to the hospital in Hull—I don't speak French and I didn't want to get some kind of runaround. So I brought her to the General and she's been there ever since.

"The doctors say she's in a coma, but they don't know how it came on, they don't why, and they don't know when or even if she's ever going to come out of it."

"Do you spend a lot of time there?" Esmeralda asked.

"As much as they let me. Judy came by to sit with me tonight—other nights, some of the other guys come by."

Esmeralda smiled. Judy looked very feminine to her. It was odd considering her as "one of the guys."

"And how does she seem to you?"

It was Judy who answered. "Lost. You look at her face and you know there's no one home."

"It's starting again, isn't it?" Blue asked. "The same business as before? Someone's stolen part of her like Glamorgana did, only this time they took so much that there's nothing left for her to run on."

"Not necessarily. I think Judy had the right idea. She's lost."

"Lost? Lost where?"

Esmeralda sighed. "I don't know. But someone's going to have to go find her."

No one spoke for long moments. Blue finished off his beer and opened a second. The others were still working on their first.

"Do you know how to do that?" Blue asked finally.

"In theory. I'll have to make some preparations."

"Like what? How long will they take? When can we go?"

"Not we—me."

Blue shook his head. "Not a good idea."

"Someone has to be here for when she gets back," Esmeralda said. "Someone she knows well and trusts. Someone that loves her. So it's either you or me that goes. Do you know what to do?"

"No, but I don't like the idea of—"

The computer beeped and Blue looked at the screen.

TRUST HER, Jamie said.

Before Jamie could say more, or Blue could argue, the phone rang. Blue scooped up the receiver.

"Yeah, speaking," he said into the phone. "What's the big . . .?"

Watching him, the two women saw all the blood drain from his face. Around Esmeralda's feet, a gust of wind stirred.

8

Smoor had the taste of ashes in his mouth as he left the corridor and walked into the private room to stand over the bed. When he used his dead mistress's spells, they always burned like cold fire in his mind and rose like ashes in his throat. He looked down at the woman, remembering. That night and his pain. The death of his mistress, consumed by her own witchfire. And all that remained, scattered on the grass . . .

The taste of ashes grew stronger on his tongue.

Leaving the bedside, he went to the window and drew a talon-like fingernail along its edges, peeling back the weather stripping. Once all around, and he pulled the huge window from its frame, not even straining with its weight. He leaned it up against a wall.

Returning to the bedside, he wet a finger on his tongue, then drew symbols on the woman's face, the saliva glistening like phosphorescence where it lay on her skin. Peeling back the sheets, he drew more symbols on the palms of her hands, her belly and the soles of her feet. Not until they were dry, still shimmering, but with a hard cold light now, did he remove her from the IV and monitoring equipment.

By the time a nurse arrived in the room, summoned by a flashing light at her station once the monitors were disconnected, he had already crawled crablike down the side of the building, the woman hoisted under one arm, and disappeared into the woods that bordered the hospital's grounds. He waited, hidden in the trees, until there was a lull in the traffic on Smyth Road, then loaded his burden into the back of a stolen Buick Skylark and got behind the wheel. The Buick's plates had been exchanged earlier in the evening with those from another car in a shopping-center parking lot.

"Spells will keep you alive," he told his unconscious captive, looking over the seat at where she lay sprawled in the back. "But not for long." He grinned as he turned frontward and started up the Buick. "Long's not needed anymore—not for you, my pretty thing."

The Autumn Heart was his.

9

Blue hung up the phone with a numb expression, missing the cradle and fumbling the receiver until he got it set properly in place. Then he just stared blankly at a spot equidistant between the two women.

"What is it, Blue?" Judy asked.

Esmeralda didn't speak. The wind had spoken to her. She already knew.

"It's Emma," he said slowly. "She's gone. Either she just . . . just got up and walked away, or somebody's kidnapped her." He sat for another couple of moments, a lost look in his eyes, then shook himself like a big dog and rose from his seat. "I gotta go find her."

"Blue," Esmeralda said quietly, but it was enough to stop him in his tracks. He turned slowly to look at her. "Where will you look?" she asked.

"Christ, I don't know. I'll start at the hospital, then work it out from there."

Judy set her beer aside and rose as well. "I'll get hold of Hacker and some of the other guys."

"Wait a moment," Esmeralda said. Again her quiet voice stopped movement. "Where will you look?" she repeated.

Blue blinked for a moment, then frowned at her. "I told you, I don't *know*. But I'm not just going to sit around here and—"

Esmeralda held up a hand. Winds stirred briefly about her, tousling her hair. Judy's eyes widened.

"Think for a moment," Esmeralda said. "Who could have taken her? For what purpose?"

"If I knew that—"

"She's right," Judy said. "If we can figure that out, we cut out a lot of running around."

Blue looked from her to Esmeralda, then slowly made his way back to his seat. "Okay," he said. "I'm thinking. You got any bright ideas?"

Esmeralda forgave his brusque manner. She was beginning to get a measure of him. It was worry that was shortening his temper.

"I could track her," she said, "but I'm attuned to her spirit, not her body, so any farseeing I might do would be of no help in this aspect of our present situation."

The computer beeped, and they turned to look at Jamie's screen. Words darted across its green background.

LOGIC DICTATES THAT THIS IS CONNECTED TO HER EARLIER TROUBLES, they read.

"They're both dead," Blue said. "Chance and the witch. I *saw* them die."

AND THE WITCH'S CREATURES?

Understanding sparked across Blue's features, waking a grim darkness. "Jesus! Those things. They just ran off."

EXACTLY, Jamie said. NOBODY SAW THEM DIE.

"But what the hell would they want with Emma?"

In the ensuing silence, Esmeralda's quiet voice seemed loud. "Vengeance?" she asked.

Blue's gaze locked on her own; then he nodded. "It's got to be them that grabbed her," he said. "And I know where we can start looking for them—Lac la Pêche, where Chance and his witch bought it."

He rose again, Judy following. This time no one called out to stop him, but he paused at the door.

"You coming?" he asked Esmeralda.

She shook her head. "There's another part of her that's still lost that I'm better equipped to look for. Godspeed."

She could see both of them remembering the wind rising up about her, a wind that had only touched her.

Blue nodded. "You, too," he said, and then they were gone.

Esmeralda rubbed at her temples, then shifted to the swivel chair, which she pulled up in front of the computer screen. "I'll need some things, Jamie," she said. "Maybe you could tell me where to go look for them to save my wasting any more time."

WHATEVER WE HAVE IS YOURS, Jamie replied.

10

Hidden from the moon's light by the deerskin flaps of his conjuring lodge, Migizi sat gathering silence from the quiet places within his spirit. His shadow lay upon his shoulders. His soul watched from outside the *jessakan*, leaning against its birch poles and deerskins, listening to the soft sound of the water drum calling the grandfather thunders, the chanting that asked Grandmother Toad for her aid.

The air was close inside the lodge, thick with sacred smoke. High above the glade, Nokomis's blossom moon *wabigwanigizis* rode the sky, listening to Migizi, accepting his smoke. When Migizi stepped outside the lodge, she bathed him with her light, adding her strength to his strength, and then they came.

A band of manitou, Nanibush's spirit guides, walked the *meekunnaug*, the Path of Souls that the spirits of the dead travel to reach the west. The moon came down to be by Migizi's side, Grandmother Toad standing there, holding his wrinkled brown hand in one of hers, the hand of his soul in her other. The spirit guides were dressed in their finest white buckskins, their braids bedecked with feathers and shells, their shirts with complex beadwork designs. Spirit drums sounded quietly in the darkness.

"K'neekaunissinaun, ani-maudjauh," they called softly. Our brother, he is leaving.

"Not I," Migizi replied softly.

Grandmother Toad turned from Migizi then to face the woods.

Drawn by the kindness that the moonlight showed in her features, the strange manitou drifted from the woods to join them in the glade.

"We bring you a sister tonight," Migizi said, for he saw now, with Nokomis's strength joined to his, that this manitou was female. "She is lost."

The sound of spirit drumming was a soft thunder all around them. Sacred smoke given sound. *Animiki* speaking.

"Come with us, sister," the spirits said.

The strange manitou hesitated.

"Come with us," the spirits called.

Grandmother Toad crossed the glade to take the manitou's hand. "I will show you the way, *nici'men,*" she said, calling her "little sister."

A moment longer the strange manitou hesitated; then she let Grandmother Toad lead her onto the Path of Souls. Migizi watched them go, the spirit guides walking all around them, the sound of spirit drums following them as they traveled west.

"Go in peace, little one," he said. *"K'gah odaessiniko."* You will be welcome.

When they were gone, he lifted his gaze to the moon of blossoms, thanking her, then returned to his conjuring lodge for his spirit pipe. He filled it with tobacco and took it with him to where his soul sat under the honeysuckles waiting for him. He raised the pipe skyward.

"Saemauh k'weekaunissimikonaun," he called softly to the manitou. Tobacco makes us friends.

His shadow nestled against his back. His soul looked westward. He lit the pipe with peace in his heart. He thought of the naming ceremony the next day would bring. Some might think it was his due, as a grandfather *mede* of his people, to name the daughter of Bebon-Waushih and Misheekaehnquae, but they were not he. Migizi considered it not his due, but a great honor that the child's parents would ask him to help her find her name.

The finding of a name was a sacred task, so he offered smoke to the thunders and asked for their blessing.

TWO

1

Esmeralda sat alone in the Silkwater Kitchen. She had changed into jeans, a flannel shirt and sturdy walking shoes. On a chair beside her lay a gray leather jacket that someone had left behind in the House when they moved away. Jamie had told her to go ahead and borrow it as she had brought nothing suitable with her. Beside it was a small leather bag, stuffed full of the things she felt she might need, collected from her carpetbag and various parts of the House. There were herbs and candles in it, charms and fetishes. And because this was no longer England, tobacco as well, for she knew her journey would be taking her into the spirit realms where the native manitou dwelled.

On the table in front of her was the copy of *The Tale of the Seasons*—the old poetry journal that she'd left behind in the

House's Library when she'd gone away years before. It had a blue
leather cover and the pages were stiff and cream-colored, covered
with tidy handwritten words in green ink. She had been leafing
through it, stopping to read a verse here, another there. Now she
looked out the kitchen window at the dark garden, the words
thrumming in her head.

> *I know where I walk you can't always go*
> *for all my strange talk, you can't always know*
> *there's a madness in my soul, a demon in my head*
> *a power born of hollow hills, gold and twilight-led*
> *I know where I walk Great Pan is not dead*

She didn't know the person who'd written those words. Not
anymore. At the same time, she knew that girl very well. The
words she had written spoke of a time when the winds that moved
inside her were a source of confusion and fear. They dated to a time
before she had learned to ride their currents, to when she still
fought the strangeness that they had brought into her life.

> *I know that my ways don't always seem kind*
> *sky-clad I grew once, root, leaf and vine*
> *if I speak of love now, speak of love for you*
> *gather in the harvest, reap the brambles too*
> *I know that my ways lead now to you*

Too often she had made of them a pretense, thought of them as
something that was charming and whimsical, and even mystical,
but not real—just as Emma had. As Emma still did. They had
seemed to be a source of creative energy, a muse, but not something to steer one's life by. She had drunk at their well in those
days, but made no payment in return.

> *there was a star once, o how it did shine*
> *fell into the shadows, time out of mind*
> *there've been so many stars that did fall*
> *hear the strains of madness, hear the demon's call*
> *there was a star once, now the dark is all*

And now? she thought, looking out to where the night lay on the House's garden. She had moved out of the shadows, risen from the darkness, to study, to explore, to learn. How the spirits moved. The sources of their powers. The vessels they chose to reside in. She had cloistered herself in years of study. Passing on the lore to those who asked, to those who came to drink at her well. She had embraced the beauty and the mystery, yet how often had she walked back into the shadows to sow the mysteries' seeds in the darkness?

Well, she was doing it now. Horned Lord, Mother Moon. She was doing it now.

"Leaving so soon?"

She looked up to find Tim standing by the kitchen counter with an empty tea mug in his hand.

"For a time," she said. "But it'll be a short journey this time." In how we reckon time, she thought. Who knew what distances she would travel, moving through the spirit realms? "Have you been working?" she added.

"I live on tea when I'm writing." He took the cozy from the teapot and filled his mug, then held the pot up, offering her some.

She shook her head. "You've reminded me that it was time I was going."

Closing her old poetry journal, she left it where it lay and rose from the table. She put on the borrowed jacket and slung the bag over her shoulder. Tim called to her as she went to the door.

"You're going the wrong way—that just leads into the gardens. I guess you forgot. The gardens are surrounded on all sides by the House. You can't get to the street that way."

"The journey I'm taking won't take me out of the House," she said. At least not by routes he would know.

He gave her an odd look, then nodded. "Like meditation?"

"Something like that. Hopefully I'll see you in the morning, Tim."

"Sure." He raised a hand. "Happy trails."

"Thank you."

She stepped out into the night and closed the door before he could say anything more.

★　★　★

The gardens enclosed in the protective embrace of Tamson House always seemed far larger than their actual acreage should allow. They were riddled with paths that twisted and wound around deep stands of trees and bushes. Statues hid in the greenery. Flowerbeds lay thick with spring growths. Little nooks with benches appeared out of nowhere, only to be swallowed again when one walked on. The paths all led to the central knoll that was Esmeralda's destination.

It was quiet there. The fountain hadn't been turned on yet and the city beyond the walls of the House might never have existed, its presence was so little felt here. Esmeralda sat on the stone lip of the fountain, her bag on her lap, and collected her thoughts. Above her, an ancient oak overhung the fountain with the wide spread of its branches. The quiet she nurtured inside soon echoed that of the tree above her, the gardens around her. Her taw, the silence that is like music, filled her with its potent strength. When she heard footsteps approaching, they seemed loud, for all that the man who came out of the trees walked softly like a cat.

He stood and regarded her, and she him. In the moonlight they could make out little more than general features.

"A strange night," the newcomer said quietly. "I never thought to find one of the Powers in this place, Lady, but then this rath delights in surprise."

"You must be Taran," she said. "The bard."

A sad name, she thought, for it meant a child not blessed by fire and water. An outcast. He moved closer and lifted one arm. The moonlight shone on a leather glove stretched tightly around a clawlike appendage that had once been a hand.

"Bard no more," he said.

Esmeralda shook her head. "That's something that can't be put on or taken off like a cloak."

"Without music . . ."

"Your heart is silent?"

He thought before answering. "No," he said finally. "But without a channel, the fire burns dim. Half of any creative gift is in how it communicates to others."

"There are musics you can make with only one hand," she said. "You should ask Blue about synthesizers."

He gave her a puzzled look.

"Never mind. I'll show you what I mean when I get back."

He nodded. "You mean to walk the Middle Kingdom?"

"I wish I was. I know it better than the spirit realms of this land."

"It's all the same realm," Taran said. "That's what the trees taught us."

"But the dwellers change."

"Or perhaps it's just how we see them." He smiled. "I've missed this sort of talk. I speak with the rath—with Jamie—but it's not the same as speech with flesh and blood. Barriers lie like hidden reefs in the written word."

"Voices lie, too—sometimes it's easier to follow what's written down."

"This is true." He glanced at the bag she carried, obviously sensing some resonance emanating from it. "You travel well prepared."

"I'm going to look for Emma—Blue's friend. Do you know her?"

He nodded. "I was a part of those who did her ill. Though she doesn't remember, I can't forget."

"You also saved her life," Esmeralda said.

Taran shifted uncomfortably at that.

"It's true," she added. "I was there—at the end."

"I remember . . . a wind. . . ." He gave her a sad smile. "I'll leave you to your business, Lady, and wish you the moon's own luck."

"We'll speak again," Esmeralda said. "When I return."

"I would be honored, Lady."

"Call me Esmeralda."

He shook his head. *"Gaoth an Iar,"* he named her. Wind of the West.

He walked away, vanishing into the woods with his catlike quickness and silence, before she could reply.

"We'll speak of names again," she said softly, then turned once more to the business at hand.

Her taw was easier to reach this time, cloaking her with its quiet strength in moments. She attuned herself like a divining rod to Emma's spirit and the Autumn Heart that lay inside her lost friend. Memories of the Weirdin she'd drawn rose up in her. The Acorn.

The Forest. The Eagle. She bound them to her seeking with threads of thought, then let the winds arise.

They gusted around her feet, rising and circling about her, carrying the scents of the garden with them, filling her with a spinning array of perceptions. Blossom scent. Moonlight. The call of a stag on a distant hill. The sweet taste of wild strawberries. Feathery touches on her skin.

Her hair whipped loosely about her head. Errant leaves, dried and escaped from last autumn, whirled in a dance around her. She rose from her seat at the edge of the fountain, bag clasped against her stomach, and took a step. Another. The third step she took was out of the garden, out of its world, following the ribbon of light that connected her to Emma's Autumn Heart.

Behind her, by the fountain, leaves drifted down to settle on the stones where she'd been sitting. The moonlight looked down through the trees, but if it looked for her, it was disappointed, for she was gone.

2

They sat in Judy's garage in Sandy Hill while they waited for Hacker and Ernie Collins, another friend of theirs, to show. The garage was filled with motorcycles in various states of repair, the air heavy with the metallic smells of grease and machine oil. Judy lounged on a bench tinkering with a Harley carb and watching Blue reassemble the shotgun that he'd taken apart to fit in his saddlebags for the bike ride over.

"How come you're riding Esmeralda so hard?" she asked finally.

Blue shrugged. "I don't know. She pisses me off for some reason."

"Because she's so self-possessed?"

"Seems more cold to me."

"C'mon, Blue. Don't shit a shitter. What's really the problem?"

He snapped the last piece into place and looked up from the shotgun. "What's she doing here?" he asked.

"Helping Emma—just like us."

"Yeah, but why now? Why didn't she show up before Emma

ended up in the hospital? Why wasn't she here last year when all that weird shit was going down? Instead she sends this cryptic message that you'd have to be somebody like Tal or Sara to figure out."

"Are you always there when people need you?"

"I try to be."

"Well, maybe that's what she's doing now. Christ, Blue. She lives in England. She flew all the way over here to help."

"I know, I know."

Judy sighed. "Has it got something to do with how close they used to be?"

"What do you mean?"

"Well, like were they an item or something?"

Blue didn't take offense at that. Unlike a lot of his contemporaries he had nothing against gays. If Emma'd been into that before she'd met him, that was her business.

"They had more of a . . . I don't know, platonic kind of a thing going," he said finally. "Emma never really wanted to talk about her much."

"Something happened between them?"

"Not so's I can figure. They just drifted apart. They had a weird kind of a relationship anyway—both of them living in the same city and just writing letters instead of hanging out with each other. I think it bugs Emma, talking about Esmeralda now. It was like Esmeralda reminds her of all the stuff that Emma wants to forget."

"Like the deal with Chance."

"More like with Chance's witch—Glamorgana."

Blue began to load the shotgun, inserting shells in the loading gate, one after the other. Each one made a sharp click as it entered the breech.

"That stuff really went down, huh?" Judy asked after a few moments.

Blue nodded. "You've been in the House—you've seen the kinds of stuff that can go on."

"Yeah, things can get a little spooky. But witches and Faerie . . ."

"I've seen weirder."

Judy leaned back, putting the carb aside. "Really makes you wonder sometimes, doesn't it? I mean, you read about some wacko spotting little green Martians, or getting taken away by a UFO, and you've just got to laugh. But what we've got here isn't a whole lot different. Not really."

"Except it's real. I don't know shit about space invaders, Judy, but this stuff's for real. If you don't take it seriously, it can kill you."

"Oh, I know something's going down," Judy said. "I just don't know what the hell it is, and I'm wondering out loud—that's all. But I'm in for the duration."

Blue loaded the last couple of shells that the shotgun would take, then dumped the remainder in the pocket of his jacket. He gave Judy a long, considering look.

"Why?" he said finally.

"Why what?"

"You don't really believe in this shit, so why're you coming along?"

"I believe in you, Blue."

Ernie Collins's Ford Bronco pulled into Judy's driveway then, with Ernie and Hacker in the front seat, and the two of them rose to meet the newcomers. Ernie was a little guy with big shoulders who had the same slicked-back hairstyle he'd worn back when the Big Bopper was making records. Beside him, Hacker looked immense—a mountain man, all beard and hair and bulk, squeezed into a pair of Levis and a faded blue workshirt. Hacker's gaze drifted to the shotgun Blue was holding.

"Aw, shit," he said. "Are we going to need that?"

"Probably."

Hacker tugged at his beard—a motion so habitual that he wasn't even aware of doing it. "Judy didn't say much—just that your girl got herself nabbed again. You ought to keep an eye on her, Blue. Good-looking woman like that—too bad she's got this bad habit of attracting the wrong kind of interest."

"Hell," Ernie said. "She hangs out with Blue, doesn't she, so what do you expect?"

Something flickered in Blue's eyes. "If you don't want to—"

"Lighten up," Judy said from beside him, giving him a poke in the ribs.

"Yeah," Hacker said. "We're here, aren't we?"

Blue rubbed his face then nodded slowly. "Yeah. Thanks for coming. I'm just so wired up right now. . . ."

"Let's just go," Judy said, leading the way to the Bronco. "Save that shit for your analyst."

She turned and gave Blue a grin. He nodded, but couldn't find a smile to give her back. Working the tension out of his muscles with a rolling motion of his shoulders, he passed her the shotgun, then climbed into the backseat with her.

"Same place?" Hacker asked as he got in.

Blue thought of something Sara's bard Taliesin had told him once, that everything is a part of a wheel. Things move in a circular pattern. You've been there once, you'll be there again, even if it all looks different. Everything fits on some wheel. The trick was to figure out which one. Well, if they were on a wheel now, then it was carrying them back into some familiar territory.

How many times did you have to do something before you got to move onto a new wheel?

"Blue?" Hacker tried again.

Blue looked up and nodded. "Yeah," he said. "Same place."

The wheel turns, he thought, but when tonight was over he planned to find them a new one. Who needed any more of this kind of shit?

"Lac la Pêche, James," Hacker told Ernie in the front seat, mangling a hoity-toity accent. "And be so good as to step on it, would you?"

3

Following the trail of Emma's spirit, Esmeralda stepped from one night into another, from garden to glade. A shadowed forest loomed all around her. The clear dark sky above held stars that were crystal sharp, a moon full and rounded. The glowing ribbon connecting her to Emma had led her into a spirit realm—a Middle Kingdom of North America's Native People.

Her night-wise gaze settled on the small curious structure standing nearby. Four poles thrust into the ground, connected by supporting branches. She took in the deerskin flaps, the pine bough on the west pole, the string of braided leather with its cowrie shells. Then her gaze traveled west, up a slope to where honeysuckles grew thick, and she saw the old man, a shadow lying on his shoulders like a cloak, his soul standing beside him.

The old man came slowly down the slope, his slow movements due not to age, but caution. His soul preceded him, passed her by, as did he. Esmeralda stood quietly, waiting, then turned.

She'd heard of this belief among some of the Native People. When you met a man, you shouldn't address him until you had passed him by. This let your souls continue on while only your bodies and shadows conversed. She knew of the belief, but didn't know why it was held.

When the old man turned, she called a greeting to him, but he shook his head. When he spoke, his words meant as little to her. Closing her eyes, she tried to remember what little she'd learned of sign language while briefly staying with a Plains medicine woman out west. Esmeralda had a gift for language, and the movements came back quickly.

She raised both hands, palms facing outward. Then, lowering them slightly, she directed them toward the old man.

Bless you, her signing said.

The old man smiled. He extended both of his open hands in a forward direction, palms down, then lowered them until his arms were perpendicular to his body. His right hand rose to his forehead, palm turned inward, middle and index fingers spread out and pointing up, the other fingers closed. The hand rose higher and made a clockwise circular motion. Then he held both hands horizontally in front of his chest, palms down, fingers together and pointing forward, and made a shaking motion.

Esmeralda concentrated, then nodded as she understood.

Thank you, manitou of the wind was what he had said.

She thought a moment, then began to sign again. *I seek the spirit of a friend.*

Her signing wasn't as quick and smooth as it once had been, but it was enough to get her meaning across. His own signing told her that this wasn't his usual form of communication either.

There was a manitou, his hands said. *She walked west with your brothers.*

Esmeralda looked in that direction. She closed her eyes, seeking that ribboned thread of light that connected her with Emma's spirit, but the thread ended here. In this place. What did he mean, walked west with her brothers? Emma was an only child, while Esmeralda herself had no siblings.

I don't understand, she signed.

The spirit guides of the west, he replied. *Grandmother Toad took her in their company.*

Grandmother Toad? Again she signed her confusion.

He made a new sign, thumb and index finger of his left hand extended with the other fingers closed, palm facing her. He added the sign for night and pointed up to the moon. "Nokomis," he said aloud while his hands shaped the signs for grandmother and toad again.

The Moon Mother, Esmeralda realized. Brigit. She had taken Emma . . . where? West. But the thread ended here. What lay west? And then she knew. The Land of Souls. Did that mean that Blue had been too late? Had Emma died and her soul now fled to the land of the dead?

The old man watched her, waiting. Peering over his shoulder, like the hood of a cloak given life, she could see the head of his shadow, watching too. Behind him his soul stood, looking eastward, into the forest.

Can we call her? she signed.

The old man made a sign of questioning. It was plain what he meant. Call who? The errant spirit or the moon?

Esmeralda stood quietly, letting the silence inside her rise up to clear her mind. Then she reached into her shoulder bag and took out the tobacco pouch that she'd borrowed from a Belgian student in the House. She rolled a cigarette, fingers awkward. It had been years since she'd smoked. When she had made the cigarette, she lit it with a lighter, also borrowed, and drew the acrid smoke inside. Careful not to cough, for all that it teared her eyes and made her throat feel raw, she offered the cigarette to the old man.

4

The being with which Migizi conversed was unlike any he had heard of before. She was like a flame, the light of her medicine shining strong inside her. Her skin was so pale, her hair a waterfall of glimmering gold in the moonlight, her clothing so strange. But he knew her for what she was when he first looked down the slope to see her standing beside his *jessakan*.

When she offered him the sacred smoke, he hesitated at first, surprised that she used no spirit pipe, more surprised still at how she woke fire from her fingers. But she was a manitou, and the ways of manitou were different from those of men.

The sign language they were using to speak to each other he had learned from a *baun* of the Sinebaun, the Stone Medicine Men, who in turn had learned it from the tribes who dwelled on the distant western plains. By this, he knew her to be a manitou of the windmaker Nibanegishik, her charge being the winds of the west.

So he accepted her smoke. *"Saemauh k'weekaunaehnaun,"* he said, and repeated the words in sign language. *Tobacco is our friend.*

She signed back, *Tobacco makes us friends.*

"Waussae/aukonae k'weeyow," he replied. *"K'okomissinaunik k'gah ondinimowaunaunih."* He repeated it with signs. *Bright with flame is your body. A mystery derived from our grandmother.*

I would meet with her, she signed back. *To seek my lost sister.*

Ah, Migizi thought. So that strange lost manitou now walking the *meekunnaug* was her kin. No wonder she had seemed so different to him. But this one—she was not lost. She walked unfamiliar roads, perhaps, but she was not lost.

Listen, he signed.

She cocked her head and heard now what his soul had heard long before either of them. Spirit drums talking. Small thunders in the night.

She comes now, he signed. *Returning from the spirit land in the west.*

The new manitou turned and a wind started up at her feet as Nokomis stepped from the Path of Souls to walk among the honeysuckles, descending the slope to stand before them. Migizi touched the wind manitou's shoulder.

Speak with her, he signed when she turned to look at him. *Grandmother Toad knows the path your sister has taken. She can take you to her.*

The new manitou nodded her thanks and turned again to where the moon stood, gleaming with her inner light.

5

Esmeralda had never seen a woman as beautiful as the one who stood before her now—nor a spirit that shone with such strength. Light gleamed from her, an inner light that lent a fire to her coppery skin. Her hair was the pure white of moonlight, her body slender under a white doeskin dress. She appeared as young as a woman in her early twenties, yet by her eyes Esmeralda knew she had looked upon the world while it was still being formed.

Grandmother Toad. What a name for a being such as this. The Weirdin named the toad as a wielder of evil power, as did the Native beliefs of many of the Eastern woodlands tribes. She knew that much. But she saw now that this was in fact the greatest aspect of the Moon's power. Swallowing evil and transforming it into light.

"Welcome, daughter," the woman said. "I have watched you from afar for many years."

Esmeralda wasn't sure what language Grandmother Toad spoke—all she knew was that she understood it.

"You . . . know me?"

The woman smiled. "Of course I know you. Did you think I was only grandmother to the Djibwe? I am whatever I am needed to be. To the Djibwe I am Nokomis—Grandmother Toad who lives in the moon. To you I am Brigit. To those who wish to believe in nothing . . . I am nothing for them."

"I always knew that," Esmeralda said, realizing the truth of what she said only as she spoke it. "I just never stopped to think about it. . . ."

"Your spirit grows," Grandmother Toad said. "You have studied long."

"One can always learn."

"True. But there comes a time for lessons to be put aside and for one to *do*."

The voice of her conscience given flesh and blood, Esmeralda thought as Grandmother Toad's word echoed the realizations she had come to while sitting in the Silkwater Kitchen, leafing through her poetry journal.

"I'm trying now," she said. "To do something *and* learn at the same time."

Grandmother Toad nodded. "Seeking your sister who dropped like a fallen star, from what she was to be reborn."

"She's . . . Is she dead, then? Am I too late?"

"Somewhere, her body breathes, but not for long. Her soul has already gone on to the spirit lands."

Esmeralda shook her head. "It's too soon."

"It was what she wanted."

"She doesn't really know *what* she wanted. Please, Grandmother. Bring her back. It's partly my fault. I went on ahead in the journey, expecting her to catch up when she lagged, instead of stopping to help her so that we could travel together."

Grandmother Toad appeared to consider that. "Three chances of choice she had—when you first met, last year when her Autumn Gift was woken once more, and then this night's journey west. But perhaps . . . perhaps your being here was to be her third choice."

"Please . . . just let me talk to her."

"I can't bring her to you—you must go to her. Will you dare the journey along the Path of Souls?"

Esmeralda nodded.

"If you fail, there will be no return for you either—you understand that?"

Again Esmeralda nodded.

"Then come," Grandmother Toad said, offering her hand. "We must travel quickly, for if her body fails while you are still in my grandson's realm, it will be the same as your failing in this task."

Esmeralda didn't need to think. She took Grandmother Toad's hand in her own, marveling at the spark of warmth that sped up her arm at the contact of their skin. The spirit drums sounded louder. She sensed shifting shapes moving around them. Then the world where the old man had constructed his conjuring lodge faded behind them and they were walking into deeper spirit realms.

6

They approached the parking lot at Lac la Pêche without lights, the Bronco coasting in for the last few hundred yards, engine dead. Ernie put on the brakes.

"Shit," he said quietly as the Bronco came to a halt. "I forgot that the brake lights'd show."

"It's okay," Blue told him. "The action's out in the woods."

There was only one other car in the lot—a Buick Skylark. Blue went to check it out while Hacker reached into the space behind the backseat of the Bronco and took out a Blue Jays baseball cap, which he pushed down over his unruly hair, the sun visor pointing backward. Grabbing a couple of baseball bats, he joined the rest of them in the parking lot.

"The Skylark's clean," Blue said.

"You figure they came in that?" Ernie asked.

Blue shrugged. "They had to come in something."

But he was remembering how the creatures had been afraid of the iron in his shotgun's pellets last time and was wondering what new human agents they had helping them now. He had a sick, desperate feeling inside. They weren't going to make it. It didn't matter how strong he was, how much he cared about her, what he tried, Emma was going to die.

"Here you go, slugger," Hacker said, tossing Judy one of the bats. "Bases are loaded—let's give 'em hell."

"What are you doing with that cap?" she asked.

"What does it look like I'm doing? I'm playing ball."

"What are we looking at here anyway?" Ernie asked Blue. "How many do you think we're going up against?" He had a tire iron in his hand that he'd pulled from under the driver's seat.

Blue shook his head. "I'm trying to remember how many there were the last time. Thing is, I figure we've got to finish them all or Emma's just going to be going through this same shit over and over again."

He saw the wheel turning in his mind's eye, going around in a long slow spin. . . .

"You think these fairies had something to do with her coma, too?" Judy asked.

"Fairies?" Ernie demanded. "Jesus H. Christ. I thought we were taking down some of the Dragon."

"These guys are worse-looking than any bikers," Blue said.

"Great. A bunch of ugly homos. What the hell are they doing with your woman anyway?"

"Not fairy like in gay," Judy told him. "Faerie like in goblins and things that go bump in the night."

"Is this for real, Blue? Are we chasing down some spooks or is Judy just shitting me again?"

Blue wished they'd stop horsing around. On one level he knew it was just their way of dealing with the situation, but all he could think of was Emma out there in the woods somewhere, the witch's creatures doing Christ knew what to her. He pumped a shell into the firing chamber of his shotgun.

"Let's go," he said, leading the way into the woods.

"Don't you just love it when he plays the strong silent type?" Hacker asked Ernie as they followed.

"What's this shit about fairies?" Ernie wanted to know.

"Can it, you guys," Judy told them.

Though it had been months since he'd been here, Blue still remembered the way to the glade where he'd found Emma the last time. Once they were close to it, he got down low, crawling forward with the shotgun held in his hands, using his elbows to drag himself along. The others followed suit, quiet now that the business was at hand.

When Blue paused, then found shelter behind a fat pine bole, Judy crept up on his right, the other pair on his left.

"See anything?" she breathed in his ear.

Blue pointed. Looking down, they could all see the stone in the center of the glade, the pale form in a skimpy hospital gown lying on top of it. From where they were, they could just barely see that some kind of glowing designs had been painted on her skin. A vague sickly yellow light emanated from her body.

The hopeless feeling grew in Blue, just looking at her. Hang in there, Emma, he thought. He raked the glade with a desperate gaze, trying to find the creatures. If they were just waiting for him to make his move, he wouldn't keep them guessing for long. Only where the fuck were they?

"I don't see anybody," Hacker whispered.

"They're here," Blue replied. "I can feel them and I'm not waiting."

"What the hell's that glow around her?" Ernie wanted to know.

"I don't know. But I'm going to find—"

Judy gripped his arm suddenly and they all saw it then. It was a squat ugly creature, thick body hair covering its lower torso like trousers. White uncombed braids of hair framed its face to fall down to past its shoulders. It carried a short staff, bedecked with bones and feathers, in its left hand. In its right, it carried a dagger. Like another staff, its erect penis swayed back and forth as it crossed the grass to where Emma lay.

"Oh, Jesus," Ernie muttered. "What the fuck *is* that thing?"

Judy and Hacker stared wide-eyed along with him, dumbstruck at the undeniable *alienness* of the creature. Blue recognized it as the leader of the creatures. Didn't matter where the others were. Not when he had this one in his sights.

"No way!" he cried, rising to his feet. "No way you're getting her, pal!"

He ran toward the stone, bringing the shotgun to bear, then hit an invisible wall and went sprawling. He lost his grip on the shotgun and rolled toward where it had fallen. By that time the others had reached him. They approached the unseen barrier more cautiously. As Blue got to his feet, the reclaimed shotgun back in his hands, they all pushed at the wall with their hands, looking for all the world like a group of mimes pretending that they were feeling the confines of an invisible box.

"Look," Judy said.

She pointed at their feet. A thin strip of phosphorescence lay on the grass, running off in either direction for as far as they could see, curving inward, obviously enclosing the glade in a circle of protection. Hacker tried to touch it with the end of his bat, but it was protected by the invisible barrier.

"We can't get through," he said.

"We've got to get through!" Blue cried, desperation now creeping into his voice.

He hit the barrier with the stock of the shotgun, again and again, so hard that his hands began to sting from the impact, but it wouldn't give. By now the creature below had taken notice of them and was approaching.

"Come to watch the rites, did you?" it asked, grinning maliciously at their helplessness. "I'll chew your pretty little thing's heart, won't I? I'll suck the marrow from her sweetmeat bones. And then I'll come for you, don't you doubt it. Then I'll come for you."

It turned away to return to where Emma lay, laughter trailing behind it. Blue howled and threw himself at the barrier, too far gone to listen to anything now.

"Hacker," Judy said quickly, "you take the left—Ernie, go right. Test this thing every couple of feet and shout out if you find a way through."

Wasting no time, both men set out, slapping their weapons against the barrier as they went.

"Blue," Judy tried, pulling at his arm. "Blue! For Christ's sake, will you listen to me?"

When he turned, she thought he was going to have a go at her. His eyes were crazy. The shotgun went up like a club. She lifted her bat to ward off the blow, but then he gave a rattling cough and leaned weakly against the barrier, the arm holding the shotgun falling limply to his side.

"It's no good," he said hollowly. His eyes shone with frustrated tears.

"Give me a boost," Judy said.

He gave her a numb look. "What?"

"A boost, for Christ's sake—up that tree." She pointed to a pine that the phosphorescent trail circled around. "Depending on how high that barrier is, I might be able to get over it by climbing up the tree and sliding down one of the branches."

She watched hope flicker deep in his eyes, and then they were running for the pine.

7

After a time of walking through trackless forests, Grandmother Toad led Esmeralda to a place where mists grew thick between the trees. Tendrils curled up to touch Esmeralda's cheek; the wind that followed her brushed them away. Against the soft sound of spirit drumming, she heard the occasional drop of moisture falling to the leaves. In the distance an owl hooted.

"This is *meekunnaug,*" Grandmother Toad said. "The Path of Souls." She indicated a wide path that appeared through the mists, tall trees rising on either side of it. "You must follow it until you come to a river—your sister will be on its opposite bank."

"I understand."

"Remember: If you fail, you remain here. If your sister's body ceases to breathe in the Outer World, you will both remain here. This is a place where the dead walk, daughter. My light allows you to travel it in the flesh, but if you abide too long, if the moon sets before you have returned, you will both remain here forever."

Esmeralda nodded. Grandmother Toad gave her hand a squeeze and kissed her cheek, then loosed the hold she had on Esmeralda's fingers and stepped back.

"Go now, daughter," she said. "And be quick."

Esmeralda hesitated one long moment, then started down the mist-strewn path. In moments Grandmother Toad was lost to sight. The spirit drums still sounded, but very faintly now. She felt invisible presences on the path with her, brushing close to her in the thick mist. Not spirit guides, these. These were the spirits of the dead, traveling west.

She walked until a face appeared suddenly out of the mist on her right. Pausing, she saw that it was carved from the living wood of a tree—an old man's face, his braids descending into bark below his perfectly crafted features. When she stopped, the carving's eyes opened and the face spoke to her.

"Give up this hopeless quest," it told her. "The one you seek is content as she is. If you burden your soul with this trial while you still live, you will retain the memory of that sorrow in Epanggi-shimuk when you die and never know peace."

"She didn't know what she was doing," Esmeralda told the face.

But the features had grown still once more. She touched its cheek and felt only wood under her fingertips. The mists swirled up between her and the tree. When the wind that followed her cleared them away once more, no face remained. Only rough bark, a knothole where she had seen a mouth. Two more where she had seen eyes. The stub of a branch, where she had seen a nose.

Turning from it, she continued down the path.

The sound of the spirit drums was so faint now, she might have only been listening to the blood move in her own veins. A second face appeared out of the mist—this time on her left, an old woman's face carved from a granite outcrop that rose tall and gray, its heights lost in the haziness. She stopped before it and once again inanimate eyes opened, the face speaking.

"Destiny governs parts of our lives," it said, "permitting certain events, preventing others. The wheel turns. Accept what has been apportioned to you and your sister."

Esmeralda shook her head. "Emma made the choice—a wrong choice. There's nothing preordained about this."

She turned and continued on before the face lost its mobility and became simply stone as the face in the tree had earlier. She hurried now, sensing the night winding away from her, the moon setting, Grandmother Toad's protection waning.

The spirit drums had fallen silent. The only sound she heard now was that of her own breath and her footfalls on the Path of Souls. One part of her feared this surreal journey, another reveled in its mystery.

Just don't forget why you're here, she told herself. It would be so easy, and time was running out.

She smelled the river through the mist, before she reached it. At its banks, she paused again. The mists cleared enough for her to look across its vast width, and she knew one long unhappy moment of failure before spying the canoe that was pulled up among the reeds and rushes close at hand. A loon called from somewhere on the water—the sound of its cry ringing eerie and distant. Hesitating for only a moment longer, Esmeralda launched the canoe and began to paddle across the river.

Strange glowing shapes under the surface of the water caught her attention as she made her way through the stands of rushes that choked the river's banks. She looked over the side of the canoe and saw faces lying in the water, looking upward, watching her. When she paused in midstroke, one of them rose to the surface and spoke to her.

"Go back," it said. "We understand your sorrow, but you do not belong here. All beings grieve when good ends, when what ought to be comes to nothing, but there is a new wheel for each that ends. Go back and build anew upon the ruins of what you have lost. Forget this well-intended yet foolish quest."

"Never," Esmeralda told it.

She turned her face away and looked forward over the bow of the canoe, dipping her paddle with hard sure strokes so that her craft shot forward, out of the rushes and onto the open water of the river. In her mind her inner clock counted the moments that were slipping by all too rapidly and she paddled harder. The mists came drifting in again, but she called up her wind to blow them away. She couldn't risk losing her sense of direction now. Time was too precious.

She could sense other canoes on the water with her. The spirits of the dead. Like her, they were still traveling west. To what lay on the far banks—Epanggishimuk, the Land of Souls.

As the shore approached, she studied it carefully. Birch woods marched back into a thicker forest of cedar and maple, elm and pine. Close by the rushes, willows grew in deep thickets. She aimed her craft to where a meadow lay against the riverbank, landing the canoe on a tiny beach of mud and clay. She pulled the canoe up onto the shore, stowing the paddle inside it, then stood up to study the new land she was in.

With time slipping away, moment by inexorable moment, she had fretted about where to even begin to start looking, but she needn't have worried. Emma stood on the bank above her, smiling down at her.

"Oh, Esmeralda," she said. "What are *you* doing here?"

8

Spirits were talking. *Animiki* grumbling their drum talk in the sky.

Migizi had dismantled his conjuring lodge, rolling the poles in his deerskins, tying the bundle with the leather thongs that had bound the cedar branches to the birch. As he worked, his thoughts turned from the naming ceremony he would perform tomorrow to what the voices of the thunders were saying. He listened to them gossip about a living being who walked the Path of Souls and how she would remain there.

It was a future they saw.

Migizi could still taste the wind manitou's smoke in his lungs and he sat now, facing west, looking where Nokomis had taken her. The bundled lodge lay beside him, his water drum by his knee. He thought of the manitou and looked for other futures for her and her sister.

Most he saw were what the *animiki* drummed.

His shadow pressed close against his shoulders. His soul reminded him that he and the wind manitou had shared smoke.

Saemauh k'weekaunissimikonaun, she had signed to him. Tobacco makes us friends.

Bringing his water drum to hand, Migizi let his fingers walk upon its skin to speak his own message to the spirit world.

THREE

1

"I've come for you," Esmeralda told Emma. "To take you home."

They sat on the riverbank, looking out across the water through the mists. The thick grass was like a cushion underneath them. Wildflowers deepened the air with their rich scents. By the shore something splashed. A frog. Perhaps a fish, surfacing for an insect. Across the water, the loon called again.

"But I don't want to go back," Emma said.

Esmeralda sighed. She turned from the view to take Emma's hand. Their gazes met.

"Why not?" Esmeralda asked.

Emma disengaged their hands. "I don't fit back there. All this weirdness . . . It was fun when we were kids. That sense of magic,

Autumn Lady and Westlin Wind, my drawings and your poetry. I'd never want to have missed any of that. But I never really thought it was real. Special, yes. Magical. Wonderful. But not real."

"Is it such a bad thing?"

"It's not a question of good or bad—it's a question of my not being equipped to deal with it. If it's not just a game, if it *is* real . . . then it's too dangerous. For me, at least."

"If you learned to use your gift . . ."

Emma turned sharply. "Learn? Where do you learn about this kind of thing, Esmeralda? I stand in line at the supermarket and read all that crap on the tabloids and I think, That's what I want to be? Some flake that gets written up in *The Enquirer?* Am I supposed to get a subscription to one of them and learn from that?"

"Your knowing so little is my fault," Esmeralda said. "I went on—I didn't wait for you. I thought you were going to follow."

"Follow you where?"

"Into the mysteries. You have a gift—"

"A gift! To talk to trees?"

"Remember last year?" Esmeralda asked gently. "When your two halves were joined again? My winds were there. I felt you use your gift through them. You eased the bard's pain. You understood the workings of the spirit world. You saw how it could be."

"I remember." Emma's voice was a soft whisper.

"With your gift you can ease the aging hearts of people before they enter the winter of their lives," Esmeralda went on. "You can give them the hope they need to carry on. You and I—people with our gifts—we're here to speak of the mysteries, Emma.

"When people are born, they're still at one with the world, but they lose that harmony as they grow older. They shut their eyes, their hearts, their minds to everything that's around them. We're here to show them the way back. I speak the language of the wind; yours is that of the trees—the old bardic mysteries."

"It's *all* a mystery to me," Emma said. "Don't you see, Esmeralda? It's all clear and laid out for you, but it doesn't work that way for me. God—just look at you coming here after me. That's the kind of person I am. When I get in deep, I need help. I can't do things on my own. I need you. I need the Blues of the world."

"We all need each other's help—that's what we're here for. To preserve the harmony."

"I need more help than anybody's got a right to ask for."

"Is that why you turned away from what happened last year?" Esmeralda asked. "Why you stilled the gift when it woke again?"

"It felt like a gift at the time. For a day or so. But then it just seemed to fray. I started remembering it like a dream. It just . . . faded on me."

"I won't go away this time," Esmeralda said. "This time I'll stay, Emma. I promise you that."

Emma shook her head. "I can't go back. How could I face anybody? Can you imagine what Blue'd think if I came to him with this kind of a story? 'Well, you see, Blue, I'm really here in this world to talk to the trees and use their wisdom to help everybody get along better.' "

"I think Blue understands it better than you do."

"It's no good. I can't go back. Everything's too jumbled and confused back there. Not the real world. I can handle my job and people and all that kind of thing. It's the weirdness—this gift stuff. Winds and trees. Being here's the first time I've felt sane in months."

"You'll just be postponing the inevitable," Esmeralda said.

"What do you mean by that?"

"You'll come back, be born again on the same wheel, and have to deal with it all then. The gift's not going to go away. What we are doesn't change, Emma—it doesn't matter what shape we wear."

"I . . . I can't do it," Emma said. "I'm sorry, Esmeralda. Maybe next time around I'll be better equipped to handle it, but not this time."

Esmeralda said nothing of what Grandmother Toad had told her, how she would have to remain here with Emma if she couldn't convince Emma to return. She could feel the time ticking away inside her, the seconds draining away, being used up, one after the other, never to be repeated. No calling them back.

"I never thought you'd take the easy route out," she said finally.

"What do you mean?"

"Suicide."

"I'm not killing myself."

"Oh, no? Your body's still alive back in the Outer World. If you don't get back to it soon, that's it. You've killed yourself."

Emma shook her head. "I just went away. I just came here, that's all."

"Euphemisms don't change the truth. Your spirit left your body and your body went into a coma. That witch's creatures kidnapped your body—Blue and some of his friends are trying to get it back right now—but that doesn't change the fact that none of this would have happened if you hadn't made the choice you did."

"Witch's creatures?"

"The same one who got you the last time."

"But Glamorgana's dead."

"Apparently. But her creatures aren't, and they've gone after you."

"And Blue's gone after them?"

Esmeralda nodded.

Emma pushed her hands against her face. "Why doesn't it stop?" she demanded. "Why does this just go on and on and on?"

"Because it takes you to stop it."

Emma stood up and walked a few paces away from the river to stare into the forest.

"Please, Emma. Things can be good again."

Emma didn't turn around. "Why do you even care about me?" she asked. "I'm so weak. . . ."

Esmeralda rose to join her. "Because you're like a sister to me. My other half. I love you—that's why. And you're not weak. You're just in over your head. Needing help and accepting it doesn't make you weak. Turning your back on what you are, giving up—that's weakness. That's the easy way out."

"You'll really stay and help?"

"I promise. I'll have my things sent from England. Jamie's kept my room in the tower for me all these years. It'll be like I never left."

Emma turned to look at her. "Is this what *you* want, Esmeralda? You're not just doing it for me?"

"I'm doing it partly for you—but I'm doing it for myself as well. I've taken the easy road, too, Emma—not the one you took, but

the end result's somewhat the same. I let the acquiring of knowledge overpower the help *I* should have been giving. Not just to
you, but to everything under my charge. I only helped when it was
convenient to my schedule, or when someone was so desperate
that there was no one else they could turn to. But our gifts are a
constant thing—not something we can turn on and off like a
faucet."

Emma looked at her for a long moment. Esmeralda couldn't tell
what she was thinking. All she knew was that time was running
out. . . .

"All right," Emma said finally. "I'll come back with you."

She gave Esmeralda a quick hug, then led the way down to
where the canoe was still pulled up to the shore. She turned back
when she reached the water's edge.

"Aren't you coming?" she asked when she saw Esmeralda just
standing in the meadow, a bleak look in her eyes.

Inside Esmeralda the ticking clock had finally run its course. She
could feel the moon set in the Outer World, Grandmother Toad's
protection fading.

"We're too late," she said.

The road home was closed to them now.

2

Even when she stood on Blue's shoulders, the lowest branch of the
pine was too high for Judy to reach.

"Stand on my hands," Blue told her.

Holding the tree for balance, Judy lifted one foot, then the other,
while Blue slipped his hands under her feet. Grunting with the
effort, he straight-armed her up until she could reach the branch.

"Got it," she called down.

She hoisted herself onto the branch, straddling it while she
caught her breath. She had her baseball bat stuck in her belt behind
her, the knob caught in the belt to keep it from slipping out.
Checking to make sure it was still in place, she stood up on the
branch and began to edge her way outward, her fingers just brushing the next branch up to keep her balance.

Watching her go, Blue held his breath. "Come on," he muttered. "Just a few steps more."

Then she was above the barrier and moving past it.

"You did it!" he called up.

Now all she had to do was get down to the ground and see if the phosphorescent ribbon that was the barrier's source could be erased from the inside. He watched her edge along the branch toward its end, her weight making it dip. It was still a long jump. Then he glanced toward the stone and saw that the creature had become aware of what they were doing.

"Heads up!" he called to her, pointing toward the creature when Judy looked down.

She nodded and kept on moving. But now the creature was heading in their direction. Cursing, Blue laid his shotgun on the ground. He took a few steps back and then ran at the tree. He leapt up, got a grip on the fat bole, and began to shimmy his way to the branch, his hands getting gummy with pine resin.

The branch had dipped low enough for Judy to try jumping. She dropped her bat to the ground, then got a grip on the branch with her hands and let herself down. She swung for a moment or two, then dropped, knees bent to take the impact. She rolled when she hit the ground, hardly shaken at all, and scrambled for the bat. By the time she had it in hand, the creature was only a half-dozen yards away. Too late to try the barrier now, she realized.

It had left behind both its knife and staff. Spitting on its hands, it came at her, arms outspread, saliva glistening on its palms with the same glow as the phosphorescent ribbon from which the barrier grew.

Judy stood her ground, pulse doubling as adrenaline surged through her system. The creature wasn't all that much taller than her, but if it ever got those paws on her . . . She waited until just before it came into range; then she swung the bat, ducking in low under its arms and aiming for one of its legs. If she could cripple it, they might have a better chance at taking it down. But the creature was faster than she'd believed possible.

It caught the bat in midblow—the hardwood smoking where the saliva on its palms touched the wood. Ripping it from her hands, it tossed the bat aside. Blue was just getting onto the branch that had let Judy into the glade—too far away to help. Hacker and Ernie weren't in sight. She was on her own.

She thought of that saliva on the creature's palms, burning her skin like acid, never mind that the sucker looked tough enough to tear her in two without working up a sweat. She took a stumbling step backward.

I'm going to die, she realized numbly.

3

"Too late?" Emma said. "What do you mean we're too late?"

"I didn't get here on my own," Esmeralda said. "Grandmother Toad helped me." At Emma's blank look she explained. "That's how she's known in these spirit realms. She's an aspect of the moon—Brigit, Galata, Albion, Metra, Mary, Maya . . . whatever name you want to give her, they all describe the same mystery. She showed me how to find the Path of Souls that brought me here, but there was a time limit on her help. We had until the moon set in the Outer World."

"So we have to wait until she rises again tonight?"

Esmeralda shook her head. "We wait until we're born again." Or at least Emma would. Present as she was in her corporeal form, Esmeralda didn't know what would become of herself in this place.

"You go on without me then," Emma said.

"You're not listening—I said we're both staying here. It's no longer in our hands now."

"Esmeralda, I don't want you to sacrifice your life just because of my mistakes."

"I made my choice," Esmeralda said. "Just as you made yours."

"Why didn't you tell me about the time limit right away?"

"You had to come with me because *you* wanted to—not out of some sense of allegiance to me or anyone else—and I couldn't leave without you. I accepted that when I chose to come."

Emma sank to her knees by the riverbank, not caring that she knelt in mud. "I've really done it this time, haven't I? Only now I've dragged you down with me."

"Emma, I wanted to come. I told you, I had something to learn on this journey as well."

"Only trouble is, whatever we've learned, we've both learned it too late."

Esmeralda sat on the grass near where Emma knelt. "At least we're together," she said. "I don't regret coming. I've missed you, Emma."

"I've missed you, too. I . . ." She broke off, head cocked as though she heard something.

"What is it?"

"Listen."

Then Esmeralda heard it, too. Drumming. So faint as to be almost inaudible.

"Spirit drumming," she said.

Emma nodded. "But not just any spirit drumming—can't you hear it? Something's calling to us."

Esmeralda's winds stirred as hope lifted inside her. "The old man," she said. "It has to be him. The shaman in the glade who brought Grandmother Toad to me."

"He brought her to me as well," Emma said. "I was too scared to go on the path by myself, but then she came to help me. Can you understand what he's saying?"

Esmeralda shook her head.

"I can," Emma said. "The wood of his drum's translating it for me. It's saying, 'Follow me home, lost spirits.' "

"I don't know. Grandmother Toad said—"

"Who's giving up now?" Emma asked. "We can at least try, can't we? Come on, Esmeralda. Get in the canoe."

Esmeralda looked at the river, where the mists now lay so thick that it was impossible to see more than a few yards into them. She let her winds rise up to sweep the heavy haze away, but they made no difference. If anything, the mists deepened.

"You get in the front," Emma said, "and I'll steer."

Esmeralda could sense the familiarity of the drumming, hear the old man's voice in its faint tone, but she could perceive no sense of direction from it. Yet if Emma could . . .

She got into the bow of the canoe. Emma shoved off and jumped aboard, the canoe swaying dangerously, then slowly settling in the water. They each took a paddle and dipped them in the river's still water, propelling the craft forward.

In moments the mists had swallowed them, so thick now that Emma couldn't see her companion anymore. But she could hear the drum. Its sound cast a thread that she held firmly with her mind. She was determined to follow it home. Esmeralda had shown her the importance of persevering, by her selfless loyalty as much as by her logic.

But now the water grew rougher. From a calm, slow-moving surface, it became abruptly violent. The canoe lurched in the turbulence. Sudden eddies spun them in circles, huge jutting rocks rose up out of nowhere. Esmeralda pushed the canoe away from the rocks with her paddle until the paddle snapped. Water sprayed over them and it was all Emma could do to steer a clear way. Then a wave, bigger than any other, rose up in front of them, lunging at them like a behemoth exploding from the mists.

"Esmeralda!" Emma cried.

As the wave crashed down upon them she threw herself forward to grip her friend's hand; then they were washed out of the canoe and dropped into a spinning maelstrom of dark rushing water. Emma held on to Esmeralda's hand with a strength born of desperation. She fought the urge to breathe in a lungful of water, and concentrated on finding the thread of drumming once more. She knew it was still there, sounding inside her on a spirit level for all that its physical presence had long since been drowned by the violence of the sudden storm on the river. When she finally snared it, she held on to it just as desperately as she did Esmeralda's hand.

Imagining it to be a fishing line, she hauled them along its length, away from the river's depths, away into the outer spirit realms to where an old man was drumming their rescue.

4

The creature struck, moving like lightning, but fear lent Judy the speed to dodge the full impact of its blow. Still, its glancing force was enough to make her lose her balance and go stumbling toward the pine. The leather of her jacket burned where the creature's saliva had touched it—the heat searing her skin. Off-balance as well from the impetus of his swing, the creature recovered only moments after Judy.

She was running for the barrier, hand outstretched to wipe away the ribbon supporting it, when the creature brought her down. The stink of burning leather arose again, followed by a reeking wave of the creature's heavy body odor. The force of its grip on either arm hurt as much as the heat that was now burning through her jacket to sear her skin. The creature started to turn her over, but then its weight suddenly left her body.

She rolled free to see that Blue had jumped down from the branch and pulled the creature off, heaving it to one side. She scrabbled out of the way as it rose to its feet to face Blue. She reached the barrier, finding it by feel. Using the elbow of her jacket, she broke the solidity of the phosphorescent ribbon. When she tried the barrier again, it was gone.

"Got something!" she heard someone call on the far side of the glade—Hacker or Ernie, she wasn't sure which and she didn't have time to go look.

"Over here!" she cried and then she went after the shotgun.

Behind her, the creature charged Blue. It came at him, arms widespread to clasp him in a bear hug. Blue dodged, moving fast, but the creature was faster. It caught Blue by one arm and threw him toward the trunk of the pine.

Blue hit hard, the sleeve of his jacket burning, his arm feeling like it was on fire, head ringing. The creature spat at him and he dodged the saliva, hearing its burning hiss as it splattered on the bark beside his head. As the creature charged him again, he rose to meet its attack.

Judy arrived with the shotgun, but the two combatants were too close to each other now for her to chance a shot. All she could do was stand helplessly by as they grappled.

5

Emma allowed her mind to focus on only two things: the grip she had of Esmeralda's hand and the thread of drumming that was their only chance of escaping Epanggishimuk now that Grandmother Toad's protection was withdrawn with the setting of the moon in the Outer World. She followed the thread, drawing them out of the maelstrom of the river to the flat rock of an island that jutted from its turbulent waters.

Waves crashed against the shore, rising high, but not high enough to wash them off. Esmeralda's winds blew them back. They lay on the hard stone like a pair of bedraggled cats, gasping for breath. The mists thickened around them, making an impenetrable wall of haze.

"Where . . . where are we?" Esmeralda asked as she finally caught her breath.

She had lost her shoes in the water, but worse, she'd lost her shoulder bag with its fetishes and charms. She sat up and peeled off her socks, sticking them in the pockets of her borrowed jacket.

"We haven't left the inner realms," Emma said.

"The drumming?"

"I can still hear it—but it's faint."

Esmeralda looked out at the mists. Waves continued to crash against the rocks, spraying them. What little they could see of the river beyond the rock was a storm of spinning waters.

"We'll have to go back in the river," she said. "We have to cross it to get out."

Emma nodded dully. Her head ached from the strain of bringing them this far on the threads of the drumming. But the longer they sat here, the fainter the drumming grew.

"I'm not giving up," she said.

Esmeralda smiled at her. "That's the Emma I remember—welcome back."

Emma wrung the water from her hair, but a new wave rose up and the spray that wasn't driven back by Esmeralda's winds soaked her again.

"Time to go," she said.

They helped each other stand and stood with their arms around each other's waists to keep their balance. The thread of drumming sounded suddenly louder, but then Emma realized that it was coming out of the mist. A new drumming. Not the thread that had been leading them home.

"Esmeralda . . ." she began, but she didn't need to speak.

The heads of two enormous serpents rose out of the water. They had huge eyes, round as moons. One was black, the roof of its head capped with antlers. The other was white, its brow smooth. The new sound of the spirit drums that accompanied the creatures joined the rhythm of the drumming that they had been following.

"Mishiginebek," Emma breathed. The drumming whispered the name of the serpents to her. Mishiginebek lived to punish those who mocked the manitou, who used their medicine for evil, by devouring their souls after death.

I've mocked the spirits, Emma thought. I refused to believe in them, refused to accept their reality.

The great beasts watched them with unblinking gazes, unmoved by the storm of waters from which they rose. Emma shuddered at the forked tongues that flickered from their mouths. She could already feel the convulsive motion of their throats, drawing Esmeralda and her down into their bellies. . . .

Esmeralda stepped forward, drawing Emma with her.

"No," Emma protested.

"They're here to help us," Esmeralda said. "Don't you see? The shaman sent them."

And then Emma saw an image of the old medicine man in each of their eyes. She couldn't read the sign language his hands were shaping, but the drumming told her what Esmeralda could read. The serpents were his patrons, as the Black Duck was his totem. They had come, summoned by his water drum to help them.

Emma turned away to look at her companion; then the two of them held hands and jumped into the roaring waters.

6

When the creature spat at Blue's face, Judy thought her heart would stop. But Blue turned his head just enough so that the gob of saliva went by his ear. His cheek and hair smoked from its accompanying spray. The pain was enough to lend him the strength to wrench himself free. Judy brought up the shotgun, now that she had a clear shot, but suddenly Ernie was there, his tire iron upraised, then flashing down.

It bit into the creature's head with a wet popping sound, breaking through the bone of the creature's skull. Blood sprayed and the creature dropped to its knees. Before it could rise, Hacker was there as well and the two men each hit the creature again. When they stood back, it lay still on the ground between them. Judy stepped forward and fired a shot into its chest for good measure.

"Jesus, Jesus," Ernie was saying, staring down at the thing. "What the fuck is it?"

Blue wiped the side of his head with a sleeve of his jacket and stepped slowly forward. His cheek was pocked with red burns.

"It's dead," he said flatly. "That's all it is."

"Are there more of them?" Hacker asked.

"There were the last time."

"Great."

But Blue wasn't listening anymore. He turned his back on the dead creature and went on down the hollow to where Emma lay on the gray stone. Judy fed another shell into the shotgun and trailed along behind him. When she reached the stone, Blue was trying to wipe the glowing symbols from Emma's face. Whatever they had been painted on with wouldn't come off.

"God, she's so still," Judy said.

"Is she dead?" Hacker asked, coming up behind her.

Blue shook his head numbly. "Jesus, man. I just don't know."

He put his head to her chest and heard the faint sound of a heartbeat.

"She's alive!"

He started to gather her up in his arms.

"Should you be moving her like that?" Ernie asked.

Blue just looked at him like he was crazy. "We've got to get her to a hospital," he said.

He hoisted her up, but then Judy touched his arm.

"Look," she said, pointing to just beyond the stone.

A pair of pale shapes stood there, ill-defined so that their features couldn't be made out, but human shapes all the same.

7

The serpents bore them out of the river, up into the sky to where the mists were deepest. The spirit drums spoke like thunder all around them. As their bodies were borne by the twin beasts, they lost all sense of physical awareness and seemed to be drifting in a grey place. For their spirits, motion had ceased. The trees of a ghostly forest rose all around them. Seated directly before them was the old shaman. He, too, seemed to be made of mist. He looked up at them, ghostly hands leaving the skin of his water drum.

Welcome, manitou, he signed to them.

As she took in their surroundings, Esmeralda's thoughts turned to the Weirdin that she'd read in Jamie's study. Three old bones, drawn from their bag. A future told in their carved faces. That moment seemed like a hundred years ago now. But she could still see them as though they lay in her palm.

The Forest. A place of testing an unknown peril.

She and Emma had been tested and known peril tonight.

The Acorn, or Hazelnut. For hidden wisdom and friendship.

They'd both found wisdom and deepened their friendship.

And the last bone? She looked at the old shaman.

Among certain tribes a man did not speak his own name, so she couldn't ask their benefactor his, and there was no third party present to speak it for him. But there was still one Weirdin unaccounted for, and she thought she knew now both its meaning and their benefactor's name.

She let go of Emma's hand and faced the shaman. Extending her arms, she waved her hands in imitation of the beating of wings, palms down, fingers outstretched. Then she brought her right hand near her nose, curving it slightly to suggest a bird's beak.

Eagle, she signed.

The Eagle. Release from bondage.

The old shaman smiled as his name came from her hands.

You must go, manitou, he signed. *Your own world calls you.*

Esmeralda nodded. But she wanted to show her respect for him. *I have a friend,* she signed quickly, *in need of his true name. Will you help him find it?*

Migizi's smile broadened. *I would be honored.*

His palms returned to the skin of his water drum and the sound of its voice rumbled through the ghostly glade. As Esmeralda took Emma's hand once more, a great rushing sound filled her ears, hard on the heels of Migizi's drumming. The place of mist tattered like smoke. There was a moment of vertigo, and then they were standing in a wooded clearing in the Outer World, drawn to the place where Emma's body awaited the return of her spirit.

They saw Blue holding Emma's body, Judy Kitt with a shotgun in her hands, and two strangers. For one long moment they held to their spirit forms; then Esmeralda's flesh returned to cloak her spirit while Emma's fled into her body. She stirred in Blue's arms, the symbols on her skin fading, evaporating away, into the late-night air, until they were gone.

"Jesus on a Harley!" Ernie Collins said softly. "Now I've seen everything."

8

It was just after dawn when Esmeralda returned to the knoll in the center of Tamson House's gardens. The bird chorus was in full song all around her, the sun's light just rising over the gables of the east side of the House.

"*Gaoth an Iar,*" a voice said softly. Wind of the West. "You've returned from your journey."

Esmeralda smiled at the crippled bard. "Journeys never end," she said. "You must know that."

"Yet your feet are still."

Winds rose to tousle her hair and his. She touched a hand to her chest.

"Only when the heart is still is the journey over," she said. "And even then . . ."

"There are rivers to cross."

Esmeralda smiled. The old Celts also believed that one crossed a great river when they died. So much seemed different in the world only to be proved that it was the same thing, merely wearing an unfamiliar shape.

"I met a man last night," she said, "who knows your true name. Will you come with me to hear it from his lips?"

"And then?"

Esmeralda looked beyond the garden to where she could see the roofline of the House through the garden's trees. "Then we'll return to this place." She smiled. "It can be as much an inspiration as a refuge, you know."

She could already hear the music that his one hand would call forth from the synthesizer that Blue was going to pick up this morning. But the bard would need his true name to make that music. And when she had eased the winter of his heart? There would be others for her to help. She and Emma. There would always be others.

Rising, she offered him her hand. By the time the young playwright Tim Gavin had made his way to the garden's knoll, to call them in for a celebratory breakfast, there was only a stirring of leaves to show where they'd been.

GHOSTWOOD

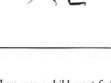

There was a child went forth
every day,
And the first object he looked
upon,
That object he became. . . .
—Walt Whitman

There are wildflowers in the
woods,
there are owls who wake and
guard
the forest paths.
—Susan Musgrave
The Charcoal Burners

Lead into Gold

The Cave—*entrance to the*
Otherworld
—Weirdin disc;
Secondary: Second Rank,
36.a

To a greater force, and to a
better
nature, you, free, are subject,
and that
creates the mind in you,
which the heavens
have not in their charge.
Therefore if
the present world go astray,
the cause is
in you, in you it is to be
sought.
—Dante Alighieri
The Divine Comedy

IT WAS TIME TO DIE.

Albert Watkins looked out the window of the house that he and his wife Eleanor were renting on Clemow Avenue. Across the street, stretching either way to the end of the block, was the enormous bulk of Tamson House. The facade it presented to the world of being a long row of town houses meant no more to him than it did to any long-term resident of the neighborhood. Everyone knew that it was all just one building; for them, the secret its facade hid was merely the odd turn of mind of the man who'd originally commissioned the building and had then overseen its curious construction. But Watkins knew the true secret its facade hid:

Tamson House was a place of power. It was a door to Otherworlds and magic breathed in its walls, mystery slept restlessly in its enclosed garden. In a world where the ancient mystery traditions had been mostly relegated to bad plot devices in Hollywood films or New Age fantasies in equally painful novels, Tamson House presented irrefutable proof that more lay beyond the scope of the shallow world than most men and women could perceive with their sleeping senses.

To comprehend the power that lay in the House's walls—the potent forces of energy matriced in the ley lines that collected under its foundations as though the building were some ancient stonework, rather than a curious, overly large structure—required a mind that demanded more of itself and its body than the autopilot thought processes and reactions with which most of humanity confronted the world. There was no one in this neighborhood awake enough to appreciate its potency. There were even people living in its maze of hallways and rooms who hadn't the first inkling of what lay underfoot, of what hummed within its walls and was stored in its perfect puzzle of stonework, glass and wood.

But Watkins knew. Reading the works of a namesake, Alfred Watkins—the name was close enough to his own to make no difference, to Watkins's way of thinking—he'd first begun to understand the complexity of the earth lines that gave the sacred sites of the world their potency. From ley lines and their mystic crossroads he'd delved into the lore that accompanied them.

Common knowledge and quaint folktales had led him into a study of ever more arcane texts and finally, through perseverance— "The superior man heaps up small things in order to achieve something high and great," the I Ching said—through studies and interviews with various spiritual teachers—Native American shaman, Eastern swami, cabbalists, Western mystics—but mostly through the sheer audacity of his own wit, he learned how the world worked. He learned of the otherworldly powers that lay waiting in this world's hidden places. He learned how to tap into their potency and so quicken his own resources. And ultimately, he learned how he could have it all.

It required one's own death, but repaid that death a hundredfold with eternity—but not in some nebulous afterworld. What use was that? No, the dividend that sacrifice repaid was a return to this world and the promise that one could be whatever one wanted, have whatever one wanted.

Forever.

Watkins was nearing the end of his natural life. The past years of his searching had taken on a fine edge of desperation. He knew the power was here in this world, waiting for the man or woman brave—or foolhardy—enough to take it up, and he had found its hiding places. A stonework in the Hebrides, another in Brittany. A mountaintop shrine in Tibet, another in the Andes. A jungle pool in Sumatra, a river in Oregon. But they were all too well protected. Their guardians were fierce and dangerous beyond compare for they swallowed not the bodies, but the souls of those who came with plunder in their heart, rather than respect.

And then Watkins found Tamson House. It, too, had a guardian, but his guardianship was eroding. He was new to his task—a novice, and an untutored one as well. His mind was still too enwrapped in the human concerns of the life he had led before he'd acquired his responsibility. The guardian of Tamson House had yet to learn how to focus on the task at hand to the exclusion of all else.

Watkins had no such difficulty. He had but one thing on his mind. When he looked at the night-silhouetted skyline of the building, he saw neither its darkened gables nor the shadowed outline of its roof, but the sparking glow of its power, a shimmering aura of power just waiting to be harvested that glimmered and spun webs of fairy-gold light from roof ridge to chimney, cornice to gutter.

Tonight it would all be his.

It was growing late. Dawn would soon be washing the eastern sky with its soft pastel light. But he knew that before the first pale ghosts of the sun's light could streak the sky, he would be dead, his spirit embracing the mystery that was Tamson House.

He had been monitoring the guardian's increasing distress with heightened eagerness. The whys of that distress were immaterial to

Watkins's concerns. What interested him was that the guardian was attempting to reach out from the confines of his guardianship—reaching, stretching himself thin, thinner—until tonight his hold on the House was so vague that Watkins knew that any moment now the guardian would lose his grip on the House and be gone.

Where he would go was also irrelevant to Watkins. All that was important was that for a time—perhaps it would only be a moment—the House would be unprotected. A moment was all that Watkins would need to slip in and take control.

He turned from the window and went to sit on the edge of the bed, lifting a glass of clear liquid from the nightstand.

"You don't have the courage to fulfill your potential," a so-called wise man had told him once. "The art of what we pursue is not to gain power, but to become more complete, to fully understand the complex simplicity that makes us what we are and by doing so, understand the mysteries of the world of which we are an integral part. Acquiring power is child's play—any half-wit can accomplish that; it takes courage to forgo the concept of self and take one's rightful place in the natural scheme of things."

Watkins held his glass up to the light.

"This takes more courage," he said softly.

The liquid was a distillation from the fruit and roots of the hemlock.

"And offers greater return," he added.

He wasn't frightened. There was no room in the tight focus of his mind for fear or doubt. He closed his eyes, his mind monitoring the spirit of the House's guardian across the street as it tugged and stretched itself away from its responsibilities. The guardian was pulled taut now, every point of his being concentrating on his effort, just as Watkins was entirely focused on his own task.

The guardian pulled free from one tower.

Watkins smiled.

There was a momentary hesitation on the part of the guardian; then he strained again and suddenly he was free.

Gone.

The House unprotected.

Watkins lifted the glass to his lips. It would be like a kind of alchemy, he thought, his passage from life, into the mystery held by the House, and then back again. Transformed.

His wife appeared in the door to the bedroom and he smiled at her.

"It's time, isn't it?" Eleanor said.

"Time indeed," Watkins replied.

The fear and doubt that could find no purchase in his mind lay creased in the worry lines of her features like the oil and grime encrusted in a mechanic's hands.

"I'll be back," Watkins told her. "I'll never forsake you. I'll be young again, Eleanor." He paused, then added the lie, *"We'll* be young again. Young forever."

Before she could speak, he swallowed the bitter liquid. He set the glass down on the table and lay back as the first shiver of pain lanced through him. Eleanor crossed quickly to the bed and sat beside him.

Ignoring the pain, he crossed his arms upon his chest and closed his eyes, concentrating on the defenses his body would require while his spirit was straying.

When he stopped breathing, Eleanor gave a small gasp. She reached out to touch him, but some invisible force repelled her hand. It pushed her fingers forcefully away just before she could touch him. Small sparks flickered and the smell of anise briefly stung the air.

It was just as he said it would be, she thought, looking down at her husband's composed features. God help them. . . .

She rose and went to the window, seeing only the dark bulk of the strange building across the street. She could see no magic aura, no mystic energy, no sign of her husband.

God help them, she thought again, then realized what she'd been thinking.

They had strayed too far from God's garden to expect His aid now.

"Just come back," she whispered.

She straightened her back then, determined to allow herself no more fear. Albert was depending on her to be strong. There was nothing she could do anyway.

Except wait.

★ ★ ★

The utter freedom of leaving his body behind almost seduced Watkins into simply letting himself go. He found himself surrounded by darkness except for a small glowing spark that seemed to lie far before him, as though it was the light at the end of a tunnel. That light woke a yearning in him that was almost impossible to ignore. It took all his will to turn from it and send his spirit into Tamson House.

With the guardian gone, it was child's play to enter the building. He raced through the matrices formed by its walls and hallways, exulting in the power that leapt and crackled in welcome to his presence. He drew it to himself and could feel himself begin to swell with its potency.

Take care, take care, he warned himself.

Too much, too soon, and he wouldn't be able to assimilate it before it consumed him. And that wasn't the only danger. He had not been alone in watching the guardian depart. Other presences clamored for the power that the guardian had left behind unprotected.

He wasn't alone, but he was first.

In the same way that he'd protected his body, he now sealed off the House, using the immense power that crackled so intensely through every particle of his being to shape a new Otherworld to house the building and all within it—an Otherworld sealed away from the greedy attentions of his rivals. He then seeded that world with a protector of his own making—the ghost of a primeval memory—so that if any spirit should manage to slip through his seals, they would still be dealt with.

Only then did he allow himself to drift away, high onto a mountaintop in his newly created world. There he floated in the dark night air, a pentacle shape, arms and legs outstretched, the five points of his body each touching the inner perimeter of yet another safeguard—a third circle of power to protect him.

He had time now to gather the full power of the House at his leisure—slowly, surely, without risk to himself. When that was done, he would turn his attention to finding a suitable victim to take the place of the sacrifice he had made of his own body.

Human sacrifice had always been the ultimate cost of such

magicking, but it was a fair price, he thought, for the rewards one could gain. Especially considering how he would soon regain all that he had lost with the subsequent death of that proxy he had still to choose.

For all his knowledge and self-acquired insight, he was unaware of how much, in such a minute fraction of time, the power had already corrupted him. He thought only of the alchemy he worked, the transformation he was undergoing.

As he congratulated himself on his success, he also deceived himself into believing that everything that existed revolved solely around him. Had he been with one of those spiritual teachers he had forsaken, they would surely have argued the point with him, little realizing that, in this pocket world he had created—neatly joined to all those myriad layers of time and place that encompassed the Otherworld—he was not so far from the mark.

The Hooded Man

The Forest—*place of testing
and unknown peril*
—*Weirdin disc;
Secondary: Second Rank,
29.a*

*Blow out the lights. Listen.
You can hear the willow
dancing.*
—*Ingrid Karklins*

1

Something wasn't right.

Tim Gavin lifted his head, cocking it like a cat who'd just heard something but couldn't quite decide what, if anything, it was that he'd heard. He'd just turned twenty on the weekend, but he looked younger—a thin ascetic in jeans and an old "Radio Clash" T-shirt, his dyed blond hair cut so short that it was only a bristle upon his scalp.

He'd been trimming the profusion of vines that had lately threatened to swallow the minotaur statue by which he knelt. Laying aside his clippers, he looked around the garden. There wasn't much he could see from his vantage point. Trees enclosed the small glade he was working in, cutting off his view of the rest of the garden. It wasn't simply those trees that stopped him from seeing the whole of the property.

Although it only took up some three and a half acres—enclosed on all four sides by the various rooms and corridors of Tamson House—the garden had always given him the impression of having a much larger acreage. So much larger that Tim sometimes got the curious notion that it wasn't so much a garden in the middle of a house the size of a city block as a door to some . . . other place. What kind of other place, he didn't know. An ancient forest, maybe. A place familiar, but strange.

But then the House itself was like that: strange.

He'd come for an evening's visit a few years ago with some older friends, then ended up moving in when he decided that he really wanted to make a go of writing plays. He'd thrived in the House's odd environment, with its tangled maze of rooms and hallways and its unique sense of *place,* and especially liked the ever-changing cast of characters that could be found wandering through its corridors at any time of the day and night.

It was sort of like a commune, he supposed, but nothing like the image he used to carry in his head of burned-out hippie Socialists living on the fringes of society. While the House definitely catered to an alternate kind of life-style, the people here didn't drift indolently through a dope-haze. Rather, they seemed to have a sense of purpose to their existence. Most of them were creative people— musicians, artists, writers—using the House as a stepping-stone, a place where they could find the time to create, to get a start on their careers, without having to scrabble about trying to make a living at the same time.

There was also what Tim referred to as the Mondo Weird Contingent—the ones that Blue called the Pagan Party, as though they were some kind of political movement, which in a way, Tim supposed, they were. He just didn't have as much patience for them as Blue did. They were the kind of people who believed everything that Charles Fort or Whitley Streiber had to say, or were into old religions—pagans, Wicca, those kinds of folks. Still, he could see what drew them here as well. The House had the feeling of a wizard's sanctum about it and there was definitely a sense of mystery—give it a capital "M"—locked in its walls.

And running loose in its garden.

He'd never met the woman who owned the building. She was always abroad, it seemed—for some reason, the people in the know usually had a funny look in their eyes when they said that—but he certainly appreciated what she was doing for the people she let stay here. He'd never felt so inspired . . . so ready to work . . . as he had when he moved in. But oddly, his priorities shifted the longer he stayed.

He still worked on his plays, yet now—as had happened with some of the other long-term residents like Blue, or Ginny, or Esmeralda—he found himself devoting more and more of his time to the House's maintenance. And not resenting those hours stolen from his writing, either. Which was weird, particularly since what he'd taken upon himself was the responsibility for the garden's upkeep and he'd never liked gardening in the first place. Still, day after day, he'd be out here, trimming and weeding and the like, while at night he read up on various gardening techniques in the magazines and books that Ginny located for him in the House's huge library.

And he was enjoying himself; feeling as much of a sense of purpose doing this kind of work as he did when he was writing.

He'd developed a whole Tao for what he did—approaching the garden with a kind of Zen creativity that utilized what was at hand, each thing in its place, sculpting, editing, adding, but always retaining the garden's original flavor. Because what the place didn't need was a look out of some *Better Homes and Gardens* glossy spread. He just saw to it that the overgrown flowerbeds were brought back to their original beauty, the hedges were clipped where they were supposed to be, allowed to run rampant where that seemed more appropriate—that kind of thing. And then there were parts of the garden—what he thought of as the Wild Walks—where he didn't trim a twig. There he just sort of tiptoed about, soaking up the ambience of the place, not even *wanting* to change—to tame—a single solitary leaf.

"You would have liked Fred," Blue told him once.

Fred was before Tim's time, but from all Tim had heard of the old man's devotion to his work, he could only agree. Apparently it was Fred who, back in the fifties, had set himself the monumental task of making some sense of the jungled garden that had been let run wild for thirty years. When Tim saw what had been happening after just the few years of neglect since Fred's death, he couldn't begin to imagine where Fred had even started.

But start he had; started, and maintained, and finally left a legacy of which any woman or man would be proud.

Sometimes Tim could almost feel—which brought him dangerously close to the Mondo Weird Contingent, he knew, but what can you do?—that Fred was still here in the garden with him: guiding his hands, or speaking softly in his ear.

It brought Tim a sense of, not so much peace, as . . . companionship.

What he heard—sensed—now wasn't that familiar spirit. It wasn't the garden's memories of the old master's hands at work, but something else that had stopped Tim in the middle of his task. An anomaly: something not quite sinister, but not quite right either; something that, well, yes, it might belong in a place like this—but more to its Wild Walks than to the cultivated areas.

When the feeling wouldn't go away, Tim finally stood up. He brushed the dirt from the knees of his jeans and started walking— no precise destination in mind, just letting himself wander, letting his subconscious become a dowsing rod focused on that oddness he felt and so steer him in its general vicinity.

When he reached the center of the garden, where an ancient oak overhung the fountain, he stopped dead in his tracks and wished he'd never come. He wanted to look away, but couldn't tear his gaze from the sight.

Hanging there, from the lowest boughs of the tree, were three naked children. Three dead children. Two boys and a girl—the oldest couldn't have been older than eight or nine.

They were thin-limbed, with knobby joints. Their skin was a kind of leaf-green, their hair the dark brown of freshly turned sod. Their dead eyes bulged froglike from their sockets. Wrapped around their necks were vines and it was from these that the children dangled like awful fruit from the boughs of the oak.

It took Tim all of a handful of seconds to see this, to have the image frozen on his retinas, burned there for all time. He saw the green skin, but it didn't register as being alien or wrong. All he really saw were three dead children. Children that someone had killed, hanging them up here to be found by the first unfortunate person who happened to come by.

And then he fled.

Back through the garden, now grown mysterious with a more malevolent mystery than it had ever held for him before.

Back to the House, where, stumbling and out of breath, he found Ohn Kenstaran sitting on the stone bench by the door that led into the Silkwater Kitchen.

Ohn was playing a zither. He was bent over the instrument, long brown hair falling forward to hide his features, one hand—a healthy hand that had a harper's dexterity and skill in every joint and muscle—plucking a melody that belled and rang forth as though it came from an instrument three times the zither's size. His other hand was a withered claw, incapable of finger movement, hidden from sight in a thin brown leather glove. He used it to steady the zither on his lap.

He looked up at Tim's sudden approach, his features creasing with worry when he saw the state Tim was in.

"There's . . . they . . . I saw . . ." Tim began, making a jumble of the words as he tried to get them out.

"Easy," Ohn said.

He set the zither aside and motioned Tim to sit beside him.

"Take a breath," he said, his good right hand resting on Tim's shoulder. "Hold it in—that's it. Steady, steady. Now let it out, but slowly. And again."

Ohn's imperturbable presence helped Tim stabilize the thunder of his heartbeat as much as the slow breathing did.

"There's these kids," Tim said when he finally stopped hyper-ventilating. "Out by the fountain. Somebody's . . ."

The image burned into his retinas flashed in his mind's eye, bringing back a rush of panic.

"You'd better show me," Ohn said.

The older man led the way back to the center of the garden, back to where the oak's branches overhung the fountain, Tim following reluctantly on his heels. When they reached the knoll on which the oak stood, there were no children dangling from its boughs.

Tim stared, the memory of what he'd seen still too fresh, too strong to be forgotten. He turned to Ohn.

"Oh, man. They were just hanging there. Three dead kids. . . ."

"This is an old forest," Ohn told him. "Haunted with ghosts. Perhaps what you saw was some memory called up from the tangle of its slow dreams."

"Forest?" Tim said. "What're you . . ."

His voice trailed off. He thought about what he called the Wild Walks, about Fred's ghost and how the garden always seemed so much bigger than it actually was, like it was a finger of some primordial forest, thrusting through space and time to lay an echo of its mystery on this garden, never mind that it was tucked away in the middle of a modern city.

"Great," he said. "Now I've joined the Contingent."

It was Ohn's turn to look confused.

"The what?" he asked.

"The Mondo—never mind."

Tim didn't know Ohn well, but what little he knew of him, he liked. He'd been told that Ohn used to play the harp, but then he had this accident with his hand—Tim didn't know the details—and he'd refused to touch one since. He'd had a different name back then, too, Ginny had said one day when Tim asked her about the harper. Ginny seemed to know everything about everybody, for all that she spent ninety-nine percent of her time moled away in the library. She told him that Ohn's name used to be Taran—that was what his present surname, Kenstaran, meant, "once named Taran"—but he'd gone off with Esmeralda one day to some kind of naming ceremony and come back with the new name.

Tim remembered Ohn as a pronounced depressive back then, always moping around and not big on talking to anybody. That had all changed when he came back. Maybe the new name had cheered him up, or maybe he'd brought back some good humor along with the new name; whichever, Ohn, for all that he was a good head these days, was still a prime candidate for the Contingent and Tim didn't feel like insulting the guy.

He looked back up to where he'd seen the dead children hanging earlier.

A memory called up from the forest's dreams, was it?

Sure. Why not. Better that than it having been real.

But as he and Ohn headed back to the House, he had to ask himself, if it hadn't been real, then how come it still *felt* so damned real? The memory of it was a whole lot clearer than stuff he knew for sure had happened. And how come the whole garden felt different now, like it was all a part of the Wild Walks? Was he going to keep seeing weird things? Maybe spaceships next? Or Elvis, sitting on one of the stone benches, crooning "Love Me Tender"?

I don't need this, he thought.

He stayed out of the garden for the rest of the day. Sitting in the nook of the Silkwater Kitchen, he drank endless cups of tea and just stared out the window at the garden until night finally fell and the familiar shapes of the garden's trees and shrubberies blurred into one large smudge of shadow.

But if he couldn't see—from the lit kitchen out into the darkened garden—he could still be seen. Hidden in a thicket of hawthorn where it nested up against a stand of silver birches just a lawn's length from the House, three children watched him; children with eyes too old for their age and too feral to be human, muffling giggles with their knobby green knuckles pressed up against their mouths.

2

There were maybe thirty-five, forty people staying in Tamson House that summer—not a full house, but more than enough so that there was always someone interesting to hang out with if you wanted the company. They were as good a bunch as had ever been guests in the place: old friends, new friends; a few strangers who'd probably become friends because that was the kind of place the House was—it just drew the right kind of people to it.

But Blue didn't want company tonight.

He was supposed to be helping Judy work on Hacker's bike— his old Norton that seemed to be in the shop more often than it was out, not the new Kawasaki Hacker drove around town. When Judy got evicted from her place earlier that year, Blue had turned over a spare garage to her to be her workshop and she'd moved her personal gear into one of the empty rooms on the south side of the House. He liked having her around, usually liked working with her, but not tonight. Fed up with his antsy mood, she'd finally sent him off a half hour ago.

"Look," she'd said, "if you're not going to help, at least make yourself useful and get us a couple of brews."

He'd started for the Silkwater Kitchen, but ended up in Sara's Tower.

Tamson House had three towers. There were two of them on the east side of the building, one on the south corner, near the ballroom, the other on the north. The observatory was in the latter, complete with telescope, star maps lining the walls and a nine-teenth-century English orrery that still worked. Sara's was in the northwest corner of the house and it was the one place, along with Jamie's study, that was off limits to the houseguests.

Unlocking the door, he'd gone in and sat down on the fat sofa in Sara's downstairs room. There he slouched against the cushions and stared moodily at the poster on the wall across from him. It dated back to when Sara and Tal were still gigging around town, before Tal got too wired on modern life and had taken off into the Otherworld with Sara in tow. The poster had a picture of the two of them—high-contrast, sepia ink on a kind of ivory parchment background, her holding her guitar, Tal with his harp. Above the picture were their names; below it were the words "Welsh harp and guitar" and the date of the gig.

Been a long time since they played a gig, Blue thought. Unless that was what they were doing wherever they were now.

Wherever they were now.

He ran a hand through his long black hair, combing it with his fingers.

Jesus, he missed her.

He found it hard to describe their relationship to people who didn't know her. It was sort of father/daughter, brother/sister, maybe most important, friend/friend. He'd watched her grow up, hung out with her; taught her, learned from her; protected her—

Missed her.

You're being an asshole, he told himself. She's got her own life to live. It's nobody's fault that it doesn't happen to connect with your own right now. She'll be back.

Sure. Someday. But he hadn't seen her since her last visit— which was, like, over a year ago now—and maybe he was being maudlin, but he'd sure like to have her walk in through that door right now.

He sat on the sofa for a while longer, his big frame slouching deeper into its cushions, and continued to stare at the poster, as though, if he looked at it hard enough and wished—*really* wished—he might be able to call Sara back from wherever she'd gone. Not forever. Just for a visit. Just so he could know that she was still okay.

Needless to say, he remained the sole occupant of the room.

Finally he got up and started to walk around, looking at pictures, fingering knickknacks, remembering. He smiled at the painting of the fox he'd done for her—Jesus, hadn't she been surprised when he'd given it to her? He paused longer in front of the small photo of her and Jamie. Look at her. She couldn't have been more than fourteen at the time.

He drifted from there into her workroom, gaze taking in the collage of old photos that was thumbtacked on the wall above the long worktable, before it caught and held on the opposite wall.

What the—?

When he caught the sonovabitch who'd snuck in here to make this mess . . .

He walked slowly across the room and stared at the marks that had been smeared on the wall. There was an order to them—they weren't just random smears, but a kind of graffiti, or maybe ideographs, though what they meant he couldn't begin to guess. They had a familiar look about them, like an elusive word that lay on the tip of one's tongue, but he couldn't place where he'd seen this particular kind of marks before.

What he did know was that someone had gotten in here—*how,* he'd like to know, seeing as how he had the only key to the tower—and went spray-can crazy. Except . . .

He took a closer look at the markings. No, this had been brushed on. In fact—a vague chill started up in the base of his spine—this looked a whole lot like dried blood.

Oh, man. What the hell was going on now?

Maybe Esmeralda would know, he thought as he backed out of the room, gaze still locked on what he thought of as a desecration of Sara's private space.

3

She had an audience of copper-skinned children, watching her go through the slow, deliberate postures of her morning ritual.

Ch'i.

Exciting the breath.

Shen.

Gathered the spirit inside.

Focus. Focus.

The children had followed her from the camp, out past the birches to where the sun sought and found the freckles of mica in the old stone by the river. It was warm, here in the morning sun. She was stripped down to just a T-shirt and shorts, her long curly hair tied back with a ribbon. Drops of perspiration beaded her brow. Her muscles shivered with tremors, although to the casual observer she seemed to be doing very little.

The children sat in the shade of the birches and watched.

She was used to their scrutiny. They were like a pack of unruly manitou, teasing little mysteries, forever following her about, asking questions, playing tricks, meeting her accusing looks with their guileless open gazes. Only in the morning, when she danced the song of the thirteen postures—

Moving, yet still.

Like a mountain.

Like a great river.

—were they quiet, content to observe. A covey of slender forms, dark-haired, darker-eyed, poised motionless like quail before they stormed into motion again. She could put them from her mind and concentrate solely on contemplation of her taw, the heart of her own mystery, that place of inner stillness from which strength was gained and where magic was born.

But not from a vacuum.

Cause and effect.

There was no gain, without conscientious effort expended. Concentration was required. Focusing. Attachment without attachments. To become nothing and so become all.

It was a long journey and after years, she was still not so far from the beginning of the road, but she was patient. And she felt no sense of hurry. Already the years had provided her with ample rewards.

In the court of the body, mind and breath ruled. Spirit. What the children's elders called Beauty. But each required the support of the other.

Chin.

Internal strength, stored up within like a drawn bow.

Focus. Focus.

Fa chin.

The energy released. Like an arrow. The body relaxes, the mind so awake, so aware, that each blade of each stem of grass can be differentiated, one from the other.

She began the slow dance into another posture, her taw growing warm and strong deep inside her, waking. Awareness spreading so that while she looked ahead, she could see behind. Could sense . . . could sense . . .

A vague anxiety touched her, like a rumor making the rounds of her body's court, and it woke a ripple of uneasiness that spread through her, making her lose her concentration. It came from the children.

She turned slowly to look at them, not angry, more disappointed that they should intrude upon her morning ritual, but then saw that they themselves were not the cause, but an effect.

A stranger stood by the birches, closer to the children than to her. A tall form in a hooded cloak. A hooded man. Sleeves joined in front of him, hands invisible in their folds. The cloak stretching to the ground, its hem damp with dew.

She let her arms fall to her sides and waited as he approached her. He seemed to almost float above the grass, rather than walk upon it.

"I am sorry to intrude," he said.

His voice was deep, resonating. And unfamiliar.

She peered under the hood, trying to make out his features, but the shadows lay deep there. Too deep. Then, with the clarity of sight that her taw brought to her, she realized that there were only shadows under the hood. The man had no face.

She shivered, her perspiration clinging cold to her skin though the sun was still warm.

"Who are you?" she asked.

Better yet, she added to herself, *what* are you?

"It is time," was his reply.

"Time . . .?"

She glanced at the children, half-minded that this was some new trick of theirs, but they were watching the encounter with wide eyes, untouched by any personal association to the hooded man's presence. All she could see in their features was the same confusion she felt herself. And the finger of fear that tapped nervously against the base of her spine.

"You must return to the Wood," the hooded man said. "To the Heart of the Wood where once you trod. There is a need."

She felt an odd sense of dissociation from the moment, as though she were with the children, one of them, watching and listening under the shelter of the birches, not standing here on her own in the glade, the sole object of the stranger's riddling words.

She cleared her throat.

"You're going to have to, ah, be a little more clear," she said. "I don't know what you're talking about."

"There is a need," the hooded man said again.

The way he repeated the words made her think of a phonograph record, stuck on a groove. It was the exact same phrasing, same intonation.

"Yeah. But—"

She broke off, her own eyes widening, as the hooded cloak suddenly fell in upon itself and crumpled to a heap on the ground. Startled, she took a step back. By the birches, the children exploded into motion like the covey of quail they'd reminded her of earlier. In moments, they were gone, running barefoot back to the camp. Their retreat was oddly silent.

They left her alone by the old stone, the sun still warm, though she now had a chill that cut deep inside her all the way to the marrow of her bones. She tracked their retreat, then looked down at the empty cloak that lay puddled in the grass by her feet.

"I hate it when this kind of thing happens," she said softly.

She was trying to lighten her mood, to ease the sudden tenseness that had her muscles all in knots.

But it didn't help.

4

"You know what I don't like?" Emma said. "It's when you're reading a book and just nothing happens in it."

Fifty pages into the new Caitlin Midhir novel, she put it aside and stared into the fire. The Templehouse Room was cozy, deep with shadows except for the pools of light cast by their reading lamps and the warm glow from the hearth. It was late in the year for a fire, but the night had gathered a chill to its bosom, and they both liked how the coals made the room seem more intimate.

"Not really," Esmeralda said. "It depends on what sort of a book I'm reading. Some books don't need things to be happening to have things happen."

Emma took a moment to digest that.

"I guess I'm just bored," she said finally.

"Where's Blue?" Esmeralda asked. "I thought you two were going into the finals of the World's Ping-Pong Championships tonight."

"That's later—first he's doing biker stuff with Judy down in her workshop."

Esmeralda set her own book aside—a study of the totemic influence of birds by the Cornish occultist Peter Goninan that Emma knew, if she was reading it, would have her falling asleep halfway through the first page.

"What's the matter?" Esmeralda asked. "Are things not working out between you and Blue?"

Emma shook her head. "No. Everything's fine. It's just—I'm not jealous or anything. I mean, I know he just happens to have friends that are women and I like Judy. . . ."

"But," Esmeralda prompted after Emma's voice trailed off.

"I just wonder about us," Emma said finally. "That's all. I love Blue—at least I think I do—but sometimes I worry that the reason I like being with him is not so much for what we have, but because he's such an interesting contrast. You know, it's like I'm enamored with the idea of a guy with his image and basically macho interests, still having the kind of sensitivity that he does. That it's the *idea* itself that I'm in love with. . . ."

She sighed and plucked at a loose thread on the hem of her sweatshirt.

"Does that make any sense?" she added.

"Some," Esmeralda said.

"And then there's this place," Emma went on. "It's like, everybody here does something. You and Blue and . . . well, just everybody. You're the kind of people that make things happen while I'm the kind of person that things happen to. I never really felt that before I moved in here."

"You do things," Esmeralda began.

"Oh, sure. But only after somebody else comes up with the idea. I used to be really . . . I don't know . . . independent, Ez. I was sure of myself; I used to do things. Now I just feel like a hanger-on."

"You know that's not true."

"Maybe not. But it feels like it is. I had a career, but I gave it up. I mean, why be an architect in somebody else's firm when I could live here and do my own art and not have to worry about paying the mortgage and that kind of thing? But I haven't picked up a brush all spring. I don't see my old friends anymore—not because Blue's uncomfortable with them. I don't think he's uncomfortable in *any* situation. I'm the one who feels uncomfortable. They ask me what I've been doing and I can't tell them anything because I don't do anything."

"Yes, but—"

"And then there's this *other* stuff," Emma went on. "You know."

She gave her friend an expectant look.

Esmeralda nodded. "The Autumn Gift," she said. "The tree magic it whispers to you."

"It still spooks me," Emma said.

"It shouldn't scare you."

"But it does. It just sits inside me, making me feel things I can't understand. It's different for you. You *know* who you are, what you're doing here. I'm still waiting for someone to explain it all to me."

"You're the only person who can—"

Emma cut Esmeralda off with a wave of her hand. If she'd heard it once, she'd heard it a hundred times. *She* had to connect with the spirit that spoke inside her. Only *she* could decide her own destiny. Except what if you just couldn't connect with that kind of thing?

She believed now—in the magic, in that whole Otherworld that lay just beyond the here and now that was its source. After what had happened to her over the past couple of years, how could she not? And she could also accept and recognize that some spirit moved inside her, spoke to her, connected her to all that spooky stuff. But she didn't know why it had chosen her. And she didn't know what she was supposed to do with its gift.

"Nothing's *clear* anymore," she said finally.

"So what's the solution?" Esmeralda said.

"Now you sound like Blue," Emma replied, returning to focus their conversation on one small part of the problem, rather than the more mysterious whole of magic and spirits in which her life was entangled. "Everything's got a solution. But I don't know if there *is* one to this. I feel like I've got to go away, but I don't want to. I feel like Blue and I are some middle-aged couple who've been married for years—you know, like we've just settled into all these *routines*—and it bothers me, but then I don't want to change it because I've never been in a relationship this solid before."

She lifted her gaze from the fire to look at Esmeralda.

"Jesus, Ez. I feel like I'm having a mid-life crisis and I'm barely thirty. I just wish something would *happen*."

She felt a tingle of uneasiness as soon as she spoke those words. What was it she'd read somewhere? Something about being careful what you wish for, because you just might get it.

"Well, nothing serious," she added quickly. "Just, you know, some kind of a change. . . ."

She broke off as the door opened and Blue stepped into the Templehouse Room. There was an odd look in his eyes that went beyond his recent moodiness—a kind of edginess that she couldn't help but feel was an immediate effect of her own current state of mind. Naturally that just added guilt to everything else she was feeling these days.

Be careful what you wish for. . . .

"Are you all right?" Esmeralda asked Blue when neither he nor Emma spoke.

Blue shook his head. "I think we've got a problem."

. . . because you just might get it.

I take it back, Emma thought.

But of course it was too late for that now.

5

She didn't want to go.

This was the week of the initiation ceremonies, when Mother Bear's drummers-to-be were welcomed into the lodges of the *rath'wen'a*—no longer initiates, but true Drummers-of-the-Bear themselves. For those initiates, it was a time of fasting and purifying the body in sweat lodges, of totem dreams and visions, and later, of ceremonial dancing and festivity. They went about their final business with expressions so serious behind their painted cheeks and brows that the children would dance about and pull grotesque faces in front of them, trying to make them laugh.

Yet if the initiates were serious, the camp itself was a hubbub of excitement. Their family and friends understood, and respected, the solemnity, but didn't partake of it themselves. Between the birchbark lodges and deerhide tents, their voices rang with laughter and song as they set about their own preparations. Quillwork and beadwork was mended on shirts, vests, breechclouts, dresses, arm-bands, collars, moccasins, legbands and garters; silver buckles and brooches were polished; claw and bead and cowrie shell necklaces were restrung in new patterns. All about the camp, carved festive staves had been planted with feather and shell ornamentation dan-gling from their heads. Roasts of venison, beaver and rabbit sizzled on spits; cookpots simmered on every fire, filling the air with their savory scents.

As Sara Kendell returned to the camp in the wake of the chil-dren, the hooded cloak now folded over one arm, she could see the preparations for the ceremony going on all around her and her regret at having to leave grew deeper.

She and Tal came every year to the initiation ceremonies, but this was the first year that they were taking an active part in the actual ceremony itself, for this was the year that both Tal and Kieran would receive their drums from the elders and so be inaugurated as drum-brothers to Mother Bear. They had worked hard—if something they loved so much could be called work—toward this day and she was proud of them both. She desperately wanted to be watching with Ha'kan'ta when the two of them left the *rath'wen'a* lodge with their first water drums in hand.

The Way of the Bear wasn't her path, but that in no way diminished her respect for the *rath'wen'a* and their harmonious melding of spiritual matters with the more practical environmental and health concerns that were so much a part of their day-to-day existence. She understood Beauty, she just sought it by following a different road.

"I don't know why you don't follow the path with us," Kieran had said when he and Tal first began their journey to the heart of the drum.

But Sara's feelings lay inarticulate in her heart. What was right for them was wrong for her.

"Saraken is like the *quin'on'a*," Ha'kan'ta had answered while Sara was still trying to frame her explanation in words that would make sense. "She's as much a manitou as she is a child of human parents. Why do you think Pukwudji offers her such enthusiastic friendship? They're like wolf pups, born in the same litter."

"Sure, but—"

"What you study," Ha'kan'ta added, "she already knows. In here"—the shaman touched a closed fist between her breasts—"where Beauty was first born."

"Lord lifting Jesus," Kieran said. "You make her sound like a saint."

But he smiled, taking the sting from what he said.

Ha'kan'ta smiled. "She still has a long road to travel before she can reach that place of Beauty and call it up at will."

Tal hadn't spoken, but then, Sara found that there was such a connection between them that words weren't always necessary. Which was why she wasn't surprised to find him waiting for her as soon as she reached the camp.

He looked odd, almost a stranger, naked except for his breech-clout, his long red hair pulled back from his head in the thirty braids of an initiate, his pale features and chest emblazoned with ghostly white clay patterns, highlighted with darker daubs of paint: berry red, sweetgrass green, the blue of Mother Bear's sky, the black of her rich forest loam.

But his green eyes were familiar, watching her from the raccoon mask of daubed white clay that surrounded them.

"I was worried," he said.

Sara smiled. "I'm okay. It's just . . ."

"We have to go."

It was uncanny the way it almost seemed as if they could read each others' minds, but she knew he was just picking up on her mood. What they had was a form of empathy that she supposed all couples developed after a while.

"No," she said. "*I* have to go. You've worked too hard for this week."

"It won't be the same without you."

She smiled again. "That's sweet of you to say, but I really want you to stay and, you know, get your drum and everything. It's important to me. Besides, it's probably no big deal."

He didn't ask, Then why are you going? But then he wouldn't.

He trusted her judgment as much as she trusted his. He reached out and touched the hooded cloak with his fingertips.

"What happened?" he asked.

Briefly, she described how her regular Tai Chi workout had been interrupted.

"This was all that was left," she said, holding up the garment she was carrying.

Tal nodded thoughtfully. "And when he spoke of this wood . . .?"

"He gave it a capital 'W' and acted—well implied, really—that I should know what he was talking about with this 'Heart of the Wood' business."

"The oaken heart of the Mondream Wood," Tal said, "where Myrddin lived awhile."

"Or something like that," Sara said, remembering when she was a child and Merlin lived in a tree in the garden enclosed by her uncle's house. "I don't think it'll be dangerous or anything," she added. "I mean, if there was a real problem at the House, someone would have come for me. Esmeralda, or Ohn."

"Unless this sending was the only way that they could communicate with us."

"Don't make it sound scary," Sara said. "It's bad enough I've got to go in the first place."

She knew it wasn't going to be easy to leave. She and Tal had been inseparable for almost seven years now. This would be their first time apart since the whole business with Tom Hengwr had brought them together initially. But she knew she had to go all the same. Not because she really thought there was any danger. It was more as though the hooded man had instilled some sort of compulsion in her so that she had to go.

What did they call it in the old Romances? A geas. Something you had no choice but to fulfill.

Tal sighed. "I've no sense of foreboding about this," he said finally. "No sense of anything at all—good or bad—and that worries me."

"But I have to go," Sara said.

He nodded. *"That* I do feel. For all our farwalking, the world of your birth retains its hold on you; Tamson House will always be your home. And your responsibility."

"I know. And I've been kind of lax about checking up on things, haven't I?"

Tal didn't seem to have heard her. His eyes had taken on an unfocused, faraway look.

"If it was the oak that called for you," he said, "that's not so bad. He offers protection and can guide you safely home, for he stands on the doorway to the mysteries, straddling the worlds. But there are other trees in the Wood who don't bear the same affection for humankind. The alder and the yew . . ."

"Don't get all spacey on me," Sara said.

Tal blinked and focused on her again.

"You'll be careful?" he said.

"Every moment. Maybe I'll even be back for the final ceremony itself. I've got four days, right?"

Tal nodded. "I'll miss you," he said.

A drum spoke out before Sara could answer. It echoed a high-pitched summoning throughout the camp.

"I guess they want you," she said.

"All the initiates," Tal said. "The *honochen'o'keh* must have arrived to hallow our drums."

Sara would have liked to have seen them. She had a special warm spot for the *rath'wen'a*'s spirits of goodwill—partly because they were Pukwudji's cousins, but mostly for their own charm.

"You'd better go," she said.

She wanted to hug him, but was afraid of smearing his clay and paint markings. They had to be just right for all these ceremonies. But Tal had no such compunction. As he drew her close, she felt a sudden tightness in her chest that had nothing to do with the pressure of his arms around her. Her eyes got all misty, but she managed not to cry.

"Go gentle," Tal said as he stepped back.

"You, too," Sara said.

She watched him go, following the rattling sound of the summoning drum to where the elders awaited the initiates, and it was all she could do not to call after him.

Don't be a baby, she told herself. You're only going to be gone a few days.

But as she fingered the cloak and watched him go, she heard the hooded man's words again.

There is a need.

All of a sudden that simple phrase took on far too many unpleasant implications.

6

The long-term residents of the House had fallen into regular duties as time went by. After Jamie died and Sara went away, Blue took over administrating the various bills and legal needs until Esmeralda had shown up and he could thankfully hand things over to her. He was back on security and general maintenance now, aided and abetted by Emma and Judy, which was how he liked it. The only thing the three of them didn't take care of was the gardening. But this spring, Tim had, if not given up, then at least set aside his ambition to be a playwright and accepted responsibility for the gardens.

Of the other three longest-staying houseguests, one was a man named Anton Brach, an Austrian chef disillusioned with the hostelry business, who had set up shop in the Penwith Kitchen, on the other side of the garden from the Silkwater. So long as you told him beforehand that you'd be sitting in on one of his meals—the timetable was strictly structured and while a dress code wasn't enforced, T-shirts and the like were definitely frowned on—you could be assured of a gourmet meal to make all others you'd had before pale in comparison. Blue basically liked the guy, even if he was a little anal-retentive.

The second was Ginny Saunders, who'd taken charge of the Library, over by Sara's Tower. She was a small Gambian woman who kept her kinky hair in a long braid that fell to the small of her back and tended to dress like a Midwestern schoolmarm from some old B-western. Blue wasn't sure what she did with all the time she spent in the Library beyond the fact that she oversaw the various students who were hired to input all the Library's books and papers into the House's computer system—that had been Esmeralda's idea. What he did know was that if you had a question, and the answer was somewhere in the Library, then Ginny knew where to find it.

The third was Ohn Kenstaran, Glamorgana's bard, reformed now. He, along with Esmeralda, helped infuse the House with its sense of spirituality—that aura of mystery that drew as many hermetic scholars and pagans to visit as it did artists. But where Esmeralda was not exactly aloof, just a little distant because she tended to be preoccupied a lot of the time with obscure matters, Ohn mingled freely with the other houseguests. He played music at the Wicca rituals, argued with the occultists, sat in on the pagan discussion groups and generally got along with everyone.

And then, of course, there was Jamie. . . .

Blue didn't really understand what had happened to his friend. Jamie's death was one thing; the hurt had lodged inside Blue and just stayed there, with nothing capable of easing it. He'd wake up nights, cheeks wet, chest tight; or turn some corner of the House, expecting to see Jamie standing there only to have the hard truth hit him all over again. Jamie was dead and nothing Blue could do would bring him back. But that first time that Jamie had spoken to him from the computer in the Postman's Room—pixeled words left behind in the trail of the screen's cursor . . .

It didn't make sense, but there it was. Jamie wasn't alive, but he'd come back as a spirit inhabiting the House that had been his home for so many years, seeing through its windows, hearing through its walls. Blue wasn't sure how much of Jamie had returned, but there was enough of him haunting the House that there was no denying who it was that ghost-spoke from the computer screen, played chess with Esmeralda, or pored over the information that Ginny's students entered with a scanning device.

It had given Blue the creeps at first. No, first it had scared him shitless, *then* it gave him the creeps. Now he just accepted it. He still missed Jamie—the flesh-and-blood Jamie that he'd hung out with—but having some part of him come back as it had was . . . well, comforting.

But Blue didn't feel comforted at the moment. By the time he returned to Sara's Tower, all the regulars were with him except for Anton and Ginny. Wordlessly, they stood beside him in Sara's workroom and stared at the graffitied wall.

"It's Ogham," Esmeralda said finally.

Ohn nodded. "The Beth-Luis-Nuin alphabet of my people."

"So what does it say?" Blue asked.

Esmeralda and Ohn exchanged glances.

"It's Ogham," Ohn said, "but the letters, when I translate them, don't form familiar words."

Esmeralda nodded. "It's either a foreign language . . . or gibberish."

But then Emma spoke up. "I know what it says. 'Oh all the past is lost and we despair,' " she read. " 'Each root, each branch . . . its memories stolen, hope lost; the river grown so wide we will never again its waters cross.' "

Beside Emma, Judy Kitt ran a hand through her frizzy blond hair, combing it with her fingers. She was wearing a pair of greasy overalls and a once-white T-shirt. Her delicate features were wrinkled in a puzzled frown.

"How'd you do that?" she asked. "I mean if Ohn couldn't read it . . ."

"I . . . I don't know," Emma said.

Esmeralda laid a hand on Emma's shoulder.

"Ogham was born from the trees of the first forest," she said. "The same forest that blessed Emma with her Autumn Gift. This Ogham must translate into the primal language that the ancient wood first taught the druids."

"You're saying some forest left this message for us?" Blue asked.

Esmeralda shook her head. "I don't know. All I know is that there's something very odd in the air tonight."

"No kidding," Tim said and then he told him about what he'd seen by the fountain earlier that day.

"This," Esmeralda said, pointing at the Ogham when Tim was done, "is a message. But what Tim's just told us . . ."

Ohn nodded. "Speaks of borders breaking. I should have seen that earlier."

"How could you know?" Esmeralda said.

"Say what?" Tim asked. "What kind of borders?"

"Those between this world and the Middle Kingdom," Esmeralda explained. "What you saw must have been bodachs—a kind of wood spirit. They like to play tricks on us—nothing really hurtful, but as Tim's already seen, they can be disconcerting. Usually they can't cross over, but if a crack's opened in the veil that separates our world from theirs, they would come through to bedevil us."

"Great," Blue said. "Like we really need this. . . ."

Although some of those who'd gathered in Sara's workroom had shared experiences beyond the norm with him, Blue was the only one left in the House at the moment who remembered a time seven years past when the House had been under siege by creatures from the Otherworld. A lot of good people had died. Fred. Jamie. . . .

"They won't be the source of the problem," Esmeralda went on. "Just a more visible consequence—a kind of forerunner to the real problem."

Tim looked nervously out a window to where the garden lay dark and shadowed.

"Well, what is the source of the problem?" Blue asked.

Esmeralda shrugged. "It's too early to tell. But look."

She crossed the room and knelt by the baseboard to point at where what looked like a kind of fungus was growing.

"Jesus," Blue said as he joined her. "It's some kind of mold."

"It's moss actually."

"Mold, moss—what's the difference? It still shouldn't be growing here."

"True, but—"

"Oh, my God," Judy said.

Turning, Blue saw what had caught her attention. Small twigs had grown out of the wooden base of a floor lamp, complete with tiny leaves. Looking around the room they saw that other wooden furniture had also sprouted sprigs of greenery.

"Oh, man," Blue said. "What the hell's going on?"

"Maybe Jamie knows," Esmeralda said. "Where's the nearest terminal—in the Library?"

Blue nodded. "Yeah, there's one in there hooked up to Jamie's mainframe—"

The floor suddenly rumbled underfoot, shaking the furniture and making them all lose their balance.

"It's an earthquake!" Tim cried, heading for a doorway.

As a second tremor shook the building, they all started to move—all except for Emma. She stood in the center of the room, riding the shock like a sailor on deck braced against a rough sea. Her eyes had a far-off look about them.

"No," she said. "It's the forest. It's coming back."

"What does she mean by 'it's coming back'?" Blue asked Esmeralda, who had caught hold of his arm to keep herself from falling as a third tremor made the floor bounce underfoot.

"I don't know," she told him. "But it can't be good."

7

Cal Townsend had always been a little leery of the pagans he met. He was a slender, intense-looking individual; his eyes a little too large and owlish behind his glasses for the narrow features that surrounded them; his dark curly hair cut so close to his scalp that he appeared to be wearing a skullcap. He had his own way of worshipping what he saw as the creative force behind the world— anthropomorphizing nature in ways that were similar to the Wicca's Antlered God and Moon Goddess—but he could never quite get comfortable with the organized pagan versions of worship. It smacked too much of the lunatic fringe to him, for all that he was basically at one with and sympathetic to their beliefs.

At least it was like that until he met Julianne Trelawny.

She made the weird seem both logical and normal to him, but he couldn't quite shake the nagging doubt that the only reason he was into all this stuff now was because he was hot for her.

If it was only looks, that'd be one thing. She was voluptuous— there was no other way to put it—with a heartbreaker of a face and gorgeous red hair that hung all the way down to her waist. And unlike most redheads, she had a dark complexion—due to one of her grandparents being a Native American—and that just made her seem more exotic and attractive to him. There weren't many women—pagan, Christian or otherwise—who could come close to how good she looked in her ceremonial cloak.

But it wasn't just looks. He could listen to her talk for hours because she always had something interesting to say, from her wry commentaries on the world at large to her ability to convey her very sincere old-religion beliefs without ever sounding like she was a space cadet. And she wasn't all deadly serious, either. She loved the old hardcore punk from the seventies, for example, as well as the new acoustic music that was currently making its mark on the charts, and she had a pixilated—a truly whimsical—sense of humor that just charmed the hell out of him.

Was it any wonder, Cal thought, that he was so taken by her?

They'd first met at the Occult Shop on Bank Street. They were both browsing through the bookshelves—she comfortably at ease in the place, while he felt as though anybody walking by outside and looking in through its window had to be thinking that he was a real basket case to even be in here in the first place. But they'd struck up a conversation and when he found out that she was living in Tamson House—or rather when he found out what kind of a place Tamson House was—he moved in as well. Not in the same room or anything, but it was almost like they were living together, wasn't it, even if the House was the size of a city block and had who knew how many people living in it?

The downside of all this was that she had no idea that he was so crazy about her—or at least she never let on that she did—because he'd never got up the nerve to tell her. He'd been very cool about everything, just hanging out with her, not coming on, being her pal, and now he just didn't know how to broach the subject.

He probably wasn't even her type. Probably she'd go for a guy like Blue, who—thankfully—already had a girlfriend. But in the three weeks he'd known her, he hadn't seen her go out with anybody, so he didn't know what her type was.

Maybe it was him.

Yeah, and maybe the Easter Bunny really did hide all those eggs on Easter Eve. . . .

Tonight it was just the two of them, sitting together in the small ground-floor parlor on the Patterson Avenue side of the House where the people interested in the old religion usually gathered in the evenings. The room was called the Birkentree Room—which was very appropriate, Julianne had told him once, seeing how the birken tree was another name for the birch, which stood for the first month of the druidic calendar of the trees and represented a time of beginning and cleansing. But Esmeralda had told Cal one day that the name actualy came about because a Scots folksinger used to live in the room. "The Birken Tree" was an old traditional song that was kind of her signature tune, so eventually people just named the room after it. When Cal had mentioned this to Julianne, she'd just smiled and told him that it didn't make any difference; it didn't change the appropriateness of the room's name.

Naturally, even though she obviously hadn't thought it was a stupid thing for him to have mentioned, he'd still ended up feeling like he was about an inch tall. He got all flushed whenever he thought about it—it and the hundred other times he figured he'd made an ass of himself around her.

"It's so weird," she was saying now.

"About your cloak?" Cal said.

Julianne nodded. "I just can't figure out what happened to it. I hung it up in my closet right after I got in from the ritual last night and it was still there when I put away my bathrobe after my shower, but this morning it was gone. Someone had to have come in while I was sleeping and taken it."

"Weird," Cal agreed.

He was still trying to ignore the image of her taking a shower that refused to leave his mind's eye.

Down, hormones, down, he commanded.

It didn't do much good. Not when she was sitting there on the other end of the sofa, her legs folded under her, looking so damn gorgeous that it was all he could do not to stare. He crossed his legs to hide the telltale indication of his more than platonic interest in her.

Julianne sighed. "Things just don't get stolen in Tamson House," she said. "It just . . . doesn't happen."

"Did you talk to Blue about it?" Cal asked.

"No. I didn't want to start up any weird vibes, because maybe it's just someone playing a prank on me. But still . . ." She turned the deep green of her gaze fully on him. "There's something different in the air tonight, don't you think? It's like something's about to happen—everything's all crackling with pent-up energies just waiting to let go."

Cal wished she hadn't used those particular words to describe what she was feeling. He knew all about pent-up energies. And he was going to get lost in those eyes. Then he realized that she was waiting for him to say something.

"I . . . uh"—he cleared his throat—"know what you mean."

Oh, brilliant. What was it about her that always left him tongue-tied and thinking about sex? He wasn't like this normally. Hell, he worked as a data processor in an office with a half-dozen beautiful women and he just hung out with them, made jokes, life was easy, they were all friends. Why couldn't he just relax for once? Or at least tell her how he felt?

She'd fallen silent, head cocked to one side as though she was listening to something just out of hearing range.

Just do it, Cal told himself. Tell her now before somebody else comes into the room.

"You know, uh, Julianne," he began.

She blinked lazily, then focused on him. His pulse jumped into double time.

"I—"

There was a sudden roaring sound and he never got a chance to finish what he'd barely begun. The sofa they were sitting on tumbled over backward and to one side, spilling Julianne into his arms, but he had no time to appreciate the moment. The air was filled with the crackle and crunch of breaking wood and then a tree—a giant, full-grown, honest-to-real, no-fooling, enormous old oak tree—came pushing up out of the floor, splintering floorboards and anything else in its way.

He tugged Julianne aside as a large branch whipped out of the jagged hole in the floor and whistled by them, cutting the air just where she'd been. Adrenaline whined through his body so that he was manhandling the big sofa before his rational mind could tell him that what he was doing wasn't possible. He pulled it the rest of the way across the room, all the way over, with the two of them between it and the wall, the body of the sofa protecting them from the other branches as they came whipping out of the floor as well as from the slabs of plaster and wood that crashed down from the ceiling as the tree continued its rapid upward movement.

And then he collapsed and just hung on to Julianne.

The air was thick with plaster dust and the sound of tearing wood, which was as loud as thunder. The floor and wall against which they were pressed shook with the violent fury of the tree's passage through the room. Julianne gripped him back, arms holding him tightly, head buried against his shoulder.

They were going to die, Cal thought.

Fear raced at a panic-quick speed through him, but for all his terror, he found himself focusing on Julianne being in his arms and realized that if they were going to die—

Well, at least I'm dying happy.

8

Ginny Saunders was putting away books in the Library that evening. Esmeralda marked the passages and chapters to be entered into the computer, and the students they'd hired did the actual data entry, but it was Ginny who knew where to find the necessary texts and insisted on replacing them on their shelves herself afterward. It was the last thing she did every night before leaving the Library, the final task of her daily routine.

She enjoyed the solitude at that time of day, the sense of orderliness and completion that the practice of tidying up left her with. She read voraciously, but was also a lover of books for their own sake. She appreciated the look of the bindings, lined up in neat rows on the shelves, the idea that so much knowledge and thought was tucked away between the boards of all those many books under her care.

She knew that there were people who thought she was a little strange—"moling away" in here, as Tim liked to put it—but it didn't bother her for a moment what people thought. She'd been wealthy in her time, and she'd been poor, but this was the first time she'd been responsible for something and she liked the feeling. It might just be a private library, in an odd old house, and she received only her room and board for her work, but it was still a full-time job and the satisfaction she derived from it more than made up for what people thought she was missing in the world that turned and spun on its mad axis beyond the Library's walls. She'd spent most of her life in that world and found only sorrow and pain there.

Neither existed for her here. Here she didn't need a shell to protect her from the world—the House itself provided that. Here she could vicariously experience what she'd never had the nerve or understanding to sample before. Here she could finally relax and be herself. And it wasn't boring. Not for a moment. Not with all these books, nor the glass display cases laden with curiosities and artifacts, nor the trickle of genuinely interesting people who made their treks into what she thought of as the mind of this fascinating building.

She hummed tunelessly under her breath as she shifted the ladder to the next shelf. Beth Norton, a second-year Carleton University student, had just left to pick her daughter up from the babysitter's and there was no one else about. The room was still, holding that special kind of quiet that only a large room can. Picking up the twelfth volume of Frazer's original *Golden Bough,* Ginny stepped onto the ladder, then paused.

The book felt odd in her hand. The leather binding was suddenly rough with an almost barklike texture. The weight was different than she remembered it to be.

Frowning, she took it over under a light. The binding looked as though someone had taken a vegetable grater to its surface. She ran a finger across the roughness and her frown deepened. The binding hadn't been marred. There was something stuck to it. She rubbed a fleck of it away to reveal the gleam of leather underneath. Peering closer, she realized that the book was covered with some kind of moldy growth that had hardened on the leather.

She looked worriedly at the shelves nearest to her, visions of mildew or worse ruining her precious books firing up in her imagination, but the spines facing her were unmarked.

Thank God, she thought. It was only this book.

But even one book was one too many.

She took it over to her desk, where she kept a box of tissues. Holding the book under the brass desk lamp, she started to clean its cover, but stopped when she realized that the book appeared to be getting thicker.

The only explanation she could come up with was that somehow the book had sustained massive water damage and the damp pages were swelling. How that could have happened in here, she couldn't begin to guess. There were no leaks in the roof—it wasn't raining, anyway. No plants that needed watering. . . .

Idly she flipped back the cover, then dropped the book as a tree branch sprang out into her face. She stared at where the book lay on the desk, the branch, complete with leaves, growing from between the signatures in its gutter. A second, then a third, branch joined the first, bursting forth—bud, to leaf, to twig, to bough— with impossible speed.

Shaking her head, she backed her chair slowly from the desk. She stood up, and retreated further, unable to keep her gaze from the bizarre sight. A small tree grew from the book now. And . . .

An uncontrollable shiver started in her calves and crawled up her nerves.

Vines crept up the legs of the desk, entwining about the lamp and various knickknacks scattered on its roll top. Moss sprouted, thickened on the blotter around the book. Twigs and small knobby buds sprouted from the wood of the desk itself.

"No," Ginny murmured, shaking her head.

It wasn't possible.

A sharp cracking sound whipped her around to find vegetation overtaking the long rows of bookshelves all around her.

"No!" she cried.

She took a half-step to the nearest shelf and began to tear the vines and branches away. She never heard the rumbling underfoot, only felt the floor begin to sway. As she backed away, the room shook. Books tumbled from the higher shelves. The display cabinets rattled. In one, a clay flute in the shape of a bird suddenly sprouted beak and feathers and began to peck away at the glass locking it inside.

She was going insane, Ginny realized.

She tried to keep her balance as the rumbling grew into thunder, but stumbled to her knees. The House shuddered around her. Dozens of books came crashing from their high perches. She brought her arms over her head to protect herself from the sudden onslaught and crawled toward the center of the room, where the hail of falling books was the lightest. There she crouched, staring with an anguished gaze as the Library was transformed from her quiet haven into a landscape that could only have grown from the imagination of some mad surrealist, armed with vegetation in place of paint and brush.

9

"Do you remember the way?" Ha'kan'ta asked.

Sara nodded. It was the first time she'd be making the journey on her own, but she'd gone often enough with Tal taking the lead to know how to make it on her own.

She'd changed into a pair of patched jeans and a tatty old sweater—they were the best she could come up with for traveling clothes that wouldn't also make her look too outlandish when she got back home. She'd decided that the beaded buckskin dresses or hunting leathers that she usually wore in the Otherworld were just a little too exotic for Ottawa's streets.

Never draw attention to yourself, Kieran had told her once, passing along one of the basic lessons that his own mentor, Tom Hengwr, had taught him. If you appeared to be the kind of person that no one would look twice at, then no one would remember you either.

Sara was all for not standing out from the crowd—to do otherwise raised the possibility of too many awkward questions, such as, Where had she spent the last year? So she'd just have to wear this stuff for now and pick up some new clothes while she was home. All that had survived this past year in the Otherworld intact were her walking shoes—and that was because she mostly went barefoot or in moccasins while she was here.

She finished tying up her laces, caught up her pack by one strap and was ready to go.

"And you're sure you don't want any company?" Ha'kan'ta asked.

I'd love company, Sara thought.

But she knew how much Kieran's part in the ceremony meant to Ha'kan'ta and wouldn't have dreamed of asking the *rath'wen'a* to come with her.

"I'll be fine," she said. "Honestly. It's just for a couple of days."

Ha'kan'ta regarded her consideringly. The blue of her eyes was a startling contrast against the deep coppery hue of her skin. She was taller than Sara, almost as tall as Tal or Kieran, and always reminded Sara of some Indian princess with her white doeskin dress and its beaded collar, the two long braids entwined with cowrie shells and feathers that hung to either side of her face, the dramatic beauty of her features.

"I was thinking of the wolves," Ha'kan'ta said.

She had two of them—Shak'syo and May'asa, Winter-Brother and Summer-Brother, respectively; not exactly pets, but they weren't wild animals either. They were just friends, Sara had realized a long time ago. The pair were lying at Ha'kan'ta's knees at the moment, regarding Sara with expressions that seemed to say that they understood every word that was being said and were now just waiting on her reply.

"I don't think so," Sara said. "It's kind of hard to go unnoticed when you're flanked with a pair of wolves. And that goes for Ak'is'hyr, too," she added before Ha'kan'ta could mention the moose that was the third of her constant companions.

She slipped the straps of her pack over her shoulder, adjusting the pack until it hung comfortably. Ha'kan'ta followed her outside the lodge.

"You know what we do?" Ha'kan'ta asked before Sara could say goodbye. "With the *rath'wen'a*?"

Sara nodded. To the Drummers-of-the-Bear fell the task of righting the wrongs, appeasing the offended and repairing the harm that the tribes brought upon themselves through unavoidable as well as disrespectful actions. They were intermediaries between the spirit world and the world of skin and bone, their charge as much the land itself as their people. They were healers, restoring harmony when discord threatened. They journeyed out of ordinary reality to bring back Beauty and nurture it in those—human hearts as well as heartlands—that had let their spirits become thin.

"You are as much a part of the journey we undertake as any drummer," Ha'kan'ta said, "only you step your road intuitively, rather than following a path that has been set out before you."

"We've talked about this before," Sara said.

"Yes. But we haven't talked about faith."

That made Sara feel uncomfortable.

"Why do you look embarrassed?" Ha'kan'ta asked.

Sara shrugged. "It's just . . . you know. It makes me think of people who are too . . . obsessed."

"Faith is important," Ha'kan'ta said. "It needn't be invested in a particular deity—most who do so, do it by rote anyway. But you must believe in something or your life has no meaning."

"What do you believe in?"

"Mother Bear."

Sara nodded. Of course.

"And you?" Ha'kan'ta asked.

"I'm not sure."

"Then think of this: Have faith in yourself. In your path. In all you do. Believe that you make a difference. Faith can make that be real."

"It's that easy?"

Ha'kan'ta shook her head. "It's the hardest kind of faith there is for you must accept it on your own. No one can do it for you."

Sara took that thought with her when she left the camp.

There were three ways to cross the borders that separated the Otherworlds from the land of Sara's birth.

The first was the most common; it required a great deal of preparation, entailing various rituals, purifications of spirit and body, and the like. It could also employ chanting, meditation, or music.

The second was to find a place—a crossroads, a "haunted" section of road or ancient stonework—where the veils of the borderland were thinner than usual and one could simply step through. The garden enclosed by Tamson House was one such site, but there were others, enough so that a whole body of folklore had grown up of mortals straying into Faerie, the modern equivalent being tales of UFO abductions. Coming back from the Otherworld by this manner required traveling through a number of such sites, depending on how deeply one had entered the spirit worlds.

The third, least common and most difficult, was by intent; to focus through the secret strengths of one's taw and *will* a passage between the worlds. This was the technique of the *honochen'o'keh,* those little mysteries that Europeans called faerie. Mortals could learn it, but to the mysteries it came as naturally as breathing.

It was by way of the latter that Sara meant to return to Tamson House. She left the camp, unattended by her usual covey of children, and made her way back to the riverbank where her exercises had been so uncannily interrupted earlier that morning. She felt a little lonesome without the children following her and already missed Tal. When she reached the old stone, its mica freckles were hidden in shadow, for the sun had already traveled too far across the sky for its light to reach the stone anymore.

She took a deep breath, exhaled slowly, then immediately set about raising her taw, hurrying as much to stop herself from summoning up regrets as to get the journey begun. She was sufficiently versed in the exercise that her taw responded quickly to her call. It began as a tiny spark in her mind, then slowly grew into a warmth that spread through both spirit and body, centering in a spot just behind her solar plexus.

Calling it was easy. But focusing it . . . that was still hard for her. For that she used "Lorcalon"—the moonheart air that had been Tal's first gift to her. She let its measures fill her until the tune resonated with the rhythm of her taw and her heartbeat. Now the focusing of her will came more easily.

She concentrated on the garden enclosed by Tamson House— the Mondream Wood of her childhood. Once she had names for all the trees in it. There was Merlin's Oak. The Penny Trees, so called because of their rounded, silvery leaves. Jocky's Home—the chestnut under which her little terrier had been buried when it died. The Scary Darks—a stand of birches that Jamie had so named to tease her, but the name stuck. And of course, there was the Apple Tree Man, the oldest apple tree in the small orchard on the west side of the garden.

The orchard had grown wild—a tangle of briar and thorn and apple trees that Fred had left alone because, as he'd told her, "It's gone wild and wants to stay that way." Since Fred's death, no one else had touched it either.

It was to that orchard that Tal always took them when they returned to the House, a route that included a number of other stops through sites that were set in worlds progressively closer to it as one traveled through the Otherworld. It was on the Apple Tree Man that Sara concentrated now, planning to go directly to the orchard rather than by the more circuitous route that Tal would choose. That was how Pukwudji would do it and since her abilities were more closely aligned to those of the *honochen'o'keh* than Tal's, that was how she would do it.

She was eager to reach the House, do whatever needed to be done, and then return to the camp—hopefully in time for the ceremony. The less time her journey took, the sooner she could return.

So she called up the Apple Tree Man in her mind. Against the rhythm and flow of the moonheart air, she focused on him, remembering his scruffy bark and the tangle of his boughs, half his trunk embraced by a tall thorn tree, the thick grass that crouched over his roots, the sharp taste of his bounty when she bit into an apple. . . .

When she had the whole of him firmly ensconced in her thoughts—not just the tree's physical presence, but his personality, the inner *sense* of him—she let her taw reach across the distance to him, stretching between the worlds, and then she took a step and let herself go. There was a moment when it felt as though she were pressed up against a gauze curtain that was held tight at every corner so that its cloth stretched to her body's contours. Her vision went gray. Silence hung in the air.

And then she was through, the border crossed, and she was stepping through grass that lay thick underfoot. . . .

Did it, she thought, pleased with herself, until she took in her surroundings.

Sudden panic rose as she looked around herself.

This wasn't the orchard in the Mondream Wood. This wasn't any place she'd ever been before.

She was in a glade, the sky overhung with clouds above her. Tall, brooding trees ringed the open ground, underbrush growing up around their trunks so thickly that she could see no place she could push through. She stepped closer to the umbra of the forest, peering into its darkness, to find that while the undergrowth waned a half-dozen or so yards in, beyond that was a riot of fallen boughs and rotting trees, creating a barrier far more daunting than that of the vegetation closer at hand.

She made a slow circuit of the edge of the glade to find that it was an island in a forested sea and she was stranded on its shores.

"Quick's not always best," she could remember Jamie telling her more than once. "You're too impatient, Sairey."

She should have gone by Tal's route. Slower, yes. But safer. She could be anywhere at the moment, in any of a hundred hundred layers of the Otherworld.

Go back to the camp and start again, she told herself.

She was tempted to try to go on, to call up the Apple Tree Man once more, this time being absolutely certain beyond any shadow of a doubt that she had him firmly focused in her mind, but reason overruled impatience this time. She'd go back.

She called up her taw once more, trying to focus on the meadow by the riverbank, the old stone with its mica freckles, the stand of birches so near at hand. . . .

And could only find a fog in her mind.

This is stupid, she thought.

Her initial panic hadn't returned yet, but she felt decidedly uneasy.

She tried, failed again. Not even the moonheart air could dispel the fog that lay heavy in her mind. Overhead, the clouds had thickened, making the light worse in the glade. When she looked at the forest, it seemed to hold far more shadows than it had just a few moments ago. Unbidden, an image of the hooded man returned to her. Cloak and hood holding a man's shape, with a man's voice issuing from under the hood, but there was no man inside. Nothing inside.

You must return to the Wood.

She had the sudden feeling that he—*it,* whatever—had been the cause of her failure to reach the orchard. He'd brought her here.

"But this is the wrong wood," she said, pitching her voice to carry into the forest. "I've never been here before, so I can't return to it."

But someone had told her once that all forests were echoes of the first forest, just as all music was an echo of the first music that ever the world heard. By that reckoning, she *had* been here before.

"Are you there?" she cried. "Is *anybody* there?"

She waited for an answer, but none came. Called out again, but received no more of a reply than she had the first time. Tried to raise her taw, only to find that fog still clouding her mind.

She studied the undergrowth, the brooding trees that over-hung it.

"I'm not going in there," she said.

Not and chance being lost forever. Wherever this glade was, for her to have reached it, it had to have some magic, some connection to the routes that could be taken through the Otherworlds. Once she left it . . .

"I'm not!" she cried again, cupping her hands around her mouth so that her words rang deep between the trees.

No reply.

"Shit."

She backed away from the forest's edge and settled down on the grass in the center of the glade, sitting cross-legged, scowling. She ran a hand through her hair, told herself to calm down and did a few breathing exercises. They helped, as did the soothing influence of the moonheart air when she called it up again. Feeling more able, more in control, she closed her eyes and concentrated on raising her taw, on cutting through the fog that beclouded her mind. Riding the moonheart air's rhythm, she called to her taw's secret strength. She didn't demand, but didn't beg it either.

Breathing evenly, she simply let her need speak for her, sent it spiraling into the mists that choked her thoughts, and waited for a response.

10

This hadn't been an earthquake, Blue thought.

It wasn't a particularly inspired realization, not when he could see, right there smack in front of him, that huge mother of a tree that had pushed its way up through the floor of Sara's Tower, shattering and splintering the hardwood floorboards on its way up into the ceiling. The room was clouded with plaster dust.

The tree wasn't the only piece of vegetation in the room either, though it was the largest. Near the walls, thickets of briar and hawthorn had grown from the worktable and other wooden furnishings. The carpet underfoot, where it hadn't been torn apart by the tree's passage, was covered with a thick moss. The windowsills, doorjambs, baseboards and other woodwork had all sprouted leafy twigs and branches.

Blue didn't want to think about what this mess meant for the House. Was it even structurally sound anymore? The lights had flickered earlier, then died, only coming back when the House's own generators had kicked in. That meant that they'd lost their hydro, probably the phone lines as well. He just hoped that was the least of the damage.

Around him, the others were picking themselves up from where they'd fallen, brushing dirt and dust from their clothing. Their faces were all pale with shock—all except for Emma's. She stood near the trunk of the tree, miraculously untouched by its violent passage through floor and ceiling, one hand laid against its bark. There was a distant look in her eyes.

What had she said, just as all this was starting?

The forest . . . it's coming back. . . .

As he started toward her, Judy caught hold of his arm.

"Blue, just what—"

"Not now," he said, shaking off her grip.

He called Emma's name as he reached her side. When there was no response, he touched her shoulder, then slowly turned her around to face him. She looked at him, but he could tell that she wasn't really focusing on him.

"Emma . . .?" he tried again.

She blinked, suddenly aware of his presence.

"You can cut it down," she said. "You can tear out its roots. But the forest's never really gone."

The others had gathered behind Blue.

"Say what?" Tim said.

Emma gave him a long considering look, then turned her gaze to where Esmeralda and Ohn stood shoulder to shoulder.

"You understand," she said. "Don't you? You know about the first forest?"

Ohn nodded slowly.

"But it stood at the dawn of time," he said.

"And now it's come back," Emma said.

"What's that *mean?*" Blue asked.

Her gaze was becoming more distant again as she turned to look at him.

"Not everything has to mean something," she said. "Some things just are."

She lifted a hand to touch his cheek.

"I have to go now," she said.

"Go? Go where?"

Blue felt like a straight man in some existential vaudeville routine.

"Just to think," Emma replied.

She brushed by him and started for the door. Blue turned to Esmeralda. Her long hair seemed to stir in a breeze that he couldn't feel.

"Help me with this, would you?" he said.

Esmeralda shook her head. "She'll be fine. Where can she go?"

"I . . ."

He watched Emma walk out through the door. When she turned down a hall and was lost to his view, he felt as though he'd lost something inside himself. A piece of his heart.

"We've got more important things to worry about right now," Esmeralda went on. "We have to assess the damage to the House, see if everyone's okay—does anyone know exactly how many people we've got staying here at the moment?"

"At least thirty," Tim said. "Maybe forty."

"All right. If you and Ohn will start checking on them, then the rest of us can—"

"Will someone please tell me just what the hell's going on here?" Judy said.

"Try to answer that very question," Esmeralda finished. "Why don't you go with Tim and Ohn? Work your way down to the east side of the House by the north hall. Blue and I'll start on the Library, then head down the south hall. We'll meet at"—she glanced at Blue, then Ohn—"the ballroom, say?"

Both men nodded in agreement.

"Let's go," Tim said.

Judy seemed to about to argue, but then she looked at the tree again, that enormous oak growing out of the middle of the floor and disappearing up into the ceiling, growing where no tree should be, where no tree *had* been just a few minutes ago. She swallowed once, then nodded.

"Sure," she said. "No problem. Let's just check things out."

It was obvious from her tone of voice that she was still having trouble just accepting that the tree was there where it was, but she trooped on out of the room with Tim and Ohn, leaving Blue and Esmeralda to take up the rear.

Outside the Tower, the damage didn't seem as bad as it had been inside. Pictures hung askew on the walls, ornaments and vases had tumbled from side tables, but there was no jungle of vegetation. No moss, no branches growing from the woodwork. No giant trees.

"See you in the ballroom," Tim said as he led the other two off down the north hall.

Blue nodded, then turned right with Esmeralda, heading for the Library.

"Why did it happen just in Sara's Tower?" he asked. He wasn't really expecting an answer, more just thinking aloud.

"We don't know that yet," Esmeralda said.

She paused at the first room they came to and opened its door. Inside, the furnishings had shifted some and a few knickknacks had fallen to the floor, but otherwise the room was in much the same condition as the hall—untouched by the forest. Again a breeze appeared to stir her hair, this time also rustling some fallen paper that lay near her feet.

It was weird, Blue thought, noting the movement. You get one strange occurrence, and then everything starts to feel like it's coming unglued right at the place where it was attached to normal reality. He started to ask Esmeralda about it, then remembered how Ohn often referred to her as a spirit of the West Wind and decided that he didn't want to know.

"Any ideas on what's going on?" Blue asked instead as they moved on to the next room.

"It's too early to tell."

"Try a guess."

Esmeralda shook her head. "It wouldn't serve any purpose. All we've got to go on is what happened back in the Tower."

"What about Tim's hanged kids? Or that mess on the wall?"

"That was Ogham."

"Whatever."

The next couple of rooms were in much the same state as the first.

"Emma told us that the forest is coming back," Esmeralda said as they continued down the hall toward the Library. "The first forest, which I assume is the forest primeval that legend says once covered the whole world—everything except for the seas. What that means, why it's happening . . . it's anybody's guess."

"What *about* Emma?"

Esmeralda paused. She turned to Blue.

"I'm worried about her as well," she said. "She's never quite accepted any of what's happened to her. Not in here"—Esmeralda laid a closed hand between her breasts—"where it counts. I thought when we came back from the Otherworld that last time that she'd finally understood."

"Understood *what?*"

"If it could be put into words, I'd've done it for her years ago," Esmeralda said. "But the Autumn Gift . . . it's a matter of spirit, of harmony and wholeness and a responsibility to the land and those who walk it that can only be furthered by the one so gifted. They're the ones—they alone—who have to accept the charge given them and make the commitment to that responsibility. No one can do it for them. And until they do so, they can't know peace.

"Emma's problem is that this time around she doesn't really remember who she is, why she's here."

Blue focused on the phrase, this time around.

"You can remember past lives?" he asked.

It was obvious from his tone that he was uncomfortable with the subject.

Esmeralda smiled. "You can't?"

"No. I mean, not really. I've had flashes of déjà vu maybe, but nothing solid."

"Does the idea bother you?"

"Smacks a little too much of the Pagan Party—you know, with their grimoires and midnight chants and everything."

"And yet," Esmeralda said, "you've spent time with Native American shaman."

She started to walk down the hall again. Blue fell in step beside her.

"That's different," he said. "The mystic stuff's a part of their lives—you can't separate the one from the other. The pagans I see around here seem to just be playing at it; it doesn't really come out of a solid tradition. It's more like they're making it up as they go along."

Esmeralda shrugged. "They have to—not quite 'make up,' let's say 'rediscover'—some things, but that doesn't invalidate what they do. And there is a strong Western mystery tradition; it's just been suppressed for a very long time." She gave him a half smile. "And still is."

"Point made. And now that you mention it, there's some—like Jools, say. I take her seriously. I can respect what she's trying to do. But most of them—"

"Are just looking for some meaning in an increasingly confused world. At least they don't hurt anybody and like your shaman, they're generally concerned with the state of the world—the health of the planet itself, rather than their own little corner of it. That can't be bad, can it?"

"But Emma," Blue began, trying to return to what they'd started discussing in the first place.

"Has got what many of your Pagan Party have been searching for," Esmeralda said, "except she doesn't know what to do with it. I'm not sure if she was always born with the gift, or if it came to her, but she has it now."

They'd reached the door of the Library then, and further conversation died as they took in the severity of what the Library had suffered. Here the returning forest had struck with a vengeance. Everywhere they looked there was a jungle of brambles and briars, thorn trees, oaks, vines, apple trees and hanging moss. For long moments they could only stare at the jumble of books and paper that was caught up in the thicket of vegetation.

"Jesus," Blue said; then he forced his way in, calling for Ginny.

Esmeralda followed in his wake, arms upraised to keep the branches that Blue pushed aside from snapping back against her face.

"Over here!" they heard Ginny call back.

They followed the sound of her voice to find her sitting at the strange gnarled and branched growth that had once been her desk, light from the computer screen giving her features a ghostly glow. Her face and forearms had sustained dozens of tiny scratches and her usually neat clothing was all torn and disarrayed.

"Are you all right?" Esmeralda asked.

Ginny nodded. "I won't say I wasn't frightened when it started, but . . . I'm not sure. I know everything's in a terrible confusion, but somehow it all feels right at the same time—do you know what I mean?"

Blue and Esmeralda just shook their heads, but Ginny was no longer looking at them. She'd turned her attention back to the screen.

"All except for this," she added, nodding at the screen.

Blue and Esmeralda made their way through the thicker clutter of growth around what had once been the desk to look at the screen. All that was on it was a flickering image that they both recognized as coming from one of the Weirdin bones that Sara had discovered so long ago.

"I looked it up in that folio that Sara brought back from Cornwall last year," Ginny said. "It's Secondary, Second Rank. The Forest."

Of course, Blue thought. What else *could* it be?

"And Jamie?" Esmeralda asked, beating Blue by a half second to the question he was about to ask himself. "Have you talked to him?"

Leaves stirred about the transformed desk as she spoke. Energy seemed to radiate from her.

Ginny shook her head.

"This is all that'll come up. I've tried rebooting, but no matter what I do, I can only get this image."

Soul of the Machine

The Owl—wisdom,
darkness,
death
—Weirdin disc;
Tertiary: Mobile, 57.b

Coyote wind howls through
a star-jawed night
Sky-gaped high lonesome
and wild.

Maybe the last buffalo—
Maybe the last buffalo soldier
Talking to his campfire late
one night
Heard from the ember-eyed
darkness
Something was not right.
—Ron Nance
"Jackalope Blues"

1

Sara gave it her best, but the fog wouldn't clear from her mind. The warm secret strength of her taw remained just a memory, its presence clouded from her approach no matter how desperately she tried to call it up. The harder she tried, the less success she had until finally even the moonheart air was lost to her.

To make matters worse, tendrils of mist had drifted into the glade as well. Unlike the fog in her mind, these were a very real physical presence that made her clothing damp and her hair frizz even more than its natural curliness. She pulled a jacket out of her pack and put it on, but still shivered, feeling cold, wet and miserable. The mist thickened into a soupy fog that grew so dense she could no longer even see the trees that surrounded the glade.

Wonderful, she thought as she got to her feet. As if she wasn't feeling wretched enough being stuck here in the first place.

She walked back and forth, the collar of her jacket turned up, hands stuck in her pockets against the chill, peering into the shadowy undergrowth that choked every approach into the forest. She wasn't sure if it was just her imagination, or her poor memory, but the brambly bushes and thorn thickets under the trees seemed to be more dense than she remembered them from when she first arrived. Earlier it had seemed possible, if a daunting prospect, to force her way through them. No longer. The undergrowth, not to mention the trees and the fog that assailed both her physical senses and her mind, were all conspiring to hem her in.

She hated this feeling of imprisonment and helplessness.

There had to be a way out.

Pausing in front of the forest—she wasn't sure which way she was facing; there didn't seem to a sense of direction in this place she studied the tangle of branch, thorn and briar. The growth was so thick she wondered if she couldn't just clamber over the top of it like a mountain climber scaling some brambly equivalent of a range of foothills.

She was half-minded to try—things couldn't get any worse just waiting here for God knew what, could they?—when she heard a sound.

A rustle of cloth against thorn.

A footstep.

The sounds came from behind her, their source hidden in the fog. She turned, uneasy with the forest at her back, and tried to look through the fog to see who—or what—was approaching. Opening and closing her hands, she wished she'd had the foresight to bring along some kind of a weapon. Even a club would feel just dandy, right now. But she hadn't brought a thing, and there was nothing close at hand that she could use, while the footsteps just kept coming closer.

A knot twisted into life in the pit of her stomach. She was torn between the desire to hide—only where?—or shout out a challenge at whoever it was that was approaching. Panic shivered up through her nerves, effectively dispelling the fog in her mind, but that didn't help much now. At this particular moment she was too anxious to try to call up her taw.

She backed up until the thorns behind her were pressed uncomfortably against the seat of her jeans. There was no place to run, nothing to use as a weapon.

Why had she never learned karate or something equally useful for a situation just like this? Better yet, why had she allowed herself to get into a situation like this in the first place? She should have taken Tal up on his offer to accompany her, or at least brought the wolves along. Who cared how memorable her arrival might be in her homeworld? Right now she'd settle just to arrive, thank you very much.

She began to sidle away along the edge of the forest, moving to her right as quietly as possible. Maybe she could get around the mysterious intruder and . . . and what? Escape? Not bloody likely. Jump him? She could use her backpack as a weapon, maybe, and—

She shrieked as a hand came out of the mist to touch her arm. Falling back into the briars, she flailed out with her hands as a figure took shape behind the arm, reaching down for her. Thorns pierced through her jeans, puncturing her skin in a dozen places. Her hair got entangled in the briars until she couldn't move her head. Effectively trussed and helpless, she could only watch as the figure took on recognizable characteristics.

All her energy ran from her and she lay limply back in her thorny prison, heedless for the moment of the pricking thorns.

"I don't believe this," she said.

If she'd been standing, he'd come up to about the middle of her chest. He was a small, roundheaded individual who seemed all eyes and grin, his broad features framed by two dozen or more Rastaman dreadlocks. Stuck into his belt was a small applewood flute.

"Hey, Sara," Pukwudji said.

"What are *you* doing here?"

The big saucer eyes went sad as a fawn's, which immediately made Sara feel like a heel.

"Don't you like me anymore?" the little *honochen'o'keh* asked.

"Of course I do. It's just—would you help me *out* of here?"

It took a few moments to untangle her hair, and a few more to get her free of the bushes whose thorny branches clung to her clothes like snagged fishhooks, but finally she was free of their uncomfortable embrace and standing in the glade once more. Gingerly, she explored the backs of her legs and her rump, wincing at all the little punctures.

"Why were you lying in the bushes?" Pukwudji asked.

She looked down into his face, the broad features turned up to her, an eager-to-please smile in his eyes. Try though she might, it was next to impossible to stay angry with him. She was too relieved just to be in his familiar company.

She sat down so that she wouldn't be towering above him and he immediately lowered himself to the grass across from her. Nothing seemed quite so grim now—it was hard for anything to seem grim around his infectious good humor.

"How did you find me?" she asked.

"I heard the call of your music—in here, hey?" He tapped his head. "And so I followed the sound of it." He looked around at the befogged glade. "Why did you come here?"

"I didn't mean to come here. It just sort of . . . happened."

Pukwudji nodded wisely as though it was an everyday occurrence. Maybe among his own people it was.

"Where *is* here, anyway?" Sara added.

"It's hard to tell," Pukwudji replied. "The forest is full of voices all talking at once."

"Voices?"

"The trees. Talking. All of them at once."

Sara sighed. "Great. The Kendell luck's running about par for the course."

"But if I don't know where we are," Pukwudji added, "I do know what this place is."

"You do?"

He nodded, dreadlocks shaking around his head like so many furry snakes.

"This isn't a forest that is or was," he said. "It's one that might have been, hey?"

Sara blinked. "Could you run that by me again?"

Now it was Pukwudji's turn to look confused.

"Where did you say we were?" Sara tried.

"In a might-be place that is," he said.

"That doesn't make much sense. How can a place that only might exist still be real?"

"It's made from a mind—just like worldwalking, hey?"

"We're in somebody's mind?"

"Not exactly," he said. "Someone's called the forest that might have been to the place where it would have stood—had it existed."

But it's here, Sara wanted to say. Growing all around us. So it does exist. But instead she just asked, "Who called it?"

"Don't know. Could be some*thing's* called it, hey?"

"This is getting too spacey for me," Sara complained. "Can we get out of here?"

"Where do you want to go?" Pukwudji asked.

"To Tamson House—to the garden."

"Okay," the *honochen'o'keh* said. He'd picked the expression up from Kieran and it always sounded strange to Sara, coming from him. "I'll look for it."

He closed his eyes, features scrunching up comically as he concentrated, and then he laughed.

"What's so funny?" Sara asked him.

"Where you want to go," he managed before a new fit of giggles came over him.

"I don't get the joke. What's so funny about my wanting to go to Tamson House?"

"But that's where we are. In its garden."

Sara looked carefully through the fog. If she squinted, she could just make out the towering shapes of the trees standing closest to them. The House's garden—her Mondream Wood—might seem at times to be larger than it really was, but there was nothing even remotely like this forest in its acreage.

She shook her head.

"No way," she said. "I've been gone a year, but there's no way the garden's going to get this overgrown in that time. Trees like that'd take a hundred years or more to get that big."

"But it's true," Pukwudji said as she turned back to look at him. "I would never lie to you. You're my friend, remember?"

"Of course we're friends."

"So you see, it's true."

"But . . ."

Her voice trailed off.

You must return to the Wood.

That's what he'd said, the hooded man who'd come to her as a ghost. She'd just assumed that by wood he'd meant her name for the garden that lay enclosed by Tamson House. She'd just assumed that everything would be the same. But if there was—to use the kind of description Blue would—a great big mother of a forest in the middle of the garden, then things weren't the same at all, were they? Things could be very wrong indeed.

She wondered if she should go back for help. If Pukwudji could take her . . .

"Do you want to see the House?" he asked.

"You can get us through all of that?" Sara replied, waving a hand toward the closest part of the forest.

The little man nodded.

It wouldn't hurt to have a look, would it? Just to scout out the situation before she went running back to Tal and the others like some little bimbo from one of those mushy romance books who was always looking for the heroes to rescue her?

"How do we get through?" she asked.

Pukwudji leapt to his feet, his grin so wide it seemed to split his face in two.

"We ask for passage, hey!"

Sara didn't rise from the ground quite so enthusiastically.

"We ask," she said.

Pukwudji nodded.

"That's it," Sara said. "It's that simple."

"What would you do?" Pukwudji asked.

"Ask, of course," Sara said.

She followed him to the edge of the trees. The undergrowth seemed, if anything, even more densely overgrown than before.

"Ask who?" she added.

"The forest," her companion said.

He laid his hands lightly on the nearest bush, his palms barely touching the tips of its branches, and closed his eyes. A moment later, the brush began to move aside, revealing a twisting narrow passage that led off under the trees. Sara took a step back.

"I don't like this much," she said.

"Don't worry," Pukwudji said. "The forest likes me."

"How do you know?"

"Because it told me so, hey!"

He stepped onto the path and looked expectantly over his shoulder at her.

"I'm coming, I'm coming," Sara told him. "I don't like it, but I'm coming."

She shivered as she stepped under the first trees, expecting something to fall upon her at any moment. But all that happened was that the path continued to open up through the jumble of brush and fallen trees ahead of them—and closed up behind them.

I hope I don't regret this, Sara thought, but then she had to laugh at herself. What was she talking about? She'd regretted it from the moment she'd found herself stranded in the glade. Brave and heroic, she wasn't. But she decided that naiveté and foolishness—*that* she carried around with her in quantities far exceeding a normal person's allotment.

2

Julianne Trelawny had never been overly fond of her hourglass figure. It wasn't that she didn't like the way she looked so much as that how she looked got in the way of her relationships with both men and women. Men tended to focus solely on her amplitude, while women were either irritated by the attention that her figure brought her, or dismissed her as a bimbo. None of which was fair, but fair in this world, where everything was judged by its packaging, was just the first third of fairy tale. She'd learned long ago not to expect fairness.

But it was hard.

Blue, for all his machismo image, was one of the few men she knew who actually looked her in the face when he talked to her; who right from the very start had treated her as a person rather than a centerfold, which was probably why she let him get away with calling her Jools—a name that came as dangerously close to sounding like prime bimbo material as she'd ever heard. Occasionally she found herself wishing he wasn't already involved with someone, but so far she'd managed to keep that line of thinking as just stray thoughts. A homewrecker she wasn't—no matter how many women prejudged her that way.

Still, Blue was the exception. Most guys fell into two camps—those who lusted and those who pretended that they didn't—which made the hope of finding a good relationship just that: a hope. And Julianne had as much faith in hope as she did in fairness. She was a doer; she preferred to just carry on, rather than wait for the world to change to suit her needs.

It was the same with her pagan beliefs. She didn't pretend to be what she wasn't; she didn't hide the fact that she was Wicca, but she was sick to death at how that was just one more thing that let people prejudge a person. She tried to explain why she followed the Goddess to those people who seemed genuinely interested in hearing what she had to say, but she couldn't offer them proof in the validity of what she believed any more than a Christian or Muslim could offer it up to authenticate their own faiths.

All she knew was that there was more to the world than what could be perceived with the five senses and that she couldn't accept that Mystery as having its source in some power-hungry god whose church's creeds were based on denial of all secular matters, as though the beauty of this world was not a thing to be cherished for its own sake, but was rather a testing ground for how one would or would not be rewarded in the afterlife.

There was magic in a forest, on a mountaintop or seashore; in the heart of a desert and, yes, even on a city street. There was beauty in humankind and the creatures with which they shared this world; and there was mystery, too. If the Goddess and her followers smacked too much of the supernatural for people, that was just too bad for them. She wasn't on a crusade. She'd campaign for environmental concerns, for disarmament, for human rights, but not for the Goddess. That was private, between the Goddess and her and those other few souls who were similarly inclined.

Everybody else wanted proof. They wanted miracles. She couldn't give them either. She'd never experienced either—just the simple truth that the world itself was a great mystery worthy of devotion.

Until now.

Like Cal, she'd initially been frightened when the tree came crashing up through the floorboards—its monstrous size, the cacophony of its passage, the sheer *impossibility* of its presence, appearing here in the middle of a house, in the middle of a city. It stripped away all her conceptions of the world and how it worked.

But only for a moment. Long enough for Cal to rescue her from the sweeping branches and find them both sanctuary behind the battered sofa. Yet that first mind-numbing scream of panic that knifed through her gave way to an astonishing calm. While Cal was still hugging her close, muttering, "We're going to die, we're going to die," she pulled herself free from his embrace to look over the edge of the sofa and watch the tree's final upward movement.

The calmness grew in her. She felt a strange sense of peace. She felt—

Validated.

Not that she'd needed proof to bolster her beliefs. But to have it so violently thrust upon her . . . it was a miracle. If such an impossibility as this could be incontestably standing there before her in the middle of the room, roots hidden by what remained of the floorboards, heights lost beyond the ceiling above . . . then what else might not be true? What other miracles lay just beyond common sight, only waiting for their veil to be drawn aside?

She rose up on her knees, leaning her arms on the sofa, and just drank in the sight.

"Look at it," she said.

Cal tried to pull her back down beside him.

"Jesus," he said. "Would you get down? Who knows what's going to happen next?"

She shook herself free of his grip and stood up.

"Julianne."

Her blood was humming at a thundering rhythm through her veins. She was no longer panicked, but the emotions that sang inside her had just as much power to dissolve away everything except for the power of what she was feeling.

"Julianne."

Drawn by her name, she finally turned to look down at him. For a long moment she saw only a stranger. It took her long moments to realize it was Cal. The reluctant pagan. He belonged to the camp of lusting after her but pretending he didn't. Usually she was able to ignore that aspect of him, but she wasn't in the mood to play that game right now. Unfortunately, the thought process that had let her recognize him was enough to dissolve the fey frame of mind she'd found herself in.

That first rush of emotion that had filled her—the awareness of the miracle and all that it meant—slipped away like water running down a hillside. She regretted its departure, but clung to the spark of it that remained inside her as she might have a talisman. Clung to it and stored it securely away so that it would always be a part of her.

Not until she was sure of its safety did she allow herself to consider more practical concerns. For now it was time to slip back into the real world. To put on all the masks and blinders once again. But it wouldn't be the same. Experiencing what she had, feeling the spark of it nestled deep inside her, she knew that nothing would ever be the same again.

"Come on," she said, offering him a hand up. "Let's see if anybody needs help."

Cal rose to stand shakily beside her, hands gripping the sofa as he stared at the tree.

"Man," he said softly. "Can you believe that thing?"

Julianne smiled. "Oh, yes," she said, her own voice dreamy rather than subdued. Then she blinked.

"Come on," she repeated and began to carefully pick her way across the wreckage of the floor.

Once out in the hallway, Cal felt as though he and Julianne had traveled a distance of far more than just a few steps. From the devastating wreckage of the room that lay just behind them, they stood now in a place that had barely been touched by the violence. Some pictures hung crookedly on the walls. A vase had toppled from a side table to the floor, but it hadn't broken, only strewn its dry flowers across the carpet. Otherwise the hall had survived virtually unscathed.

Cal looked back into the room.

"It's weird," he said. "It's like it only happened in the Birken-tree."

Julianne nodded, then called out a greeting. Coming to them from the hallway along the right were Tim and a handful of others. Cal recognized Ohn, Blue's friend Judy and a student from Ireland he only knew as Barry; the rest were strangers.

"You guys okay?" Tim asked.

"A little shook up," Julianne said.

"A little?" Cal muttered. He stuck his hands in his pockets to keep them from shaking and then raised his voice as the others drew near. "Anybody know what the hell's going on here?"

Tim shook his head.

"All we know so far," Ohn said, "is that the only parts of the House affected are those in which somebody was present. If the room was empty, it was untouched."

"Man, this is spooky," Cal said. "We were just sitting in the Birkentree when all of . . ."

His voice trailed off as he realized no one was listening. Turning, he saw what had caught their attention. It was Julianne. She'd moved a little farther down the hall and was staring out the win-dow to the street. She almost seemed to be glowing, she was so entranced with what she looking at.

"What do you see?" he asked, knowing that he didn't want to hear the answer but unable to stop himself from asking.

"It's the city," she said.

She turned to look at them. She was, he realized with a transcen-dental insight that had him looking past her physical beauty for once, transformed in that moment. Her face seemed to shimmer with a light that came from beneath the skin. Her green eyes were deep with hidden lights. And secrets discovered.

"It's gone," she said. "There's just a forest out there."

As she turned back to the window, the others pressed forward and Cal's moment of insight fled. He saw only Julianne there now. She was in no way lessened in his estimation, but there seemed less of her. For one brief instant he felt as though he'd been allowed a glimpse of her soul and that glimpse would forever overshadow the flesh and bone that her spirit wore to walk in this world.

Snatches of conversation rose and fell in his hearing.

"I never thought to look outside—"

"—it's not possible—"

"—you can say that after—"

"—what are we going—"

But he remained transfixed, staring at her, trying to recapture that glimpse. She seemed to sense the weight of his gaze upon her and turned from the window.

He opened his mouth to speak, to somehow try to capture in words what had just happened to him, but the ability to articulate his thoughts seemed to have just drained out of him.

"What's wrong, Cal?" she asked.

He shook his head. She was forever transformed for him now.

He'd put her on a pedestal—not *her,* but the face and body she wore that could be physically recognized as her—and only now understood how he'd let that color his feelings for her. It was what lay inside the physical shell that had been important, but he'd lusted too much after the shell itself. His attentiveness, his not coming on to her, his trying to just be her friend—they had all been moves in a game that, when and if he won it, would result in his acquiring that shell as its prize.

He realized that she'd known it all along. And tried to ignore it. Tried to pretend that he was a friend.

And all the while he was letting her down because he kept the game going. Because while he liked *her,* what he'd wanted was her body.

She could look like an ape now, he thought, and he'd still love her. But he was no longer worthy of her.

She didn't say that. Nothing in her stance, her features, her eyes, told him that.

It was what lay inside him that spoke. The spirit that wore *his* body as a shell.

3

They hadn't been following the path for that long—though it seemed far longer than it should logically take to reach the House from any part of the garden—when Sara tapped Pukwudji on the shoulder. He turned to face her.

"Look," she said.

She pointed up to the lower limbs of the trees where ranks of owls were perched, row on row. Their round eyes gazed down at the pair of them, unblinking. Tufts of feathers rose up like horns from their heads. She'd first noticed them a little farther back on the path, spying first one, half-hidden in the branches, then another, then a pair, until now the trees were fairly riddled with the birds.

Pukwudji gazed up at them, his own round eyes blinking twice.

"Owls," he said.

Sara didn't know whether to laugh or give him a whack.

"I *know* they're owls," she said. "What I want to know is what they're all doing here."

Pukwudji shrugged.

"Tal says that owls are corpse birds," Sara added, wishing she hadn't thought of that as soon as it came to mind, but she plunged on. "They gather in places where death's near." She swallowed dryly, her throat suddenly feeling too thick. "You don't think . . ."

Now she really couldn't finish what she was about to say: What if something *had* happened at the House? Bad enough the thought had come to mind in the first place; she felt that voicing it might just make it real. Guilt rose in her. It had been so long since she'd visited the House, seen Blue. If anything had happened to him she'd never forgive herself.

"Redhair's wrong," Pukwudji told her. "Owls are Grandmother Toad's friends, wise and filled with the mystery of days to come. They're manitou—just like us."

Just like you, Sara thought. But she'd long ago given up on arguing the point with him. Just like Ha'kan'ta, he was convinced that she was, if not a *honochen'o'keh* herself, then at least a cousin to them.

"They can see into the future?" she asked instead.

That just added weight to Tal's argument, she felt.

"They live outside of time—or in all time. Only Nokomis knows everything."

"So they *can* see into the future? They could gather if something's wrong?"

Pukwudji nodded. "But seeing them is a very good omen, hey?"

"I suppose."

"It's not far now," Pukwudji added.

He started to turn, but Sara caught his arm.

"How can we be in the House's garden and somebody's mind at the same time?" she asked.

"We're not *in* someone's mind," he explained. "Only in the forest that mind called up. The forest never was; what it might have been intrudes on what is."

"I'm not sure that makes any sense."

Pukwudji grinned. "That's the trouble with *herok'a*," he said, using the *quin'on'a* term to describe anyone without magical abilities. "They think too much. You should forget you ever were one, Sara. Just be—like me, hey?"

Just be? Be what? She couldn't be anything but what she was and she still hadn't quite got a handle on what that was—just like ninety-nine percent of the other people in the world.

Pukwudji gave her a poke in the side with a stiff finger to get her attention, then set off once more. Sara trailed along in his wake, all too aware of the dozens of pairs of eyes that watched their progress from the branches above.

Why did things always have to get complicated? She'd been planning to come back to the House soon anyway—sometime after the initiation ceremony. Definitely before winter. Just pop in unannounced the way she and Tal always did, catch up on news, hang around for a few days until the pace of the city, the sheer *volume* of its people and all the rush and noise, the whine of electricity that was always in the air and the endless traffic and crowding . . . until it all got to be too much for them again and they fled back into the peace that the Otherworlds hoarded like this world's people hoarded investments.

She couldn't stay away forever. She still had some responsibilities here—mostly tied up with the House and her inheritance; there were always meetings with brokers and attorneys, papers that needed signing, never mind how much Esmeralda handled that stuff for her. And then there were her friends.

She always came back. She just didn't like coming back in these particular circumstances.

Above them, the owls continued their vigil. Sara pretended not to pay any attention to them, but she couldn't help giving them sidelong glances about every half-dozen steps or so. Either the entire forest was riddled with them, she decided, or it was just one particular flock that was keeping pace with Pukwudji and her. Whichever, they made her nervous. As did the constant rustling that she could hear coming from the forest just off the path.

Sly movements.

Just animals, she told herself. But no matter how much she peered into the thick growth on either side of the path, she couldn't see a thing.

Whispering.

Just the wind. Except why did it sound like words?

Stifled giggles.

"Pukwudji," she began, but he had already stopped.

His head was cocked to one side like a bird's, listening. If he could figure out what was going on, Sara thought, then—

He turned suddenly.

"Quick, Sara!" he cried. "Can you climb one of these trees?"

She was taken aback with the sharp tension underlying his voice. But then she heard it, too. A crashing sound as something large forced its way through the undergrowth. Something large . . . and fast.

"I . . ."

He didn't wait for her to reply. With that strength that always surprised her, considering his size, he had her hoisted onto his shoulder, head dangling down his back, legs up bundled against his chest, and he was scrambling up the trunk of the nearest pine, finding finger- and toe-holds where she would have seen none. In moments, they were almost ten feet up from the ground, perched high on a branch.

When he set her down, she saw the owls all around them, staring. But not at them. She clutched the trunk of the tree and looked down at what had caught their attention.

On the path where they'd been standing just moments ago, an

enormous wild boar had burst from the undergrowth. It circled around, snorting and grunting, sharp hooves tearing up the ground. The coarse bristles of its hide varied from a blackish brown to a light yellow gray. It stood almost three feet high, five feet long and had to weigh close to four hundred pounds.

Sara began to shake as she imagined how long they would have survived if it had caught them on the ground.

"Ha!" Pukwudji called down to it. "Can't catch us, hey!"

She turned to find the *honochen'o'keh* sitting on his heels, tiny feet precariously balanced on the branch as he bounced up and down, shaking a finger at the enraged creature below them. That just made Sara hug the trunk more tightly.

"I . . . I thought you said the forest liked you," she said finally.

Pukwudji nodded. "It does."

"But then—"

"That's not part of the forest," he said. "It's an angry thought."

Sara looked down at the boar. It was butting its head against their tree now, little pig eyes glaring up at them. She could feel the force of its attack vibrating through the tree trunk.

An angry thought. Right.

"Whose angry thought?" she asked.

Pukwudji shrugged. "Don't know. The forest is filled with a mix of them, some friendly, some not so much so."

Sara thought about the sounds she'd heard as they'd been following the path. Rustling and whispers and giggles. These were . . . thoughts?

"He's going now," Pukwudji said.

Sara glanced down again. Sure enough, the boar had given up on them and plunged into the undergrowth on the far side of the path. Somehow she'd thought it would have been more tenacious in its pursuit of them. She followed its progress mostly by sound. Her adrenaline rush began to fade as distance swallowed the immediacy of the boar's passage, leaving her feeling weak and not quite all in her body.

Get ahold of yourself, she thought.

Shen.

Gather the spirit inside. Focus.

"Let's go down now," Pukwudji added.

Sara hung on to the tree as he reached for her.

"Ah . . . don't you think we should, you know, give it a few more minutes? Just in case it decides to come back?"

"He won't be back," Pukwudji said. "See, the *memegwesi* have chased him away."

Her gaze followed his pointing finger. What looked like three little green-skinned children were dancing and laughing on the path where the boar had been just moments ago. When they spied her looking at them, they all put their hands to their mouths and, stifling giggles, ran off into the undergrowth, following the trail that the boar had forced through the dense vegetation. Unlike the boar, their passage was silent.

For a long moment Sara just stared at where they'd been.

"The forest's a lively place tonight," she said finally, attempting, but not quite succeeding, to keep her tone light.

Maybe too lively, she added to herself.

"The forest is always lively," Pukwudji agreed.

"But not like this."

He laughed. "Always like this. You just don't always choose to *see,* hey?"

They made their descent back down to the path, this time with Sara clinging to Pukwudji's back. She didn't feel a whole lot more dignified, but it was better than being carted around over his shoulder like so much baggage. The ground felt blessedly firm underfoot. The night seemed very still around them, almost silent. Then there was a sound like a sudden wind, but it was only the owls taking flight. They left their perches and flew off in the direction that Pukwudji was leading her.

Another couple of minutes' walking showed Sara the owls' new perch—the eaves and gables of Tamson House. She stared at the huge structure, relief flaring in her until she realized that it was much darker than it should be. What lights there were seemed dim. And there was no sound coming from beyond the bulk of the House where the city should be. That was when her troubled gaze settled on the trees—monstrous cousins of the forest through which they'd just come, except their upper branches poked through the roof of the House itself.

"The forest . . ." she began.

"Has come visiting," Pukwudji said, not at all alarmed by the sight.

Sara sighed. Naturally he'd view the House as the intruder, rather than the trees. But then she realized that the House *was* intruding. That was why she couldn't hear the city, or see the glare of its lights from beyond the roof of the House. The trees hadn't come to the House; the House had been pulled into the forest— just as it had that time when they were having all the trouble with Tom Hengwr. Except this time the contents of the House hadn't shifted to another outer shell set in some convenient glade; this time they'd been transported to an outer shell that the forest had reclaimed.

As she glanced to her right, her gaze was caught by the lights of the ballroom that spilled from its leaded-pane windows out onto the transformed garden. She could see the movement of people inside. Hopefully Blue and Esmeralda were there. With answers to make some sense out of all this.

"Let's see if we can find out what's going on," she said.

She started for the ballroom, pausing when Pukwudji didn't follow.

"Aren't you coming?"

He shook his head. *"Herok'a* and buildings—that's not for me."

"But—"

"I'm a secret," Pukwudji said. "Your secret, the forest's secret. It's not for them to know, hey?"

"Blue'll be in there," Sara tried. "You know him."

But Pukwudji simply took a side step and was gone.

I'll wait for you here, she heard him say, his voice tickling in her mind, rather than physically heard.

Sara looked at the spot where he'd vanished, waiting to see if he'd change his mind, then sighed and continued on to the ballroom on her own. Though she tried to ignore them, she was all too aware of the owls following her progress from the eaves above with their silent, round-eyed gaze.

4

"I've been here before," Blue said. "In this situation."

Judy cocked an eyebrow, waiting for him to elaborate.

The two of them were sitting on the small stage at one end of the ballroom with Esmeralda, waiting for the rest of the House's residents and guests to arrive so that they could decide what they would do from this point. The latter had been arriving steadily by ones and twos over the past few minutes. They gathered in small groups in various parts of the cavernous room, their mood ranging from operating on automatic pilot to delight at their predicament.

The Pagan Party, Blue noted, were the happiest, once they got over the initial shock.

Esmeralda was sitting on the piano bench, picking out a few desultory bars of some sonata. Rachmaninoff's No. 2, Blue decided, recognizing the familiar tempo change from the second movement. She looked up as Blue spoke, fingers stilling on the keys.

"You mean that business a few years ago with Tom Hengwr?" she asked.

"I told you about that?"

Esmeralda shook her head. "Actually, Sara did."

"Well, I haven't a clue what you're talking about," Judy said.

She was handling the whole situation well, Blue thought. A hell of a lot better than some. Over by the double doors that led into the ballroom, a couple of would-be poets were trying to comfort a third of their number who was crouched on the floor, arms wrapped around his legs, a wide-eyed look of panic in his eyes, limbs shaking as if from palsy.

The good thing was that no one had been physically hurt. A small miracle, considering the damage he'd seen in some of the rooms.

"Earth to Blue," Judy said. "Come in, Blue."

"Well, there was this guy," he began, turning his attention back to Judy.

Esmeralda switched to Chopin as Blue gave a brief rundown on the previous time Tamson House had gone world-hopping. The music played a gentle counterpoint to his story and Blue found himself falling into its rhythm as he spoke, appreciating its presence. Somehow it made the weirdness of his story easier to relate. But more important, he realized, the quiet piano-playing was having a soothing effect on the various and sundry occupants of the House who'd just happened to be present in the building when it shifted into the Otherworld.

"You could've warned me," Judy said when he was done. She shot him a quick smile to show that she wasn't being too serious. "I mean, this kind of thing'll play hell on business. Guy'll come looking for his bike that I've been working on and not only is the bike gone, but the whole frigging House. What's he going to think?"

"Maybe it'll remind him of that joke about the magician who went downtown and turned into a restaurant," Esmeralda said.

Judy laughed. "Yeah, right."

"The music I can take," Blue said, "but not the bad jokes."

Esmeralda only shrugged and pretended to flick the ashes from an imaginary cigar.

"So Jamie," Judy went on after a few moments. "He died . . . right?"

Blue nodded.

"Only he's still here . . . kind of like a ghost?"

"He's part of the House," Esmeralda said, taking over from Blue. "Think of him as a guardian spirit."

"So where's he gone now?" Judy asked.

Esmeralda looked down at the keyboard. Her hair fell forward, hiding her face. Strands moved, as though touched by a breeze that only they could feel. She played her fingers lightly over the keys, only just brushing their smooth ivory surfaces. Her touch was so soft that not one hammer came in contact with a string.

"I wish we knew," Blue said.

5

It had been odd at first, thinking he was dead, then slowly coming back to awareness.

Body lost; gone forever the flesh and bone and the heartbeat that sent blood pulsing through every artery and vein. Sensations were stimulated through other means of awareness now.

They were ghostly impressions in the beginning. Confusing ones. A hundred different views, as though he had an eye in every part of his body. A thousand sounds, as though he had an ear for each eye. A hundred thousand scents, as though each pore had acquired its own olfactory organ.

It wasn't until his father spoke that he knew what he'd become.

It's yours to guard now, James. Cherish the burden.

It.

Tamson House.

He'd *become* the House.

He wasn't just a ghost, haunting the maze of its halls and rooms. He was the House. Alive in its wood and glass and stone. Its walls were his ears. Its windows, his eyes. He was aware of every minute occurrence that happened within the scope of its rooms and towers and halls.

He thought he'd go insane.

But he learned to cope. Just as men and women learned to sift through the confusing barrage of stimuli that assaulted their senses every moment of every day and focus on only one or two details, just as their bodies carried on their life functions without the necessity for direct attention from the consciousness, so he learned to be particular as to what he focused upon.

Sanity returned. He allowed the residents their privacy.

And he found a place to store the core of what made him who he was—a spark of identity that he kept separate and nurtured so that he would always be Jamie, still individual, not just the ghostly spirit of the House in its entirety. His father had done the same, he realized, when he found residual memories of Nathan Tamson's presence in the observatory. That part of the House had been his father's choice as to where he would maintain his individuality; just as Jamie's grandfather Anthony had chosen Sara's Tower in his own time of ghostly custodianship.

Jamie chose Memoria—the computer mainframe that had become so much a part of his life in the last years that he was flesh and blood. He had been an Arcanologist then—a self-coined word to accompany another that he'd also created to describe his life's work: Arcanology, the study of secrets. As time passed, he discovered he could maintain that work in his present state, though due to the limitations that were inherent in lacking a physical body, it wasn't an easy task. And it wasn't the same.

But this new life-after-death could *never* be the same as the life he'd left behind. Survival of the mind, of his identity, was a godsend—he couldn't deny it—but there were things he missed with an intensity that sometimes had the madness that had plagued his first few weeks in his new existence come licking at the corners of his mind once again.

The lack of physical sensation was one of the worst.

He could feel the sun, the wind, the rain on the roof and walls of the House, but those tactile impressions couldn't begin to compete with the memory of sun-warmed skin and the wind in his face, the glory of a summer rainstorm when he would stand on the porch, the rain splattering against the legs of his pants, dampening the cloth, the air crackling with energy, being half-blinded by flares of lightning, deafened by thunder. Or skating on the canal on a winter's day when the air was so cold your breath froze, the sun like diamonds on the ice, every sense and thought shocked into exaggeration. . . .

Being *alive*.

How could anything compete with life?

Running a close second to the loss of physical sensation, he felt the lack of the exchange of ideas that had filled so many of his days in his earlier existence. Through Memoria, he could communicate with Blue and others. He had access to all the material he'd entered into the computer's memory banks before he'd died. Blue and, later, Ginny read articles to him from more recent journals. But none of that was—*could*—be the same, either.

What he had really missed was the voluminous correspondence he'd maintained with like-minded individuals in every part of the world. He couldn't write to them, because for all practical intents and purposes, he was dead.

It was Esmeralda who'd found a solution to that—a solution so simple he wondered that he'd never thought of it himself. With her help, he created John Morley, a "close and dear friend of Jamie

Tams" who took it upon himself to get in touch with all of Jamie's old correspondents. New—for them—friendships blossomed, and soon "John Morley" had as voluminous a correspondence as ever Jamie'd had. John Morley began to contribute to the same journals that Jamie once had, and if anyone noticed the similarity in writing style between Jamie's previous work and that of his friend, no mention was made of it that he ever saw.

Esmeralda was also the one who'd seen to the transfer of the Library's more pertinent texts into his memory banks. She spent long hours talking with him, playing chess or Go, sometimes just sitting in his study and reading, knowing that her company—her *awareness* of him and his particular needs—was more comforting than any verbal communication.

He appreciated the part Esmeralda had come to play in his life—appreciated it more than he could ever hope to convey to her. His only regret in their relationship—was that what defined humanity? he wondered sometimes; our apparent need for regrets and guilt?—was that it wasn't Sara playing this role in his life. This didn't in any way diminish his feelings for Esmeralda; he just missed Sara.

Before his death, it had always been he and Sara, paired against the world. But while she spent time with him whenever she returned to the House, he knew she was uncomfortable with their new relationship. It wasn't real to her. No matter how much they could talk of old times, he knew that she still viewed him as a stranger; a familiar stranger, perhaps, like an old friend one hasn't seen for a very long time, the distance of years lying between now and the familiar memories of then, but a stranger all the same.

She'd suffered the hardest with his death; but rather than coming to accept his ghostly return as Blue had, every time she was with him he could see a deep sorrow well in her eyes. Though she would never admit it, he was sure that it was her inability to come to terms with the present turn their relationship had taken that sent her into the Otherworld, more than any other reason.

Those who hadn't known him before his death—or those like Esmeralda who'd been gone so long, or were so matter-of-fact when it came to what smacked so strongly of the supernatural—were nonplussed with his present state. But Sara . . .

It was because of her that he began to concentrate his studies on the Otherworld. He pored over all of its aspects, the myths and legends, the rumors he read, the facts that Esmeralda could share with him. He concentrated on how its borders related to this world. How one crossed over. How the journey could be made without a physical body.

It was the latter which proved to be his undoing.

He'd practiced reaching out from the House, stretching his spirit from where it was bound to the building, outward and inward, for the Otherworld lay in either direction, depending on one's perception of it. And as he practiced, he realized it was possible. He *could* reach out, not just to view, but to step out, as it were, of the body that the House had become, like a spirit traveling beyond the confines of its flesh-and-bone body. It could be done.

But with success so close at hand, his father's voice would reverberate in his mind.

It's yours to guard now, James.

And it was true. The House did need to be guarded. It was a center of power, a crossroads between the worlds. A place where magic lay deep in every stone and plank and tile of its making. And there were always those who yearned to breach its defenses, to take its power and invest it in themselves. Dissipating it upon their own concerns, rather than allowing it to continue its cyclic pattern of maintaining a community—building and residents, each fueling the other with solace and comfort, riddles and questions, understanding and always mystery.

It did need to be protected. Jamie saw how his father, and grandfather before him, had utilized their strange relationship with the building to keep it a haven of open-mindedness and learning. Those with destructive impulses could be turned away. Hermetic scholars following their left-handed paths might seek to tap into the lifespring of the House's energy source—the garden, the ancient wood it hoarded in its memory—but such psychic assaults were rare and they, too, could be turned aside. The House had the strength; it only needed one such as Jamie or his ancestors for its focus.

It's yours to guard now, James. Cherish the burden.

Guard it he did, but it was a burden. For he wanted to reach out—to Sara. Wanted her to understand that for all the alienness of his present situation, he was still her uncle, still the Jamie she'd always known, and she was still his Sairey. It didn't have to change. They'd been given a gift; he'd cheated death. What they could have between them would be different, but it would still be meaningful. The magic didn't have to die.

If she could just understand that, then he would be content.

He would put away regrets and guilt.

He would do his best not to yearn for what he couldn't have, but concentrate instead on what he did.

So he continued to reach for the Otherworld, to reach for her. And one day he stretched far enough so that all connections binding him to the House snapped and his spirit went sailing off into those uncharted realms.

It didn't go at all as he'd expected.

The Otherworld was not one place, but a hundred thousand places and times, all overlapping, one over the other like the layers of an onion. From his present point of view, and with his inexperience, he found it impossible to focus on any one world, little say find Sara in it. His senses overloaded with a surfeit of images and impressions. He had no body, not even a center from which to define his focus as he could with Memoria in the House, so what came to him, came from every side and direction.

There was no up, no down. No east, no west. No past, no future. No left, no right. Here it was all now, and here, seething and roiling, a chaotic stew from which he found it impossible to extricate himself.

He realized two things at that moment: he was hopelessly lost, and he'd failed his charge by leaving the House unprotected. And worse, he could sense that someone . . . some*thing* was already taking advantage of his failure.

One small tenuous thread still connected him to Memoria. It was less a physical presence, more just a memory, or a hope of a memory. It wasn't enough to show him how to return, to let him pull himself back. All he could do was send a warning back.

The message he sent was complex, a string of ideas and thoughts all bound together in what he'd learned, what he'd been, encapsulated as best he could in one brief flare of communication. But what reached the other end of the thread linking him to what he'd lost became distilled in its passage into—

The symbol upon the Weirdin disc of the Forest.

A ghostly cloak to carry a message of warning.

Then the apocalyptic stew in which he swirled and spun simply tugged his spirit apart and scattered the pieces into a hundred thousand Otherworlds.

6

Julianne wasn't ready to become part of the crowd that was gathering in the ballroom. Not yet. She told Cal to go ahead, she'd catch up with him later, and while it was apparent that he didn't want to leave her—because he honestly didn't feel it was safe, she realized, rather than for his usual reasons for being with her—he did as she asked. Finally alone, she opened one of the House's many front doors. Stepping outside, she let the night swallow her.

The paved width of an inner-city residential street should have been laid out before her. But O'Connor Street was gone, and with it the houses on its far side, the streetlights, the sound of traffic, the city itself. . . .

There was only the forest—the primal forest that had thrust itself into the House with its giant trees that were no more than the tips of fingers when compared to the forest's immense bulk as a whole. The trees were like redwoods—cathedral huge, enormous, stately and secret, resonant with mystery. They beckoned to her, almost audibly calling her name as they had from the first moment she'd looked out the window to find the city gone. Her body trembled. She ached to step away under their boughs, but then oddly enough she found herself thinking about Cal and the immediacy of the forest's pull on her was diminished.

Something had happened to Cal when the forest entered the House. Not the same kind of something that she had experienced, but he'd sustained an epiphany as intense as her own sudden validation of the miraculous depths that lay behind the world. They'd each undergone a personal shift of perception that changed their world. For her, Mystery had been transformed from intuitive belief, secreted within herself, to tangible reality, while he . . .

When she considered how he'd looked at her in the hallway after they had left the Birkentree Room, how he'd spoken to her, she realized that his shift in perception had encompassed a simpler, though no less profound, change in how he viewed the world. He'd been looking at her as a person, first, rather than as a body he lusted after. He'd realized how their relationship had been colored by the game he'd been playing and he'd been . . . embarrassed. Perhaps even shamed.

Though she had no interest in him as sexual partner, she was not so hard-hearted as to be unable to empathize with what he was going through. She'd like to be friends with him. And they could be real friends, too, if he was able to put away his pretenses and simply be himself with her, if they could get past the understanding that their relationship could only be platonic.

She'd like that. If he could deal with it, she'd like it very much. Real friends were too important, too rare, to lose.

She gazed at the forest. Her longing to partake of its mystery, to walk under its cathedraling boughs and let its secrets fill her heart, thrummed like a drumbeat inside her. It called to her and she yearned to answer, but she turned away, back to the House to look for Cal. The door creaked as she opened it and she sensed something stir in the shadows nearby at the sharp sound. Peering more closely, she could just make out a figure standing in the dark, as still and silent as the trees of the forest that encircled the House.

"Who's there?" she called.

The figure turned slowly in her direction, then stepped out to where the light from a window fell across her features. It was Emma, Julianne realized. Emma Fenn. Blue's girlfriend.

It was hard to tell for certain in the poor light, but the first impression Julianne got was that Emma seemed only half present, as though her body was going through the motions of being animated, but her spirit had long since gone off rambling on its own. Julianne remembered some odd stories she'd heard about Emma from Ginny, something about how Emma's spirit had been stolen once before. . . .

She'd put it down to just the odd sorts of stories that tended to circulate in a place like Tamson House, such as other ones that said that Ohn was really an ancient bard who'd once been a member of some faerie court, but looking at Emma now, with the forest surrounding the House where the city should have been, that kind of a story didn't seem odd at all. Worry stole its way inside her, leaving her feeling increasingly uneasy with each soft footstep it took.

"Emma," she said. "Are you okay?"

For a long moment there was no answer, but then Emma smiled. Her eyes gleamed with sudden life, her features took on a radiance.

"I'm fine," she said.

Julianne studied her for a long moment. There was no trace of the zombielike look about Emma that had first made her anxious, but the uneasiness that had lodged inside her didn't fade.

"Would you do me a favor?" Emma asked before Julianne could speak. "Would you tell Blue where I've gone? I don't want him to worry."

"Gone?" Julianne repeated. "You mean that you're out here?"

Emma shook her head and pointed away from the House.

"I'm going into the forest," she said. "It's calling me and I have to go."

The forest.

As Emma spoke those simple words, Julianne's own need to walk and experience its mysteries returned like a sharp ache. She yearned to just go. Close the door, and step away into the wonder that lay hidden beyond those first few trees, but she knew that Cal needed her more right now than she needed the forest. The spark of what she'd experienced, the glowing truth, was hoarded deep inside her and would never go away, while Cal's shift in perspective could easily leave him embittered if she didn't go to him now.

Still, she couldn't escape a sudden stab of envy. Emma had Blue, and now she got the forest, too. . . . And Julianne couldn't help but resent the fact that she was the one who'd chanced upon Emma and had to deliver a message to Blue that she knew he wasn't going to like. They didn't kill messengers anymore, not like they did in the old days, but who wanted to be the bearer of bad news? If anything happened to Emma . . . every time Blue looked at her, he'd remember who it was that had first told him. . . .

She tried to put those feelings away before they could take root. They weren't worthy and they made her feel not just uncomfortable—knowing that they were there in the first place—but unclean as well.

"It's probably not such a good idea to go off exploring on your own," she said.

Never mind that she'd been about to do the same thing herself. But there was a difference, she decided. People might think she was a little spacey sometimes, but Emma—Emma didn't seem to be so much answering the call of the forest that Julianne had heard herself, as being driven to go out into the night. Under the trees. Into the unknown.

From that perspective, it seemed a dangerous, even foolhardy thing to be doing.

"We don't know what's out there," she added, the words sounding lame as she spoke them.

Emma just looked at her for a long moment. Then she said, "You know."

Julianne fell silent. She did know, didn't she? She wanted to go, but she felt it was more important to go to Cal right now, to help him get through what was going to be a bad moment for him, to try to make it something he could look back on with wonder, rather than shame.

"What do you know about trees?" Emma asked suddenly.

Julianne gave her a puzzled look. "What do you want to know?"

"Well, you people—Wicca—you worship them, don't you?"

"Hardly. We respect them."

Julianne's gaze traveled past Emma to the awesome forest that lay beyond the House. The trees called to her still, a bittersweet air that once again sparked her longing to step under their sweeping boughs and partake of their Mystery.

"We listen to them," she added, her voice soft.

Emma nodded, obviously understanding the sense of wonder that the forest had woken in Julianne. But of course she would, Julianne thought. She heard the call too, didn't she?

"So . . . will you give him my message?" Emma asked.

"But Blue . . ." Julianne began.

If she had a relationship with a guy like Blue, she'd want to share this with him. The Mystery. The wonder of it. She couldn't understand that Emma didn't want to share it.

"When you're talking to him," Emma added, "would you also tell him—or Esmeralda, if you see her—that I've finally found the answer." Her eyes took on a dreamy look again. "I'm finally going to find out how to use my gift. . . ."

Julianne wasn't quite sure what that meant so she simply stored it away and tried again to dissuade Emma.

"I don't think that's such a good—"

Julianne broke off as Emma just drifted by her, heading for the forest.

"Emma!"

Emma paused, facing Julianne at the call of her name.

"I'm okay," Emma said. "Honestly, I am. Just give them my message. Please?"

What do I do now? Julianne thought. Try and stop her from going by force? That just wasn't her style.

So helplessly, she watched Emma turn again. In moments, Emma was under the first trees and then the forest accepted her and she was lost from sight.

Julianne looked at the trees for a very long time, wanting to go, wishing Emma hadn't.

"Shit," she said finally.

Sighing, she went back into the House.

7

"The last time we were here I met this shaman," Blue was saying. "A guy named Ur'wen'ta. He's one of Ha'kan'ta's people—the ones that Sara and Tal are staying with. I think we should try to track him down, or maybe we can find some of the other *rath'wen'a*. See, this is their turf and if anybody's going to know what's going down, I figure they're the ones to. . . ."

The ballroom had been steadily filling while he, Esmeralda and Judy talked on the small stage. From time to time, Esmeralda woke music from the piano—a few bars of Chopin, one of of Micheal O

Suilleabhain's keyboard settings of an Irish air and the like—but her fingers were still more often than not. There were almost thirty people gathered on the dance floor. Ginny and Tim had seen about bringing in chairs and benches for them to sit upon. A part of the wall by the door had been converted into a makeshift kitchen by Ohn with plates of sandwiches, teapots with steam curling from their spouts and dozens of mismatching teacups and mugs laid out on a pair of folding tables.

An odd calm had come over most of them—even the poet who'd been so shaken at first, though his earlier panic could still be seen in his eyes, just waiting to spill out. From time to time, one or another would drift to the stage where Blue and the others were talking, but most seemed content to wait, sipping tea and talking among themselves.

Esmeralda let Blue finish talking about the *rath'wen'a* shaman before she spoke. "I don't think that's such a good idea, Blue."

"Have you got a better one?"

Oh, don't go all macho on me, Esmeralda thought.

"How would you begin to find him?" she said.

"I'd . . ."

"There's not just one Otherworld," Esmeralda went on, "but so many that they can't be numbered. They exist on different planes, in different times. . . ."

As she watched his face sag, Esmeralda wished she *did* have a better idea to offer him, but she knew from her own limited experience how bewildering the Otherworld could be.

Tim came up just then, effectively postponing their discussion.

"It looks like everybody's here now," he said. "I think Julianne was the last one we were waiting on."

Esmeralda looked out over the dance floor and was surprised at how many she didn't know. She knew the regular residents, of course, and recognized a lot of the other faces, but she didn't *know* as many of them as she'd thought she would.

I've been doing it again, she thought. Stepping back from life and observing instead of partaking in it. And not even observing it all that well. She should know these people. If they were drawn to the House, then they had something worthwhile to share.

She was disappointed in the realization of how easily she'd fallen back into her old habits. It was so easy to just let her studies swallow all of her time.

"So, are you going to talk to them?" Tim asked.

Esmeralda nodded and turned to Blue.

"You handle this," she began, but then she realized something. She scanned the crowd again, not finding the face she was looking for.

"Emma," she said. She turned to Tim. "Has anyone seen Emma?"

She could sense Blue's immediate tension.

"Jeez," Tim said. "Now that you mention it . . ."

Blue stood up, his chair scraping on the wood floor of the stage. Out on the dance floor, conversation stilled, heads lifted, gazes settled on the group on the stage.

"You said she'd be okay," Blue began, turning to Esmeralda, features clouding with anger.

Judy rose at his side and put a hand on his arm. "She's not Emma's keeper, Blue."

"But—"

"It's not Esmeralda you're mad at," Judy added.

No, Esmeralda thought. He was mad at himself, frustrated with the ups and downs of his relationship with Emma, confused at the new turn it was taking. She wished there were something she could say to make him feel better, but knew that he and Emma had to work this out on their own.

"She just needs some time to herself," she told Blue. "We'll go talk to her after we get done with the business at hand."

"You might want to prepare yourself for a bit of a trek, then."

Esmeralda turned to see that one of the resident Wicca had joined Tim where he was leaning on the edge of the stage. It was she who'd just spoken.

"What do you mean?" Blue demanded.

"I've seen her," Julianne said, taking a step back from Blue's looming presence. "She asked me to pass on a message to you."

Esmeralda's spirits dropped lower as she listened to what Julianne had to pass on. Blue slammed his fist down on the top of the piano, awaking a discordant ring from the instrument's strings. The violent impact startled Esmeralda.

Don't lose it, she wanted to tell him. Not now. We can't afford it.

But her throat couldn't seem to shape the words. She knew the kind of man Blue was—a study in extremes. If you were his friend, you were his friend for life and he'd do anything for you. If you were his enemy, you were unequivocally and forever so. Where he lost it was in the shades of gray: when a friend did something hurtful, or confusing; something that didn't fit in with Blue's perceptions of what the person was.

For one moment she was certain that he was going to do some serious damage to the piano, but then he just leaned on it with both hands and bowed his head.

"I just don't get it," he said, oblivious to the audience that was watching from the dance floor. His troubled gaze turned to Esmeralda. "Why won't she *talk* to me about this kind of thing?"

Esmeralda couldn't answer that. She was surprised when Julianne spoke up.

"Maybe she doesn't know how," Julianne said.

Blue just looked at her for a long moment, then slowly nodded.

"Maybe you're right," he said. "Doesn't make me feel any better, though. She should be able to talk to me about anything—wouldn't you think?"

"Heads up," Tim said before Julianne could answer. "Looks like you can ask her yourself."

He pointed to where the ballroom's doors opened out onto the garden. The slight figure of a woman stood there, hand raised to knock on one of the leaded panes.

But it wasn't Emma.

"Sara!" Blue cried.

He was off the stage and halfway across the ballroom floor before Esmeralda had time to register that it really was Sara. A flicker of uneasiness stirred in Esmeralda. She liked Sara, but as she watched Blue embrace her in a bear hug, she couldn't help but remember the last time she'd seen Jamie's heir. She'd wished more than once in the year since that afternoon that they hadn't had that argument.

It had grown partly from Sara's ambivalent feelings toward Esmeralda—Sara simply couldn't deal with Jamie's ghost, living inside the House; the guilt that woke in her had ended up shifting into a resentment toward Esmeralda for the good relationship that Esmeralda herself had with Jamie. They both knew that Esmeralda had taken Sara's place in the hierarchy of the House—not so much because Esmeralda wanted it, as that Sara didn't.

Esmeralda wasn't sure if Sara ever admitted that to herself. What she did know was that Sara perceived the other half of the problem to be Esmeralda's fault.

"You manipulate people," Sara told her. "It's real subtle, but every time I come back I can see it happening. You give one person a little push here, another one a push there, always for 'their own good.' Maybe they can't see it happening—they're too close to the situation or something—but I can see it and I don't think it's right."

"You're not being entirely fair."

"Yes I am."

Esmeralda had shaken her head. "There's a big difference between giving advice and being manipulative."

"I agree. But the way you give advice makes it seem like it's the other's person's idea and I'd call *that* being manipulative."

"But—"

"I'm not saying that you don't do good; to be really fair, you're usually right, but I think it's the wrong way to go about 'helping' people. It's not honest."

And the way you treat Jamie, Esmeralda had been about to say then. You'd call that honest?

But she'd kept quiet, not wanting to aggravate the situation. Not wanting to talk about it in the House, where Jamie could hear and be hurt by what they all knew was the truth.

"I don't believe in standing back and seeing my friends hurt themselves" was what she had said.

"Sometimes people need to make mistakes."

"I see."

Sara frowned at her. "Look, all I'm saying is if you're going to meddle around with people's heads, at least be up front about it. Give them your advice and then let *them* decide if they want to take it."

They'd left the argument on that note, knowing it wasn't really resolved, but also knowing that any further discussion would merely be repeating things they'd already said.

Remembering the tension that had lain between them when they'd parted, Esmeralda was a little wary as Blue led Sara back to the stage, but Sara just smiled at her as though they'd never had the argument, which made Esmeralda realize that Sara was probably more like Jamie than she'd ever thought. Jamie never held a grudge; once he'd had his say, that was it. Life carried on.

She stepped from the piano bench and sat down on the edge of the stage.

"Hello, Sara," she said. "You've come at an opportune time."

"I'm not so sure—"

"You're Sara?" Tim interrupted.

When Sara nodded, he seemed embarrassed for a moment. "I just thought you'd be older," he added and then realized that he really wasn't making a whole lot of sense.

"You're . . .?" she asked.

"Tim. Tim Gavin. I never seem to be around when you come by, and I just . . . I don't know. . . ."

Esmeralda laid an arm across his shoulders.

"Tim's been taking care of the gardens," she said. "At least he was until all of this started."

"What *is* going on?" Sara asked. "I got the weirdest . . . sending, I suppose you'd call it. . . ."

She took off her pack as she described the hooded man and his message that had brought her back to the House, pulling out the cloak as she spoke.

"That's my cloak," Julianne said. "The one that disappeared from my room this morning."

There was quite a crowd gathered up around the edge of the stage now. Questions started coming at Sara, fast and hard.

"What's out there?"

"Is the city really gone?"

"Where did you come from?"

Esmeralda waited for a moment, giving Blue, or Sara, the opportunity to take charge, but they both turned to her. Esmeralda sighed and held up her hands.

"Let's just all slow down a minute," she said. "Thanks," she added when she finally had everyone's attention.

The various residents and House guests waited expectantly for what she had to say, but she turned to Sara first.

"Sara," she said. "Did you want to freshen up, or maybe have something to eat, before we get into this?"

"Is there any coffee?" Sara asked.

"I can get some," Ohn replied.

"Then let's get to it," Sara said.

8

Julianne, Blue, the House, her past . . . everything fell by the wayside as Emma stepped under the trees. There was just the forest. Trunks like immense spires so that she felt she was walking on the rooftop of some ancient unimaginable city with strange wooden chimney stacks rising up high on all sides of her; boughed branches above like the domed ceiling of an enormous chapel; a reverent silence in the air that spoke not just of mysteries, but of some deep profound secret that, could she ever understand it, would irrevocably change her.

Around her there were trees felled by lightning and disease, but wherever she walked, the way was clear. The ground was springy underfoot, thick with mulch. She thought she heard a flute playing and paused to listen. At first it seemed to come from deeper in the forest, but then she realized that its source lay behind her—back by Tamson House.

She remembered turning to look at the House when she first reached the edge of the forest. By the bright moonlight she saw that its roofs were covered with birds.

Owls.

Birds and House were forgotten once she entered the wood, but the memory of them came back when she heard the flute. And that made her think of Blue and Esmeralda. . . .

She drew in a deep breath, let it slowly out.

For once she felt in control. The forest had called to her, it was true, but answering that call had been *her* choice. It wasn't like Blue

convincing her to get back into her artwork—more by making her
feel guilty because she wasn't doing anything with her life, than
through his support, though that, she knew, was her problem, not
his. He was genuinely supportive. It was just that he always had so
much on the go that she couldn't help but feel guilty around him
because she never seemed to do anything.

And Esmeralda.

She supposed what bothered her the most was how Blue and
Esmeralda were able to invest a sense of importance in whatever
they did—whether it was fixing a bike, making dinner, or looking
up some obscure reference in an even more obscure book. Everything had meaning for them—some things more than others, naturally, but they managed to go through life never having to question
the validity of what they were doing. Or at least that was the
impression they gave.

Emma questioned everything. But the worst thing, to her way
of thinking, was the way she seemed to automatically adjust her
personality depending on who she was with and what kind of
mood they were in. She'd be contemplative with Esmeralda. With
Blue it was split between jockish things like tossing around a
football with him and Judy and some of their buddies, or watching
movies on the VCR that she wasn't even sure she liked, and going
to art galleries or classical concerts at the National Arts Centre.
She'd talk to some of the Pagan Party and want to join them in
their rituals. When she was with Tim there seemed to be nothing
more fulfilling than working in the gardens. . . .

But deep down inside she was never satisfied. She never knew
who she was. Never really believed that anything had meaning,
little say what she did and never mind this "Autumn Gift" she had.

It didn't make her feel special the way Esmeralda seemed to
think it should. It just made her feel confused.

When she was a teenager she'd have given anything to step into
a fantasy world. The odd correspondence relationship in which she
and Esmeralda had participated then, with its poems and drawings
and shared mythologies, had been as perfect a substitute as she
thought either of them would ever get. A kind of foil against the
real world that had, at times, seemed *more* real. But, unlike Es-

meralda, she'd left that world behind. She'd grown up. Matured, she thought, when she reread some of those old letters.

Only to find that the fantasy world was real.

Only to find that there really was something inside her that could reach out to anthropomorphized elements of nature and actually communicate with them. A kind of . . . power that carried with it responsibilities she wasn't ready, or able, to accept; a power for which others were willing to kill.

It scared her so much that all she could do was shut it away and tell herself that it didn't exist. She couldn't talk to trees. She didn't have some healing ability that could make good the wrongs of the world, no matter how small she started.

But while in the real world she could pretend all she wanted that it wasn't real, that it didn't exist and so she certainly had no part in it, it wasn't so easy to do that here. Because here she could lay her hand against the rough bark of a tree's trunk and *feel* it talk to her. A slow, sleepy conversation that wasn't so much communicated by words as directly from the spirit of the tree into her own.

The flute-playing had died away, returning the earlier stillness to the forest, and with that stillness, she found her worries fading just as the music had. She walked on, feeling as though a great weight had been lifted from her heart. Things weren't any clearer—she wasn't *that* changed—but they were no longer so frightening.

Ahead of her the trees opened into a small glen. As she first stepped out onto its thick matted grass she thought there was a dog or a wolf sitting on its haunches at the far side of the glade. She hesitated, her pulse quickening, but then she realized it had just been a trick of the light—her eyes confusing her as she stepped from the shadows under the trees into the brighter moonlight.

There was no dog sitting there. Just a man.

She moved forward again, curious now, caution forgotten.

The man looked up at her approach and she felt a nag of familiarity at his features. There was something about his thinning hair and full beard, coupled with the intensity of his gaze, that had her casting back through her memory trying to remember where she'd met him before. And then she realized that she hadn't. He only looked familiar because of the pictures she'd seen of him on the walls of the Firecat's Room that she shared with Blue.

"You're Jamie Tams," she said.
The man smiled. "So it would seem."

9

Julianne liked the way that Esmeralda could just take control of a situation. While everybody else was milling about, some dazed and confused, others caught by the wonder of the forest but no less perplexed, Esmeralda knew that the first priority was to get them all doing something and *then* they could figure out what was going on. After Sara, sitting close to Blue, had had a chance to tell her story and they'd spent some time discussing how it fit with their own situation, Esmeralda organized work parties, sending them all off in groups of threes and fours to take inventory of their provisions, clean up the areas where the forest had intruded on the House, patrol the halls and the like.

Julianne tried to get paired up with Cal, but he was studiously avoiding her, the shame plain in his face whenever he did glance her way. She wanted to tell him that it was no big deal, but couldn't, because his attitude toward her *had* been a big deal. It might not seem like much on the surface, but it underlay the whole problem she perceived to lie between the sexes and just enforced people's perceptions of each other's roles.

She believed that an awareness of that was the simple truth that had come to Cal in his moment of epiphany. What she didn't understand was how he couldn't see that she'd be willing to forgive and start over again. All his self-recrimination was going to do was embitter him.

She wanted to confront him, to just shake some sense into him so that what he'd learned wouldn't be wasted, but she knew she couldn't do that here. Laying his problems out in front of everyone the way that Blue had stripped his heart bare earlier would only aggravate the situation.

So she let him go, watching him trail after Tim and a couple of the Irish students to inventory Brach's larder in the Penwith Kitchen, then turned to Blue and Judy, with whom she was supposed to check out the garages to see if there'd been any damage done to the House's vehicles, particularly Blue's collection of trail bikes. Growing up with three brothers who were all dirt bike enthusiasts, Julianne knew almost as much about the machines as did either of her companions.

Much of Blue's tension seemed to drop away as he entered what was, for him, familiar territory. But instead of starting on the bikes, he dropped onto the car seat that was bolted to the floor across from his workbench, and laid his head against its back to stare at the ceiling.

"You okay?" Judy asked.

Blue sighed. "I feel like a fool, going on in front of everybody like I did."

Judy pulled up a wooden crate and sat down in front of him.

"Hey, you were worried," she said.

"Blind's more like it. Man, I should have *known* things weren't going well between us." He looked from her to Julianne and shook his head. "Who am I kidding? I did know. I just didn't want to admit it. I mean, I really wanted this to work out—for both of us. So I was trying hard. Being myself instead of trying to fit somebody else's perceptions, supporting what I thought she wanted to do, but giving her space. . . ."

His voice trailed off and he stared at the toes of black cowboy boots.

"Uh, maybe I should go," Julianne said. "Give you guys a chance to talk and everything."

Blue looked up, his gaze locking onto hers.

"A time like this," he said, "I appreciate having my friends around me."

He got hold of a smile from somewhere; it didn't quite reach his eyes, but it was there. Julianne found herself smiling back, trying to keep the wistful way she was feeling out of her own features.

"Okay," she said.

She dragged a battered old wooden chair over to sit beside Judy, turning it so that she could rest her arms on its back. There was a moment's awkward silence.

"You guys are both women," Blue said finally. "You know what you want from a man, right? So tell me, what was I doing wrong?"

Judy laughed. "Jesus," she said. "How're we supposed to know?"

"I'm being serious."

"So am I."

Blue sighed again. "Okay, so that came out wrong—but you know what I mean."

"Maybe you were trying too hard," Julianne said.

A small voice was nagging in the back of her mind, asking her what she was doing. If Emma was out of the picture, then that just left things open for her, didn't it?

But Julianne ignored the voice. She'd rather Blue was happy, period, with Emma or whoever he wanted to be with. The one thing she wasn't interested in doing was taking advantage of an unfortunate situation.

"What do you mean?" Blue asked.

"You know—what you were saying. Giving her space, being supportive—it's like you were handling her with kid gloves, or maybe always standing back to check out that you were doing the right thing."

"She's been through some weird shit."

"I know. But we all go through it, don't we?"

"Not like she went through."

"It doesn't matter," Julianne said. "Say your best friend gets hurt in a car crash and you were driving. That kind of thing just stays with you. Is the way you hold on to that going to be any less than how Emma's dealing with what she went through, or just different?"

"Okay. I see what you mean."

"But the thing of it is," Julianne went on, "is that you've been shielding Emma, protecting her from any kind of a bad scene, right?"

"Well, sure. But what's that got—"

"I get it," Judy said. "It doesn't give her a chance to be strong on her own."

"I was *giving* her space." Blue leaned forward and flipped his hair back over his shoulder. "Man, if I gave her any more space we wouldn't be living together anymore."

"I know," Julianne said. "That's not the answer. It's just that you've got so much *presence,* Blue—"

Judy nodded in agreement.

"—that it might have been hard for her to ever feel like she actually had any space of her own." She smiled to take the sting out of what she was saying. "When you're in the House, I always know where you are."

"What—I'm too loud or something?"

"What Julianne's trying to tell you," Judy said, "is that when you're around, everybody's aware of it. Not 'cause you're loud, or pushy or any of that kind of crap. It's because you're you. You know what you want and you go for it. You're not"—she smiled, then corrected herself—"you're *usually* not confused about anything."

"So I've got to be different?"

Julianne shook her head. "It's Emma who's got to work things out. But that leaves you with the hard part. You've got to be there for her, but you've also got to be patient and give her time to see it all through."

"It's a shitty deal," Judy said.

Blue nodded slowly. "Tell me about it." He turned back to Julianne. "So I should just let her do her thing in the forest?"

"She'll be okay," Julianne said. "Haven't you *felt* those trees, their magic . . . their wonder?"

Blue closed his eyes for a moment and Julianne wondered if he was reaching out to the forest. Even in here, with no window to look out, she could feel its presence herself. The Mystery whispered to her, making the spark that was nestled inside her flicker and glow.

"Yeah. I can feel it," he said. "But I've learned that there's two kinds of wonder: the kind that heals and the kind that hurts. That forest . . ."

His voice trailed off. Judy looked from Blue to Julianne.

"You think it's dangerous?" she asked.

Julianne had thought that of all of them, except perhaps for Esmeralda, Judy was handling this the best, but she heard now the anxiety underlying the smaller woman's voice.

"I don't sense any danger," Julianne said.

"Well, I guess you'd know," Blue said.

"Because I'm one of the kids in the Pagan Party?"

Blue looked embarrassed. "You're just more in touch with this kind of thing."

"He thinks you're their momma," Judy added, regaining her own humor as Blue's neck got redder.

"I know," Julianne said. "I'm still trying to figure out if that's a compliment or not."

"You know I'm not cutting you down," Blue said.

Julianne nodded.

"It's just," Blue went on, "that the last time the House went on a vacation like this we didn't exactly have a fun time."

"Does the man have a way with words or what?" Judy asked.

Blue just shook his head. "Man." He rubbed his face with his hands, then looked up at the pair of them. "What say we check out the bikes like we got sent here to do?"

"If we do go out scouting," Judy said as they all got up, "we can look for Emma, too. Hell, with the way you keep your engines tuned, Blue, she'll be able to hear us coming even if she's in the next county." She turned to Julianne. "Do they have counties in this place, do you think?"

"Oh, sure," Julianne said. "Counties, townships, the whole works. Everything'll be laid out nice and orderly for us."

Julianne glanced back to see Blue still standing by the bolted-down car seat. She could see that he was making an effort to stop worrying, but his smile still didn't reach his eyes. Judy followed Julianne's gaze with her own.

"What are you?" Judy asked Blue. "The supervisor?"

Blue shook his head. "No. I was just wondering why neither of you came with a mute button."

"Cute," Judy said as she crouched down beside the engine of the nearest bike to check its distributor cap. "Real cute. Reminds me of this guy I met in the LaFayette one night. He was just as witty as you, Blue—at least he was until I took him out back and thumped him."

"You didn't," Julianne said.

"Get this," Judy went on. "Guy called himself the Porker. . . ."

10

"Everybody's looking for you," Emma said.

Her momentary fear at coming across the man had vanished now that she knew who he was. She sat down on the grass in front of him and regarded him with a frank curiosity that he didn't seem to mind.

So this was Jamie Tams, she thought.

She'd been hearing about him from Blue and Esmeralda ever since she'd moved to the House. Now, finally, she was getting the chance to meet him.

That he had died some seven years ago didn't seem odd. Not in this place. Not in this forest. Not after having been aware of his presence in the House for the past couple of years. What was odd was finally seeing him in the flesh, one hand stroking his beard, the intensity of his gaze lightened by a flickering twinkle that lay in the back of his gray eyes.

"People are always looking for me," he said. "And then, when they find me, they're not always pleased."

Emma smiled. "I'm not scared," she said. "Blue's told me all about you. He said you can get spacey, but you're certainly not dangerous."

"It's not that I'm a physical threat," he said.

I guess not, Emma thought, taking in his small frame. He looked to be in his fifties and though he didn't seem particularly frail, he wasn't exactly Arnold Schwarzenegger either.

"Then what is it about you that bothers people?" she asked.

"I tell them things they don't want to hear."

"Like . . . ?"

He smiled. "Through what you perceive to be a quirk of fate, but which was, in fact, inevitable, you acquired a gift that allows you communion with what most would believe to be the supernatural. Though there are many who hunger desperately for such a gift, you deny it. You have been shown, not once but many times, how it can not only enrich your life, but allow you the opportunity to leave the world a better place than it was when you were born into it, yet you refuse it."

Emma shifted uncomfortably as he spoke. The hint of humor had disappeared from his eyes. His gaze seemed to impale her with its ferocity.

"I . . ." she began.

"Your attitude bespeaks not only immaturity, but a grave irresponsibility. What you do belittles not only you, but the gift itself."

What he was saying struck too close to home.

"I don't even know what it is," she said. "I don't understand it!"

He had absolutely no sympathy for her.

"You haven't tried to learn."

"But I have. It's just that whenever I talk to Esmeralda about it, my head starts to spin and I get sick to my stomach."

"That's only fear," he said.

"I'm not like you and her," Emma said. "I don't get off on all of this weird stuff. I didn't ask for anybody to give me anything."

He shook his head. "That's not true. You called to the spirits of this world, time and again; you walked in the forest and spoke their names. Season by season, you paid homage to mysteries, great and small."

Emma looked at him like he was insane, but then she realized what he was talking about. It was when she was in her teens. When she and Esmeralda were corresponding. When the well of creativity that first started her drawing seemed bottomless and the sketches and paintings came alive under her fingers with almost no conscious effort or thought.

She used to walk in the woods and fields around her parents' house and literally talk to the trees as though they could understand her. She'd feel the touch of a breeze on her cheek and call out a greeting to Esmeralda, for wasn't Esmeralda the Westlin Wind, just as she was the Lady of Autumn, who carried the heart of the season in her breast?

"I was just a kid then," she said.

"The spirits don't judge a being by its age, only by its integrity."

"You're not being fair!" Emma told him. She was only just holding back tears. "I'm not a dishonest person."

But he only looked at her.

"I'm not."

"You share your feelings with others?" he asked. "You don't hurt those you love with your silences?"

"I . . . I . . ."

The torrent broke from inside her. She wept, head bowed, face in her hands. He made no move to comfort her, only waited until the tears ebbed, the torrent subsided.

"I . . . try . . ." she finally said in a small voice.

She looked up and saw, through a tear-blurred gaze, that he was grinning at her.

"Do you see?" he asked.

"See?"

"What I meant. No one likes to hear what I have to say."

Anger arose like a dark cloud in her at the smug tone of his voice.

"You bastard!" she cried, her voice still husky from her tears. "This is all some big joke to you, isn't it?"

"To ignore humor is to view the world with only one eye."

"You're not Jamie. You're not at all like Blue said you were."

His features went suddenly serious. "Understand this, Emma Fenn. The Otherworld changes people. Without a strong sense of self, or of purpose, it will transform you into your deepest desires or fears."

It wasn't so much what he said as how he said it that cut through Emma's anger, eroding its hold on her. An uneasy feeling stole through her.

"What do you mean?" she asked.

"Half the world is night," he told her. "Do you understand what I mean by that?"

Emma nodded. "That's because of the way the earth turns on its axis. It's always night somewhere. . . ."

Her voice trailed off as he shook his head.

"No. It's nothing so simple, yet it's the most basic truth you could ever learn. A hard truth." He tapped his chest. "Inside us lies every possibility that is available to a sentient being. Every darkness, every light. It is the choices we make that decide who or what we will be.

"On your world, they speak of one's environment, how it affects individuals in their formative years. Your family, your friends, your social standing, your schooling . . . they all shape and mold you into the person that you become. By the time you gain an awareness of the process, you've already *become* who you will be. It's only those with a great strength of will, and a vigorous awareness of self, who can change themselves.

"Do you follow me so far?"

Emma slowly nodded.

"In the Otherworld, this is accentuated. If they abide here too long, the weak-willed go mad; even a strong personality can have his or her strengths undermined, can be made weak and so be affected."

"I don't understand why you're telling me this."

"I've a twofold purpose," he replied. "The first is to warn you that you and those who have come with you to this realm are in danger—from themselves as much as from the influences of the Otherworld. The second is to explain what it is that makes your gift so important. Because of the understanding—the insight—that it allows you, you are capable of helping those who turned to the night by showing them their options. Not in words, not by long tedious explanations or manipulations, but by simply making them aware."

"But the trees . . ." Emma began.

They didn't talk to her about this. They simply whispered a sense of mystery to her.

"Places can be affected in a similar fashion. Have you never felt uncomfortable for no good reason in one place, yet perfectly fine in another?"

She nodded, waiting for him to go on, but he fell silent once more.

"So," she said finally. "I'm supposed to be some kind of do-gooder, running around saving people and places from themselves? Is that what you're saying?"

He shook his head. "No. You are a vessel into which the potential to help has been poured. No one—no person of your world, no spirit of this world—can make you be what you're not or what you don't wish to be."

Emma sighed. "I . . . I'm just not much good at that kind of thing. My own life is screwed up enough without my thinking I can tell people how to live theirs."

"It isn't necessary for you to confront each person on an individual basis. Can you remember how you felt when you *were* communicating through your artwork? Not just the sense of completion, but the sense of rightness—the sense that you had brought to life something that could live beyond your sphere of being, that held in it far more potential than you ever realized you were imbuing in the work?"

Emma shifted uncomfortably. It had been so long since she'd felt good about anything she did. But thinking back to those days, she could remember—not so much what she had lost, as that she had lost . . . something.

"Vaguely," she said finally.

"And were you ever moved or changed by the creative work of another?"

"Oh, sure. But—" She paused. "I see."

"Good."

"And the places?" she asked then.

"You can only do what you can when you find yourself in a place that requires your help."

"I still don't think I can do it."

He smiled. "You don't have to."

Emma just looked at him. After this huge pep talk in which she'd learned far more about the Autumn Gift than she'd ever thought she could—learned and not been scared of the knowledge—he was now telling her that none of it mattered?

"I don't get it," she said.

"You can leave it behind—here in the Otherworld. Return it to those who gifted you with it in the first place."

Emma looked at the cathedraling trees that encircled the glen and wondered if he meant them.

"Just like that?" she asked.

"No. But I could show you. It's not an entirely . . . arduous procedure."

Emma's eyes narrowed, suspicion flaring in her. There'd been those who'd tried to tear the gift from her. Was he just trying a different approach to reach the same goal?

"What's in it for you?" she asked, wondering why she even cared.

Because wasn't this what she wanted—to be free of the damned thing? To be free of influences—the gifts, those of the people around her. . . .

"I want nothing from you," he said, then added, "no, that's not entirely true. I do require your help, but in an unrelated matter."

"Which is?"

"Tamson House. It needs rescuing."

Emma looked at him, not sure she'd heard him correctly. "Come again?"

"Tamson House stands at a crossroads between the worlds. It is our entrance to your world, your entrance to ours. There are very few such places still extant in your world, and fewer still so . . . pure. Why do you think it is the gathering place of so many creative individuals?"

That was true, Emma thought. She might not get much inspiration in it, but it certainly drew more than its share of artists, musicians and writers, not to mention those who were interested in the paranormal or the old-religion people that Blue called the Pagan Party.

"There is a certain man in your world," he went on, "who . . . covets the House's power. He has been sick for a very long time—a special kind of sickness: other people simply don't exist in his worldview. He isn't alone in this illness, but in him it has become an art in amorality. He means to use the power of the House to rejuvenate himself."

"But isn't that kind of what everybody does there?" Emma said. "Esmeralda always talks about how it's a haven, that it gives people a chance to open themselves up that they'd never get outside its walls and then the House fills them with its energy."

"True, but they return as much as they take. This man will take it all and give nothing back. When he is done, Tamson House will be a building like any other—a little larger perhaps, but it will have lost its bond with the Mystery. And the man—an amoral such as he will be capable of great harm once he has taken the potency of Tamson House's spirit into his own.

"Normally the House's guardian is there to deal with such a

situation. Tamson House is not a place which suffers the mean-spirited lightly."

That much Emma knew. She'd overheard more than once in its halls people talking about how the House seemed to take care of itself. Bad things just didn't seem to happen in it. She'd even felt a sense of that herself, though she'd never really thought about it until just this moment.

"With the House's guardian gone," her companion went on, "the House lies helpless. And this man . . . he has already begun to feed."

Something bothered Emma about what he was telling her, but she couldn't quite put her finger on it.

"You must find a way back to where the House stands in your world; then you must find and stop this man."

That brought her out of her reverie.

"What—me?"

He shrugged. "Whoever will do it. Your friend Blue perhaps?"

"Why don't you do it your—" she began, but then she had it. Now she knew what had been troubling her. "You're supposed to be the guardian," she went on. "Why don't you just stop it?"

"I can't get through. I've tried. The man was expecting my interference and set up certain . . . safeguards to ensure that I would be unable to stop him."

Emma studied him for a long moment. "You're not Jamie Tams," she said.

This time she spoke from logic, rather than anger.

"I never said I was."

"But you never said you weren't either. And you look just like him."

"I wanted to appear in a shape that would seem nonthreatening to you, yet one you might also hear out."

"So what do you really look like?" she asked, not really sure she wanted to know.

"That's not important."

"Okay. Just tell me who you are."

"Someone you wouldn't trust if you knew."

"I don't trust you now."

"You'd trust me less if you had my name," he said.

"But you still expect me to help you?"

"You're not just helping me; you'll be helping yourself . . . and your friends."

"How do I know that?"

The only answer he gave was a shrug. She tried to stare him down, but he returned her gaze with just a hint of laughter in the back of his eyes. The worst thing about all of this, she realized, was that—God knew why—but she *did* trust him. Maybe it was because he'd managed to articulate things for her that she'd never been able to grasp before. Esmeralda had tried often enough, but for some reason, the words just weren't there for her to use.

"I'll have to talk to the others," she said finally.

He nodded. "Just remember, time's running out. Every hour you stay here is that much more dangerous for many of those who accompanied you to this place. And every hour, our enemy grows stronger."

"Okay. But I still have to talk to the others."

"Do what you must."

"What's this man's name?"

"I don't know."

"Well, where can we find him?"

"I don't *know*. If I could track him, I could reach him, and if I could reach him"—a feral hunger woke in his eyes—"this conversation would be unnecessary."

"Except for what you told me about the gift," Emma said.

His eyes softened. "Except for that. After, when all of this is done, we will speak of that again. If you choose to leave it here, I *can* help you."

"But you won't tell me what you get out of helping me."

"Not the gift at any rate," he told her. Laughter spoke in his eyes once more. "I don't need it. After all, I'm part of what gifted you in the first place."

"You're—"

"Look!" he cried suddenly, pointing in alarm at the forest behind her.

There's nothing there, she told herself. It's just some stupid trick. But she couldn't help looking all the same. When she turned back, she was alone in the glade.

She scrambled to her feet, turning wildly to look in all directions, but he was really gone. That quick. That supernaturally quick.

A shiver of dread crawled up her spine.

Well, what did you expect? she asked herself. In this place, being what he said he was.

I'm part of what gifted you in the first place.

Was that true? Was any of what he'd told her true?

Too much of it, she realized.

The Otherworld changes people. Without a strong sense of self, or of purpose, it will transform you into your deepest desires or fears.

She took a moment to get her bearings and then hurried back to the House. Passing through the trees, this time she barely noticed them except as obstacles in her way.

11

"He's really gone, isn't he?" Sara said, looking at the rolltop desk that housed the mainframe of Jamie's computer.

Although the Postman's Room had become Esmeralda's study and contained the clutter of her work on the desk and side tables, in the stacks of books and papers leaning up against the bookcases, no matter where Sara looked, she was reminded of Jamie. Especially familiar was the old-man hum of the computer, clearing its throat as it searched through its disk drives. She remembered Jamie's name for it, remembered all his names. Memoria for the computer. Aenigma for his files. Arcanology for his studies.

Oh, Jamie, she thought.

A tight feeling grabbed her chest and she had to wipe at her eyes with the sleeve of her sweater. From beside her, in the twin to the club chair in which she was sitting, Esmeralda reached out a hand and laid it gently on Sara's shoulder. Ohn sat on his haunches, his back leaning against a bookcase. Ginny was at the desk, frowning as she worked the keyboard.

"There's no sense of his presence anywhere in the House," Esmeralda said. "God knows, I've searched for some trace of him, but it's as though he never came back."

Died, Sara thought. And then came back. But what was it that had come back? Not really Jamie, she'd believed. There had always been a ghost in the house, a spirit living in it, looking after things like the Hobberdy Dick from that Briggs story that she'd loved as a little girl. She hadn't been able to believe it was Jamie, until now. Now that he was gone.

"But did he leave voluntarily, or was he coerced into doing so?" Ohn asked.

"I'd say voluntarily," Esmeralda said. "He'd been talking for some time of finding a way to visit the Otherworlds. I just don't think he realized what would happen if he deserted the House."

Like I deserted him, Sara thought.

"You believe it followed him?" Ohn asked.

Esmeralda nodded. "The House must have been drawn into the backwash of his departure. At that point he would have realized that something was wrong, but it seems that there was nothing he could do about it. The Weirdin he left on the screen, the cloak he sent to Sara . . . these were all he could do to warn us of the danger."

Ginny looked away from the computer screen to study the two of them.

"What are you talking about?" she asked.

"Jamie Tams," Esmeralda said. "The previous owner of the House."

"But he's supposed to be dead. You're speaking of him as though he were still alive."

"He was," Esmeralda said. "In a way. His spirit lived in the House; it spoke to us through Memoria."

Ginny looked at the computer where the Weirdin symbol still flickered on the screen.

"I always thought that was just the way you spoke about your software," she said slowly. "I never took it literally. The way everything here has its own name. . . ."

"Jamie was real," Esmeralda said. "More real than many people who have a body to carry them around in the world."

Sara shivered. She watched Ginny study Esmeralda's features, looking for the joke that wasn't there.

"I . . ." Ginny began; then she shook her head and turned back to the computer. "Never mind," she added and began to work the keys again.

"How can we . . . find him?" Sara asked.

The look in Esmeralda's eyes lacked her usual confidence.

"I don't know," she said. "He could be anywhere. The Otherworlds are scattered through so many temporal as well as spatial layers that I can't think where to begin. I reach for him—for that individual essence that sets him apart from everyone else—but it's like he's everywhere. Or nowhere."

"While each moment we stay here, our danger increases," Ohn added.

Sara nodded. She knew that much about the Otherworld. To those unprepared for the potency of its mysteries, the Otherworld was less a place of marvels than a source for madness. It wasn't simply the imagination of storytellers that was the source for all those tales of mortals straying into Faerie coming back as either poets or mad.

"Like the boar that attacked me?" she asked. "Or those *memegwesi* that Tim and I saw in the garden?"

"The bodachs," Esmeralda said. "They themselves won't do us any harm unless we begin to believe their illusions. But the boar . . ." She rubbed wearily at her eyes. "We're like a disease, insofar as the Otherworld is concerned. Continuing with that analogy, the boar is an antibody, trying to expel us from the Otherworld's body. The longer we stay here, the more potent its defenses will become until we're finally gone.

"It wouldn't be so bad if there were just a few of us—but we've the House itself and close to forty people, most of whom aren't in the least bit prepared for what they're undergoing. . . ."

"We were here before," Sara said. "The House and a bunch of people."

"But you had a protector in the House then," Ohn said. "This time we're on our own."

"If we could find Jamie," Esmeralda began.

"I've got something!" Ginny called.

They crowded around the computer to see images of the Weirdin symbols flickering rapidly across the screen. Sara tried to pick them out, but they were going by too fast for her to focus on any single one of them.

"It's like that story about the *I Ching*," Esmeralda said, speaking more to herself.

"What's that?" Sara asked.

"Someone was supposed to have asked the book to define itself. In response, it gave back six moving lines when the yarrow stalks were thrown."

"Which means?" Ginny asked, a half breath before Sara spoke.

"If you follow the moving lines through in their proper progression," Esmeralda explained, "it gives you all sixty-four hexagrams—the entire *I Ching*. That's what we're seeing here. All of the Weirdin, every disc."

"But—"

"Shhh. Let me concentrate."

Esmeralda closed her eyes. The light from the screen flickered on her face, waking strange shadows that were here, gone again, there. Sara could feel something like a static charge building up in the room. A breeze seemed to have sprung up, although there was no window open.

"Got . . . something . . ." Esmeralda said.

"Take care," Ohn told her, but Sara could tell that Esmeralda hadn't heard him.

Esmeralda turned from the screen and took two steps into the center of the room.

"It's closer," she said. "I've almost . . ."

The breeze turned into a sudden wind, spinning paper from the desk and tossing Esmeralda's long hair about her shoulders. She took another step and then it was as though she'd stepped behind an invisible wall. There was a slight sound of air being displaced, then the wind was gone.

And so was Esmeralda.

Ginny stared open-mouthed at where Esmeralda had vanished. Sara was almost as surprised, for all that she was used to the abrupt magical appearances and disappearances of Pukwudji and his kin. Only Ohn seemed calm.

"*Goath an Iar,*" he murmured.

Sara automatically translated the Gaelic words into English. The first time she'd met Tal he'd given her the gift of tongues. Westlin Wind, Ohn had named Esmeralda. Now she understood that mercurial feyness that she had always sensed around Esmeralda. She was like the little mysteries of the Otherworld, an air spirit with the secret of the wind hidden in her breast.

"I fear for her," Ohn added.

With a vague sense of surprise, Sara knew that she did too. Somewhere between the argument they'd had when they'd parted a year ago and this moment, she realized that while perhaps she didn't exactly like this woman who'd assumed all of the responsibilities that Sara should have herself, she did admire Esmeralda.

"Does she know her way around?" Sara asked, thinking of how easily she'd lost herself in getting here.

Ohn nodded. "I believe that she is as at home in the Otherworlds as she is in her own, but I doubt that all the knowledge in either will be enough."

"Why? What do you know?"

Ohn turned to look at her. "Esmeralda is like your Jamie was: she collects knowledge and lore and seeks to understand the worlds better through both. Her strength is in how she can open roads for others—both physical roads, and pathways of the mind and spirit. She has no power of her own."

"You call vanishing like she did having no power?" Ginny asked.

It was obvious from the tone of her voice that she was still having trouble assimilating what she'd just seen.

"There are two kinds of magic," Ohn said. "One involves personal abilities, such as how Esmeralda can step between the worlds and her gift of vision which allows her to see beyond the physical to the heart of a matter so that she *knows* its essence. The other is more complex as it involves the actual manipulation of matter, the ability to impose one's will upon an object or another being and transform it.

"I sense the hand of an adept skilled in the latter art involved in all of this."

Sara and Ginny were still mulling that over when Emma came bursting in through the study door.

"Where's Esmeralda?" she asked. "I've got to talk to her. I know what's going on."

Wonderful, Sara thought. Why couldn't Emma have shown up five minutes earlier?

"Your timing's the pits," she said.

The Oldest War

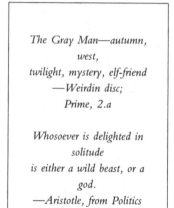

The Gray Man—autumn,
west,
twilight, mystery, elf-friend
—Weirdin disc;
Prime, 2.a

Whosoever is delighted in
solitude
is either a wild beast, or a
god.
—Aristotle, from Politics

1

She knew, Cal thought every time Julianne looked at him. She knew exactly what had happened to him.

He could tell that she wanted to talk to him about it, but that was something he just couldn't handle. Every time he thought about how he'd been treating her, his shame rose like a tidal wave inside him, making it impossible to breathe. It was as though she'd caught him masturbating with a picture of her in his free hand, which, in a way, was exactly what he had been doing. Not physically, perhaps, but it really didn't make much difference, did it? He'd still been doing it.

How was he ever supposed to face her again?

If they ever got out of this weird forest, the first thing he was going to do was pack up and move his things out of the House. Maybe he'd even move out of the city.

"You okay?"

He started at Tim's voice, then realized that he'd been standing at a cupboard, staring at the ranks of canned soups, pad in one hand, pencil immobile in the other. He was supposed to be taking inventory with Tim and the two Irish students, but he hadn't written a thing down in five minutes.

"Yeah," he said. "Just dandy."

Before Tim could continue the conversation, Cal got busy tallying cans of soup. He gave a sigh of relief as Tim turned away and went back to his own counting, but it wasn't long before his concentration drifted again.

Man, he thought. For a gourmet cook, Brach sure stocked a full larder of canned goods. He could understand the dry goods—flour, teas and coffees, spices—but he'd always thought that real hotshot chefs preferred fresh vegetables, pasta and the like to the canned and packaged varieties. You'd think—

A thump on the door close to where he was standing brought him back to his surroundings once more.

"What—?" he began.

A heavy grunting on the far side of the door—followed by a second, louder thump that made the wooden panels shudder—cut him off. Tim rose up from the floor cupboard he'd been investigating. The Irish students stepped out of the pantry.

The Penwith Kitchen, like the Silkwater on the far side of the House, looked out onto the garden, which was completely enclosed by the House. There shouldn't be anybody out there, Cal thought as the door took another blow. This time one of the panels cracked. The grunting was louder—angry. A fourth blow knocked out the cracked panel and then they could all see the snout of the wild boar that was attempting to break in.

"Jesus!" Tim said.

Seeing them, the boar went into a frenzy, battering the door, hooves scrabbling on the porch outside. Tim gave one of the students a push down the hall that led deeper into the House.

"Get out of here!" he cried. "C'mon—*move!*"

The other student hurried to follow. Tim tugged on Cal's arm, but Cal hardly felt the touch. He was transfixed by the boar's fury as it fought to widen the hole it had broken in the door. The creature's enraged gaze settled on him.

That should have been Julianne's reaction, he thought. She should have been angry with him, she should have hated him for the lie he'd held between them. Instead, she'd forgiven him. He'd seen it in her eyes.

How the hell could anybody be that compassionate?

Maybe he should just let the boar—

"Have you got a death wish or something, Townsend?" Tim asked.

His grip tightened on Cal's arm. Without giving Cal the chance to protest, he hauled him out of the kitchen and slammed the door shut.

"Shit," Tim said. "If it can get through that outside door, this isn't going to hold it back at all."

Cal finally focused on his companions. He shivered as he realized what he'd been thinking. Letting the boar attack him—that was just being crazy.

"We've got to warn the others," one of the students said.

Tim nodded. "And get Blue to haul out some of his artillery."

They could still hear the boar worrying at the door. There was the sound of tearing wood, a heavy snorting, bangs as it threw its immense body against the breaking wood.

"Let's *go!*" Tim cried.

He started off down the hall at a run. The students followed. Cal hesitated for a long moment. He listened to the boar's fury and tried to understand what had gotten into him back there in the kitchen. Then he heard the door leading into the garden give way and he bolted after the others. Vaguely he heard a sharp report from the other side of the House—like the backfire of a car, or a gun being fired—but he was in too much of a hurry to give it more than a passing thought.

Blue had already broken out the artillery. He kept his old Winchester and a 12-gauge pump-action Remington shotgun for himself, passing along another pair of shotguns, a Marlin lever-action

.22 and a Browning single-shot rifle to those who were taking the first patrol through the House's corridors.

Ohn had been teamed with a sculptor named Sean Byrne—a huge, strapping man with features as roughly chiseled as his art was in its initial stages. He carried one of Blue's shotguns cradled in his arms as the two of them patrolled the long hallway that ran along the north side of the house. Ohn had refused Blue's offer of a weapon himself, holding up the claw of his hand when Blue tried to argue with him.

"Christ," Blue had said, "I wasn't thinking. . . ."

Ohn had simply laid his good hand on Blue's shoulder, giving him a squeeze before he followed Sean out on their patrol.

"Some weird scene," Sean said as they reached the door to the Library and were about to start back.

Ohn nodded. He paused to look at the jungle of vegetation that had overtaken Ginny's workplace. There were rustlings in the undergrowth that lay thick against the bookshelves, twitterings and small rappings against the glass display shelves.

"Makes you wonder," Sean went on.

Ohn wondered constantly, about so much that it couldn't possibly all be catalogued. But that was what the Mysteries did: they made one question and wonder. Ohn didn't believe that they existed for that purpose; the Mysteries simply were. If anything, perhaps man had been created to question them and wonder.

"And where does your wondering take you?" he asked his companion.

Sean shrugged. He shifted the shotgun from the crook of his arm so that its barrels lay against his shoulder.

"Well," he said. "You hear about things like this all the time— UFO abductions, Bigfoot, all that weird stuff—and you have to just laugh at it. You see those hokey faked-up pictures they run in the supermarket tabloids. . . . That's what'd happen if we went to anyone with this story. It would sound just as phony. Except it's real."

Ohn's gaze drifted back to the wild thickets that had taken over the Library.

"Indeed," he said.

"So it makes me wonder," Sean said. "How much of that stuff I used to laugh at—how much of *it* was real?"

"One marvel does not necessarily beget another," Ohn replied. "I don't doubt that some of what you speak of was real, but logic dictates that it can't all be so."

"You can say that, even looking at all of this?" Sean asked, waving a hand at the Library. "Even being where we are?"

"Perhaps especially so," Ohn replied. "There is a great world of difference between Mystery and nonsense, between glamour and fantasy. What we are experiencing will remain with us forever— that is part of its gift to us. It changes us." He tapped his chest. "Here, within—where it matters.

"Those others—the ones that are written up in the broadsheets of which you spoke—their lives don't seem changed to me. The only difference it has made in their lives is that it brought them some momentary fame; their neighbors regard them with either sympathy or mockery, but they learned nothing from their experiences. They weren't changed." He turned to look at his companion. "How can anyone experience this and *not* be changed—irrevocably so?"

"People react differently to things," Sean said. "Just because they don't seem changed doesn't mean that what they saw or felt wasn't real."

"Granted," Ohn said. "But in my experience, it's best to simply keep an open mind and—"

He broke off at the sudden clatter of hoofbeats that came from the hallway that ran along the south side of the House. Both men stepped from the doorway of the Library. As Sean brought the butt of the shotgun to his shoulder, a stag came around the corner of the hall into their view. Its hooves slid on the floor, digging long runnels into the hardwood's finish; then it bounded toward them.

It was a beautiful beast, Ohn thought, with at least twelve tines per antler. A majestic stag, loosed from the wood to find itself lost in the House like a stray thought.

He started to draw back into the Library, out of the creature's way, when he realized that Sean was about to fire.

"No!" he cried, pushing the barrel of the gun up into the air just as Sean pulled the trigger.

The roar of the shotgun was deafening. Off-balanced as Sean was, the kick of the weapon tumbled him to the floor. The stag tried to stop, legs scrabbling, hooves sliding, dignity stolen as it sought purchase on the smooth floor. It bumped against the wall, its antlers striking the doorframe not three inches from Ohn's head.

Ohn ducked as the wood splintered. His own sense of balance was all awry from the ringing in his ears. He leaned against the doorframe, watching as the stag slid to a stop a few yards farther down the hall. It turned panicked eyes in his direction for one long moment; then it fled off down the hall.

"Jesus," Sean said, picking himself up from the floor. "What'd you do that for? It could've killed us."

"It wasn't trying to hurt us," Ohn said. "It was just scared."

"Scared. Right. What the hell was it *doing* in here?"

"It didn't want to be here any more than we do," Ohn replied. "It's the forest—it's growing stronger."

"What do you mean?"

"I'm not sure how to explain. I just know that the longer we stay here, intruding on the forest, the more perilous it will become for us." He turned to Sean. "We don't belong here, you see—not the House, not so many of us, all at once. Our presence here angers the forest and its anger is transmitted to the creatures that inhabit its reaches, spreading panic and fear and anger among them.

"They don't mean to hurt us, but they will."

"We'd better get back and tell the others," Sean said.

Ohn nodded. "Though I don't doubt that they are already aware."

His gazed returned to the jungle that the Library now held. He thought of Jamie's spirit lost and of Esmeralda gone in search of it. His fear for her safety—a fear which had lain heavy in his thoughts since the moment she'd vanished from the Postman's Room—grew into a sharp blade of pain.

She will survive, he told himself. She had to.

He gave the interior of the Library a last look, then hurried after Sean.

Judy didn't like guns but considering their present situation, not having one seemed a worse proposition than carrying one, so she found herself hauling around one of Blue's rifles. Knowing her luck, she'd probably shoot herself in the foot with it.

"It's just a twenty-two, so it doesn't have too much of a kick," he assured her. "But it doesn't have that much stopping power either, so don't go getting cocky."

"I'll leave that for you he-man types," she told him.

Blue had seemed surprised at how few of those trapped with them in the Otherworld had any experience with weapons. There was a guy named Willie McLoughlin who was one of the Pagan Party, the sculptor Sean and—this surprised Judy the most—one of the poets, John Haven, reed-thin and the softest-spoken of the bunch of them. She figured Julianne could probably handle one too, what with having a handful of brothers and the way she knew her way around the dirt bikes, but Julianne never spoke up.

"When I was a kid, everybody had a BB gun," Blue had said, "and you just waited for the day you got your first twenty-two."

"The closest I ever got was a GI Joe doll," Judy told him. "I got him for the accessories—you know, the jeep and stuff."

Blue just nodded, then said, "If you're going to go out on patrol, I'd rather you carried one."

So she'd taken it, never saying anything about Ohn not having to lug one of the ugly things around. She just hoped she didn't have to use it.

Her partner as she patrolled the second floor was Willie. He looked like a bit of a space cadet, she'd thought at first. He was wearing one of those collarless Indian cotton shirts and baggy cotton pants, with a couple of strands of beads and a little leather pouch that had who knew what inside dangling from his neck. His hair was almost as long as Blue's but he didn't tie it back, and he had one of those goatees that drove Judy nuts. They always made her think of B-movie villains.

But if he looked a bit spacey, he didn't act it. And he carried his shotgun with an easy familiarity that made Judy feel a bit more confident than she would have if all of their protection had relied solely upon her.

They were on their way back to the Postman's Room, when they heard the dull boom of a firearm being fired almost directly below them. She turned from the doorway that they'd been about to enter and looked nervously down the hall to where she could see a set of stairs leading down.

"What the hell do you think *that* was?" she asked, her hands getting sweaty where they gripped the rifle.

Willie had gone ahead into the room. When he replied, it wasn't to answer her question.

"Look at this," he said. His voice sounded strained.

She backed up to the doorway until she could look in but still see down the hall just by turning her head.

"Look at what . . .?" she began, but then she saw what he was talking about and her throat got suddenly dry and just closed up on her.

The window to the room stood open; the room itself was full of owls. They perched on the backs of chairs and on lamp stands, on dressers, the headboard of the bed, the windowsill and the window itself. The latter swung back and forth with two of the wide-eyed creatures sitting on it, their heads swiveling so that while their bodies moved back and forth, their gazes remained fixed on her and Willie.

"Suh," Judy said. She cleared her throat and tried again. "Sara said something about owls. . . ."

One rose suddenly and flew straight for them. Willie ducked and Judy backpedaled out of the way as the bird swooped past them, then sailed off down the hallway. In moments the rest of the birds were in flight. The air was filled with the sound of their wings as they rose one by one from their perches and flew into the hall. There they split up, some going down the hallway in one direction, some the other.

"This is too freaky," Judy said.

She leaned weakly against the wall, the gun clutched against her chest. She wasn't even aware that she was still holding it.

"We'd better tell Blue," Willie said.

"I think they're going to get to him before we can," Judy said.

She pushed away from the wall and went into the room. Laying her rifle on the bed, she walked to the window and gingerly looked out. In the darkness she could just vaguely make out the looming presence of the forest. Shivering, she shut the window and bolted it.

"Maybe we should leave it open," Willie said. At Judy's raised eyebrows, he added, "So they'll have a way to get out."

"And then something else'll have a way in."

"I didn't think of that."

Judy picked up the rifle. "Let's just get back."

Willie stared at the closed window, then nodded. Side by side, starting at each natural creak and groan the House made, they followed the owls back to the east side of the House.

John Haven stood at the window, rifle held in one hand, its muzzle pointed at the floor, and looked out into the night. He was a slender, almost effeminate-looking man in his late twenties. His hair was fine, short on the top, longer in the back where it was gathered into a short ponytail. When he was beside him, Blue felt like some hulking football player towering over a little kid.

"It's really something, isn't it?" John said softly, turning from the window. "All that forest out there."

Blue nodded. "You're handling this better than your friend . . . uh . . ."

"Richard," John supplied. "Richard Fagan."

"Yeah, him," Blue said.

Fagan had started to freak again, just before the first patrols set out. Julianne and John had tried to talk him down, but eventually all they could do was give him a couple of Valium from somebody's prescription and just hope that he'd get it together.

"Richard's not a strong person . . . physically, I mean," John said.

"But you're doing okay."

John smiled. "You just can't see the way I'm shaking inside."

"Tell me about it."

"Or maybe it's because I've got some Romany blood," John added, "so I can handle the weirdness better." At Blue's raised eyebrows, John went on, "It's on my father's side. My grandmother was a Gypsy; she quit her clan—or whatever it is that they call them—to marry my granddad. That made her 'unclean' to her people."

"I've heard about that stuff," Blue said. "I used to know a couple of Gypsies—back in the days when I rode with the Devil's

Dragon. They live by all kinds of taboos—or at least the older ones do."

"They've got some strange ideas, all right," John agreed, "but then I guess every cultural group looks a little odd to those who aren't a part of it. Anyway, the reason I brought that up is that she used to talk about things. . . ."

His voice trailed off for a moment and he looked back out the window. Blue wasn't sure what John was seeing, he just knew that it wasn't whatever lay outside the window.

"What kinds of things?" he asked.

John looked back at him and shrugged. "Magic things," he said with a bit of an embarrassed smile. "We used to laugh at her stories—my sister and I—but now . . ."

"Now you believe?"

"No. I mean, of course I do. But I wonder why I couldn't accept what she was telling me back then. I loved her; I trusted her. Why couldn't I at least allow her the dignity of her beliefs without making fun of them?"

"It's a hard call," Blue said. "If it seems impossible—"

John cut him off. "I *know* all of that. The point is, I should have had more of an open mind, but I didn't. I put her in a box labeled 'grandmother with weird ideas,' but never stopped to think of how we all get put into boxes. I'm a poet and I'm not all that rugged, so people think I'm twee or gay, but I'm neither. I've got a sweet side to my thinking and a bitter side. What I am—what any of us are—can't fit into one convenient box or label."

"It's worth remembering," Blue said. "Sometimes it's hard, but you've got to work at it."

John nodded. His gaze returned to the darkness beyond the window.

"She's dead now," he said. "My grandmother. I just wish . . ."

He didn't finish, but then he didn't have to. Blue knew what was going through his mind. He wished he could roll back time to tell his grandmother that he believed her, or maybe just that he believed *in* her. He wished, like everybody who took the time to think about it did, that he could just stop stereotyping people.

"We'd better get a move on," Blue said.

John turned from the window. "Life goes on," he said.

Blue nodded, but the muffled sound of a gunshot rose up from the ground floor before he could speak. John stepped quickly from the window to join Blue, who had already moved out into the hall. Blue pumped a shell into the firing chamber of his Remington.

"Maybe somebody just got nervous," John said.

"Yeah, maybe."

But Blue didn't think so. He started off down the hall to nearest stairway leading down, pausing at the head of the stairs. He held a finger to his lips as John was about to speak, then pointed down. John moved quietly to his side.

"What are they?" he whispered as he looked down to the foot of the stairs.

Blue shrugged. He'd never seen anything like them before himself except as pen-and-ink illustrations in books on prehistory. They stood like men—the tallest couldn't be more than five feet tall—but they were covered with fur and had faces like apes. Yet they weren't apes either, because they carried spears and wore leather headbands or armbands from which dangled bunches of feathers and strung shells. And they seemed to be conversing among themselves.

They hadn't looked up to where he and John were standing, so he touched John's arm and drew back out of sight. John followed, stepping carefully so that the floor wouldn't creak underfoot.

"They look like primitive men," John said quietly.

Blue nodded. "Like the drawings you see of the Java man."

"That gunshot we heard earlier . . .?"

"I don't think it had anything to do with them," Blue said. "They didn't look agitated enough to have been shot at. Seems to me that they're just scoping out the building, but I don't like the fact that they're *in* here. That means the House isn't secure anymore."

"Who was patrolling downstairs?"

"Ohn and Sean took the north side, Judy and Will had the south."

"Somebody fired a shot down there," John said.

Blue hadn't forgotten. He looked at his watch.

"Let's get back to the ballroom," he said. "It's about the time we said we'd be getting back anyway. We can do a head count then and move everybody upstairs who isn't already there."

"And then?"

"Let's just take it one step at a time," Blue said.

He glanced back at the stairway, but he was thinking of the glass wall of the ballroom where they'd left those who hadn't been given a specific assignment.

They should have stayed together, he thought, never mind that it made good sense to get a handle on their provisions and set patrols.

"I just hope the ballroom's still secure," he added as he set off down the hall at trot.

Julianne had already organized the exodus from the ballroom. It started with Richard Fagan screeching—only this time he wasn't suffering from another of his shock-induced hallucinations. The three green-skinned children who had their faces pressed up against the glass were enough to give anybody a start. She didn't find them alarming herself—her fright was reserved for when the bodachs fled and the bear came looming out of the shadow-thick garden, moving into the light thrown by the ballroom's windows.

"Everybody *out!*" she cried.

She hauled Richard to his feet and half-dragged, half-carried him to the big oak doors that led out of the ballroom into the rest of the House.

For a long moment those gathered in the room were frozen in place; then they made a general rush for the doors. Julianne passed Richard to the first pair of them to go through, then stood aside, hurrying people on while keeping an eye on the bear, which had come up short against the window.

What were you supposed to do when you ran into a bear in the woods? she asked herself frantically.

Then it came to her: avoid eye contact and retreat in a non-threatening manner. Right. Like she or her companions were threatening.

The only firsthand knowledge she had of bears was from seeing them in the zoo—and once in a circus. She'd left the latter halfway through the performance, disgusted with how the animals lost all their dignity as they were put through their paces by their trainers. Those bears—black and brown, and the grizzly in the zoo—were diminutive compared to the size of the one outside. It was huge, an enormous cousin to the ones she'd seen—more like some exaggerated cartoon of a creature than a real bear. But it *was* real—a giant, primitive ancestor to the bears that presently inhabited the world.

The world, she thought. She wasn't *in* any world she knew. Not anymore.

"Don't panic," she told people as they crowded the doors. "Take it easy. Help each other."

The bear seemed to be staring directly at her. It laid a paw against the glass, then rose to its full height of almost eleven feet.

Please, she thought. Just go away. There's nothing for you in here.

Except there was food scattered all about the room. That would be enough to draw it here, wouldn't it?

But the bear didn't seem interested in the food. Just in her. And its anger . . . She tried to avoid eye contact with it, but couldn't tear her gaze away. The rage in its eyes struck her almost like a physical blow.

The last of the people were through the door now. Julianne hesitated in the doorway, her own gaze still locked on the fury that burned in the bear's eyes. Then it drew back a paw and batted the window. The pane broke under the blow, glass falling to shatter against the tiled floor.

Julianne didn't stay any longer. She darted through the doorway and shut the two massive doors. She called to one of the stragglers and had him come back to help her drag a heavy walnut sideboard over from the wall and push it up against the doors. Leaning on the sideboard, her breath coming in ragged gasps, she listened for sounds from within the ballroom. She heard the sound of more glass breaking and window frames snapping as the bear forced its way inside. And then she was aware of another sound—a swishing sound that seemed abnormally loud because of the adrenaline that was racing through her, forcing all of her senses to operate at their peak.

She turned to see an enormous owl sailing down the hallway

toward them. She and her companion ducked as the bird flew by, the air filled with the soft whispering of its wings. More owls followed the first—a half-dozen or so, all told.

"Oh man, oh man, oh man," her companion was mumbling, his face pressed up against the sideboard.

The doors suddenly shook as the bear threw itself against them. The sideboard shifted an inch or so. Julianne pushed it back against the doors, but the bear's next impact moved it back again. It clawed at the door, then hit it once more with the full weight of its body. Julianne could actually feel the floor shiver under the impact.

How long would the doors hold? She wasn't going to wait around to see.

She grabbed her companion's hand and helped him stand; then the two of them fled for the stairs where the others had gone. Behind them the bear continued to attack the door.

2

Esmeralda wasn't lost. Unlike Jamie, she knew how to navigate the bewildering array of times and places that made up the Otherworld. For her it was a matter of viewing it not as it was—infinite worlds and times layered one upon the other, separated often by no more than the flimsiest of gauzes—but as she imagined it to be: a beehive of worlds and their various timelines, sectioned and partitioned from each other in orderly honeycombs. With the skill of a *honochen'o'keh,* or the winds that were her cousins, she stepped through the various worlds with her eyes closed, viewing her progress solely through the sight of her own inner vision.

The path she followed was a spiraling corkscrew that started with the spark of familiarity that had leapt into her mind from the flickering Weirdin images on Memoria's screen in the Postman's Room and took her from oak forest to redwood, from jungle to arctic tundra, from lowland fen to desert, from mountain ranges to seashores. She kept track of each world she passed through and was always aware of the road that would lead her back to the origin of her journey.

She wasn't lost; but Jamie was.

He was everywhere, he was nowhere. Every world and time she touched seemed to have the taste of him in its air, but no sooner did she arrive than the winds of that place told her it was only the echo of his presence that they carried, not his presence itself. She lost count of the worlds she walked before she finally found one thread of him stronger than any other.

She followed its unraveling to its source, to a part of a world that was like the highlands of the Andes Mountains of her homeworld. There, where the howling winds lent her their strength, she found not her Jamie, but Emma's:

He was a coyote-headed man, sitting on a stone outcrop. The cliff side fell away behind him for a half-mile. He was perched at his ease, careless of the drop so close at hand, dressed in scuffed cowboy boots and jeans. He wore a blue flannel shirt tucked into his jeans with a leather vest overtop that was decorated with bead- and quill-work. His eyes were mismatched—one blue and one brown. On his head was a flat-brimmed black hat; holes had been cut in the brim to allow his ears to poke through. Two long braids, tied with leather thongs at their ends and decorated with feathers, hung to either side of his face. She couldn't tell if the braids were really his, or just attached to the inside of the hat.

It didn't really matter, she supposed, for she had recognized him as soon as she saw him. He could look however he wanted, be anybody he wanted to be. That was part of his magic.

She sighed, then walked over to where he was sitting and settled on another stone nearby.

"The jeans and boots aren't that Native," she said. "Come to think of it, neither are the shirt and hat."

"I didn't say I was trying to look Native."

"Then why the vest and braids?"

His only reply was a wide grin.

So that was the way it was going to be. She concentrated for a moment, then reached into her pocket, taking out a pouch of tobacco and a package of papers that hadn't been there when she'd started her journey. Not looking at him, she rolled a cigarette. She licked the paper, pinched off the ends. Stowing the tobacco and papers away, she started to concentrate on matches, but before she could reach into her pocket, he was offering her a light from a burning twig.

"Cute," she said, but accepted the light.

She took a long drag on the cigarette, drawing the smoke deep inside, and concentrated on not coughing, no matter how much the smoke burned her lungs. She held it in for a moment, then exhaled. Blowing the ash from the end of the cigarette, she casually offered it to him.

He grinned, knowing just as she did that he could never resist a smoke, knowing as well what sharing it implied. She didn't say anything until he'd taken a couple of drags and handed it back to her. She shook her head.

"Keep it."

She waited until he'd finished the cigarette and ground it out under his heel. He pinched the butt with his long brown fingers, then stowed it away in a pocket of his shirt.

"So," she said. "Has this all been your doing?"

"All what?"

"Tamson House shifting from its homeworld, Jamie lost, *my* being *here*."

"Some," he admitted. "But I didn't start it."

"Of course not. You never do. You just happened upon the situation . . . innocently."

Her voice was mild as she spoke, but her eyes flashed dangerously.

"You have a sharp tongue," he said.

"The truth hurts?"

He gave her his coyote grin. "It just stings a little."

"So what happens now?" she asked.

"That's up to you."

Esmeralda sighed. She seemed to do that a lot around him, she realized.

"Okay," she said. "Can you help me find Jamie? The House needs him."

"The House needs someone—he's lost his chance."

"But—"

"Tamson House," he interrupted her, "is important to us: where it stands, what it has become. It requires a guardian with a sense of responsibility. We gave Jamie a great gift—to continue on his Wheel, though its turning was done. It wasn't lightly gifted.

"As things stand now, he deserted his post, allowed the House to cross over into the Otherworld and left its strengths open to attack. That wasn't in the contract."

"You never showed him a contract."

"He never asked."

"He made a mistake," Esmeralda said. "People make mistakes."

"We have no time for mistakes."

"You've never made one?"

"That's not relevant."

"The hell it isn't," Esmeralda said. "Where would you be if Grandmother Toad hadn't forgiven you *your* mistakes? Jamie deserves another chance."

The mismatched eyes studied her for a long moment, their expression unreadable.

"It will cost you," he said finally.

Esmeralda shook her head. "You get just as much out of Tamson House as we do—more probably. It's an easy gate for you to a world that's growing steadily more difficult for you to reach. The way I see it, you owe us."

"Someone must pay."

"I don't think so," Esmeralda said. "Jamie already has—scattered the way he is over a thousand worlds—and no one else was responsible except for you."

"You can't have everything," he said, changing tack. "Take your friend Emma. We gifted her and all she does is deny her gift. You people want it all, but you aren't willing to pay for any of it."

"What's happening with Emma is between her and you. We were talking about Jamie."

"I know. I just thought that perhaps Emma would be willing to pay in Jamie's place."

The smolder in Esmeralda's eyes fanned into sudden flames. She stood up and a wind arose that moved counter to those that already whistled across the cliff top. It whipped her hair about her head.

"Don't even think about it," she said softly.

He shrugged. "Or I could make you pay."

Esmeralda's winds gusted, lifting him from the rock and blowing him over the side of the cliff. A whirlwind of spinning air held him aloft as she stepped to the edge and looked over at him.

"Fire and air don't listen to you," she said. "But the wind listens to me."

There was no alarm in his eyes; they mocked her with the same coyote grin that lay laughing on his lips.

"You won't let me drop," he said.

"Maybe, maybe not. But think of this: if you don't treat us fairly, we won't treat you fairly. Maybe I'll see that the House is sold and they build an office building in its place—a few acres of concrete and glass and steel. How will you use the building then?"

"We would stop you. We—"

"Or maybe I'd just burn the place down."

The laughter in his eyes faltered.

That's got to him, Esmeralda thought. He might know that she wasn't capable of letting him drop, but he could see that she could, and would, make good her threat to burn the House.

She let her winds bring him back to the stone where he'd been sitting. They dropped him unceremoniously so that he fell in an untidy tangle of limbs. He was on his feet like a cat, casually brushing the dirt from his shirtsleeves and jeans as though nothing untoward had occurred, but he couldn't fool her. Her last threat had shaken him.

"You wouldn't," he said, his voice betraying his uncertainty.

"Try me."

"But you love the House."

She nodded. "But I love the people more. I'll take people over a building any time."

He seemed to deflate. All humor left his features. He sat down on his ankles, hands on his knees, back leaning up against a stone.

"Can I have another cigarette?" he asked.

She passed him the tobacco and papers and waited patiently while he rolled himself a cigarette. When he was done and had it stuck between his lips, he reached out with a hand that seemed to disappear into a hole in the air, making it look as though his arm ended at his wrist. When he drew the hand back, it held another burning twig.

Somewhere, in some world, Esmeralda thought, surprised faces were looking at a fire near which a hand had appeared to snatch up that twig. She wished she could pull that feat off as easily as he did, but the best she could do was use a pocket or a pouch and have something of her own that she'd left back at the House appear in it. While she didn't smoke herself, she kept the tobacco on hand for those times she fared into the Otherworld. She'd left so unexpectedly today that she hadn't had time to collect any of her usual traveling gear.

"That was some trick with the wind," her companion said as he lit his cigarette.

He was rapidly regaining his composure, but then he'd always been quick to bounce back. He had to be to survive as long as he had with his particular nature. Blue-gray smoke clouded around his features before the wind blew it away.

"It's only because we're so far into the Otherworld," Esmeralda said, "and the winds here lent me their strength."

"Still . . . I don't remember you being so hard before."

She smiled for the first time since she'd met him. "I learned that from you."

"Did you now?"

Esmeralda ignored what was no more than a rhetorical question.

"Will you help me find Jamie?" she asked. *"Without* bargaining?"

"It's in my nature to always try to turn a profit."

"It's also in your nature to make the simplest thing complicated," Esmeralda said. "Why couldn't you have just asked me instead of making us go through all of this?" She waved a hand vaguely around her. "And bringing the House here . . ."

"I didn't bring it—Jamie drew it in after him. I'm cleaning up messes this time—not making them."

"Will you help?"

Now it was his turn to sigh. "All right. But it's not just finding Jamie that's the problem."

Esmeralda nodded. She knew. Her companion might be able to bring back all the parts of Jamie from where they were scattered on who knew how many worlds, but that didn't mean that they would all come properly back together again. They could easily end up with a spirit that was as mad as a Bedlamite.

"It's not what you're thinking," he said, "although that's another part of the risk."

"Then what are you talking about?"

He took another drag from his cigarette, exhaled. They watched the wind take the smoke away.

"It's what's happening to the House in its homeworld," he said.

The grin that came to his lips at her look of confusion had no sense of victory about it.

"What are you talking about?" she asked.

So he explained it to her as he had to Emma earlier.

"So that's what's causing the forest to intrude," she said when he was done. "This man has woken a ghost of the first forest to enter the House and is using it to protect himself while he siphons off the House's energy. But doesn't he realize that while the ghost of the forest can be wakened, once awake it takes on a life of its own?"

"How do you know that?"

"I thought everyone knew that about the first forest. That's why so few people dare to wake even the ghost of one of its trees."

"Not that," he said. "How do you know he woke the first forest?"

"Well, what else can it be that caused the forest to enter the House itself? You know, and I know, that the House straddles more than one world, but those places are always in clearings— never in the middle of the woods or in a swamp or a lake."

Her companion laughed. "Of course. You're right. But that's perfect. We don't have to do a thing—the forest itself will take care of him for us."

"*And* the House," Esmeralda said. "When the forest is done with it, I might as well have burnt it down. Tamson House won't exist anymore. Not on any world."

Uneasiness played across her companion's features again.

"Then what do we do?" he asked.

"That's simple." Esmeralda ticked the items off on her fingers. "Call back Jamie and install him back in the House. Deal with whoever it is attacking us. And strike a bargain with the forest."

"That's beyond my abilities."

"Mine, too. But we'd better think of something. We can start with bringing Jamie back."

He nodded, but still seemed distracted. He was probably thinking, Esmeralda realized, of just how he was going to explain the seriousness of the situation to those who held him accountable. She felt a moment's sympathy for him.

"Whiskey Jack," she said.

He had as many names as he had shapes, but that was how he had named himself to her the last time she'd met him. It was a corruption of the Anishnabeg word *wee-sa-kay-jac* and meant Bitter Spirit. The time before that he'd called himself the Hodja—that was in Turkey. She'd known him as a small spider-man in Africa, a round-faced Robin Goodfellow in a Sussex forest, a raven-headed woman in Oregon. Trickster had a thousand and one shapes and names. Sometimes she felt as though she'd met every one of them.

"The sooner we begin," she added, "the sooner it can be ended."

He nodded. "We'll need a vessel—something to put him in until you take him back to the House. Without it, he'll just scatter again as you make your return journey."

He looked down at the tobacco pouch that was still on his lap, then shook his head and stowed it away in the pocket of his shirt. Esmeralda said nothing. As he'd said, it was in his nature to look for payment, and if that was all that his help would cost her today, then she was coming out far ahead. From the other pocket of his shirt he drew out what looked like a small dead bird.

It *was* a dead bird, she realized as he handed it over to her: a stuffed kingfisher, its wings tied tightly to its body with overlapping leather thongs and decorated with beads and feathers; it was a kind of magic charm that Native American warriors had once worn into battle. She accepted it gingerly.

"Now what?" she asked.

"Now we call him." His mismatched eyes caught her gaze and held it. He pointed to the fetish she held and said, "Don't drop it."

That familiar grin returned to his features. He bounced lightly on his heels, eyes closed, head tilted back, and began to bark. The winds caught up the *yip, yip, yip* of his voice and sent it spiraling off into the Otherworlds.

In Esmeralda's hand, the dead bird began to twitch.

3

Everything was falling to pieces, Blue thought. Jamie disappearing, being stuck in the Otherworld and having the forest intrude on the House had been bad enough. Then Esmeralda had to take off, looking for Jamie, and she'd been gone for hours. Who knew how long *that* trip would take her? But to top it all off, they'd been under siege for the past few hours and it didn't look like it was going to get any better.

What if they were permanently trapped in the Otherworld? What if there was no way back?

The first danger, Emma had explained—passing on what the weird guy she'd run into in the woods had told her—was the way the Otherworld worked on people. Blue could already see the strain in his companions. Richard Fagan was the worst; he'd just stepped out of his head and maybe his mind was never going to return. But it was touching them all to some degree.

They were more on edge than he remembered any of them to be. Arguments started quickly, and escalated even more quickly. And there was a constant nagging in the back of everyone's head— not just the worry that they were trapped here, maybe for good, but that there was something changing in their thought processes. Their minds were making weird connections, crazy ideas kept cropping up, and there was an incessant rattle and murmur of inner conversation that didn't always feel like it had its origin in one's own head. It was as though the sanctity of their minds had been breached and they were all slowly being turned into crazy-eyed fanatics like the Radio Man back home who walked up and down the bike path by the canal having long, loud conversations with the radio he carried on his shoulder; a radio that didn't work.

And if they were growing steadily mentally unstable—Emma said that it was because there was the House and so many of them intruding on the Otherworld that the deterioration was so rapid—

they were also cut off from their food supply. The flight up to the second floor had happened so quickly that no one had thought to bring any provisions with them. They had water, courtesy of the washroom just down the hall from the Postman's Room, but no food. Night was coming and Blue was worried about some of the Otherworld's creatures getting at the generators and cutting off their light supply as well.

But there was nothing they could do about any of it. They were trapped here on the second floor, hiding behind barricades that they'd hastily erected out of stacked dressers, sideboards and tables to block off the east side of the House's second story from the rest of the structure. From their vantage points at either end of the north/south corridor on this side of the building, they could see an increasingly varied array of beings and creatures that were wandering through the House:

Some fought among themselves, like the monkeymen he and John had seen earlier and an enormous boar; the monkeymen had won, but only after losing two of their number.

Others tried to breach the barricades to attack them. The bear had been the worst; it had taken all their combined firepower to stop it. Poor sucker wouldn't normally have come near them, Blue knew, but something had driven it into a frenzy. Blue felt like a shit for having to kill it.

Still others just watched them like the owls that Emma said were manitou, drawn to them by the heavy use of magic it required to maintain the House in this Otherworld.

When Tim came to spell him at the barricade, Blue started wearily back to the Postman's Room, which had become their command center. He was bone-tired—like most of them, he hadn't slept for over thirty-six hours—and depressed about the bear. In direct contrast to his depression, the nagging in his head was like a toothache, making him want to just strike out at something. Anything. It was becoming a major effort just to think clearly.

It was okay when he was talking to someone, but as soon as he was alone with his thoughts, the inner jabbering started up like an angry buzz that wouldn't go away. He knew he wasn't alone in that. There was a lot of forced conversation going on around him.

They weren't holding up well, he thought. Sara and Ohn were handling it the best, but then they were used to the Otherworld. His own experience in it was limited, but he figured that part of his own problem was that he'd been messed up before the House ever got shifted into the Otherworld.

That made him think of Emma. Oddly enough, she was hanging in strong as well. In fact, with Esmeralda gone, it was Emma who was holding them together. He guessed that Julianne had been right. He *had* been overly protective with her. Given a chance to show her stuff, she was proving her mettle. She'd just needed the opportunity to draw on that core of iron she had inside her.

Ginny and Julianne were doing pretty well, too: Ginny because she was concentrating so hard on making sense of the computer's own brand of craziness, while Julianne had been too busy taking care of their own wounded to think of anything else. Richard Fagan had finally stopped freaking enough to drop into a drugged slumber, as had a girl Blue remembered seeing out in the garden doing watercolors before all of this began. Her panic attack had caught everybody off guard; it took three of them to haul her back from the barricade when she started clawing at the heaped furniture, screaming, "Let me out, let me out!"

Then there was one of the Irish students, the one named Barry, who'd dropped his side of a sideboard on his leg and opened up a gash about a foot long that needed to be sewn shut again. A couple of others had been hurt in a tussle with some humanoid creatures that looked like they had iguanas a few generations back in their ancestry.

They were lucky that so few of them had been hurt so far, but Blue knew it wasn't going to last.

Julianne was sprawled wearily in one of the club chairs when he stepped into the Postman's Room. Ginny was still at the keyboard, worrying over the flurry of images that were continually flickering past on Memoria's screen. Emma was with Sara. They were standing by the window looking outside.

Emma looked over her shoulder as he came in. "All that noise earlier," she said. "Was that the bear?"

Blue nodded. "We had to shoot him. Sonovabitch wouldn't pay any attention to our warning shots."

"You left Tim in charge?"

"Yeah. He's with Cal and a couple of others. Sean's on the north barricade. We've got a bit of a lull. I think all that gunfire freaked them."

Not to mention the way it left his own ears ringing. Rifles and shotguns were not meant to be fired in enclosed spaces like this.

Blue propped his Remington up against a bookcase and slid down on the floor beside it.

"We've got to do something," he said. "Otherwise, I don't think we're going to make it through the night."

Emma nodded. "Sara's going back."

Blue sat up a little straighter. "Back to where?"

"Ottawa. We've got to stop the man who's doing this to us. If we can do that, and if Esmeralda finds Jamie and can bring him back, maybe the House'll return to where it belongs."

If, if, Blue thought. His gaze shifted to Sara.

"How're you planning to do that?" he asked.

He'd thought that they were trapped here, but if Emma and Sara had come up with a way out . . . Hope rose in him, momentarily quelling the whispers and constant nattering that worried at the edge of his mind.

"With Pukwudji's help," Sara said. "Whatever caught me in the glade and kept me there didn't seem to affect him. If I can get to the garden where he's waiting for me, I think he can take me back to Ottawa."

"And then?" Blue asked.

Sara looked puzzled. "Then what?"

"That's what I want to know. What are you going to do if you *do* get back? How're you going to find this guy? Where would you even start to look?"

"He's tapping into the House, right?"

"I guess."

At least that's what the man in the forest had told Emma. Blue wasn't so ready to put as much faith in what he had to say as Emma was, although he had to admit that the man had been spot on the money so far—especially when it came to how the Otherworld was going to mess up their heads.

"I'm a Tamson," Sara said. "Just like Jamie and his dad and his granddad. I can feel the connection that Jamie has with the House. I'm hoping to use it, to tap into however the man's drawing off the House's energy and following that trail back to where he is."

"You can do that?"

"Not here—with the forest blocking me—but away from its influence, I think I can."

It sounded like clutching at straws, Blue thought, but he didn't have anything better to offer. That brought him around to the other thing that was worrying him.

"Just say you do find this guy," he said. "He'll be dangerous—seriously dangerous."

Sara nodded.

"That's why we thought you should go with her," Emma said.

And leave you? Blue thought. If Sara and he *did* manage to return to Ottawa, there was no guarantee that they'd be able to get back here. Thinking of Emma trapped here woke a sick feeling in the pit of his stomach.

She seemed to sense what he was thinking. Crossing the room, she sat on her heels in front of him and laid her hands on his knees.

"It's not that I want you to go," she said.

"You mean that?" he asked.

She leaned forward to kiss him. "We've got things to work out, I don't deny that, but I want to work them out. Before we can do that, though, we've got to deal with this."

"I hear you," Blue said.

She smiled. "You're the best we've got, so it's got to be you who goes. I don't see any alternatives."

As she rose to her feet, Blue stood up with her. He enfolded her in his arms, marveling—as it seemed he hadn't had the chance to in ages—at just how perfectly their bodies fit against each other. For all his weariness, he felt renewed. The nattering at the edge of his mind dimmed, faded, and was gone.

When she finally stepped back from his embrace there was a wistful look in her eyes that made Blue's heart sing. He knew then, as he always had, that he'd do anything for her.

"I'll be back for you," he said.

"I know you will."

He looked over Emma's shoulder to where Sara stood watching

them. She had that scared-but-I'll-be-brave look in her features that was so familiar to him, but there was a happiness for him there as well.

"Okay," he said. "Let's figure out how we can get to the garden."

"It's funny," Tim said.

He leaned up against the wall, positioned so that he could look over the barricade and down the length of corridor. His line of sight took in the top of the nearby stairway, where he could see the hindquarters of the bear that they'd been forced to shoot earlier. It lay where it had fallen, gathering flies. Sitting on the banister just above the corpse was one of the owls, wide eyes regarding him with an unblinking gaze.

The birds freaked him, making him happy to be armed. The butt of his shotgun was on the ground by his right foot. He had the barrel in his hand, held against his thigh. The cold smoothness of the metal was comforting against his palm. He glanced at Cal to see if Cal was listening, then returned his gaze to the corridor.

"Used to be," he went on, "that my biggest problem was whether to write a play in verse or regular dialogue. Now I wonder if I'm still going to be alive this time tomorrow."

Talking helped ease the weird feeling in his head that came clamoring up through his thoughts each time the conversation lagged. Because it had been quiet for twenty minutes or so, he and Cal had the watch to themselves, allowing the others to get some well-earned rest. He doubted they were sleeping. Tim liked Cal well enough, but he wished he were here with someone else—someone who wasn't quite so morose.

"So what's with you and Julianne?" he asked.

That brought a quick response.

"Why?" Cal asked. "What did she say?"

"She didn't say anything. It's just that you're usually about as close to her as a burr that got snagged on her sweater, but now you're avoiding her like she's got the plague or something."

"Maybe *I've* got the plague," Cal said.

Normally, Tim wasn't one to pry. But he needed to talk—just to keep the weird feeling in his head at bay—and since he'd exhausted a number of other lines of conversation already with little response from his companion, he decided to just press on. At least he'd gotten some return on this particular subject.

"What?" he asked. "You guys have a fight or something?"

"You wouldn't understand."

"Try me."

For a long moment he thought he wasn't going to get an answer, but then Cal sighed. He didn't look at Tim, just stared down the corridor across the top of his side of the barricade and spoke in a subdued voice.

"When everything first started," he asked. "When the forest just appeared the way it did—did anything happen to you?"

"Happen to me how?"

"Like inside you," Cal said. "Did it *change* you?"

Tim considered the emphasis his companion had put on "change." He remembered being freaked, but then everything started to happen so fast. . . . He'd also had the benefit of being around Esmeralda and Blue, who seemed not just more together in terms of organization, but used to this kind of thing. That had helped.

"I don't think so," he said. "I mean, I see things differently, I guess. . . ."

And wasn't that the understatement of the year? His entire perspective had undergone a jolting shift. Mostly he tried not to think about it because, when he did, the first image that came rolling up behind his eyes was that of three green-skinned children, hanging like dead fruit from the old oak by the fountain. He didn't think that that was quite what Cal was driving at.

"Something happened to you?" he added.

He glanced at his companion in time to catch him nod.

"Oh, yeah," Cal said.

And then Cal explained that moment of piercing insight that had come to him, standing there in the hall and looking at Julianne as she seemed to glow with her own inner light. He started out haltingly, obviously embarrassed, but he carried on all the way to the end.

When Cal was done, Tim didn't say anything for a long moment. He could empathize with Cal to some degree—anyone who didn't think Julianne was gorgeous really ought to have their hormones checked—but he felt that Cal had blown the whole thing way out of proportion.

"But it's all part of a game," he said finally. "The whole courtship thing."

"You don't understand," Cal began.

"No, I do. Really. But think about what you've been saying."

"That's all I ever do."

"Try it from a different perspective, then," Tim said. "Look, there's nothing wrong with a man finding a woman attractive and fantasizing about her; women find men attractive and do the same thing. You didn't want to do any weird shit with her, you just wanted to make love with her. There's nothing wrong or twisted about that."

Cal shook his head. "It's the *way* I was coming on to her. I knew she was the kind of woman who always had guys hitting on her, so I deliberately tried to just be her pal, figuring I'd be her friend first and then maybe the other stuff would happen. I was *pretending,* you see? Our whole relationship was based on a lie because while I was being her pal, all I really wanted was her body."

"So you never liked her."

"Of course I liked her."

Tim shook his head. "You're just screwing yourself up, man. What you should do is talk to her. If she doesn't want to be your lover, that's going to be a drag, but maybe you could still be friends."

Cal didn't appear to have heard him.

"It's like there was something missing inside me before," he said. "Compassion, or empathy. I should have taken the time to see how it would look from her perspective."

Tim glanced down the hall toward the Postman's Room.

"Well, heads up," he said. "Here comes your chance to make things right."

Tim thought Cal was going to vault across the barricade and just bolt when he saw Julianne approaching them, but he held his ground. A flush colored the back of his neck and he stared down at his shoes.

"Blue needs a hand from one of you guys," Julianne said.

Tim started to step forward. Talk about your perfect timing, he thought. Maybe somebody could salvage something worthwhile out of all this crap they were going through. But Cal moved more quickly.

"I'll go," he mumbled and hurried by Julianne, clutching his rifle against his chest and not looking at her.

Julianne's gaze followed his retreating figure, then returned to Tim, who just shrugged.

"Guess he just likes being useful," he said, but he could see in Julianne's eyes that she knew exactly why Cal had fled.

Julianne sighed and took up Cal's position on the other side of the barricade. She carried her shotgun with familiarity, but didn't seem particularly happy about having to lug it around. She looked over the barricade and down the corridor, but things were still quiet. The dead bear remained by the stairs, the buzz of the flies on its corpse getting louder as more and more of them arrived for the feast. The owl still watched them with what Tim couldn't help thinking was an unforgiving gaze.

His gaze shifted back to his companion. He'd take looking at Julianne over all of this weird shit any time. Long before Cal had shown up at the House, he'd done his own shuffle and dance with her until she made it plain—but nicely—that she wasn't interested in being more than friends. What she offered as a friend more than made up for his disappointment, but it didn't stop him from teasing her.

"So," he said. "What's a nice girl like you doing in a place like this?"

She gave him a quick smile that didn't quite reach her eyes, but Tim could see that she appreciated his attempt at levity.

"I could ask you the same thing," she said.

"But I'm not a girl."

"Or nice?" she asked.

She arched her eyebrows as she spoke—trying to get into a bantering mood, Tim thought.

"Depends on your definition of nice," he said and he launched into a silly description of what he thought the word meant that, by the time he was done, had her smile finally reaching her eyes.

★　★　★

It took Sara a moment to place the intense young man who joined them in the room directly across the hall from the Postman's Room. She'd been meeting too many people today to keep them all straight without a fair amount of concentration. His name came to her just a half breath before Judy noticed him.

"Hey, Cal," Judy said. "How're you holding up?"

"I'm okay," Cal said.

Sara didn't think so. He didn't look scared, but there was a paleness to his features and a haunted look in his eyes that spoke of some emotional turmoil. She couldn't have said why, but she didn't think it had anything to do with their all being trapped here in the Otherworld.

"Have you ever done any rope climbing?" Blue asked him.

"Some—back in high school."

They were all crowded around the window overlooking the garden. Blue and Judy had removed the sliding windows from their grooves, passing them to Sara and Emma, who stacked them up against the wall out of the way. What they were doing now was lowering a rope out the window to check its length. The rope had been made by tying sheets together—something that Sara didn't think was ever done except in the movies.

"We're trying to keep this low-key," Blue said, "because we don't want to get people's hopes up."

Cal nodded, though it was obvious to Sara that he didn't have a clue as to what Blue was talking about.

"We're trying to get down to the garden," she explained.

"Sara's got a friend there," Blue went on, "who might be able to take us back to Ottawa where we can deal with the sucker who's got us trapped here."

"You've really got it figured out who's responsible for all of this?" Cal asked.

"We're working on it," Blue replied. "We'll know better once we get back to Ottawa—if we can get back."

"And this friend of Sara's . . .?"

"He's a manitou," Sara said. "One of the little mysteries that make their home here in the Otherworld—but he's shy, so we can't go in a crowd."

"Oh . . . kay," Cal said.

He was obviously still confused, Sara thought, but seemed willing to go along with things until they started making sense.

"So what do you want me to do?" Cal added.

"What we need," Blue said, "is someone without a whole lot of weight to go down this rope and stand guard until Sara and I get down. I'd go myself, but we're not so sure that the rope's going to hold me, so I'm going last."

"No problem," Cal said.

"The thing is," Blue went on, "if the rope breaks when any of us are going down, you're going to be stuck in the garden—cut off from everybody else."

"Why can't I just go with you?" Cal asked.

"Pukwudji knows Blue," Sara said, "but if anybody else is with me, he might not show up at all. He really is shy—almost to the point of it being a phobia."

"I was going to do it," Judy said, "but Mr. Big Shot here"—she nodded her head toward Blue—"says he wants me to stay."

"I don't want to sound crass," Blue said, "or to belittle anybody else's talents—including your own, Cal—but if something happens to us, if we don't make it back, you're going to need her mechanical expertise."

"Julianne seemed to know her way around the bikes," Judy complained.

Sara noticed the way Cal flinched at the mention of Julianne's name and then she knew what was bothering him. She remembered the way he looked at Julianne and then put it all together. There was nothing worse than a one-sided love affair.

"Julianne knows how to use them and maybe change a spark plug," Blue was saying to Judy, "but she can't take things apart and put them back together again the way that you can. That—and any kind of medical knowledge—are going to be primo skills if you guys are stuck here."

"And Esmeralda seemed to think that Julianne knows a lot of herbal lore," Emma said.

"So you should take care of the both of them," Blue said.

"Get him," Judy said. "Like we're only as good as the services we provide. Sounds pretty cheesy to me."

Blue gave her the finger.

"Why don't you just go down the stairs?" Cal asked. "It seems quiet enough now."

Blue shook his head. "There's things moving around on the ground floor. How many or what, we don't know, but we can hear them from Sean's side of the corridor. Haven't you guys heard anything on your side?"

"Like I said, it's been quiet."

"Well, we've been watching the garden for a half hour now," Blue said, "and there's nothing moving out there. Seems to me it's the better risk. So what do you say—are you up for it?" When Cal nodded, Blue offered him a pair of cloth garden gloves that had coarse gray leather on the palms and fingers. "These'll help you keep from slipping."

Emma took Cal's rifle and attached a shoulder strap to it while Cal put on the gloves. With Judy and Sara's help, Blue shifted a big walnut dresser over to the window to which they'd attach the rope. When they had it tied and flung it back through the window, Blue peered down.

"Okay," he said. "We're ready to roll."

Sara studied the nearest trees over Blue's shoulder. The forest had marched almost right up to the House, filling the garden with its tall outgrowths. There didn't appear to be anything of a threatening nature hiding under the boughs, though it was hard to tell because the light from the windows only went as far as the first few trees. There could be any number of the forest's motley army of creatures hiding down there, just waiting for them to touch the ground.

"It looks clear," she said, "except for those damn owls."

She was sick of the birds. They were everywhere, watching, staring, prying. If she leaned out the window and looked up on either side of the window, she would see a half-dozen of the bloody things, perched on the eaves, staring back at her. Emma might think they were manitou drawn here by the magic that was being used to keep the House in the Otherworld, and she was probably right, but they weren't acting like any of the manitou with which Sara was familiar. There was something profoundly disquieting about their silent scrutiny, as though they *knew* something. . . .

"Let's do it," Blue said.

He stood aside so that Cal could swing his leg over the sill. Sara watched as Cal tentatively tested his weight on the makeshift rope, then began his slow descent.

I'm next, she thought.

The idea of having to make her way down two stories on that flimsy sheet-rope made her feel a little queasy. The way the Kendell luck seemed to be running these days, she'd probably lose her grip about halfway down, fall and break her neck.

Don't think about it, she told herself and concentrated on watching the shadows under the trees, looking for movement. Beside her, Blue was going over last-minute instructions with Emma for the umpteenth time.

"Just hold everybody together up here," he was saying. "Keep the guards rotating so that nobody gets too bored or tired and misses something."

"I know, Blue."

"And if things do seem real quiet for much longer, you might try to get a work detail together to move some of those corpses out past the barricades. They're already drawing flies; when the smell starts to hit—"

"Enough already," Emma said.

Cal had reached the ground, dropping the last few feet and landing, awkwardly but safely. When he'd regained his balance, he unslung the rifle from his back and hung it over his shoulder where he could bring it up quickly if he needed to. Keeping an eye on the forest, he steadied the rope for Sara.

Sara took a deep breath—

Chin.

Store up the inner strength like a drawn bow.

Focus.

—and swung her own leg over the sill. She grabbed hold of the rope, her hands sweating inside their gloves, and glanced inside. Judy gave her a thumbs-up. Emma was kissing Blue. She stepped back and pushed him toward the window.

"Be careful," she said, including Sara in her caution.

As soon as Sara started her own descent, the muscles of her back and shoulders tensed and started to cramp. She drew on the focused energy of her taw and forced herself to ignore the cramping muscles. Bracing her legs against the wall the way that Cal had, she slowly made her way down. The end of the rope came far sooner than she expected it to. Cal stepped aside to give her room and she let go, landing as awkwardly as Cal had, but all in one piece.

"Everything still seems clear," Cal told her.

He spoke over his shoulder, his attention concentrated on the forest in front of him. Sara moved out from under the rope. She looked up, frowned at the owls, then held the rope for Blue as he made his descent. Just as he landed on the ground, knees slightly bent to absorb the shock, there came the crashing sound of a large body moving through the underbrush.

Cal brought his rifle up to his shoulder. Blue scrambled to get his own unslung. Sara stood frozen, expecting she didn't know what—another bear, another boar, maybe a dragon for all she knew—but it was a stag that came bounding out from between the trees. It skidded to a halt on the grass, antlers glinting white in the light that spilled from the House's windows as it turned its head back and forth.

"Hold your fire," Blue said softly.

They waited a long moment. Sara wondered if this was the same stag that Ohn and Sean had confronted inside the House.

Don't let it attack, she thought. She hated the idea of their having to shoot anything that looked so beautiful.

The stag held its ground for a few heartbeats longer, then turned and walked slowly away, following the thin strip of lawn that still lay between the garden's forest and the House. Sara let out a breath she hadn't been aware of holding.

"Let me give you a leg up," Blue said to Cal.

"You sure you don't want me to come along—just in case you need an extra gun?"

Blue put his hand on Cal's shoulder. "We need you here more," he said.

He cupped his hands. When Cal stepped onto them, Blue gave him a boost up. He and Sara waited to make sure Cal reached the window; then Blue turned to her.

"Which way do we go?" he asked.

Sara just pointed straight ahead to where the shadows lay thick in the tangled undergrowth.

Blue stepped forward. "Man. How're we going to get through that?"

Let's see if Pukwudji's trick works for a *herok'a*, Sara thought.

She moved ahead of Blue. Laying her hands upon the nearest tangle of boughs, she closed her eyes and reached out to the forest with her heart, asking it for safe passage. The strains of the moon-heart air sounded in her inner ear; a moment later she sensed a response to that tune that Tal had given her. The twigs and leaves moved away from under her hand. She heard Blue whisper a muffled "Jesus," then opened her eyes to see a path leading into the forest.

They waved one last time to those watching them from the window; then Sara led the way onto the path.

"Where do we start looking for him?" Blue asked when they'd been following the path for a couple of minutes.

"I guess we'll just call him," Sara began; then she paused. "Can you hear that?"

Blue shook his head. "I don't hear any—no, I guess I do. It sounds like a flute."

"It's Pukwudji," Sara said.

As though trained to see to her needs, the path veered in the direction of the music. The flute-playing grew not so much louder as more present with each step they took—an accelerated process as though somewhere there were a volume knob being turned up.

It was the forest, Sara thought. However far Pukwudji had really been when they'd first heard his flute, the path was using its magic to transport them quickly to where the played.

It took only a few moments before the path opened up to a space under an apple tree—the Apple Tree Man himself, Sara realized, still here in what remained of the House's garden. The undergrowth was cleared away from the tree. Leaning against its trunk, sitting on his heels, was Pukwudji. He brought the flute down from his lips as they approached, but the echoes of his music continued for a few breaths longer than it seemed they should have.

"Hey, Sara!" he cried, scrambling to his feet.

Sara was so happy to see him that she closed the distance between them in a few quick steps to give him a hug. She hadn't realized until this moment just how worried she'd been that he might not have stayed to wait for her.

"You remember Blue, don't you?" she said.

"Oh sure." Pukwudji thrust his flute into his belt. "Blue-Rider-of-Thunder, that's what Ur'wen'ta named you, hey?"

Blue smiled. "Something like that."

"But you have no thunder to ride tonight."

"Didn't want to scare up any more ghoulies," Blue said.

Pukwudji nodded seriously. "The forest is full of unhappy thoughts tonight and unhappiest of all is the forest itself." He turned to Sara. "Are we going now?"

"We're going," she said. "But not home. Can you take us back to Ottawa?"

"What for?"

Sara waved her hand in a motion that took in the forest. "To stop the one's responsible for all of this."

Pukwudji didn't say anything.

"What did you mean about the forest being the unhappiest of all?" Blue asked.

"It's like a baby," Pukwudji replied, still looking at Sara. "It's newborn, but already it begins to die."

"Who's killing it?"

Now Pukwudji turned to Blue. "All things die—except for Grandmother Toad's little mysteries, hey?"

"If you say so. But that doesn't tell us who—"

"Someone woke this forest," Pukwudji said. "Called it up from where its ghost lay sleeping in the ancient of days. Once called, a force such as this forest is not easily controlled—that takes a great magic that only very few *herok'a* may wield. But the one you seek, who called up and controls this forest, is that strong; strong enough even to kill it.

"To try to count coup against such a being is the same as taking your own life, hey?"

"We don't have a whole lot of choice in the matter," Blue said.

Pukwudji looked at Sara. "Is this true?"

Sara nodded.

"You want to go?"

"No," she said. "But we have to."

"If we die, I won't see you anymore. I'll come back, but you . . ."

Sara swallowed thickly. "I know."

"I'll miss you," Pukwudji said. His saucer eyes were suddenly shiny with unshed tears.

Blue kicked at a twig that lay by his feet. "This guy—he's really that strong?"

"He's a maker," Pukwudji said, as though that explained it all.

Blue turned a questioning look to Sara.

"The *rath'wen'a* say that there's different kinds of magic-workers: users and makers," she explained. "Most use what's already in the world; they're the ones who recognize a being or object—or even a place—by its true name. By naming it, they can manipulate its properties: heal it, change it, use it."

"And these makers?"

"They can create something out of nothing—like make real a forest that never was."

"But that's like naming it, isn't it?" Blue asked. "I mean, this guy knew about the first forest and just called up a piece of it, right?"

Pukwudji shook his head. "This part of the first forest never existed before—it's only what might have been, not what was—so there wasn't even a memory of it to name. The man responsible for all of this created the forest—he *made* it—using a memory of that first forest, a ghost impression, but creating something entirely new."

"And this is . . . rare?" Blue asked.

"Almost unheard of," Pukwudji said.

Sara nodded. "There are stories about the makers, but they're just legends—even in the Otherworld."

"Can they be killed?"

"All things die," Pukwudji began.

"I know," Blue said. "Except for the little mysteries. So a maker can be killed." He looked from Sara to Pukwudji. "Anybody know how?"

"By someone stronger," Pukwudji said. "Do you still want to go?"

"Knowing all of that doesn't change a thing," Blue said. "We've still got to try—right, Sara?"

Sara hesitated. What she really wanted to say was: Why can't somebody else take the responsibility for a change? We've already been through something like this once before and we only just survived by the skin of our teeth. Nobody gets that lucky twice.

But she knew that because of their ties to the House and Jamie, it *was* their responsibility.

If Jamie hadn't disappeared, if the House hadn't been left unprotected . . .

"Sara . . .?" Blue said.

Sara didn't trust her voice, so she just nodded.

"All right," Pukwudji said. He took Sara's left hand in his right, clasped Blue's free hand in his left. "I'll take you."

His voice was subdued. The touch of his small knobby fingers felt dry against their palms. There was a vague sense of vertigo—here and gone in less time than the space between one breath and another—and then the overpowering presence of the forest surrounding them was suddenly lifted.

They still stood under an apple tree, in the garden's orchard in the middle of the House, but the forest was gone. Beyond the gables of the building they could see the glow of the city's lights, hazing the stars.

They had returned from the Otherworld to their own.

"You did it!" Blue cried.

His momentary happiness at knowing there was a way to get back faded as he looked at Sara. She stood shivering, her hand still clasping Pukwudji's.

"Oh, God," Sara said in a small voice. "I can feel him. He's so close; the touch of his mind is so cold. . . ."

Blue couldn't look at her. He looked away, back to the roofline of the House, only to see owls perched there—two, three, a dozen of them, all in a row, staring right back at him.

"Maybe this wasn't such a good idea," he said.

Neither of his companions responded.

4

When the dead bird twitched, Esmeralda was so startled that she almost opened her hand and let it fall from her grip. Her coyote-headed companion grinned at her, but she just gave him a fierce glare in return until he looked away. The fetish continued to twitch and move in her hands, filling with Jamie as Whiskey Jack drew the scattered bits and pieces of Jamie's spirit from all the countless Otherworlds to which they'd been scattered.

Though Esmeralda would never admit it to her companion, or even let it show on her features where he could read it, the movement of the fetish spooked her.

There was magic and then there was magic. Most of it was logical enough, once you accepted that the natural boundaries of the world stretched a little further than the physics with which scientists had snared them: if Otherworlds existed, then it made sense that passage could be found between them; if the wind and the stars and the trees all had spirits, then of course you could communicate with them, once you knew their language; if you allowed that men and women had souls, then why couldn't there be ghosts—spirits that hadn't yet passed on to wherever it was that the dead finally went?

It was magical—wondrous—but then so was the transformation of caterpillars into butterflies, the flight of a hawk, the change of the seasons, the voice of the tide, the child growing in its mother's womb. It was all part of what the First People called Beauty. But what Whiskey Jack did now—investing the fetish in her hand with the scattered parts of Jamie's spirit—that seemed more like some wild-card magic; a magic where the rules were thrown out the window, where anything went.

With her zealous need for order and organization, this wild-card magic of Whiskey Jack left Esmeralda feeling as uneasy as it did those people she'd left back in the House, those who had no experience with magic of any sort. It was like being in a room and suddenly realizing that the walls went on forever; that they could be both solid and a veil that was easily drawn aside to reveal a world where the underpinning logic one used as a basis of reference no longer applied.

The jerk and quiver of the dead bird in her hand made it very easy for her to empathize with Richard Fagan's panic attack. His poetry, the leaping and breadth of his imaginative process, hadn't made him any more immune to the reality of the preternatural than her own otherworldly experiences would let her be immune to Whiskey Jack's wild-card magic now.

A shiver of pure dread went scurrying up and down the length of her body before she could force herself to be calm. She told herself it was only Jamie's spirit filling the fetish—gentle, soft-spoken Jamie; the man she'd had a mad crush on when she first came to Tamson House all that very long time ago. Jamie wouldn't hurt her and Whiskey Jack couldn't—at least not physically. They'd dealt with that a long time ago.

"It's done," Whiskey Jack said.

Esmeralda suddenly realized that his *yip, yip, yip* cry had long faded. He sat watching her, an unreadable expression in his mismatched eyes. The dead bird struggled in her hand, but she held it firmly.

"Is he . . . intact?" she asked.

Whiskey Jack shrugged. "It's hard to tell. You'll know when you return."

"How will his spirit transfer back into the House?"

Again he shrugged. He dug the tobacco pouch from his pocket, built himself another cigarette and repeated the trick with the burning twig.

Exhaling blue-gray smoke, he added, "Just press the fetish against some part of the House and that should do it. His spirit won't be able to help itself from entering the House."

"No tricks?"

"Why would I lie to you?"

Esmeralda could think of a hundred reasons.

"I believed all your lies once, Jack," she said. "The first time we met. I won't believe them again."

But she could still feel the pain of that betrayal. That was something that would never go away. She wondered sometimes how she could sit so calmly with him, when that hurt lay inside.

Because he was Coyote, she supposed. His betrayals weren't malicious, they were just his way.

"I've nothing to gain from lying to you now," he said, using the only argument that he knew she would accept.

"All right," she said. "Thank you, Jack."

He took another drag from his cigarette, rising to his feet as she stood.

"There's a war between the living and the dead," he said, his voice oddly casual as though it were just a bit of idle conversation he was making. "That's what ghosts are—spirits that won't step from one wheel to another."

"Nobody wants to die," Esmeralda said.

"Yes, but some people will do anything—any evil—if they think it will allow them to maintain their familiar position on the wheel of their life."

"Why are you telling me this?"

"I just want you to know that there's still going to be a price paid before this business is finished."

"You said—"

"It won't be old Whiskey Jack asking for payment."

"What kind of payment?" Esmeralda asked.

"The usual: blood. A life; lives." He looked away from her, out across the mountains, cigarette smoke curling incongruously from his coyote nostrils. "You see," he added, when he finally turned back to her, "that man who's causing us all this trouble in your homeworld—he's one of those people who'll do anything to hold off death."

"Can't you speak any plainer than that?" Esmeralda asked.

She didn't really expect an answer; she might as well ask a river to run uphill. But he surprised her.

"Someone's going to have to take him by the hand and lead him down the Path of Souls," he said.

He tipped a brown finger against the brim of his hat, coyote grin laughing on his lips, though it never reached his eyes; then he stepped over the edge of the cliff and was gone.

Esmeralda didn't bother to step to the edge and look down. He wouldn't have fallen; he just liked to make a good exit. Right now he'd be in some other time, some other place, making mischief for someone else. Esmeralda just had to smile. He made it hard to stay mad at him—always had; always would.

But she thought of what he'd said and her smile faded.

Someone's going to have to take him by the hand and lead him down the Path of Souls.

In other words, for them to get rid of the man that was draining the House's energy—what Sara would call its taw—someone was going to have to die with him. To show him the way.

Great. Were they supposed to pick straws?

Well, she wouldn't let anyone else do it. She just wouldn't tell them.

You see, Jack, she told the empty place where he'd been standing, I don't want to die either, but if this is where I have to get off my wheel, I'll do it. Not for you, not for the House, not even for the people. But for Beauty, because Beauty encompasses it all.

But I'm scared, Jack.

In a perfect world, he would have returned to comfort her, but there was no perfect world—except perhaps for what lay at the end of the Path of Souls. She'd been close to that land once; now she was finally going to see what it really was like. And maybe there'd be a coyote-headed man waiting there for her, one who didn't know how to lie, or if he did, knew how to say he was sorry when he did.

Somehow, she didn't think so.

Gripping the fetish, she closed her eyes and followed the thread of her journey back through the Otherworld to where it had begun.

5

The first half hour after Blue and Sara left seemed to drag on forever. When it had passed and there was still no sign of otherworldly invaders roaming about the House, Emma made the decision to dismantle one of the barricades. She sent Sean and Cal out ahead to scout the lower floors, then divided those that remained into three teams: one stayed to hold their position on the second floor, keeping the Postman's Room as its nerve center. Another was responsible for consolidating as much of the provisions as could be scavenged from the kitchens and ferrying it up to the second floor. The third worked on a cleanup detail, removing the corpses from the House and depositing them outside.

The latter was brutal, ugly work. None of them—except for

Sean and Ohn—had ever had such a close-up experience with death before. The animals were bad enough. Some of them were half-eaten, chest cavities torn open with the organs and intestinal matter spilling out on the floor. Their fur was matted with congealed blood. The air around them buzzed with flies and had already taken on an unpleasant odor.

But it was the ones that were almost human that were more troubling: the monkeymen with their all too human faces and the strange iguana-like beings with their scaly head crests and reptilian eyes. They were like dead people.

"Forget they were ever alive," Sean said as they hauled the bodies outside.

That was easier said than done, Julianne thought. She'd never considered herself to be a squeamish person before, but her stomach kept doing flips when she was confronted with the stiffening corpses. Blood collected on her clothes and smeared her hands and forearms, while the sightless eyes of some of the creatures seemed all too reproachful. She wasn't the only one to lose the contents of her stomach when they first started.

They found the bear to be the worst to deal with—and not only because of its size. In death, its features had taken on a noble, almost bittersweet cast. There wasn't one of the twelve it took to push the carcass down the stairs and drag it down the hall that wasn't affected by its death.

They had posted guards down the lengths of the corridors where they were working, but the crazy onslaught of the Otherworld's creatures wasn't repeated. Tim muttered something about the calm before the storm, but fell silent as more than one person shot him a dirty look. When they finally got the bear's corpse outside, dawn was streaking the eastern skies. Julianne found herself slouching against the wall beside Cal. She was exhausted—mentally as well as physically—but she reached out a hand and touched his arm to get his attention. It left a red smear on his shirtsleeve.

"Sorry about that," she said.

Cal gave a short bitter laugh and spread his arms to show the bloody mess of his clothes.

"Like it's going to make a difference," he said.

"We have to talk, Cal."

She expected him to get up and walk away, or just withdraw behind the barrier he seemed to erect behind his eyes whenever she looked his way, but the brutal work on the cleanup detail had left him as drained as it had her. All he did was stare out at the giant trees of the forest that reared up in front of the House like monolithic holdovers from the dawn of time.

"What's to talk about?" he said finally.

Julianne sighed. "The world's not black and white," she told him. "It's not divided up into the good people and the bad people. There's just people."

"What about Hitler—are you saying he had his good points?"

"You might as well ask, what about Jesus, like he had bad points."

Cal turned to her. "That sounds weird, coming from you."

"I've got no fight with Jesus," she said, "or anything he tried to teach. The only problem I've got with him is what people do in his name, but that's not what I was talking about. Sure, there are exceptions, people who are impossibly good or evil, but that kind of thing doesn't have a whole lot of relevance for ordinary people like us. Most of us are just a mix of good and bad; the best of us try to leave the world a little better place than it was when we got here."

"But—"

"What I'm saying is that it's not as important what you've done, as what you do. If you make what you believe to be a mistake, learn from it and try to do better, but don't brood over it until it takes over your life. None of us are here long enough for that kind of shit."

She put an arm companionably around his shoulder and gave him a small hug.

"Do you understand what I'm trying to say?" she added.

Cal nodded, but before he could speak, the quiet that had descended on the House after that long onslaught of the forest's creatures was suddenly broken with the sound of drums. They started with a solitary drumbeat that was quickly picked up by more and more instruments from every quarter of the forest until the air itself seemed to thrum with their combined rhythm.

Julianne withdrew her arm from Cal's shoulder and they both

stood up, joining the others who were already trying to peer between the trees to find the source of the eerie drumming. Cal retrieved his rifle from where he'd leaned it up against the wall and worked its action, pumping a shell into its firing chamber.

"Jesus," someone said, Julianne wasn't sure who. "I don't think I can go through this all over again."

Ginny was alone in the Postman's Room. She pushed her chair away from the desk, and leaned back with her arms behind her head, trying to ease the tightness in her neck and shoulder muscles. Memoria's screen had stopped its flickering roll call of Weirdin images, settling on just one again: the symbol for the The Gray Man's disc.

She realized that she might as well pack it in. What was happening here had nothing to do with software problems. It was magic, plain and simple; the same kind of hoodoo that had transported the House into the Otherworld, that made a forest take root in its rooms and had whisked Esmeralda away with the spin of a wind that had no logical source of origin.

Her experience as a systems analyst was meaningless here. In her time she'd designed dozens of programs, customized hundreds of different kinds of software, even built hardware from scratch, but the root of this problem was magic and it needed a magician to fix it.

She wasn't a magician. The tricks she knew to get obstinate systems up and running might seem like conjuring to anyone unfamiliar with what she was doing, but they were just that. Tricks. This required real magic.

She slumped in the chair for a long moment, then rose wearily to her feet. It drove her crazy to have to give up, but it was time she started doing something useful. She got as far as the doorway before the loose paper in the room began to swirl around once more. She froze, eyes widening as Esmeralda seemed to step out of nowhere into the room.

You should be used to this by now, she told herself, but she knew she never would be.

Her pulse was jackhammering and it took her a moment to regulate her breathing. Esmeralda nodded to her, than walked toward the computer. She held a bird in her hand that twitched and struggled against her grip until she reached the desk and pressed the bird against Memoria's screen. As Ginny watched, the bird's struggles grew frantic; then it suddenly went limp.

Esmeralda opened her hand and looked down at the bird lying in her palm. With her fingers removed from around the bird, Ginny could see that its wings had been tied against its body. The leather thongs used to do that were decorated with beads and feathers. The bird looked dead.

"That should do it," Esmeralda said.

She laid the bird on the desk beside the keyboard, then turned to Ginny.

"Where is everybody?" she asked.

"Uh . . ."

Ginny stared at Memoria's screen. The symbol of the Weirdin disc was gone. Replacing it was a familiar menu.

Esmeralda drew a finger along the body of the dead bird.

"I found Jamie," she said. "He's back in the House now, but I wouldn't try calling him up just yet. He's going to need a little time to reorient himself."

"Uh . . . right," Ginny finally managed.

She remembered what she'd been thinking just moments ago, how what they needed was a magician to fix the computer's problem. Somehow, for all that had happened in the past day or so, she hadn't really been serious, but the way that Esmeralda had just solved the problem with the computer—using a dead bird, for God's sake!—that brought it all home with a rush of fear that made her head ache. She was finding it hard to breathe again.

"Are you all right?" Esmeralda asked.

Ginny blinked. She took a deep breath, exhaled, took another, then slowly nodded.

"Where is everybody?" Esmeralda asked, repeating her earlier question.

"Outside," Ginny said.

And then the drumming began.

When the figures came walking out of the forest, Ohn stepped forward. He touched Cal's arm as he passed him, then Judy's.

"Stay calm," he told them. He turned slightly so that what he said next could be directed at everyone who held a shotgun or rifle. "Point your weapons at the ground and don't make any threatening gestures."

"You're shitting us, right?" Sean said.

Ohn shook his head.

"Look at them," Emma said, supporting the harper's request. "None of them are armed."

The newcomers stood just under the umbra of the outermost trees, half in shadow, men and women both, with only a few yards between each of them. They were dressed in ceremonial garb, beaded tunics and leggings, quill-decorated dresses; their faces were painted with white clay and dyes. Some had feathered headdresses, others wore the cured heads of wolves and other animals as hoods, which gave them the appearance of being an an odd mix of animal and human. They all had drums hanging from their belts. Their fingers continued to dance rhythms from the taut heads of their instruments; their features were unreadable.

"Who are they?" John Haven asked softly.

"Better ask *what* are they," Sean said.

"They're shaman."

Emma gave a happy cry when she saw Esmeralda standing in the doorway behind them.

"You're back!"

Esmeralda nodded. "When they did get here?" she asked, nodding to the drummers.

"Just a few moments ago," Ohn said.

"Are these Blue's *rath'wen'a*?" Judy asked. "Those Drummers-of-the-Bear he was telling us about earlier?"

Esmeralda look at the men and women, half-hidden in the shadows of the forest, and shook her head.

"I don't think so," she said. "They're drummers, all right, and they *are* shaman, but they've got the feel of the first forest about them."

"Born from the mythic timber of its darkest wood," Ohn agreed, "but flesh and bone now."

"What do they want?" Sean asked.

"That's simple," Esmeralda said. "They're exorcising us—or at least they're trying to." She looked around the small crowd. "Where's Blue?"

"He and Sara are trying to get back to Ottawa," Emma said. "Sara thought her friend Pukwudji might be able to take them back."

"How long have they been gone?"

"For a few hours now."

Esmeralda frowned.

"What's the matter?" Emma asked.

"I have to reach them before they try to confront the man who's responsible for all of this." At the unspoken question in Emma's eyes, Esmeralda added, "Because I know how to stop him."

"That's great! What do we do?"

"I can't tell you," Esmeralda said. "It's a special kind of magic that can't be talked about."

Following their conversation as everyone was, Ohn frowned.

She was lying, he thought. But why? What had she learned on her journey?

"Did you find Jamie?" he asked.

Esmeralda nodded. "But I think it's going to be a few hours before he's got himself together enough to shift the House back to Ottawa." She looked past Ohn's shoulder to where the drummers were still tapping their rhythms from the heads of their instruments. "We'll just have to brave it out with these folks until then."

"And hope they don't call up something worse while we're waiting," Sean said.

"I'll try to talk to them."

She stepped past Ohn, moving closer to the forest. The gazes of the shaman tracked her motion, then settled on the quick deft movement of her hands as she used sign language to explain that they meant no harm to the forest; their coming here had been an accident and they would be leaving soon.

The drums stopped with an abruptness that left their ears ringing.

One shaman—an old woman with more gray in her hair than black, her features horsy and wrinkled—spoke. Her voice was gruff, her words clipped and guttural; her hands echoed what she said in sign language similar to what Esmeralda had used.

"What does she say?" Ohn asked.

"Too much death," Esmeralda translated. "You have slain our—" She frowned. "I don't know that word she just used. It could have been heart, or spirit. . . ."

"It's the bear," Emma said. "She's talking about the bear we had to kill."

"You killed a bear?" Esmeralda asked, but then her gaze traveled to where the corpses were piled. "My God, you killed *all* those creatures?"

"They were attacking us," Judy said. "What were we supposed to do—let them kill us?"

"No. Of course not. But—this is serious. Some of those animals were clan totems."

The shaman spoke sharply. As she did, they could all hear something large moving in the forest behind her. A collective gasp whispered through them as the source of the noise stepped forth from between the trees.

The creature was almost seven feet tall and had the physique of a bodybuilder. Not until it drew closer could they see the fine downy hair that covered its body. The large bull bison head that sat on its shoulders was real, not part of a cured pelt. The two short, curved horns glinted in the growing light; a long dark mane fell to its shoulders. It wore no clothing. Between its legs hung an enormous flaccid penis and testicle sac.

The shaman's hands were busy echoing the harsh words that issued from her mouth.

" 'Our plains brother comes to our aid,' " Esmeralda translated as she finally drew her gaze away from the bison's features and looked at the woman again.

Ohn watched Esmeralda's hands as she replied.

The shaman shook her head, responding with a short cutting motion of her hand.

He touched Esmeralda's shoulder. "What's the matter?"

"I asked her if they would wait."

"And she said no?"

Esmeralda shook her head. "Not exactly. She just told me to send out our champion to meet theirs."

"Our . . .?"

Esmeralda just pointed at the bison-headed man.

"That's theirs," she said. "We've got about a minute to pick one of us to fight him."

"Why don't we just shoot it?" Sean said, lifting his rifle.

Esmeralda pushed the barrel of the gun away. "You can't do that."

"Why not?"

"Because first, they'll just send something else after us—"

"I thought all we needed to do was buy some time?" Sean interrupted.

"—and secondly," Esmeralda went on as though he hadn't spoken, "the karma would be devastating."

"It doesn't have to be a physical battle, does it?" Julianne said.

Ohn nodded in agreement. That was well considered, he thought.

Esmeralda agreed. "You're right. The actual word she used was 'challenge'—I just naturally took it to mean physical combat."

"I don't know," Judy said dubiously. "He doesn't look like the kind of guy who would settle for a verbal debate."

"I think it's like a riddle," Julianne said. "You know, where the most obvious answer isn't necessarily the correct one? They're mad at us because of how many of the forest's creatures we killed—I know," she added as Sean started to protest. "We didn't have any choice. That's given. It's over and done with. But now's our chance to show that we don't just automatically shoot whatever's threatening us."

"You mean well," Sean said, "but you're full of shit. I'm not standing around to let that thing gore me."

"You won't have to," Esmeralda told him. She turned to Emma. "Can you get everybody into the House?"

Emma shook her head. "I'm staying out here with you."

"Don't be silly."

"I'm not. Two years ago you risked everything to help me. I'm not walking out on you now."

The others began to agree—even Sean—but Esmeralda wouldn't have it.

"How can we expect them to believe we don't mean them any

harm," she asked, "if we're all standing out here with our rifles and shotguns like some lynch mob?"

"Yeah, but—"

"Please," she said. She turned from Sean to address Julianne and Ohn. "You know I'm right."

Julianne nodded. "But that doesn't mean we like it."

"I'm not going," Emma said.

"All right," Esmeralda said. "But the rest of you—"

The drums of the shaman spoke suddenly.

Esmeralda glanced at them, then quickly turned back.

"Our time's up," she said. "Please?"

Finally they began to file into the House until only Ohn and Julianne were left.

"Take care of them," Esmeralda said.

"It's not really my thing," Julianne said. "I don't even like asking somebody to go down to the store for me."

"But . . .?"

"But I'll try."

"Thanks."

"Remember your winds," Ohn said, before he left. "As a last resort."

"What did he mean by that?" Emma asked as she and Esmeralda turned to face the shaman and their bison-headed champion.

Esmeralda didn't answer except to let a breeze gust up and flick her long hair about her head. Emma's lips made a startled "O," but then she nodded, understanding that they weren't necessarily as helpless as they seemed.

Esmeralda used her hands to speak to the old woman shaman. *We will not fight. What was done here was done in defense. We are sorry for the unhappiness this has brought to you, but we were given no choice but to strike back when we were attacked. What we will not do is compound that tragedy with yet more unnecessary violence.*

The shaman frowned. *You are the intruders,* she signed.

I know, Esmeralda replied. *Yet we are not here through any choice of our own. We—*

A startled cry from the House behind them interrupted the flow of the words that sprang from her hands. Esmeralda turned to see Julianne in the doorway. At first she could see no reason for

Julianne's alarm. Then she realized that she could see right through her.

"Esmeralda!" Julianne cried. "Come quick."

But it was already too late. Julianne became a ghost, and then she was gone, along with the contents of the House. The structure made an alarming lurch. Wood creaked and groaned until suddenly the entire building fell in upon itself. It collapsed in an odd kind of silence. In the wake of its destruction, Esmeralda and Emma exchanged worried glances.

"It's Jamie," Esmeralda said softly. "He's taken the House back. Either that or . . ."

"Or what?"

"The enemy has stolen all of the House's power. But whichever it was, it leaves us abandoned here."

"Uh, Ez," Emma said. "I think it's a little worse than that."

The shaman had begun drumming once more, all except for the old woman. Her hands danced with conversation.

Our magic has driven the evil away. Now only you two daughters of the darkness remain.

"What's she saying?" Emma asked.

"They're taking credit for the House disappearing."

"Well, that's okay, isn't it? I mean, if they want to think that they did it, why should we argue with them?"

"Because they think the House was evil," Esmeralda said, "and that makes us evil and also their last two pieces of unfinished business."

The bison-headed being stamped his feet on the ground, keeping time to the drumming, which had taken on a frenzied rhythm.

"Your winds," Emma said. "Can they take us out of here?"

"Let's give it a try," Esmeralda replied.

Now that the others were gone, there was no reason for Emma and her to stay here. She closed her eyes and called her winds up, but after the prolonged use she'd put them to in fetching Jamie, it seemed that they could move her hair about and little else. The forest around them was peculiarly still—there wasn't even a breeze for her to borrow—and she wasn't deep enough into the Otherworlds for her to augment them in other ways.

"It's no good," she said.

Emma hid her disappointment. "You tried."

A quick rattle of drumming drew their attention back to the shaman.

It was ill chance, not evil that brought us here, Esmeralda told the woman. *Harm us if you must, but we will fight no more. On your heads will lie the guilt of further violence.*

There is no guilt in slaying enemies, the shaman signed back.

"What did she say?" Emma asked.

She looked worriedly from the old woman to the bison-headed man. His penis was beginning to harden, thickening like the bough of a small tree and rising up the length of his thigh until it stood erect, bouncing slightly as he continued to dance to the drumming.

"Basically," Esmeralda said, "it boils down to us saying our prayers."

"Oh, shit."

Esmeralda nodded. "In a nutshell."

She didn't feel nearly as calm as she was pretending to be. But for Emma's sake she tried to keep her panic at bay as she desperately looked for a way out of their plight, but without her winds she couldn't step them out of this world. Given time, allowing them to replenish their strengths, she could do it, but the shaman and their champion didn't look as though time was something they were offering.

This had to be Whiskey Jack's doing, Esmeralda realized suddenly. He'd lied to her again. She should have known. No matter what he'd promised, there was always a price to pay.

The bison-headed man began to shuffle toward them. Emma made a small sound in the back of her throat. Esmeralda took her hand and gave it a comforting squeeze, then stepped forward so that she was between Emma and the bull-man.

She thought she could hear the distant sound of a coyote's cry, its *yip, yip, yip* sounding far too much like laughter. She sent her winds after its fading sound with a last final curse before the bison-headed man was upon her:

Damn you anyway, Whiskey Jack. Damn you to whatever your kind knows as hell.

Then she faced the bull-man, her face an expressionless mask.

She knew she was going to die, but she refused to give them the pleasure of seeing her fear.

6

The owls were starting to get to Blue as well. He hated the way they just sat there in a long, silent row along the eaves of the House, staring down at them with their unblinking gaze. Their constant presence worked its way under his skin. It wasn't so much an itch as a coldness that traveled relentlessly along the spiderwebbing road map of his nerves to settle in the marrow of his bones.

He felt like putting his rifle to his shoulder and picking off a few of them, but then he realized it wasn't the owls giving him the creeps—at least it wasn't *just* the owls. There was something about the House itself, a kind of diminishing of its presence, as though the mysteries that always lay at its heart had suddenly been pulled into the light, where they were revealed to be just so many conjurer's tricks.

He looked at his companions. Sara was shivering; her features seemed unnaturally pale, even in the poor light. Pukwudji appeared even more freaked out. He held one of Sara's hands and leaned against her, his big eyes looking mournfully at the House.

I can feel him, Sara had said. *He's so close . . . so cold. . . .*

Yeah, Blue thought. Our heebie-jeebies have got a definite source; we just don't have a make on the sucker yet.

"C'mon," he said and ushered them toward the nearest doors. "Let's get in out of the open."

The eyes of their enemy—like the eyes of the owls—seemed to fill the sky, bearing down on them with an intolerable pressure. He thought they'd feel better once they were inside, but it was only worse. Their footsteps on the floor of the empty ballroom echoed eerily and the pressure of their unseen enemy's gaze seemed stronger than it had been outside.

At least we left the owls behind, Blue thought until he looked up at the top of the window frames that ran the length of the garden side of the room. There were birds perched there, looking in. Owls.

Blue led his companions out into the hall. They looked into one or two of the rooms along the way, but everything was empty. The interior of the House had moved to the Otherworld; all that remained was a shell—just the structure itself, as much under siege as its interior was in the Otherworld.

"If we ever get the House back," he said, "there's going to be one hell of a mess to clean up, but at least we don't have to worry about structural damage. Doesn't seem like the forest did any damage to the building in this world."

Sara nodded glumly. Pukwudji just held her hand and didn't respond at all. But Blue felt he had to talk. The echoes of his voice gave him a creepy feeling, but the silence bothered him more.

"You know what really gets me?" he said. "The way this all feels so . . . random. It's like there's nobody to confront, nobody to point the finger at and say, 'You're the bad guy. Your ass is mine.' "

"There's someone now," Sara said.

Blue shook his head. "Intellectually, I know what you're saying, but it doesn't feel like there's a tangible enemy. It's just some faceless thing—a cipher. How the hell do you go to war with something that's just a feeling? This guy's just a ghost."

"I can do more than feel him," Sara said, her voice betraying her tension. "I can lead us to him."

Blue didn't say anything for a long moment. Finally he lifted up his rifle and slapped its barrel against his left hand.

"Then let's do it," he said.

"He's not far," Sara said. "A street over, maybe two at the tops. I can feel him just sucking the vitality out of the House." She touched her right temple with a finger. "I can see him in here."

She put her back against the nearest wall and slid down until she was sitting on her heels. Pukwudji crouched down beside her.

"But we can't just go and shoot him," Sara said.

Blue hunched down until his face was level with hers. "Why the hell not?"

"Because we're not in the Otherworld anymore," she replied. "You can't just walk down the street, carrying a rifle. Someone'll call the cops before we get to the end of the block."

"It's night, Sara. Who's to see?"

She shook her head. "It's not going to work. Let's say that nobody sees us and we get to whatever building he's in without being stopped. If we just walk in and try to shoot him—that's saying he'll even let us get that far—we'll have police all over us. He's not doing anything that we can prove is illegal; he's not doing anything we can prove is real at all. And even if you should manage to kill him, you're going to go to jail for doing it."

"Then what should we do?"

"I don't know. I thought I'd know when we got here, but he's so strong and I don't have any magic—not the kind I'd need to take him on."

"What about you, little buddy?" Blue asked Pukwudji.

The *honochen'o'keh* could only shake his head.

They fell silent then. Blue ran his hand up and down the cold metal of his rifle's barrel. The presence of their enemy was almost palpable in the air—a thick, cloying sensation.

"If we don't have magic to use against him," Blue said, "then we're going to have to do it my way."

"We can't," Sara said.

"Maybe *we* can't," Blue said, "but I've got to. Besides, it all makes a kind of sense. The House has always had a kind of mythic feel about it, so maybe it's time I played out my part of the story—sort of like the king of the wood."

"What are you talking about?"

"It's in one of Jamie's books. Back in the old days there were these societies who picked some guy and made him their king, you know? He could do anything he wanted, have anything he wanted. You name it and it was his. But this only lasted for a few years—I can't remember how many—and then when his time was up, they'd kill him."

"You're not making any sense," Sara said, but Blue could tell she knew what he was getting at.

"You see, before I met you and Jamie, I was a real loser," he went on. "I rode with the Dragon, I did all kinds of bad shit. Man, I was a mess, heading straight down the highway to hell. But then I met Jamie and he brought me back here and suddenly I had options—that was something I'd never had before. That's something you and Jamie and the House gave me: a chance to be one of the good guys."

"What's that got to do with this king-of-the-wood business?"

"Well, you see, it's like I've been the king of the wood for the past bunch of years. I've been able to do whatever I wanted. I've had my past wiped clean like it never happened and got the chance to start all over again, to be the kind of guy I might've been if I hadn't taken a wrong turn way back when."

"That still doesn't—"

Blue cut her off. "I figure it's time for me to put something back now. Lots of those guys went willingly, you know. I figure it's because they knew that their dying meant something. It renewed the land, made everything okay for the tribe. I can get into that."

Sara shook her head. "That's not what's going on here."

"I think it is," Blue said. "I think it's going to cost us something to get things back to the way they were before. Even Pukwudji said that."

"But—"

"We've all got to die sometime, Sara. If I've got to go, I'd rather have my death mean something than just be another statistic on the obit page."

When he stood up, Sara scrambled to her feet.

"I can't let you do it," she said.

"I don't see that we have a choice."

"But—"

"Think of all the good the House does. Think of all those people we left in the Otherworld. You don't think they're worth dying for?"

"Not all of them."

"Everybody's worth helping, Sara."

"You know what I mean."

Blue found a tired smile. "Yeah, we'd all rather see a stranger get it than someone we know."

"Well, I'm going with you," Sara said.

"You're going as far as it takes to point me in the right direction," Blue corrected her. "Then you and Pukwudji are out of here. We've only got one gun; only one of us can pull the trigger at one time."

"I don't want to do this, Blue."

"Shit, and you think I do?" He lifted a hand to her hair and ruffled the curls. "Things'll work out."

"It's not fair."

"Well, you know what Jools says about fair."

Sara shook her head.

"It's just the first third of fairy tale and you won't find either in the real world."

"This *is* the real world and we *are* in the middle of a fairy tale."

"So sue me. Or her."

"You're not the king of any wood," Sara told him. "You're just a king of fools."

"So what does that make you?"

"Who said you were *my* king?"

It was tough making jokes, Blue thought, feeling the way they did, but it was that or cry. If Sara started to cry he didn't know if he could go through with this.

He found himself wanting to say things to her: how much he cared for her, how much he'd missed her, how much she was a part of his becoming the person he was now, but he knew that would just make it harder. Then he thought about Emma, waiting for him back in the Otherworld, and all the friends he was leaving behind. Judy. Esmeralda. Ginny. Ohn. Jools. They were good people. They were worth the sacrifice, but man, he was going to miss them.

"This is why the owls are here," Pukwudji said suddenly.

"Say what?" Blue asked.

Pukwudji stood up from where he'd been crouched on the floor, his hand creeping back up until it was nestled in Sara's once more.

"They gather at the birth of great deeds," he explained.

"Well, hell," Blue said. "Let's not keep them waiting." He turned to Sara. "Which way do we go?"

"He's somewhere near the south side of the House," she said. She looked miserable; her voice was strained. "I think he's in one of the houses on Clemow."

Blue led the way to the closest of the doors on the east side of the House that led out onto O'Connor Street. When they were out on the street, he kept the rifle close to his body so that it couldn't be easily seen. Sara walked on his right as they headed down the block to Clemow, Pukwudji's hand still in hers.

There was a sound on the air—a kind of whispering that made them pause and lift their heads to look around. Blue and Sara exchanged troubled looks, then started off again. Above them, the owls followed, flying from house eave to telephone pole. Still silent; still watching.

"This is the place," Sara said.

Blue changed his hold on his rifle. He wiped his right palm on his jeans, then took the grip in that hand again, finger snaking into the trigger guard. He looked up at the building. They were halfway down Clemow, between Bank Street and O'Connor. The house was an older, two-story brick building with hip-and-valley roofs, set snug in between its neighbors, the houses all standing in a neat row on this residential street. There were a few lights on inside, but heavy curtains killed any hope of a view. It was the only building on the street with any lights.

It looked about as threatening as day-old bologna, he thought. Maybe less. You could get food poisoning from bologna.

"This guy's in there?" he asked.

Sara nodded. She took a step up the walk, pausing when Pukwudji didn't move with her.

"We have to do it," she told the little *honochen'o'keh*.

"I know," Pukwudji said. "But it only requires one of us. This is a bad place, Sara."

Only one of us, Blue thought. Well, he was the guy with the big gun, wasn't he?

Before he could start down the walk, Sara let go of Pukwudji's hand and went ahead of him. He hurried to catch up, but she was already on the porch by the time he reached her.

"I told you before—you're only here to point me the way," he whispered. "You've done that, so why don't you just leave the rest to me."

The look she gave him in return allowed for no argument, but Blue tried anyway.

"Look," he said. "Someone's going to have to take charge of the House."

"Esmeralda will do that."

"Yeah, but . . ."

"We're in this together," Sara told him. "I don't want to argue any more—that's why I just went along with what you were saying earlier. Now are we going to do something or not?"

Blue sighed. "Like what? Ring the bell?"

Sara shrugged. "Why not? He knows we're here."

As she lifted her finger to push the bell, Pukwudji caught her hand and stopped her.

"Don't," he said.

Blue was in agreement. If the enemy knew they were here, why had they even come in the first place? They were supposed to be surprising the guy; considering the kind of power he had to work with, they didn't have a hope in hell otherwise. But this . . . Ringing the bell and then shooting whoever answered didn't seem like the best course of action.

"You didn't tell me he'd know we were coming," he said.

"I can feel him in here," Sara said, tapping her temple again. "He doesn't see us as a threat. He doesn't know about the gun. He . . . That's all the surprise I think we're going to get."

"He's got to threaten us," Blue said. "I don't think I can just . . . shoot him in cold blood."

"It's not like we've got a whole lot of choice," Sara said. "If you want to give me the rifle . . ."

Blue couldn't see much of her features, they were cast in shadow because her back was to the streetlights, but he could hear the emptiness in her voice. She wasn't any more prepared for this than he was. It was one thing to take somebody down in the middle of a running battle; something else entirely to just walk in off the street and shoot them.

"We've got to be sure he's the one," he added.

Sara nodded. "We'll be sure."

Once again she reached for the doorbell, and again Pukwudji stopped her.

"This is a bad place," he repeated. "It's not all quite part of this world, hey?"

"I can feel that," Sara said.

"What is it?" Blue asked, peering more closely at the doorbell. "Is this thing booby-trapped?"

Pukwudji shook his head miserably. "It's a door to the Other-world—but not to any part of it that we know. He's made his own echo of the Otherworld here; a shadow cast by the bitterness of his spirit. The rules it follows answer only to him. Do you understand?"

Blue nodded. At least he thought he understood. The house might look innocent but, just like Tamson House, there was more to it than met the eye. He figured what Pukwudji was saying was that their enemy had invested a part of himself in the building. It wasn't the doorbell that was booby-trapped; the whole building was a trap.

He could feel something—a presence in the air, a coldness—that he realized was emanating from the building. It wasn't overtly threatening, but it had the same taste to it that he'd sensed back at Tamson House; something was watching them, just waiting for them to make their move.

He looked back at the street. Owls were perched on telephone poles, streetlights and the roofs of houses. One was on the hood of a parked car on their side of the street. They were here for the show, for—how did Pukwudji put it?—the "birth of great deeds."

Right, he thought. Taking notes for some otherworldly PBS special. Well, let's not disappoint them.

He worked the lever of his rifle, filling the firing chamber with a shell.

"Skip the bell," he said. "Just try the door. If it's unlocked, swing it open and stand back."

Sara nodded. She took a breath and put her hand on the door-knob, but as soon as she touched it, she collapsed like a marionette with its strings cut. She slumped against the door and slid to the floor of the porch, her muscles completely limp. It was as though her bones had all turned to jelly.

"What . . .?"

Blue crouched down beside her. He laid his rifle down so that he could gather Sara up from where she had fallen. The door opened when he had her in his arms. Light spilled out, half-blinding him. He blinked in its glare, then found himself looking up into the tired features of a woman who appeared to be in her early sixties.

She was dressed all in black, like the old ladies down in Little Italy—long black dress, black sweater, black stockings and shoes, black kerchief around her head. But for all her grim wardrobe, he didn't get any sense of menace from her—couldn't sense anything at all except for that weariness that was undoubtedly responsible for the heavy lines in her features.

He glanced helplessly at Pukwudji, but the little man had vanished. Beyond the porch, he could sense the owls, their attention sharpened into such a tight focus upon him that it felt as though they were pecking at him with their beaks.

"You shouldn't have come," the woman said.

Blue turned back to look at her.

"He was almost finished," the woman went on. "He would have taken the House, and been content with that, but now . . ."

Her voice trailed off. Blue waited for her to continue, but she just regarded him with her sad, tired gaze.

"Now what?" he asked finally.

The woman pointed to Sara lying limp in his arms.

"Now he has her as well," she said. She regarded him for a long moment, then finally stood aside, adding, "You might as well come in now."

None of this was playing the way it was supposed to, Blue thought.

"Come along," the woman added a little peevishly. "I don't have all night."

Blue shook his head. This was nuts. They'd come here to kill somebody, and now this woman was asking him in like they'd just dropped by for tea.

He looked again for Pukwudji, but there was still no sign of the little man. Retreat was definitely in order, he thought. Instead, he rose with Sara in his arms and carried her inside.

"You can lay her down here," the woman said, indicating a couch in the room just off the front hall.

The room was comfortably furnished. There were framed samplers and reproductions of landscapes on the wall. A TV set sat in one corner with the picture on, the sound off. There were a couple of easy chairs, the couch, a coffee table. Knickknacks stood in a genial array on the mantelpiece.

He hesitated in the doorway for a moment, then laid Sara on the couch. Her breathing seemed steady, but there was still no alleviation of her limpness. Her head lolled sideways until he supported it with a pillow. The woman watched him, stepping back into the hall when he rose from the couch.

"You don't really need it," she said when he glanced to the porch where the rifle was lying, "but if it'll make you feel more at ease, by all means bring it in."

Blue was no longer certain about anything that was going on, but he did know one thing: she might not think he needed the rifle, but he sure as hell was going to feel better with a weapon in his hand.

He retrieved the rifle from the porch. When he stepped back inside, the woman made a follow-me motion with one hand and started up the stairs. Blue hesitated for a long moment. He closed the front door, looked in on Sara, whose condition didn't seem to have changed, then finally went up the stairs. The woman was waiting impatiently for him on the landing.

She led him to the front bedroom, motioning him to enter.

It was colder still in the room—the drop in temperature coming in waves from the still figure that lay on the bed. Blue thought it was a corpse at first. The man's skin was pale, almost translucent. But his chest moved, his breath lightly frosting the air around his thin lips. Blue felt that he could see the man's eyes moving under his closed lids. He was in his seventies at least—maybe older. His hair was thinning and gray, his frame slender almost to the point of emaciation.

He gave no indication that he was aware of either Blue or the woman's presence in the room, but Blue could sense that watchfulness growing sharper.

"This is who you were looking for," she said. "But you're far too late. You can't hurt him."

She picked up a book from a side table and threw it at the figure.

Just before it hit the man, there was a quick bright flare of light—like bare wires sparking against each other—and then the book was flung across the room. The man remained immobile, untouched by the book, unmoved by the incident. A smell that reminded Blue vaguely of anise drifted briefly in the air, then faded.

"Nothing can hurt him," the woman said. "Not anymore."

"What . . . what the hell's going on here?" Blue finally asked.

The woman smiled at him. "You know."

Yeah, Blue thought. He knew. The man lying there was siphoning off Tamson House's vitality.

"What's in it for you?" he asked the woman.

"Youth. Eternal youth. We'll be young together—forever."

Blue shook his head. He lifted the rifle until its muzzle was pointed at her.

"I'm betting you don't have some fancy force field to protect you," he said.

"You're right, of course. I don't."

"So tell him to stop. Tell him to stop and let Sara go or so help me God, I'll shoot."

"You don't have it in you."

Blue's gaze went hard. "Lady, you don't know what I'm capable of when my friends are being hurt."

The woman laughed. "It really doesn't matter. Go ahead and shoot me—he'll just bring me back to life again."

Was that possible? Blue wondered. He could see that the woman sincerely believed it was. His own reservations withered when he thought about all the impossibilities he'd experienced in the past twenty-four hours.

"Go away," the woman told him. "He's not interested in you. Your friend has a certain . . . vitality that he can use, but he has no need for you."

"Fuck you," Blue said.

He moved the muzzle from her to the figure in the bed and fired from the hip. The bullet sparked just before reaching the man, ricocheting off to embed in a wall. The aniselike smell stung Blue's nostrils. His ears rang from the loud report, but the woman appeared completely unfazed.

"I think it's time for you to go," she said.

Her voice seemed to come from a great distance. Blue worked another round into the firing chamber and swung the rifle back so that it covered her.

"Sit down," he said.

She moved to a chair and sat. The weariness in her features was now touched with a mocking amusement. Blue looked around the room, spotted a handful of ties hanging from a tie rack on the closet door, and grabbed a couple.

"Tie your legs to the chair," he told her, tossing the ties toward her.

"This isn't going to prove anything." She looked at the man on the bed. "As soon as he's finished, he'll—"

"Just do it."

When she finished tying her legs to the chair, he took a few more ties over to where she sat and bound her arms behind her. After checking and tightening the bonds on her legs, he set the rifle aside and moved to the phone.

"I've told you. There isn't anybody who can help—"

"Put a cork in it, lady."

He dialed a number and waited impatiently for the connection to be made. It took six rings before a sleepy voice answered on the other end of the line.

"Tucker? Blue here."

"Do you have any idea what—"

"I don't give a shit what time it is. I need your help, John."

"Why is it that the only time I ever hear from you it's when you need a favor?"

"This is serious. It's got to do with Sara."

That was enough to get Tucker's attention.

"Okay," he said. "What's up?"

"I've got a situation here that's going to get real messy."

"You're at the House?"

"No," Blue said. "We're just across the street, on the south side of the building." He gave the address.

"You want me there officially?" Tucker asked.

Tucker was a cop who usually tried to play by the rules. But he was also a friend.

"I don't think that'd be such a good idea," Blue said. "I just need you."

"I'll be right over," Tucker told him.

7

Esmeralda had grossly miscalculated how long it would take Jamie to recover. He hadn't exactly died so much as fragmented this time out, but his return to awareness followed a similar pattern. By the time Whiskey Jack had gathered all the lost parts of his soul into the vessel of the dead kingfisher, he was already dealing with his recovery.

It took him a little longer to get his bearings once Esmeralda returned him to the House. The spark of his being leapt immediately into Memoria's electronic circuits; it was relating to the sheer size and scope that his spirit inhabited in its guardianship of the House that took the extra time. It was like putting on a familiar suit one hadn't worn for a few years. You knew which sleeve went where, how the zipper and buttons functioned, but it just didn't *feel* right at first. It seemed tighter across the shoulders, perhaps, and the trousers didn't hang just right. Still, it only took wearing it for a short while until you adjusted to the fit.

As he did with the House.

But by the time he was back in control, Esmeralda and Ginny had already left the room and there was no one with whom he could communicate. He started to follow their progress, looking inward through the windows, listening to the hollow tread of their footsteps on the hardwood floors, the more muffled steps on carpets, but he soon withdrew back to his nerve center in Memoria.

There was a far more pressing concern at hand than speaking to his friends.

He'd sensed the drain on the House's vitality as soon as he was lodged in the interlocking patternwork of its wood and glass and stone. He traced the origin of the siphoning back to the House's homeworld, a process that gave him his first awareness that the building had followed him into the Otherworld.

In the matrices of Memoria's memory banks he had long ago

created a physical representation of himself and his study. It wasn't a place anyone else could visit, for it existed solely in electronic impulses—an odd mingling of those that were native to the human mind with those that the computer required to function; it existed solely for him. The pretense of a physical body and surroundings helped him to focus more clearly on individual issues as well as allowing him a respite from the constant barrage of stimuli that the House fed him otherwise. As Tamson House was a haven to those who required a respite from the sometimes overwhelming concerns of the world beyond its walls, so this small block of electronic impulses in Memoria's enormous memory banks was his.

It was to that place he retreated when the full enormity of the situation settled in him.

His first impulse on discovering the intruder had been to cut off the man's access to the House's magical essence. That had proved futile. The intruder was simply too strong, effortlessly blocking every one of Jamie's attempts. What was worse, he was using the House's own energy to do so. So Jamie withdrew to the privacy of his haven—even the intruder didn't seem able to access it—but while he was safe from the man's scrutiny, he was also at a loss as to how to proceed from here.

"God, but you've been a fool," he told himself. "How can you stop him, when he controls more of the House than you do?"

"You have to go to him," a disembodied voice said.

The shock of being addressed by someone in his most private of retreats was enough to make him momentarily lose control of the pretense of form he had given himself and the study. When he recovered enough to call them back into their semblances of reality, he was no longer alone in the room.

Sitting in the other club chair was a familiar figure whose presence made the hairs rise on the nape of Jamie's neck. The newcomer looked like a fairy-tale gremlin—a tiny wizened figure with a floppy hat and a baggy overcoat. His nose was hooked; his beard, and what could be seen of his hair poking from under the hat, was grizzled. His eyes were startlingly bright and seemed to bulge birdlike from their sockets.

"You can't be here," he said.

"Why not?"

"Because you're—"

"Dead?" His uninvited guest laughed. "And you're not?"

It was a question that Jamie had pondered over a great deal in the years since he'd taken over guardianship of the House, but it wasn't relevant here. With the man's laugh he realized who his guest was. It wasn't Thomas Hengwr sitting here with him—the same man who'd been indirectly responsible for all the odd occurrences that had troubled Tamson House and eventually resulted in Jamie's own death so many years ago. No, this was Whiskey Jack in one of his thousand and one guises, following up on the results of his earlier handiwork with Esmeralda.

Jamie had seen him pass through the House often enough in the years of his guardianship to recognize him no matter what shape he wore.

"What do you want?" he asked the trickster.

"The same as you—a return to how things once were. Unfortunately, that won't be entirely possible, but we can only do our best."

Jamie nodded slowly.

"It's up to you to stop him," Whiskey Jack said. "Let me tell you what I know of him, little enough though it is."

"Why don't you stop him?"

"Because it's your responsibility," Whiskey Jack replied. "And because I can't get near him."

"And I can?"

Whiskey Jack nodded.

"I've already tried to stop him, but he's too strong."

"That's why you have to *go* to him. You're part of the House once more now—all you have to do is follow the trail of energy he's stealing away."

"And then?"

Whiskey Jack didn't bother replying.

Jamie sighed. "All right. Tell me what you know."

Whiskey Jack flickered out of existence when he'd finished speaking, vanishing like a hologram when the lights were turned off. Jamie took a moment to digest what he'd been told. He looked around the pretense of his study, looked down at his hands.

We never know when we're well enough off, he thought.

We're given great gifts, but we never appreciate them for what they are. We keep wanting more and more, until one day our greed forces it all to be taken away.

Well, he had no one but himself to blame.

He rose from his chair and let the illusion of body and room disappear. His spirit hovered for a moment in Memoria's electronic web; then he allowed the intruder to siphon him away with the vitality of the House that he was so busily stealing.

As he was drawn back to his homeworld, he drew the House and its inhabitants along with him.

8

John Tucker pulled his car up to the curb in front of the address that Blue had given him and killed the engine.

He was the head of security for a special branch of the RCMP that investigated the paranormal. The official name for the branch was Mindreach, named after a project in the early eighties dedicated to researching and documenting the viability of psychic resources; since then their mandate had been broadened to encompass the entire gray area of experiences that could be collected under the term paranormal. To the other horsemen, the men who worked that branch were known as the Spook Squad.

Tucker was in his mid-fifties and still in top physical condition. He was a big man, just topping six feet and weighing in at two hundred pounds. His hair and eyes were gray; his squared mustache almost white. He'd been with the force for thirty-six years—ten years of that time heading up the Spook Squad—but the weirdest thing he'd ever been involved in hadn't been a part of his work, although it had started there. It had all gone down in that strange block-long building directly across the street from the address where he was now parked.

He'd been skeptical of Mindreach's mandate until that time, but the events in Tamson House had changed all of that. Whenever talk came down of cutting the small branch's budget, he was on the front line, cashing in favors to keep it viable. Tangible evidence was hard to come by, but he knew their work was important, because one day, somewhere out there, another Tom Hengwr was going to show up. The difference was, this time they'd be ready when the shit hit the fan.

His belief in Mindreach's importance even overrode the guilt of what he'd had to do in the final cleanup after what had happened in the House. Hengwr hadn't been the only threat at that time; J. Hugh Walters, a business magnate, had also been involved. He was too high up to take down, had too many connections in the local and federal government, so Tucker had dealt with him using the only option left.

That assassination, necessary though it had been, had him sitting at his desk more than once, typing up his resignation. Mindreach was what made him tear it up each time—Mindreach and his wife, Maggie. She'd been through the same shit; she'd helped him make the decision. And it was only because he knew that her respect for the law—she was a Crown attorney—was as great as his that he let her talk him out of it.

"We didn't have a choice," she'd tell him, always making it a collective deed, although he'd been the one to pull the trigger. "And if you walk out on Mindreach now, you're throwing it all away. Because it's going to happen again. We know now that it's possible; next time we might not get so lucky. Next time it might not be contained the way it was with Thomas Hengwr. And if you're not there . . ."

She didn't have to finish. He kept working; he kept the branch alive. But some days he couldn't help but wake up wondering if it wasn't all a lie. Maybe the ends had justified the means—that time. But who was he to call the shot? He'd been right once; there were no guarantees he'd be right a second time. And solving the problem the way he had, how did that make him any different from the bad guys?

It was a circular argument, with no easy answers. Hearing from Blue, seeing Tamson House, brought it all back again.

He studied the long dark building now, then turned his attention to the house where Blue and Sara were waiting for him.

Everything looked normal, he thought. Maybe Blue was overreacting.

But then he noticed the owls.

The birds were everywhere—on the eaves of houses, on trees, streetlamps, telephone poles, even on the car parked in front of him.

"Shit," he muttered.

He took his revolver from the seat beside him and got out of the car, clipping the holster to the back of his belt where his jacket would hide it. Blue had the front door open before he reached the porch.

"Thanks for coming," Blue said, stepping aside to let him in.

"No problem, Farley."

Tucker smiled at Blue's pained expression. Glen Farley was the name on Blue's birth certificate; there weren't many people who could get away with razzing him about it. Only this time, Tucker didn't get a rise out of him.

Tucker's smile faded into a frown. Things were definitely serious.

"So what's going down?" he asked as he stepped into the front hall.

Blue just pointed to the couch in the living room. Tucker took a few quick steps over to where Sara was lying and knelt down beside her. He put a pair of fingers up against her throat, then looked over his shoulder at Blue.

"Did you call an ambulance?" he asked.

Blue shook his head. "She needs magic, not medicine."

Magic. Right. That shit again.

Tucker sighed. "Do you want to run the whole story by me?"

Blue pulled up the coffee table. Sitting on its edge, his gaze shifting from Sara's still features to Tucker's face, he filled Tucker in on all the details as he knew them. He finished his explanation upstairs where the residents of the house were. The old woman regarded them with amusement, for all that she was bound to a chair. Her companion lay on the bed as motionless as Sara did on the couch downstairs.

Tucker dug a quarter out of his pocket and tossed it at the man. Just as Blue had said it would, the quarter sparked against something just a fraction of an inch from the prone figure on the bed and was hurled across the room. Tucker watched the quarter spin on the floor, then finally lie still. An odd, pungent odor stung his nostrils, but it was gone before he could place it.

"You see?" Blue said.

Tucker nodded and drew Blue back out into the hall.

"What did you want from me?" he asked when they were out of the bound woman's earshot.

Blue ran a troubled hand through his hair. "Fucked if I know," he said. "Have you still got the same gig—chasing spooks and Elvis pretenders?"

Tucker nodded.

"Well, I was hoping your people might have developed something by now that we can use." At Tucker's puzzled look, Blue added, "You know. Like something to cut through that guy's force field or whatever it is that he's got protecting him. Maybe something to contain his magic so that he can't turn it on anybody else."

"Sounds like you're talking about the kind of gizmos that the Ghostbusters used," Tucker said.

"Is that so farfetched?"

"Fercrissakes, Blue. That stuff's just a fantasy."

"And this isn't?"

Tucker started to reply, then nodded. "Okay. I get your point. But you're clutching at straws. We don't have anything like that. Christ, we don't even have any hard evidence that this shit's on the level, little say having gotten around to developing equipment to deal with it."

"We're talking about Sara here," Blue said.

"And I'm leveling with you. This isn't security-clearance bullshit. You do realize that ninety-nine-point-nine percent and then some of our loyal taxpayers haven't a clue that something like Mindreach even exists in the first place?"

Blue nodded. "I've just got to do something for her. It's eating me up, John—you understand what I'm saying?"

Tucker was worried about Sara as well, but the larger proportion of his concern was directed at the nameless figure that lay on the bed in the room they'd just quit. From what Blue had been telling him earlier, this guy could be even more powerful than Hengwr had been and that was something he *didn't* need.

"I hear you," he said.

"So talk to me," Blue said. "Give me some feedback. What the hell do we *do?*"

"We wait," Tucker told him. "I'll call Maggie and have her come over. She can sit with Sara while we watch in here."

"And then?"

Tucker shrugged. "We play it by ear. There's nothing else we can do."

It wasn't enough. He could see that in Blue's features—where frustration warred with resignation. He felt the same himself, but what else could they do? There were no other options.

"Okay," Blue said.

His voice had taken on an uncharacteristic dullness. He hoisted his rifle and stepped back into the bedroom. Tucker hesitated for a moment, then went downstairs to look for a phone. He'd spotted one in the bedroom, but didn't see any reason he should let their captives be privy to any more information than they already were.

He paused in the doorway of the living room to look in on Sara again.

"This sucks," he said.

He headed farther down the hall to where he could see a wall phone hanging just inside the kitchen door.

9

It happened so fast, Sara didn't have a chance to protect herself. One moment she had her hand on the doorknob, the next she could feel her spirit being sucked out of her body into . . .

Elsewhere.

She was no longer on a porch, no longer in Ottawa, no longer in her own world. She experienced a stomach-wrenching sensation of vertigo. A sound like flies trapped against glass buzzed in her skull, droning against the breathy airing of a distant flute that soon faded. The buzzing remained until she opened her eyes.

The place to which she'd been taken appeared to be a wide mesa top. She had the sense of physical form, but she knew that although she could feel a desert wind touch her cheek and brush against her hair, although the ground felt solid underfoot, it was all an illusion.

She could still sense her body, lying where it had collapsed on the porch of that house on Clemow—but her awareness of it was like looking through thick gauze. The mesa top, the night sky above, brilliant with stars, the endless expanse of desert that stretched off in all directions from the mesa, the pretense of a shape she wore now, were far more immediate, far more *real*.

She remembered what Pukwudji had said about their enemy creating his own Otherworld and realized that it was there that she'd been taken. She turned in a slow full circle, sand gritting realistically under her shoes. It was only when she completed the circle that she realized she was no longer alone.

A figure stood at the edge of the mesa, in a direct line of sight from where she'd first appeared. It had its back to her. A shiver of dread traveled up her spine, but when it turned, she wasn't confronted with the enemy she'd been expecting.

The man who returned her gaze bore an uncanny resemblance to her Uncle Jamie. Remembering what Emma had told her of her meeting in the forest, Sara stifled her first impulse to run to him.

"Sairey?" he said. "Is that you, Sara?"

The voice was perfect, but she didn't trust its perfection. If the enemy was capable of creating a perfect pretense of her own body in this place, when she knew it lay slumped on an Ottawa porch, then he was similarly capable of calling up a perfect replica of her uncle.

"What are you doing here?" Jamie asked.

For all her distrust, it was hard to ignore his presence—hard to ignore the possibility that, somehow, this really was Jamie calling to her.

"Is that you really you, Jamie?" she said, unable to stop herself from hoping.

He nodded and stepped closer to her.

"Jack's being kind," he said. "I would have given anything to see you one more time, but after all the mistakes I've made, I never had the courage to ask."

Sara couldn't help herself. The closer he came to her, the more she fell into believing that this really was Jamie. All the years of mourning his death dissolved under a rush of affection.

"Who's Jack?" she found herself asking, as comfortable with

him as though they were sitting in the Postman's Room again, having one of their rambling conversations.

"Whiskey Jack," Jamie said. "The coyote man."

He stood just an arm's length away from her now. He seemed more diffident than she remembered him to be, but she realized immediately that that was because she was putting distance between them.

"I've missed you," she said.

She stepped into his arms and returned his hug. He felt the same as always—sturdy and just a little stout. His hand moved on her back in a familiar pattern. He smelled of pipe tobacco and old books. She held on to him for a long time before she would let him go.

"What are you doing here?" he asked again.

She explained briefly, then added, "Where is 'here'?"

"We're in the mind of our enemy," Jamie told her. "Or more correctly, in a world created from his thoughts."

Sara thought of what Pukwudji had told her when he found her trapped in a glade of the first forest.

"Like the ghost of the forest he created that's trying to swallow the House?"

"The House is back where it's supposed to be," Jamie told her. "I've done that much right."

"But the forest's still a threat, isn't it?"

"Not as much as the enemy is."

"Who *is* he, Jamie?"

"I know what he is," Jamie said. He described the man as Whiskey Jack had to Emma and Esmeralda. "His name's not important."

Sara nodded. She looked around the mesa top. The wind still blew its hot dusty breath in from the surrounding desert; they were still alone. Above them, the constellations hadn't moved. Time, it seemed, stood still in this place.

"What are we going to do?" she asked.

"I have to take him down the Path of Souls," Jamie said.

Sara was surprised at Jamie's indirectness. He was usually so plainspoken.

"You mean kill him, don't you?" she said. "Blue was going to do that—that's how I ended up here."

"He's already dead," Jamie explained. "He had to die—that was the price for making his attempt to acquire the House's power. Everything has its cost, Sairey, especially magic. You know that."

"That doesn't make any sense. What use is the power if he's dead?"

"With the power, he can bring himself back to life."

"But there has to be a price. . . ."

Jamie nodded. "When the House's magic is his, he'll have the power to make somebody else pay in his place. Somebody else will die, while he returns to life—revitalized. Perhaps even immortal."

"That's possible?" Sara asked.

"It is."

"Well, then why didn't you ever come back?"

"I wasn't willing to sacrifice someone else, Sairey. It's that simple."

Sara felt stupid and a little ashamed. Of course, Jamie wouldn't do that. To cover her embarrassment, she turned the conversation a few steps.

"So you're going to show him the Path of Souls?" she asked.

Jamie nodded. "Take him on it, yes."

"And then what happens?"

"Then his threat will be ended and things will be back to normal except that the House will need a new guardian."

It took Sara a moment to digest that.

"Wait a minute," she said. "You're the House's guardian. . . ."

Her voice trailed off as what he was trying to tell her finally dawned on her.

"You can't do it, Jamie."

"I have to do it. The only way to be rid of him is for a willing soul to take him."

"But then you . . ."

"I've had a good life, Sairey—and an extension to it that few are allowed. And death isn't an ending—it's a beginning. Jack's told me about the wheels of our life. We step from one onto another. Change is natural."

"Whiskey Jack is a liar."

"This time he's telling the truth."

Sara shook her head. "You can't *know* that."

"But I do. Don't forget—I was almost there once. But the wheel of the House took me back before I could finish my journey."

"Jamie . . ."

"I'll miss you, too," Jamie said.

He tousled her hair, then put his arm over her shoulder and began to walk her to where he'd been standing when she first saw him.

"Remember what Ha'kan'ta's people have told us of the Place of Dreaming Thunder?" he asked.

Sara nodded, not trusting herself to speak.

"That's where I'll wait for you."

A hundred protests rose in her, but they couldn't get past the thickness in her throat. And then they were at the edge of the mesa and she was looking down at their enemy.

He hung in the air, arms and legs outstretched and surrounded by a nimbus of light that was both a circle and a square so that he looked like a physical representation of da Vinci's *The Proportions of the Human Body*. But unlike da Vinci's famous sketch, the man who hung here was neither young, nor well proportioned. He was instead an old man, his features sharply defined, his skin almost translucent so that the blue veins made a networking pattern, his body a sad image of scrawny torso and scrawnier limbs.

Sara shivered. There was nothing overtly threatening about the man. If anything, he seemed pathetic; but the nimbus of light that surrounded him crackled with a raw, dark vitality—stolen vitality—and she didn't doubt either his evil or his power for a moment. She understood immediately why he had to be dealt with—now, before he returned to her homeworld.

He seemed entirely unaware of them—eyes closed, his features confident and reposed—or perhaps he didn't consider them enough of a threat to worry about. When she thought of how easily he'd pulled her out of her body and brought her here, she decided it was the latter.

"I . . ." she began. She turned to Jamie. "It's not fair. You . . . you've already died once. . . ."

Jamie squeezed her shoulder, offering a comfort she couldn't deal with yet.

"The dead are only those who can't accept change," he explained. "They refuse to continue their journey from wheel to wheel and so they haunt the places of their past as ghosts and can't ever know peace or fulfillment."

"But—"

"I have to do this, Sairey," he said. He lowered his head to kiss her brow. "It's not so much atonement for being the catalyst to this situation, as my time to go on."

"But the House," Sara tried. "It'll need a protector. . . ."

"It will find what it needs, or it will be provided. Its guardian doesn't have to have stepped from the wheel of life. Remember, when my grandfather first built Tamson House, he was both alive and its spiritual guardian."

But that hadn't been Sara's real concern. It was losing Jamie again. It was guilt for not accepting him when he was part of the House.

"How . . . how are you supposed to do it?" she asked.

"I only have to touch him."

Sara swallowed dryly. "Let me do it," she said. "Let me go instead."

"I already know the way. You don't."

"How hard can it be?" Sara asked. "We must all know it, somewhere inside us, or no one would ever get there."

"It's my turn, Sara."

She turned from the awful sight of the man spinning in his nimbus of light below them and wrapped her arms around Jamie, burrowing her head against his shoulder.

"I . . . I don't want you to go," she said. Her voice was muffled, but she knew he could hear her. "I've been such a shit, Jamie. I just want to . . . make up for hiding from you all these years."

He disengaged her arms gently and held her at arm's length.

"There's nothing to make up for," he said. "But you can do one thing for me."

The tears she'd been trying to hold back were swelling up in her eyes, making his face blur in her vision.

"What . . . what's that?" she asked.

"Give Esmeralda your support."

"Esmeralda . . .?"

"Your road isn't mine, Sara. I don't think it ever was. You need movement and space and journeys and . . . Tal. Esmeralda's a lot like me. She needs to get her nose out of her books and involve herself a little more in life, but I think that's something she'll learn. She'll learn it more quickly with your support and affection. I think she'll make a good guardian."

But she manipulates people, Sara wanted to say. She thinks she knows the best for everyone, but instead of helping them see their options, she tricks them into doing what she thinks they should.

The argument was there, but she didn't voice it. Not because she didn't want to argue with what was, in its own odd way, a dying man's last wish, but because she realized that Esmeralda really was a lot more like Jamie than she'd ever realized.

Jamie had been a manipulator as well—she just hadn't seen it because her love for him had clouded her perceptions of that part of him. But what else could explain the way he'd brought out the best in Blue and countless others, including herself? Sometimes people needed that dispassionate outside view to steer them—to use that expression of Ha'kan'ta's people that Jamie had been using—onto a more appropriate wheel.

It was manipulation, true. But in the end, it was the people themselves who made the real choice. They had the option to just walk away. Maybe so few of them did because they realized that the wheel they'd been shown was what they'd always been looking for.

"I . . . I'll try," she said.

Jamie kissed her again. She plucked at his sleeve as he stepped away and walked to the edge of the mesa.

"I love you, Sairey," he said.

She blinked back tears. "I love you, too," she managed.

She didn't think she could look, but she was at the edge of the mesa in a few quick panicked steps when he stepped off. He didn't fall so much as float to where the enemy hung in his glow of light. There was an implosion of light when the two figures touched. Everything went black—the nimbus of light, the stars, everything.

Then Sara saw a pinprick of a spark that enlarged until it was a small glowing circle the size of a silver dollar.

She could see two small figures in it, walking toward its center-most point. Their backs were toward her, but she could tell which was Jamie by his straight back and sure tread. The other one kept trying to pull away—a small struggling figure, all its stolen power useless because of Jamie's sacrifice. He was held firm by the grip of Jamie's hand, but he never stopped struggling, not until they were just tiny specks in the light, and then were gone.

Sara sat on the edge of the mesa as the tunnel of light winked out. Tears streamed down her cheeks. The night sky returned, sprinkled with stars. The Otherworld their enemy had created continued its existence—for such things were always more easily brought into existence than unmade.

She bowed her head and wept for a long time until the sound of faint drumming made her finally lift her head and turn around to find its source.

10

Esmeralda cursed the coyote and his cry that sounded so much like laughter, but his mocking *yip, yip, yip* awoke another reaction from the shaman and their champion. The drummers' fingers faltered on their instruments. The drums fell still. The shaman's dark brown eyes went wide under their animal and feather headdresses, their skin paled. The bison-headed man halted his advance. His penis shrank and fell back against his thigh.

The coyote's cry sounded again, closer still. Turning, Esmeralda and Emma saw Whiskey Jack come walking out of the ruins of Tamson House. He was dressed the same as he'd been when Esmeralda had seen him earlier, wore the same coyote face in place of human features.

"Who . . . who's that?" Emma asked.

"You met him earlier," Esmeralda said, "when he looked like Jamie Tamson."

Emma's gaze shifted from the approaching figure to Esmeralda's tight features.

"You know him, don't you?" she said.

Esmeralda nodded. "Remember Jack Wolfe?"

Emma frowned, then said, "He was that guy who had a relationship with you back in the early seventies, wasn't he? The one who said he fell in love with you as an experiment—he just wanted to know what it would feel like."

"That's the one."

"You never said he wasn't human."

"I didn't know then."

Whiskey Jack had come up to them by then.

"You knew," he said. "You knew all along."

Esmeralda shook her head, the tightness momentarily leaving her features.

"How could I know?" she asked. "I was just a kid."

"You had your winds—that was never the bounty of a child."

"It's old history," Esmeralda said, though it was obvious from her voice that though the hurt was old, it hadn't been forgotten. "It doesn't matter anymore."

Whiskey Jack turned to Emma. "I never knew it could hurt so much," he said.

"What could?"

"Love."

"So what do you want?" Esmeralda asked, tired of the conversation. She'd been through variations of it almost every time she and Jack met. "Did you come to see the results of your handiwork?"

The coyote eyes blinked in confusion. "My . . .?"

Esmeralda waved a hand to where the bison-headed man had withdrawn into the ranks of the shaman. The drums remained silent; the drummers watched, unreadable expressions in their eyes.

"You interrupted their party," Esmeralda said. "Our friends here were about to deal with the 'daughters of darkness.'"

"You think their enmity is my doing?"

Esmeralda nodded. "Who else could be responsible?"

Whiskey Jack laughed. "But I've come to rescue you."

Esmeralda could sense Emma relaxing beside her. The next words she spoke were hard to call up.

"No thanks, Jack. I told you before, I'm done with your bargains."

"Esmeralda!" Emma cried.

Whiskey Jack lifted his hands, spread them palms up. "No bargains, no strings, Westlin Wind."

Emma gripped Esmeralda's arm, but Esmeralda's suspicions weren't so easily allayed.

"What's the catch?" she asked.

"Think of it as atonement for past wrongs," Whiskey Jack said.

"You're stepping out of character."

The coyote head grinned. "One thousand and one faces—remember? Even you haven't seen them all."

"But—"

"Don't complicate matters," Whiskey Jack told her. "Tamson House has been returned to its homeworld and the threat against it has been dealt with. All that remains is your rescue."

Esmeralda centered in on that one phrase, *The threat has been dealt with*. Her heart sank. Tears welled in her eyes.

"Jamie . . ." she said softly.

So Whiskey Jack had found a way to make Jamie pay after all. She knew she should be angry, but all she felt was a deep sorrow to join the hurt Whiskey Jack had put there inside her all those many years ago. She was too worn out to be angry.

"Jamie did what he did of his own free will," Whiskey Jack said. "I promise you that much."

"Not without your help he didn't."

His gaze rested on her, but he didn't reply. The familiar mismatched eyes held a sorrow that she had never expected he could know.

"You have let the hurt I caused you so long ago color your life for far too long," he said finally. "I'll admit freely that I can never be the most trustworthy friend, but I mean no one real harm. I meant you no harm. Had I known how I would hurt you, I would . . ."

"You would have what?" Esmeralda asked when his voice trailed off.

"I had to know," he said simply. "I had to know how such a simple bond between two beings could have such power. Was that so wrong?"

"It was wrong to hurt me the way you did."

Whiskey Jack nodded. "I know that now. But it was also wrong of you to let the hurt I caused you build a wall between yourself and the rest of the world. You don't eschew relationships because you're too busy with your studies, Esmeralda."

She glared at him, but under his sad gaze, the blue eye and the brown, touched with sorrow and empathy, she couldn't maintain her anger. It wasn't just weariness; it was that what he had just said wasn't a lie.

"I . . . I know . . ." Esmeralda murmured.

Her tears could no longer be held back. She wept, not knowing if her tears were for Jamie, for the empty place inside her that she'd been too scared to allow another relationship to fill, or for what she'd had and lost with Whiskey Jack. Perhaps it was a little of all three.

Emma put a comforting arm around her friend. When Esmeralda turned toward her, Emma drew her head down to her shoulder and stroked the long gold and brown hair that stirred restlessly under her fingers, although she could feel no wind touch her own skin. She gazed at Whiskey Jack over Esmeralda's shoulder.

"You didn't lie about one thing, that's for sure," she said.

"What's that?" he asked.

"No one likes to hear what you have to say."

He inclined his head in tired agreement. "And yet, they are things that someone must say."

"I suppose."

The tableau held for a long moment, but finally Esmeralda stepped back from the circle of Emma's arms. She wiped her eyes on her sleeve. When she sniffled, Whiskey Jack took a red bandanna from his pocket and offered it to her. She regarded it for a long moment, then sighed and accepted it. She blew her nose. She found a halfhearted smile as she started to hand the bandanna back.

"I think I'll let you keep it," Whiskey Jack said.

Esmeralda stuffed it into her own pocket. She gave Emma a look of thanks for her comfort, then turned her attention to the shaman and their champion. The drummers had remained in the shadows of the first forest's tree for all this time, watching, drums silent. The bison-headed man was just an oddly shaped silhouette, deep in the trees.

"What happens now?" she asked.

"I send you home—unless you're strong enough to go on your own?"

Esmeralda shook her head. "And them? What happens to them and this ghost of the first forest?"

"Our enemy made this Otherworld, but it won't be unmade. They will remain here, as will the forest, though a finger of it will remain in the House's garden."

"There was always a finger of the first forest there."

Whiskey Jack nodded. "Until the next time we meet, then," he said.

"Not if I see you first," Esmeralda said, but she wasn't sure if she meant it.

"I was speaking to Emma," Whiskey Jack said. "She and I still have unfinished business—but I will only come," he added quickly at the flash in Esmeralda's eyes, "when called. For now, I'll simply see you home." He paused, then smiled. "You'll make a good guardian, Westlin Wind."

"Guardian?" Emma asked.

But Esmeralda was shaking her head. "You said no bargain, no strings. Who says I even want to be the House's guardian?"

"It was Jamie's last request—ask Sara if you don't believe me."

Esmeralda sighed. "Oh, I believe you, Jack."

"And?"

"Just send us home."

One moment they stood in the shadow of the first forest, the next they were on Patterson Avenue. The forest was gone. The ruins of the otherworldly shell of the House were replaced by the sound structure of the true building. It wasn't long past dawn, but there was already traffic on Bank Street. After the time they'd spent in the Otherworld, even an early morning in the city seemed filled with noise and unnecessary movement.

"Jesus," Emma said softly.

Esmeralda nodded. She linked arms with Emma and walked with her toward the nearest door of Tamson House. As she stepped over the threshold, she shivered. The mantle of the House's guardianship settled upon her, at once both a ponderous weight and an uplifting epiphany. She was simultaneously aware of all that went on inside the building as well as the stimuli caught and gathered by her own senses.

But her gladness at the embrace of the House was quickly tempered by memories too recent to be put aside. Sadness welled inside her. She missed Jamie already. But worse, she also missed Whiskey Jack—just as she always did after seeing him.

"Damn you," she said softly.

Emma gave her a questioning look, but Esmeralda could only shake her head.

"They're waiting for us in the Postman's Room" was all she said.

11

Once Maggie arrived to sit with Sara, Blue and Tucker returned to the upstairs front bedroom. Nothing had changed. The man on the bed still lay in his apparent coma, eyes moving under his closed lids, the blue veins more prominent than ever under his translucent skin. The woman looked up when they entered and regarded them with sardonic good humor.

"She gives me the creeps," Tucker said, speaking as though she weren't present.

Blue knew exactly what Tucker meant. Having them here, sitting bound in the chair, didn't seem to mean a thing to her. It was like she was wired into a whole different reality which, when he thought about it, probably wasn't that far off the mark.

"But we can't leave her tied up like that," Tucker added. At Blue's questioning glance, Tucker said, "Fercrissakes, what's she going to do? Jump the pair of us?"

"It's on your head," Blue told him.

He crossed the room and took a pocketknife from his jeans with which he cut the ties that held the woman to the chair. Except for rubbing her wrists, she made no other move.

"Thank you," she said.

Blue looked at Tucker and rolled his eyes. Tucker pulled a chair up to where the woman was sitting. He turned it around and sat down, resting his forearms on its back.

"Keep an eye on our friend in the bed," he told Blue.

Blue bridled at Tucker's immediate assumption of his authority, but then shrugged and fetched his rifle from where he'd leaned it up beside the door.

Screw it, he thought. If Tucker wanted to take over, he was welcome to it. If it weren't for Sara, he'd be just as happy handing the whole mess over to Tucker and bowing out. But there *was* Sara to think about, not to mention all the people still trapped in the otherworldly incarnation of the House.

He moved closer to the bed, taking up a position from which he could watch both the man on the bed and Tucker's interrogation. Tucker pulled his billfold from the inner pocket of his sports jacket and flipped it open so that the woman could see his RCMP identification.

"Why don't you tell me your name," he said.

"Eleanor Watkins," she replied promptly.

"And the man on the bed?"

"He's my husband, Albert."

Blue shook his head. Albert Watkins. It didn't have even the vaguest ring of villainy about it. If it weren't for what had happened to Sara and the icy draft that seemed to emanate from where Watkins lay on the bed—not to mention what happened whenever you tossed something in Watkins's direction—he could almost think they were in the wrong house.

"Would you like to tell me what's going on here, Mrs. Watkins?" Tucker was asking.

"We haven't broken any of your laws."

"I didn't say you had."

"And you have no right to be here in our house. Don't you need some kind of search warrant to come barging in on a body like this?"

The amicable tone of Tucker's voice acquired an edge. "Probable cause," he said.

"I beg your pardon?"

"When we become aware of a situation that appears—"

Blue had been worrying over the implication of the woman's

phrase "your laws"—did that mean she and her husband were from some other country, or some place even more distant?—so he almost missed the change in Watkins. But a glimmer of light caught his peripheral vision. He turned in time to see a glowing aura take shape around Watkins and then the man began to move the way a person will when having a nightmare—his head rocking back and forth, his body twisting, limbs flailing.

"Tucker!" he cried, interrupting the inspector's explanation of Canadian civil rights.

Watkins was violently thrashing about on the bed now. His eyes were open, but it was readily apparent that he wasn't seeing the room around him. But whatever he *was* looking at made him mad with fear. Blue lifted his rifle and aimed it at the flailing figure, unwilling to take the chance that this wasn't some grandstanding play on Watkins's part.

"What the hell?" Tucker said, rising from his chair.

Eleanor Watkins was quicker. She was up and across the room, before Tucker could grab her.

"Albert!" she cried. "Albert!"

So her smugness could be breached, Blue had time to think, but his momentary satisfaction dissolved as the woman reached for her husband. There was a flare of sparks and the aniselike scent stung the air. Watkins's protective shield flung his wife bodily away, directly against Tucker. She hit Tucker with such force that she pushed him halfway across the room before they both fell in a tangle of limbs, Tucker under the woman.

Blue returned his gaze to Watkins, his finger tightening on the trigger of his rifle. But he held his fire. He grimaced at the change Watkins was undergoing. The translucency of his skin grew more pronounced until he was like a figure from some horror film— muscles, veins and bone had all become visible through his skin. His mouth was open; it looked like he was howling, but no sound came forth.

By now his wife had regained her feet. She stared at Watkins with open dismay.

"No!" she cried.

She rushed to him again, but this time Tucker caught her before she could touch her husband. She struggled in Tucker's arms, crying wordlessly now as the enveloping aura that surrounded Watkins began to fail. His skin became opaque again. His struggles grew weaker; then finally he lay still. The aura was gone. All that remained was a dead old man, lying in the bed.

Blue poked cautiously at the body with the butt of his rifle. He touched an arm that had been flung out and now lay hanging over the side of the bed. There was no spark, no movement at all. The prodded limb gave way to the pressure he put on it, then fell back when he pulled the rifle butt away.

"No," Eleanor Watkins said, her voice soft and broken now.

When Tucker let her go, she fell to the side of the bed and threw her arms around the corpse. She laid her head on its chest, her shoulders shaking convulsively. Her pitiful sobbing had Blue feeling as uncomfortable as Tucker looked.

"What the hell happened?" Tucker asked.

"Beats me. Looks like he just . . . died."

"Died," Tucker repeated.

"Have you got a better explanation? Maybe the House had some last line of defense that he wasn't aware of and it just kicked in."

Tucker looked out the window. "The House is supposed to be in the Otherworld, right?"

"The insides are," Blue replied. "You know—the way it happened the last time."

"Yeah, well, if the House is gone, then how come there's lights on inside it?"

Blue crossed the room to where Tucker was standing. Looking out the window, he saw that Tucker was right. All along the length of the block that was Tamson House, lights burned in dozens of the windows.

"It's back," he said. He turned to Tucker with a grin. "We did it!"

"Did what? I didn't see us doing dick."

Before Blue could reply, Maggie called up to them from downstairs. Blue's grin widened.

"And Sara's back, too!"

He was out the door and clomping down the stairs, taking them two at a time, before Tucker could even reach the hallway. Blue found Sara sitting up on the couch. She looked woozy and obviously needed the supporting arm that Maggie was giving her. Blue leaned his rifle up against the wall by the front door and beamed at her.

"Oh, man," he said. "You had me worried, Sara."

She gave him a weak smile that never reached her eyes.

"Yeah, well I didn't have a whole lot of choice," she said. "He just took me away."

"Took you where?" Tucker asked as he joined them in the living room.

Sara explained what had happened. No one interrupted her until she spoke of Jamie.

"Wait a second," Tucker said. "What Jamie are we talking about here? The only one I know connected to the House died about seven years ago."

"He kind of came back," Blue said.

Tucker gave him a considering look. He started to speak, but then just shook his head.

"Never mind," he said. "I'll take a rain check on that for now." He turned back to Sara. "So then what happened?"

Blue watched Sara's eyes well up with tears as she spoke of Jamie's second death. An emptiness grew inside him—a cold, dark wasteland of despair. He reached out and took her hand, taking as much comfort from the contact as he gave.

"I didn't know what to expect when I heard the drumming," Sara said, finishing up. "It didn't even matter by that point. But when I turned, I found it was Pukwudji. He'd gone to bring the *rath'wen'a* back to help us, but they were too late for Jamie. Ha'-kan'ta said that they couldn't have done anything anyway. She said he'd dealt with the problem in the only way that . . . that was open to him."

She couldn't go on. Blue took Maggie's place on the couch and held her to him. There wasn't anything he could do to ease her grief; all he could was share it.

Tucker and Maggie left them alone. Maggie went up to help Eleanor Watkins while Tucker got on the phone to call in some members of his squad to deal with the cleanup. He returned to the living room when he hung up.

"You'd better get going," he said when Blue looked up. "This place is going to be crawling with my men in about ten minutes and I don't think either of you are ready for that just now. I'll come by the House and talk to you tomorrow."

Blue nodded. He helped Sara to her feet.

"Thanks," he said. "This is one I owe you."

"I'm not keeping a tab," Tucker told him. "But I do want to know more about all of this—Jamie, the House, the whole shot."

"I don't know about that," Blue began.

"This isn't idle curiosity," Tucker told him. "It's got to do with national security, Blue. I need to know some things." He glanced at Sara. "But I'll give you some time."

Sara looked up at him. "I'm not the one you want to talk to," she said.

"You're the one who owns the House."

Sara nodded. "But Esmeralda is its new guardian. You'll have to talk to her."

Tucker sighed. He'd met Esmeralda before.

"I'd have better luck getting information from a stone," he said. "That woman should be a poker player."

"She is," Blue told him. "And she almost always wins."

The simple walk across the street to one of the Clemow doors of the House seemed a far longer journey than it actually was. The only thing Blue really noticed was that the owls were finally gone. When he mentioned it to Sara, she gave an answering nod, but she didn't seem much interested. They both paused when they stepped inside the building. They expected the House to feel different, to reflect the sorrow that lay so heavily on them, but while there was a sense of bittersweetness in the air, Jamie's second death didn't appear to have made much of a change.

Esmeralda met them in the hallway.

"We'll all miss him," she said, aware of what they were feeling. "The House itself, perhaps most of all, but its Mystery turns on its own wheel. It can't ever focus on simply one individual. If it did, it wouldn't be the haven it is to so many."

"But Jamie . . ." Sara began.

"It's not the House remembering him, but how we do, that will give his death meaning," Esmeralda said.

"He said he'd wait for me—in the Place of Dreaming Thunder."

Esmeralda nodded. "But he wouldn't want us to hurry to that meeting. There's still a lot we have to do here, before it's our time to go on."

She slipped her right hand into the crook of Sara's arm, her left into Blue's.

"The rest of them are waiting for us in the Postman's Room," she said. "They'll want to hear what happened. Do you think you're up to it?"

"I guess so," Sara said.

They were waiting, but there weren't many of them. Emma met them in the doorway and embraced Blue. Ginny sat in the chair by the desk, Judy on the desk itself. Ohn and Julianne were on the floor, using a bookcase for a backrest. Tim was sitting in one of the club chairs, but he got up when they came in.

"What happened?" Blue asked. "Where is everybody?"

"As soon as we got back," Emma said, "they all took off."

Judy nodded. "Can't say as I blame them. This kind of thing happen often here, Blue?"

He shook his head. His gaze traveled across their familiar faces until it reached Julianne.

"Even Cal?" he asked.

"Maybe especially Cal," Julianne replied. "But I don't think it was for the same reason that the others did. Still, I think he'll be okay. And he might even be back to help with the cleanup."

Esmeralda led Sara to the club chair that Tim had vacated and sat down in the other one.

"I want you all to listen carefully to what Sara's got to tell us," she said. "You might not have known Jamie, but if it wasn't for him, the Tamson House that we all know would never have existed. His story's as much a part of the House's mystery as the House itself."

Blue had thought it might be too much for Sara to go through it all again, but while her eyes were still shiny, her voice was strong and sure as she began to speak.

★   ★   ★

The day came and went. As its light began to leak into evening, Blue, Esmeralda and Sara stepped into the garden and walked to where the Apple Tree Man kept watch over his orchard. Pukwudji and Ha'kan'ta waited for them there, a wolf standing to either side of the *rath'wen'a.*

"I made Tal go back," Sara had explained to them earlier. "Because of the initiation. But the only way he'd agree was if I returned tonight."

"We understand," Esmeralda had replied.

"You know you've got my support—all of it," Sara told Esmeralda now.

Esmeralda nodded.

Sara turned to Blue. "I'm not going to stay away so long anymore," she said.

"You've got your own life to live," Blue said.

"Yeah, but you're a big part of it." She kissed him, then Esmeralda. "We'll all come back to help with the cleanup," she added. "We'll even drag Kieran back, so don't try to do it all by yourselves."

"Tell that to Ginny," Blue said. "She's determined to have the Library back in order by the weekend."

Sara just shook her head. She looked around the orchard. It was that moment of the twilight when everything seemed incredibly defined, that moment just before it gave way to night.

"Jamie used to read me Pooh books out here," she said.

Then she turned and walked to where Ha'kan'ta and Pukwudji waited for her. The little *honochen'o'keh* took her hand. Ha'kan'ta and Sara waved farewell, and then they were gone.

"I remember the Pooh books," Esmeralda said. "Piglet and Eeyore and the Hundred Acre Wood and all. Do you remember them, Blue?"

"Sure," Blue said. He gave her a tired smile. "Only it was Sara who used to read them to me."

"Everything connects," Esmeralda said. "Especially here."

"Especially here," Blue agreed.

He stayed a while longer in the orchard, standing alone under the Apple Tree Man, looking up at the cross-hatching of its branches silhouetted against the sky.

"I'm going to miss you," he said softly after a while. He wasn't sure if he was talking to Jamie or Sara. Then he followed Esmeralda into the House.

The Wheel of the Wood

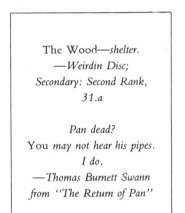

The Wood—*shelter.*
—*Weirdin Disc;*
Secondary: Second Rank,
31.a

Pan dead?
You may not hear his pipes.
I do.
—*Thomas Burnett Swann*
from "The Return of Pan"

1

Summer was almost gone and autumn was in the air. The day had been warm, but the wilting humidity of August was finally a thing of the past. The evening was cool. A light breeze stirred the leaves of the Penny Trees, making them shimmer like spinning coins in the fading light. The noise of the city beyond the House's walls didn't penetrate into the garden. The only sound was the bell-like notes of Ohn's zither that, by some odd trick of the garden's acoustics, carried from where he sat by the door of the Silkwater Kitchen all the way across the garden to where Emma was walking.

She came up to the fountain and looked up into the branches of the old oak tree that still stood guard over it in the center of the garden. It was in its branches that Tim had seen the three green-skinned children hanging, she remembered.

"But why did they pretend to be dead?" Tim had asked Esmeralda one day while the three of them were cleaning out the debris from one of the rooms.

"It was a joke," Esmeralda said.

"A *joke?*"

Esmeralda nodded. "Their kind of a joke. I don't pretend to understand their sense of humor."

"But it doesn't make sense," Tim had protested.

Emma had silently agreed.

"If you want sense," Esmeralda said, "don't look to bodachs for it. Although . . ." She had paused a moment, considering. "There are things they can teach us. Sometimes they do the things they do just to shock us—to wake us up and make us see things differently."

Emma was seeing things differently now, though she couldn't decide if it was due to the events they had all experienced in the Otherworld, or a natural change she would have grown into in her own time. The source of the change wasn't important, anyway; just the change itself.

The House had a new roster of guests—the fullest house it had had in years, according to Blue—but Emma had the garden to herself this evening. Blue was doing bike things with Judy again, Esmeralda was actually out on a date with one of John Tucker's assistants and Emma had managed to slip out on her own before anyone else could corner her.

She walked on until she came to one of those parts of the garden that Tim called the Wild Walks. There she stood quietly for a while, her hands stuffed in the pockets of her jacket, listening to the distant sound of Ohn's music and remembering the seventeen-year-old girl she'd once been.

Dark hair a-tangle, she'd climb out of her ground-floor bedroom window at two or three o'clock in the morning and go for walks in the woods and fields around her parents' house. Everything was more magical at night, and she was enamored with magic. She would feel a wind touch her cheek and when she got home she would draw a picture of herself, standing in a moonlit field with Esmeralda nearby, Esmeralda's hair blowing in the wind, strands of those gold-and-brown locks reaching out to touch Emma's cheek.

She'd write on the back of the drawing: "Last night I walked out past the Fields We Know to a hilltop where your wind remembered me. I found this picture in my mind when I came home. Were you there? Could you hear me singing?" Into an envelope the drawing would go, off to Esmeralda in the morning mail.

And inevitably—a few days, perhaps a week or two later—an envelope would arrive from Esmeralda, stuffed with poems and a brief note, all signed with a flourishing "Westlin Wind." It was Esmeralda who first told her she carried the Autumn Gift in her heart, who called her the Autumn Lady, who made magic seem real.

But that seventeen-year-old girl grew up, went to college where she took commercial art, never had time for midnight walks in the woods and fields, met a different crowd of people from the ones who hadn't had time for her in high school because she was too wrapped up in her art to be normal. Her fellow college students, and later coworkers, loved real art just as much as she did, for all that they made their livings designing logos, illustrating advertisements and posters and the like.

She wasn't sure what magics they had known when they were younger, if any. All she knew was that she'd lost hers.

Esmeralda still wrote, but they never talked about Westlin Winds and Autumn Ladies. Esmeralda seemed determined to be a perpetual student. She moved to England; she spent her summers traveling through Europe and the Middle East. There were hints of arcane mysteries couched in her letters, but they were only the vaguest of whispers, easily tuned out. Magic was gone, if it had ever been.

Until that night she met Blue.

Until she'd finally had to accept that magic had been there all along; she had simply turned a blind eye to it.

The Autumn Gift wasn't a ghostly memory. It was real. And it carried a grave responsibility that she'd been fighting for some three years now.

"You must be so fed up with my wishy-washiness by now," she'd said to Esmeralda a few nights ago.

Surprisingly, for all the hectic activity of getting the House back in order, and how tired that left them all in the evenings, she'd

begun drawing again. She and Esmeralda were sitting in the Silkwater Kitchen's nook that evening—Esmeralda doodling words on
a pad of yellow foolscap, Emma doodling pictures.

"You never get fed up with the people you love," Esmeralda
replied.

Emma laid down her pencil. "This Autumn Gift," she said,
finally broaching the subject she'd been trying to bring up for days.
"What if it's all that makes me special?"

Esmeralda lifted her eyebrows.

"You know. I get along easily with people. People seem to like
me; they like my art. . . . What if it's only because of the gift?"

"You had a magic of your own long before the gift was drawn
to you," Esmeralda said. "It was your own magic that brought it
to you."

"But I can't seem to come to terms with it and that makes me
feel like a failure."

"You're not a failure—you're just redefining yourself. We all do
it from time to time. We have to, or we stagnate."

"But—"

"It was a mistake for me to push at you the way I did," Esmeralda said.

Emma shook her head. "You were just doing what you thought
was right."

"But I was acting as though I had nothing left to learn about the
world myself," Esmeralda said. "I have to keep in mind that the
real world's more important than the secret one of my studies—or
rather that it's the way they interrelate that makes them important.
I have to get out with people more, just to relate to them instead
of trying to make sure that they fulfill what I perceive as their
potential."

She smiled and laid her hand on Emma's. "No matter what you
decide to do," she said, "I won't stop loving you."

Which was what Blue had said when she'd brought it up with
him later that same night.

"It's you I love, Emma, not some gift."

Things were a lot better between Blue and her now. With Sara
coming back more often—twice this month already, the second
time for a whole week—he was more relaxed and giving her space

in a way that wasn't so obvious anymore. Emma supposed she should be jealous of the relationship he had with Sara, but she liked Sara too much herself to be anything but happy when Sara and Tal came by. Sara, like Judy and Julianne, were friends, and as such, related to parts of him that she couldn't, which didn't lessen their own relationship. If anything, those friendships enriched it, just as her own friendships with others did.

As Ohn put it, "Our affection for others is the one thing that is an infinite resource. We can never care too much, or for too many."

He hadn't seen *Fatal Attraction,* Emma remembered thinking when he said that, but she got the point.

The twilight had eased into night. She couldn't hear Ohn's zither anymore. An owl hooted once, waking a little shiver in her, but when she looked around to find it watching her from the branch of a nearby tree, she saw that it was here on its own. It was just an owl, not an omen. But the thought of omens got her feet moving once more.

She left the network of the garden's paths when she reached the orchard and walked slowly across the dewy grass to the tree that Sara called the Apple Tree Man.

He was waiting for her there. Whiskey Jack. Jack Wolfe. Whatever his name was. He had a man's head on his shoulders tonight, but it was too dark for her to be able to make out his features.

"You knew I was coming, didn't you?" she said.

She'd come out into the garden tonight for the express reason of calling him to her, but she hadn't been able to figure out just how to do that. It was something she didn't feel right about asking Esmeralda, considering how Esmeralda's feelings toward him ran. Now Emma realized she needn't have worried.

His teeth flashed in a quick grin, but his only response was to ask her if she had a cigarette. She took the pack she'd bought earlier in the week for this express purpose and started to hand it to him, but he shook his head.

"You light it," he said.

"But I don't smoke."

He made no reply, so she removed the cellophane and put it in her pocket, then took a cigarette from the pack. She was awkward about lighting it—it took three matches—and when she finally did, the smoke made her cough. A hand tapped her comfortingly on the back and then took the cigarette from her fingers. He stuck it between his lips and took a long drag. With smoke wreathing from his nostrils, he relieved her of the cigarette package and matches. Both disappeared into his own pocket.

"So you've decided," he said.

She wasn't sure if it was a question or a statement, but she had something else she wanted to ask him first.

"Did you really love Esmeralda?"

She wished it weren't so dark so that she could read his expression.

"I did," he said, his voice soft.

Something in his voice woke a sudden insight in Emma.

"You still do, don't you?" she said.

Again he made no reply.

Emma plunged on. "So why don't you do something about it?"

He laughed softly, but the sound held no humor. It rang in Emma's ears like a coyote's bark.

"It doesn't matter whether I do or I don't," he said. "We're too different."

"You mean because you're not . . . human?"

She caught his quick nod.

"But she's—she's got her own magic," she said. "Her winds."

"And perhaps we're too much the same as well," he told her a little sharply. "Don't meddle in what doesn't concern you."

"You're one to talk."

He shook his head. His quiet laugh returned, but this time it wasn't self-deprecating.

"You've been listening too much to Esmeralda," he said. "Did she put you up to this?"

"What do you think?"

Again silence. Then he sighed. "There are times we do things that we can only regret later," he said finally. "Sometimes it's best to leave them as past history. That way we can learn from our mistakes, rather than repeat them."

He took a last drag from the cigarette, ground the butt under his heel and bent down to retrieve it. Straightening up, he put the butt in his pocket and lit up another cigarette.

"But we're not here to talk about what Esmeralda or I might want or will do," he said. He blew out a stream of smoke. "We're here because of you."

Emma nodded. She'd made the decision, but it was hard to voice it. What if she was making a terrible, terrible mistake? She knew that if she changed her mind later, there would be no going back.

She took a deep breath, slowly let it out.

"I want to give it back," she said finally.

He nodded gravely. "I thought you would."

He stepped closer to her and put his free hand against her chest, just between her breasts. Emma flinched, but forced herself not to move. He kept his hand there for a moment, then slowly turned it around. What looked like a small dead bird lay in his palm.

Emma gave a tiny gasp. Deep inside her, she felt as though something had died, as though the source of all her life's possible joys had just winked out.

"It . . . is it dead?" she asked.

He shook his head. "Such a thing can never die."

"But . . ."

It lay so still on his palm and there was such an ache inside her, such an emptiness.

"Everything is on a wheel," he told her. "You, I, this wood, your gift. The Great Mystery is that we can step from one to the other. We can be all things."

"Then . . . what's going to happen to it?"

"It will find a new home."

As he spoke the last word, he seemed to drift apart as though he had no more substance than the smoke that had been trailing from between his lips. One moment there was a hazy outline of a man standing with her in the orchard, the next she was alone.

Alone with that awful emptiness inside her.

She stood for a long time under the Apple Tree Man, trying to tell herself that she'd done what she had to do. She'd done the right thing.

Then why did it hurt so much?

Because the gift had been part of her for so long. It was like losing a part of her childhood, like a precious bit of memory being erased.

She looked up, past the fruit-laden boughs of the Apple Tree Man, up to the sky. A thousand stars looked back at her from its dark vault.

The emptiness remained, but she realized that a great weight had been taken from her shoulders. In its own way, her decision to-night was the first responsible thing she'd done since she acquired the gift, all unknowingly, so many years ago.

Yes, the emptiness remained, but she would fill it. With her art. With Blue. With her friends.

As she walked back to the House, her steps were lighter than they had been for a very long time.

2

Julianne Trelawny stood in another part of the House's garden that same night. She could feel the ghost of the first forest all around her. There seemed to be faces in the bark of the trees, watching her, smiling at her. Their branches rustled, not with wind, but with whispers.

She was tired. They'd worked hard today, as they had every day since the House's return, and things were finally getting back into some semblance of order. With everybody pitching in, the work went faster than she would ever have thought possible. Teamwork was the rule of the day—all except for in the Penwith Kitchen. Anton Brach refused to let anybody else set a foot in it until he had it spotless once more—to his criteria, thank you very much, and please don't come by to interrupt him again or he'd never get anything done.

She smiled, thinking of Cal's perfect mimicry of Brach's reaction on his return to the House. She'd told him then, as she'd told him before, that he really should consider a career as a stand-up comic.

"What?" he would protest. "And give up my promising career as the office's resident software expert?"

He was off with his girlfriend to see a band at Barrymore's

tonight. Lisa wasn't a pagan—but then Cal wasn't much of one either, when it came right down to it. But all of that was irrelevant. They were both good people and she was happy to see them together. Lisa had come by with Cal to help out almost every night since they'd gotten together. Julianne had quit working earlier than she normally would tonight just to get the two of them off doing something for themselves for a change.

It was cooler in the garden than she'd expected. She wrapped her shawl a little closer around her and considered going back into the House, but the peacefulness she'd found out here tonight seemed too precious to desert so early.

She looked up and saw a shooting star cut a sharp bright line across the sky. It reminded her of her childhood, when she would stand outside her parents' house waiting for a star to fall so that she could make a wish.

She thought of the ghost of the first forest, felt its spark glow warm inside her, and made a wish now. As though in response, she heard a footstep along the path she'd taken earlier to reach this spot. Turning, she saw someone stepping closer. As he drew nearer, she wasn't surprised to see that the man had a coyote's head on his shoulders.

In this place, at this time, with memories of the first forest ghosting through her, it seemed entirely appropriate.

He stopped beside her. The smell of cigarette smoke and forest loam rose from his clothing. Shaking a cigarette from a package he took from his pocket, he lit it and after taking a long drag, offered it to her. She didn't smoke, but she took the cigarette from him all the same and brought it up to her lips.

"I have a gift for you," he said as she took a drag.

Deep inside her, the spark that had entered her when she initially looked upon the first forest flared with a bright warmth.